Enjoy!

9/24/01

FALLING ROSES:
THE YEARS BETWEEN

ROSEMARIE PIEMONTE

Rosemarie Piemonte

Bloomington, IN

authorHOUSE®

Milton Keynes, UK

AuthorHouse™
1663 Liberty Drive, Suite 200
Bloomington, IN 47403
www.authorhouse.com
Phone: 1-800-839-8640

AuthorHouse™ UK Ltd.
500 Avebury Boulevard
Central Milton Keynes, MK9 2BE
www.authorhouse.co.uk
Phone: 08001974150

First published by AuthorHouse 4/16/2007

ISBN: 978-1-4259-9934-6 (sc)

Library of Congress Control Number: 2007902291

Printed in the United States of America
Bloomington, Indiana

This book is printed on acid-free paper.

For My Children Nicholas & Matthew

"My Mommy wrote a book and I am proud of her."
—Nicholas

"I love you more than an alligator loves his mama."
—Matthew

"I love you more than Falling Roses."
—Mommy

Acknowledgments

My Editor, Autumn Conley Bittick
Photo of me, John Piemonte
Front Cover, Irene Nichols

Also By
ROSEMARIE PIEMONTE

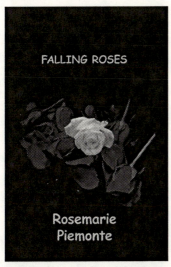

FALLING ROSES

Rosemarie
Piemonte

"Rose Piemonte pens an exciting romantic thriller with her first novel, Falling Roses. A teenager gets hit by a car and spends two months in a coma. A rock star visits the hospital to visit sick children and becomes enamored with this comatose beauty. The fairytale comes true, albeit with some deadly twists and turns. Roses characters have depth, warmth, charm, and plenty of rock and roll. If it weren't for the doings of the evil Bernadette and her wacko half brother, Johnny and Gabrielle could live happily ever after. You'll have to read the book to find out more! Enjoy the journey..."
Cynthia Brian, Media Coach, Writer, Author, Speaker, TV/ Radio Personality, Spokesperson.

"*Falling Roses* will hook you from the very beginning and you will want to find out what happens before you put the book down."
Fallen Angel Reviews

"...a roller coaster ride where every twist and turn in Johnny and Bobbie's life leads to danger. And one asks, will it ever end? Will they find peace?"
Gotta Write Network

Visit Rosemarie Piemonte's Web site at:
http://k.1asphost.com/fallingroses/
or
www.falling-roses.com

Email the Author at:
rosemariepiemonte@yahoo.com

Is this a fantasy? Or is it reality?

I cry. The fire, the raging fire. The explosion. I can do nothing.

I want to run toward the flames. Someone holds me down. What's burning intensely? Too much. It's all too much to bear. Flames everywhere. The babies. My babies!

Who are you? What is your name? I'm scared. I'm frightened. I'm wet. I'm itchy. Itchy, very itchy. My back, my legs, my arms, my head, my face. Something is crawling on me. It burns. It's running through my veins. It won't stop. Make it stop!

I feel someone or something underneath me. I feel the side of my face plastered against his chest. Is he alive? He's breathing. He's alive. Let me see you. Who are you? Why are you here with me? He's breathing ... A man is with me. We're buried. We're buried alive in a coffin. I know it's a coffin. We're in a box, in a box, in a box...

She felt the tourniquet tighten around her arm. She opened her eyes. "Who are you? What are you doing? Michael! What are you doing? What is that? No! Michael! No ... No ..."

PART ONE

~

Chapter 1

John Ravolie exited the doorway and stepped into the hall. A step beyond his wife's hospital room, he raked his hands through his unwashed hair and wiped his swollen nose with a fist. Just outside the door, J.J. Shedel sat in a chair against the wall. In his lap, three-year-old Robbie faced him. John noticed father and son playing thumb wars. John brushed his knuckles over Robbie's head and playfully messed up his mop of blond hair. Shedel looked over his left shoulder, looking for an answer that John wouldn't give him just yet. John closed his tired eyes and briefly shook his head.

In the hallway, many people were waiting for a response from John. Already, others were grieving, John noticed, as husbands held their sobbing wives. Gabrielle's parents seemed to be glancing angrily at him. They had to blame someone, John figured. He still blamed himself, and the weight of the guilt stabbed him painfully.

John noticed Michael Newtonendie staring over the rim of his Styrofoam cup; her father took a sip of his coffee. His precious Bobbie, his only daughter, would be gone soon, John thought, if she hadn't departed in her sleep. Then he wandered mournfully through the hall.

Almost a half-hour had passed since Gabrielle's head had drooped, her muscles weakened and her pale face sagged with no emotion. John could still hear the echo of his young daughter's voice. "No Mommy! Don't die. You'll miss the party."

Perhaps Jackie thought if her mother had heard her pleas, she would open her eyes again. Maybe if the crowd screamed with her, Gabrielle would have opened her eyes.

John thought when Gabrielle sat in the wheelchair nearing the group and her narrow eyes grew wider there was still a chance that she'd live to see tomorrow. He remembered she had smiled. Possibly, for a second, Gabrielle had forgotten that death was coming for her. Warm heartedly, she peered toward her friends and family. They faked their cheerful expressions while

1

looking into her direction. Since he had as well, he was sure she had noticed tears welling in their eyes.

There was no shouting of surprise. Actually, the room was quiet—too quiet. But John knew Gabrielle was in high spirits while she viewed the friends and family she loved so dearly. And she knew they adored her.

John had picked Jackie up in his arms. He held her close; she continued to cry. He had buried her face into his shoulder. It didn't muffle her outburst though, while he held his own desperate sobs silent within the strands of her brown hair.

Suddenly, Jackie's head had turned. While releasing her mouth from his shoulder she wailed, "No Mommy!"

Her tone and those two words pierced John Ravolie's mind, his heart.

John entered the hospital's chapel. He visited the chapel many times in the past month. It was a small room lit by smoked red, cylinder-size candles. Behind the candles, a stain glass picture of the Lord hung on a brick wall. The thorns crowned Him. Imitated droplets of blood splashed across his forehead. At his cheek, a strand of beaded blood flowed downward. With opened palms, the image stared at John. Again today, John stared ruefully back at Him.

Reaching forward, he picked up a long matchstick and lit a candle. "This is about me?" John asked Him. "Isn't it?" John bent a knee to the floor. "You didn't take her after the car hit her. You didn't take her after she had the babies. You didn't take her while We.Were.In.That.Damn.Box. She.Loves.Life. She loves her kids. And she loves me. She loves me," he sobbed. "Let her live. I'll make sure she's happy for the rest of her life. I need her. The kids need her. I *need* her."

Someone entered the room. A hand curved around John's right shoulder. John lifted his chin to see Gabrielle's father peering down at him. "Bobbie," Michael said to John. "She's gone."

"Damn you!" John stood; picked up the candle he had lit for her, and threw it at the picture. The glass shattered over the candles. He fumbled out of the room. With an unclear mind, he traveled the hallway back to Gabrielle's room.

Still, people from the party gathered in small groups within the hallway. When John returned their stare, they looked away. John barely heard J.J.'s words when he mumbled, "I'll stay here with Robbie, until you're..."

John entered his wife's room. While looking at the tiles, he walked up to the bed frame. When he sat in the chair beside her, he glanced at her face. Gabrielle lay with her eyes closed. With death, she rested peacefully.

"So beautiful. So young. Gabrielle. Why? Why?"

John stayed with her. He held her hand; his head rested beside her. He cried.

"MR. RAVOLIE, IT'S TIME."

John kissed his wife on her lips. Once, then twice. Her lips were still lukewarm. John walked the hall again and entered the other room where he had left their daughter, Jackie.

But, Jackie was gone.

John went to the nurses' station, worried and panicked. "Where's my mother?" John asked a nurse. The woman just shook her head. And not one person knew where his daughter was. The doctor, who had examined her for shock, had disappeared. Then he noticed Maria Ravolie coming forward. "Where's Jackie?" John frantically asked his mother.

"Isn't she in the room?" Maria questioned.

John cupped her shoulders and said, "Jackie's gone."

"I just went to the drinking fountain. John, I swear. I only left her for a minute."

"What's going on?" John's best friend, Mick Harrison asked them.

"Jackie's missing," Maria said. "She's not in her room."

John stumbled down the hall as if he was the center of a whirlwind. "Have you seen Jackie?" he asked J.J.

"No, I've been sitting here the whole time with Robbie."

Gabrielle's body lay underneath a sheet as two male nurses pushed the gurney to the coroner's wing. "Wait!" Carefully, John removed the sheet covering her side. He lifted Gabrielle's wrist, kissed her palm. Still warm to his lips. Slowly, he removed the three wedding rings from her finger.

Beside the gurney, John sat. Patiently, the nurses waited for John. But, he couldn't tell them to take her away. Michael stepped forward. He lifted the sheet from his daughter's face to view her. He then made the sign of the cross on her forehead and re-covered her lifeless expression.

John buried the wedding rings into the pocket of his jeans and watched while the nurses wheeled Gabrielle's body to the morgue.

Jeffrey Rolando arrived. He knew how to make a grand entrance, John mused. If it weren't for him, Gabrielle would still be alive. Rolando gave up looking for them. *He just gave up!*

John watched Jeffrey walk towards him. The twenty-one year old had short black hair, the same color of the expensive Armani suit he wore. His four bodyguards stood around him as if he were a celebrity. And John Ravolie knew that Jeffrey Rolando was no celebrity. Jeffrey was the son of a dead Don, but he himself was weak and pathetic. His schemes, his plots, his ideas, his plans had always failed.

John rose from the chair, walked briskly, until his walk turned into a jog. Without thinking, John raised a fist and punched Rolando in the face. "You gave up! You bastard!" With John's right arm forced behind him, he clutched his left hand into a tight, angry fist and gave another blow to the man's face. The wall broke Rolando's fall.

"Don't touch Ravolie!" Mick Harrison shouted at Rolando's men.

John's friends yanked him away as he yelled, "She wouldn't've died if it weren't for you!" His back hit the opposite wall. "Gabrielle's dead! You sonofabitch! She's dead!"

J.J. handed his son Robbie over to Felecia Harrison. Her husband Mick stood between John and Jeffrey.

Jeffrey drew his fingers to the blood that dripped from his lip. "How long has Jackie been missing?" he asked.

"Who called you?" John growled. Immediately thinking there was a traitor in the group. Realizing, his best friend Mick would take care of Rolando, against the wall, John lowered his body somberly to the floor.

"How long has Jackie been missing?" Jeffrey turned to Mick.

J.J. crouched. "Ravolie—"

"Make sure our son is safe, then go find my daughter."

J.J. SHEDEL tried not to mourn the loss of the woman he loved. There was no time for mourning just yet; he had to find her daughter.

Five years earlier, a drunk driver slammed into Gabrielle Newtonendie while she strolled the length of a sidewalk searching for a payphone. For two months, she was in a coma. When she awoke to celebrity heartthrob Johnny Ravolie at her bedside, it made the headlines. Gabrielle was fifteen-years-old when the magazine with their photos hit the newsstands. She was so young. To J.J., she was beautiful. Unbeknownst to J.J. Shedel, Gabrielle had come to Long Island to be with the man she fell in love with—Johnny Ravolie. She was fifteen, engaged to twenty-four year old Ravolie. When J.J. met her, she was then pregnant with Jackie.

J.J. wondered what would have happened if she had awoke to him, the drummer for the rock band Intensity, instead of the lead singer of Ra'vole, sitting at her bedside.

J.J. had come to The Recording Studio owned by Ravolie. As he walked to the revolving glass door, J.J. noticed her arms wrapped around Mick Harrison at the curb, and then J.J. watched as Gabrielle kissed him, and turned around to Ravolie, merely to yell, 'You've been replaced!'

That afternoon she amused him, J.J. remembered. She had spunk.

It was Gabrielle and John's first argument ever about Bernadette Malone and J.J. knew first hand that it wouldn't be their last.

J.J. kept his focus on Gabrielle, and it wasn't long before he realized she worked at The Recording Studio and that her work was highly admired. He needed her expertise on Intensity's club tour CD, since she had done such an excellent job on Ra'vole's. J.J. went to visit Gabrielle Newtonendie at the beach house where she lived with John. As soon as she opened the door and asked if his eyes were green and he noticed immediately that hers were blue, J.J. was in love with her. Later he learned that she was committed to Ravolie, pregnant with his kid.

J.J. took what he had to accept; their friendship meant everything to him. After another argument had occurred between her and Ravolie, J.J. had spent one night with her. It wasn't just sex, he recalled. He had had *just sex* with many women. But with Gabrielle, he had made love. He memorized her body, drew in her taste. He wanted to be close to her. For once, *he* felt loved.

Before that night, he had wanted more than friendship and made that clear to her a few times. He remembered when they had their first argument he told Gabrielle he wanted to be her husband. She fired back with, 'I don't love you, J.J.!' She only cared about him as a best friend. That night, he almost lost her friendship.

The day after they slept together, she went back to Ravolie. J.J. knew she would. J.J. realized he'd never be able to force Gabrielle to fall in love with him. But in that one night they spent together, he knocked her up. It took a while for Gabrielle to tell John and J.J. the truth. J.J. learned from Felecia Harrison that he indeed had a son.

J.J. DECIDED to take a break from searching the hospital for Jackie. Perhaps someone had already found her anyway. The whole hospital seemed to be looking for the four-year-old. *Why was Rolando here? He couldn't find a dog if it pissed on his shoe. Who called him? Felecia?*

Little Jackie had turned four today and her mother—only twenty. *August tenth, the day of hell.* Again, J.J. held back his tears. He stood in front of the counter, ran the faucet. He rubbed the stabbing cold water over his eyes and cheeks.

"Bobbie," he muffled Gabrielle's nickname. "I bet you know where your daughter is."

Suddenly, he looked to the floor. Under the counter of the sink, he noticed Jacqueline Marie Ravolie's pink shoe.

He almost smiled when crouching. "You do realize hiding from the people who love you isn't right, don't you?"

"I know it's wrong," said the little voice.

"Rolando is here, and the hospital is surrounded by muscle men wearing expensive suits." He changed his tone and attempted to make the little girl smile. Cautious, he thought. She just lost her mother. "Do you know everyone is looking for you? Your daddy is going crazy 'cause he can't find you. He thinks someone kidnapped you."

"Don't tell Grandma she was driving me nuts. I just wanted to be alone."

"So you come in here?"

"What are you doing in the girls' bathroom, J.J.?"

He sat on the floor, crossed his legs, and said, "This is the men's."

"Oh."

"You wanna talk about it?"

"Grandma or Mommy?"

"Either."

"No," she said.

"Should we go tell your daddy you weren't kidnapped by aliens?"

She gave a brief nod.

J.J. lifted her from the floor and sat her on the countertop with her little pink-shoed feet dangling over the edge. He loved her as if she were his own. She was Bobbie's. A younger image of her. He could see Bobbie in Jackie's blue eyes. He could feel Bobbie's skin when holding Jackie's hands. After wiping her cheeks with his fingertips he said, "I love you munchkin."

J.J. scooped her up, and carried her through the hallway and into the direction of where he knew Ravolie would be sitting. Ravolie sat with his back against the wall, studying the tiles of the floor.

Ravolie looked up from running his fingers through his dirty blond hair. Immediately, he stood and dashed down the hallway towards them.

Maria entered the hall. "Oh thank God," Maria spoke to herself. "Jackie."

J.J. put Jackie on the floor and she ran to her daddy. John scooped her up. He hugged and kissed his daughter.

Jackie spoke softly, "I'm sorry Daddy. Is it true that Mommy's dead?" she asked.

John gave a brief nod. Hugging her tightly, he turned toward J.J. "Where'd you find her?"

"Men's room."

"Men's bathroom? Huh?" He turned toward Rolando. "Stay away from me, man. You hear me. You don't come near me; don't come near my children. Stay away from my home—"

Gabrielle's father spoke, "Rolando, I don't want you or your wife attending my daughter's funeral. You or your people are not welcomed there."

Pointing a finger at Rolando's face, John said, "You're nothin'."

Chapter 2

Father and daughter lay on top of the blanketed mattress inside a hotel room, the side of their heads pressed firmly into their pillows. Side by side, they looked at one another.

Jackie broke the silence. "Daddy? What will we do without Mommy?"

"Good question." He tucked a loose strand of dark brown hair behind her ear. "She took care of us. It's a good thing I know how to cook, huh?" he asked; she smiled. He kissed her forehead, stood, and draped the comforter over her.

There was a knock at the door.

John opened the door to see his best friend Mick Harrison and his wife Felecia standing in the hallway. "How's Jackie?" Mick asked.

"She's almost asleep. Come on in," he said in a mere whisper. "I gave her a dose of this—" he showed them, and then stuffed it into the carry-on bag "—to help her sleep. I should've gotten a prescription for myself, but I didn't trust—"

"Robbie is confused," Mick interrupted. "J.J. needs your help fathering that little boy. I never want to hear you say—"

"I won't." John shrugged, blew out air. He sat on the edge of the bed.

Mick sat in the chair, while Felecia remained standing. "How're Gabrielle's parents treating you?" Mick asked.

"They're so damn ignorant," John said.

"They just lost their daughter," Felecia said.

"It's still unacceptable," Mick told her.

John struggled to understand why the Newtonendie's were treating him with complete disrespect. He was her husband, and they had loved one another. They had been together for five years. They almost died together. Even though they buried Gabrielle today, a huge part of him died with her.

9

"Do you know where you're going to live?" Felecia asked. "Are you going to live at your estate?"

"Since Shedel's been living there, I might sell to him. He's selling his condo. He can't live there 'cause—"

"Why would you do that?"

"I'm thinking about buying something smaller," John said, ignoring her critical tone. "Something with a basketball court or a one lane bowling alley," he joked; Mick chuckled. "The tennis court is not yet finished. The pool isn't complete. The other day Gabrielle told me to get a few horses so I could teach the kids to ride. Maybe I'll do that next. If only I'd asked her for a list, I'd know what my next step should be. Tell me I'm nuts."

"Hey, man. If Gabrielle was my wife, I would've done the same."

"What do you mean by *that?*" Felecia asked; Mick averted his eyes. "I talked to Roxy today," Felecia told John. "*She* called me. Jeffrey wants to rebuild the beach house."

"Why?"

"Guilt perhaps," Mick answered.

"He's already started," Felecia said. "He's going to put it up on stilts. Three floors, an elevator, four-car garage. A huge kitchen, since you like to cook," she added. "Six bedrooms and three fireplaces." She paused. "Oh, and a hot tub out on the deck that'll seat six."

"Why not eight?" Mick groaned.

"I haven't been back there, since it blew. There's stuff in there." John wiped his palms on his slacks. His forehead gained an extra wrinkle. The agitation began to grow.

"Roxy said that all your possessions not damaged in the fire or destroyed by water were collected," Felecia said. "Jeff's storing it away for you, so when you're ready to pick and choose what items you want, he'll have your stuff at his house."

"Felecia, will you stop!" Mick growled.

"Was there anything that was saved of Gabrielle's?" John asked an annoyed Mick. "I want everything. I want her clothes. I want her perfume. If her robe was hanging in the bathroom—"

Felecia commented, "A safe made it through, and the vase Bobbie made in school and some jewelry."

"I know Rolando has the jewelry box I gave Gabrielle for Christmas five years ago," Mick said. "Since the house was sprinklered—"

Felecia interrupted, "There was nothing left of the kids' room or play room. At that end of the house, nothing was salvaged from the fire. But, whatever was under your bed or near the Jacuzzi came out all right."

"There's got to be at least a million dollars worth of necklaces and earrings and rings in that box you gave her," John told Mick. "She kept the jewelry box in the bathroom near the Jacuzzi."

"When are you going to get the jewelry from Jeffrey?" Felecia asked John. "I'll pick it up for you."

"*I* will bring it to you," Mick said sternly. "Tomorrow."

"Our wedding pictures and some video tapes were in the safe. I don't know all the things she stored in there," John said. "She used the safe almost like a time capsule. I know there're things like the kids' birth certificates and our marriage certificate. The day before we were married in Hawaii there was a champagne bottle I had opened and she kept the cork and put it in there. There was also a rock that she and I used to carve our initials into the stone wall inside the cave behind the waterfall." He grimaced, shaking his head a bit. "She placed a rock in a safe." He paused. "What else did Roxy say?"

"He already started bulldozing it and Jeffrey would mail you the keys when it was done," Felecia said.

"He can't demolish it without my consent," John said angrily.

"All taken care of," Mick said. "He hasn't started."

John blew out a sigh of relief. "I won't be able to live in this new house. I can't live there."

"Maybe we can live there when it's done, Mick?"

"I can't believe you," Mick said, shaking his head.

Felecia continued, "He knew you didn't want to live there, that's why he's not going to charge you for the demolition or the rebuilding."

"Did Roxy say that too?" John asked, sarcastically.

"Yes," Felecia said.

Mick rubbed his temples. "John, is there anything we can do for you?" he asked. "We're here to ask you if there's anything you need. Not to make matters worse," he said, giving Felecia a dirty look.

"I need you to get my belongings from Rolando tomorrow," John said. He gave up looking for Gabrielle and me. That night keeps playing over in my head. Where was he? Why didn't he come to my house? The burglar alarm notified him as soon as Bernadette's entourage fired at the front door. Outside, Gabrielle and I, we stalled, just so he ... While we were in that damn box Mick, I kept saying Rolando will find us. I told Gabrielle that he'd find us. In the five years we lived at the beach house, not once did we ever have a false activation."

"I know, man. I know," Mick said. "I'll go with Trevor, Brandon, and Lenny. We'll get everything."

"The Recording Studio," John said. "I want to change the name to Bobbie's Place. Can you get this moving for me?"

"No problem, man."

"Fe, I know Gabrielle was your friend, too," John said. "You two grew up together. I'll find something of hers for you that I know she would've wanted you to have."

"I'll make a list for you. Actually, I have one here in my purse." She began to rummage through her black bag. "Are you going to stay in New York?" she asked, while she looked for her list.

"I have full custody of Robbie, but Shedel lives in New York. Out of respect for him, I won't move out of state with the kids. Maybe we'll live together. But, I'm not sure if that'll work. I don't know. Mick?" John looked to him for advice. "I just don't know if it would be a wise choice for the two of us and the kids to live together. I can see the headlines now, and Gabrielle would be rolling over in her grave," John said. "I owe him my life. I can't believe he and the kids found us. I still can't believe that Jackie got a hold of Shedel's gun and if she didn't kill Bernadette at Shedel's condo, he sure did."

"Where is J.J. now?" Felecia asked John.

"Shedel flew back to Long Island with Robbie?"

"Are you going to keep Robbie?" Felecia asked.

"Robbie stays with me until he's thirteen. Then he'll have the choice of staying with me or living with Shedel. Gabrielle wanted it that way."

"Is J.J. all right with this?" she asked.

"Shedel knows Gabrielle didn't want the two of us to fight for custody, so I know he's going to go along with what she wanted."

"J.J. could take Robbie away from you—"

"Will you shut up! Christ," Mick said. "You always have to say the wrong things at the wrong time. I apologize John. She's just so ..."

"It's okay Mick."

"No, it's not. You embarrass me sometimes," he told her. "No, you embarrass me all the time!"

"I'm just telling him what reality is. J.J.'s going to fight for Robbie," she shouted back.

"There's a Will and I already have full custody and since Robbie has been living with me and his mother since he was born, no judge will allow for him to be taken away from me."

"It doesn't matter anyway, Felecia," Mick said. "Shedel won't try to take Robbie away from John and you better not start any rumors. I apologize, John. There's no excuse for her."

"You don't need to apologize for me, because I haven't said anything *wrong*. It probably will happen, John. He's going to try."

"Our flight leaves in a few hours. Would you like for us to take Jackie back with us, so you can finish things up with Gabrielle's parents tomorrow?" Mick asked.

"I don't know. I want Jackie to stay with me. She's keeping me from drinking—"

"I'll go with them, Daddy." Jackie sat up.

He turned to look behind him. "Are you sure, cutie?"

She crawled toward him. He set her in his lap and weaved his fingers through a few strands of her hair near her ear.

"I'll see you tomorrow, right?" she asked her father.

"You sure will." As he kissed her head, he lovingly tugged softly on her ponytail. John handed her to Mick and she set her head on his shoulder. "I have a bag over here for her," John said, and he handed it to Felecia. "Some cookies; some juice. She'll probably sleep. Here's her bear." John grabbed Teddy from under the blanket and handed the soft brown bear to Mick.

"Is there anything else you need?" Mick asked him.

"No. I'll see you tomorrow. Probably around five."

"Bye, John," Felecia handed him her list before she exited.

SEVEN MONTHS LATER

WEARING A HOSPITAL NIGHTGOWN, Kathryn Morris stared at herself in the full-length mirror.

She was a woman, not yet twenty-one. Short black hair; blue eyes. With her lips pursed, she wouldn't form a smile or a frown. Creasing the ends of the nightgown to her sides, she gazed down at her nakedness.

Basketball-size, she thought, while looking at her belly. She placed her hands firmly around it, while gently rubbing her stretching abdomen.

She was nine months pregnant. That's what they had told her. Soon, she wouldn't be pregnant nor would she be holding a baby in her arms. She felt her unborn child's kick and watched the child's elbow snail it's way underneath her skin. Perhaps, at the moment, he or she wanted to suck its thumb.

Kathryn tied the front of her nightgown and sat on the bed behind her.

She waited.

She had kept her body in shape, watched her diet, and stayed healthy. There was something about this baby, a connection perhaps. A correlation to her past. A link to her future.

She could dress and run from this house. But it was too late. The induction of labor had begun. If she ran now, she'd be able to keep her baby forever. She could run to a hospital. No, they'd find her.

She had nothing that she knew of. No possessions, no money, nothing. How could she run? In what direction would she go? She knew no one. She had no other family. Nor did she have any friends. The ones who called themselves her parents seemed to be. Yet, there were days when she wished they weren't.

Her father appeared to be a good man. Her mother was loving and kind. They traveled a lot. He spoke at conferences. Kathryn had attended one of his lectures once, before her pregnancy was revealed.

Her pregnancy had caused them embarrassment. But, it was her life as a prostitute, which was causing them shame.

She couldn't remember her life. Let alone being a prostitute. Why did she do *that?* Still, she wondered. Didn't she have some other skills? They had helped her with her past as best as they could. But somehow, she was suffering from a memory lapse. Some traumatic event had caused her to forget—everything.

It was almost as if she was born only seven months earlier. She awakened in a dark motel room with two police officers standing over her. Their flashlights shined into her face. After opening her eyes to the bright light, she noticed the cocaine smeared on a small-size mirror on the nightstand beside her.

She remembered wearing a hot pink leather skirt no longer than mid-thigh. Her pierced belly button was revealed below a spaghetti strap pink cami. At least she was dressed, she mused.

An officer cuffed her. While she stood next to the bed, she noticed the roaches on the dirty, torn square-tiled floor, scurrying from the beam of the flashlight.

Why was she there? How did she get here? Who was she? What was her name?

Later, the person who called himself Reverend Richard K. Morris had come to bail her out of jail. He claimed that he was her father. Her name was Kathryn Lyn. He had called her Katie. She swore she had never seen this man before. But, she left with him. He had taken her to this house.

Kathryn knew what she had to do. What the reverend and his wife had told her to do. She had to trust them. They were her parents. They knew what was best for her. But mainly, what was best for *their* family. And, they seemed to know her, even though she didn't know herself.

Still, she didn't know if the baby was a boy or girl. Her parents thought it would be best for her, for them, not to know. No matter what was growing inside of her, Kathryn didn't want to let go. She didn't want to give her baby up for adoption, even though she had already signed all the papers. She wanted to keep her baby even if her past cocaine use may have retarded the fetus. She wanted to care for her baby. She'd work through any behavioral problem or excessive crying. Kathryn was strong willed. For the reverend and his wife, she remained cooped up in this house for seven months. She made it this far, inside these four walls.

Who was her child's father? Probably a crackhead or heroin addict. She couldn't remember the man she had slept with, or if she had slept with many men. She assumed she had, since she had been working the streets. Yet, she didn't remember any of the men that called for her. In the past seven months, no one had telephoned her. Not a girlfriend, not a boyfriend, nor a relative. Only her parents called from wherever they were to make sure she was all right. She was eating, taking care of herself. Taking her pre-natal vitamins, as well as the pills the doctor prescribed so that her memory would one-day return.

Hours later, three people were with her in her bedroom, but she couldn't see them clearly through the blur of tears and the mind and heart twisting pain of labor. A mid-wife she met previously, a doctor, and a heavyset man wearing a suit and a black hat that overlapped his forehead and covered his dark eyes stood in the shadows of her bedroom. Kathryn's heart raced—the sweat trickled down her spine. Her sweaty black hair screened the terror in her watery-blue eyes.

Her parents hadn't arrived yet, but she knew they wanted to be here for her.

"Don't take my baby!" she yelled. "*Please,* don't take my baby!" she wailed, while reaching out.

The pain of giving birth was nothing to the break in her heart that she was feeling now knowing her baby would be ripped away from her before the contractions ended.

"It's a girl," the mid-wife said softly.

Kathryn sobbed loudly. "Please don't take her! Please!" she wept even louder.

The nurse swaddled the crying baby, covered with Kathryn's blood, in a white flannel blanket and handed her to the dark-eyed man within the shadows.

That same painful evening, Kathryn received word that Reverend Richard K. Morris, and his wife Hailey would not be returning home at all. The engine on their plane had failed. The pilot lost control. They were dead. Vanished from her life.

Again, Kathryn had nothing. No parents. No baby. And no clue to whom she was at all.

Chapter 3

"I hate boats," Angelina said.

"This is a yacht," Michael replied.

"I hate yachts. And why do you keep looking out the window?" she asked.

"To see if there's anyone out on deck besides Germaine."

"Can you put the gun away? I hate guns."

"Angelina, I always keep a gun on me."

"I know and I hate it."

"Is it all there." He turned to view her sprawled out on her belly on the black and white striped bedspread. With her knees bent, her feet were swinging in the air.

"I'm still counting. Six hundred eighty-four, eighty-five, eighty-six. Why can't you just give me seven one-hundred dollar bills?"

"Trust me," he said. "It's all there."

"That's what you told me last week and you were three dollars short."

He laughed. "Angel, I added three hundred the week before last."

She giggled. "I know, and last week you were three dollars short. My fee is seven hundred dollars for this one night a week thing."

"And, the past twelve weeks, you've been worth every penny." He sat beside her, kissed her lips. Michael placed two fingers on her chin and raised it a tad. He looked into her eyes and said, "You're beautiful, funny, and smart. I want you as my wife. You're beautiful—"

"You've said," she groaned.

He kissed her lips. "I look forward to our one night a week together."

"I don't," she said then smiled.

"I'm leaving Australia."

"What?"

"Look into my eyes," Michael said. "And tell me that you'd come here everyday just to get out of your roach infested motel—"

"How do you know where I live?"

"I'm obsessed with you."

"You are not!" She laughed.

"You have some feelings for me, don't you? Even though you're a prostitute, you've got to feel something."

"I'm not a prostitute. I'm a call girl," she added with an insulted eye-roll. "I don't like that name either. But, I wouldn't be here if you didn't pay me. I hate boats—"

"Yacht."

"Whatever. And, my heart is made of glass, I don't feel anything for you and I don't care that you're leaving Australia and—"

"A heart made of glass can shatter easily." His lips were close to her cheek.

"Not this one," she replied.

"You want me more than I want you." He nodded.

"No I don't," she said with annoyance in her voice. "Let me put my money away." She stood to walk to the dresser to shove the bills in her pink sequenced purse.

"Can I undress you slowly this time?" he uttered.

"Nope."

"Why not?" He chuckled. "I'm paying for it."

"You're paying for me to be here on this boat in the middle of the night and to have sex." She turned around. "Not to un—"

Swiftly, he lifted her into his arms and kissed her passionately then lowered her gently to the bed. He began to undo the buttons of his dress shirt, while she looked up at him staring lustfully down at her.

"If I were your husband, I'd give you the world."

"You'll never be my—"

"I'm having my wife killed tonight," he murmured.

"You can't be serious. You serious?" she asked, as he kissed her neck and slid his fingers up her thigh. "Are you serious?" she repeated.

"I'm in love with you," he whispered. "I want only you. You're all I ever think about."

"But you can't kill your—"

"Stop talking," he whispered, placing a finger over her lips. "Go in the bathroom and put on that negligee I bought for you."

"Okay. But you can't have your wife—"

"What's your real name?"

"Angelina *is* my real name."

"No, it's not."

"Yes. It is."

"You told me Candy last week; Roberta the week before. When we met, you were Libby—"

"I'm Angelina tonight, okay?"

"Go put that gown on in the—"

"Why? When you're just going to take it off me."

"Go." He pointed.

"I'm going," she snarled. She walked into the bathroom. While leaving the door opened a crack, she wiggled out of her thigh-high red satin skirt and continued undressing by pulling her shirt over her shoulder-length blond wig.

Michael walked in behind her. He placed his lips on the back of her neck and his arms around her waist, sending shivers into the pit of her stomach. With eyes barely opened, she turned to face him.

He took the cherry-red satin negligee off the hanger and she raised her arms while he slid it slowly over her. When it was fitted, he held her face merely to bring her mouth close to his. Their tongues meshed and they kissed fervently. Her head tilted as he traced her neck with his mouth and tongue, down to the fabric barely covering her breasts. He lifted her up and her legs wrapped around his waist, their bodies yearning to unite. While walking backward toward the bed, he kissed her passionately.

He turned and lowered her slowly to the bed.

Straddling her body, he continued to kiss her aggressively. As he kissed her neck, he cupped her breast then squeezed her nipple through the satin and her lace bra. She placed her hands at his waist and popped the button to his black slacks. The gun, he held within the waistline of his pants.

"I love you, Angelina," he whispered.

"Get rid of the gun," she grumbled.

"I can't," he said in the same tone.

A bright light flashed through the nighttime darkness then passed through the window startling both him and her.

"The lighthouse," Michael said. "We're close. I'm going to take you to the top and make love to you there."

"One day, right?" she whispered.

"Tonight."

Pop. Pop. Pop.

He jumped up and she slid to the floor.

Swiftly he pulled the gun and buttoned his pants. He moved the curtain a tad. "Can you swim?"

"Yes, yes, I can swim."

"There's a life vest under the bed."

Pop. Pop. Pop. Pop. Pop.

Frantically, Angelina pulled up the bed-skirt and reached under the bed. "There's only one, what about you?" she asked, putting her arms through.

"Don't worry about me, love. I want you to jump and swim to the lighthouse. It's about a quarter of a mile." He clicked the strap into place, fastening the life jacket snugly around her beautiful body.

"What's happening?" she asked him.

"Someone is redecorating the boat."

"Do you know what's going on?" She grabbed her purse from the dresser, placed the strap over her head and shoulder.

"I'm sure Germaine is now dead."

"Oh my God! Why?"

"This isn't my boat."

"You stole it?"

"No, borrowing it. It's Jeffrey's," he said between random gunfire out on deck. "Jeffrey Rolando. He's like my third cousin, twice removed."

"What's that mean?"

"*He's* the cold-blooded killer, Angelina. *He's* the rich one."

She averted her eyes. "I should've known—"

"Will you still marry me?"

"Are you even married?"

"Not yet. Angelina, listen to me. Will you come with me to America?"

"Yes." She nodded frantically. "Yes."

"Find your way to the lighthouse. If I don't make it there'll be a boat for you in the mornin'."

"You'll make it, Michael," she said. The tears began to well.

"Angelina, I know you've said you don't know who you are. You don't know what your name—"

"It's Katie."

"Katie." He kissed her quick. He opened the door, lifted her up over the three rails, and she jumped into the water, beginning her journey toward the lighthouse.

"MEET ME IN THE TUB." He laughed.

John positioned himself in the bathtub, made sure the water was at the right level and just the right temperature for them. And, he couldn't forget the bubbles. There were a few floating rose petals in the water as well.

John had picked the white flowers from the rose garden at the estate they owned. And Gabrielle knew this. She still wouldn't go there and he still wouldn't sell.

She took her clothes off in the bedroom, while he tested the flavors of the paint. She entered the room with him sitting in the tub licking the brown paint from his fingers.

"Taste good?" she asked, releasing her terry cloth robe.

"Not really. Maybe the paint has to be on you, so your salty goodness and the paint mix, and then this yellow one will taste like banana."

"I highly doubt it," she told him. Gabrielle grabbed the washcloth from in-between his legs, and set it over the side of the tub. She stood in the water with her back facing him.

"Wait. Stop. Don't sit down," he said politely.

"Why, so you can look at my ass a little more?"

"This flavor is supposed to be chocolate. I'm gonna paint something right above your butt."

"No," she snarled. "You're not going to paint while my ass is in your face."

"It will only take me a minute." He wanted to be serious. Gabrielle stood still. She almost giggled when she felt the paintbrush trail across her tailbone.

"What are you writing?" she asked.

"I'm drawing a picture."

"It doesn't feel like you're drawing a picture. I know what you're writing. You're writing 'John Ravolie was here' right above my ass and you'll probably draw an arrow. I'm not going to keep that on for tomorrow, you know."

"No, I'm writing 'Property of Ra'vole' with no arrow."

"Figures," she smirked.

"Okay. You can't sit until it dries."

"I'm sitting now, and there will be no pictures of your artwork tomorrow." She sat in-between his legs slowly; his hardness aligned with her.

"Could you—um—stand back up? Just a tad now, then—um—sit back down—slowly."

"Sure," she told him, "like this." He penetrated her. "Mmm."

"I need to paint," he whispered.

"No painting—we're intimate." She moaned, and her body crumbled.

"This one is supposed to taste like apple and its green. Do you want a taste?"

"No—No more ... painting." On top of him, she moved her body.

He opened the jar. After he dipped the paintbrush, he placed the bristles to her back. She continued to move her body, while he tickled her spine. "You are disturbing the artist's concentration."

"Your concentration seems to be just right to me," she said softly.

He placed the jar onto the edge of the tub. "This is not fair," he whispered. "How am I supposed to practice on my lady love if she doesn't let me paint on her?" He kissed her back with his lips, his tongue.

"Does it taste like apples?" she asked as he stopped moving.

"Like nasty cinnamon," he told her. "Yuck. I like the chocolate better." He grabbed the other jar and began to paint. He used her entire back as an etch board, all the way up her spine. "One day, I *am* going to draw you in the nude."

"Why? When you can draw on me when I am nude? What are you drawing?"

"Something brilliant on your beautifully tanned back."

"Are you almost done?" she asked.

"I just started." He remained at her neck flipping the brush as if he were a painter. His face was serious, his mouth slightly opened, and his tongue parted his lips.

She then reminded him they had a photo shoot to do tomorrow. "What would we do if this paint doesn't come off my back?" she joked, while sounding quite serious.

"It will." He took the washcloth, dipped it in the water, and began scrubbing the right side of her back, above her kidney. Again, he continued with the soap in the towel.

"Okay—stop what you're doing, you're hurting me."

"It won't come off."

"Whaddya mean?" she said, worried.

"I'm scrubbing this leaf I drew. I'm using soap but it won't come off."

"Try another spot."

He did. "It won't come off," John repeated.

"Don't go messin' around now. You know what I'm wearin' tomorrow and practically my whole body is gonna be uncovered. And I better not have red blotches or paint on me when doin' this photo shoot."

"Well, the five of us will be holding you up, while you're laying in our arms half dressed. The photographer won't be able to see your back."

"No, but the five of you will. This isn't funny, John." She stepped out of the tub. She walked to the mirror and noticed where he had scrubbed. She indeed had a red blotch, and the paint was not coming off her skin.

"Do you like what the artist drew?"

A chocolate rose with apple leaves. He had written, *'Property of John Ravolie'* above her derriere. "Yes, it's a nice rose, but I want it off my body now."

"If it makes you feel any better I have some on my waist. I'm wearin' an open vest tomorrow." He began to scrub the brown and green paint that had dried directly under his navel.

"Call Lily, now! Ask her what we can use to remove this." Gabrielle handed him the cordless phone. He pressed the buttons and told her that voice mail had picked up. "Try Courtney. Maybe she'll know." Still there was no answer at her and Brandon's place. It was late at night and the four perhaps remained at the party or already in bed. "Are you playing a joke on me, 'cause this isn't funny?" she said.

"Look, Gabrielle. I have this paint on me too. It looks worse on me than it does on you. I'm pissed." He stood.

Gabrielle handed him a towel, and he draped it around his waist. "Do you have the box these little jars came in?" She searched a jar for the label.

"No. I took the three jars and placed them in my pocket. Lily just said it was edible paint. She told me banana, apple, and chocolate. I told her I'd bring the jars back to her tomorrow if there was anything left—"

"Give me the phone," Gabrielle told him and she attempted Trevor's cell. "This is Gabrielle. Lily, as soon as you get this message call me right away. John and I were using this edible paint and it won't come off. The photo shoot is tomorrow and we'll have to cancel if the paint doesn't come off us. Call me back at any time tonight. The kids aren't here so let the phone ring until we pick up." She hung up the phone. "This isn't funny," she said, yet almost smiled at him.

"I know." They sat together on the bed. "Are you still in the mood?" he asked.

"No."

"Me either."

THE NEXT MORNING John and Gabrielle went to The Recording Studio. They knew Lily would be there, but *when* was the question. Husband and wife stomped into their separate dressing rooms. They were both still stained with colorful paint, and John wondered, even if Lily did get to The Recording Studio in time, if she would know how to get rid of the dreadful paint.

Gabrielle was to wear a black leather outfit, which made her look like a dominatrix. Practically Gabrielle's whole body was uncovered and her tanned back—completely exposed. She placed on a leather jacket, which covered her figure to her knees, as she wore black fishnet panty hose with gloss-heeled boots trailing to her thighs. She even had a whip.

While Gabrielle walked into the bathroom, he was sure she noticed the smell of cigarette smoke.

Gabrielle walked into the stall beside him and stood on the toilet. Peering over, she looked down at his head. He sat on the toilet cover, looking at a magazine, and he had a cigarette dangling from his bottom lip.

"I know it's you," he told her. "I'm busted. I'm smoking a cigarette. Are you gonna hit me with your whip?" He stood, lifted the cover, and threw the cigarette in, flushed, and then walked out to stand by the sink counter. "This is a cool picture of us," he mentioned, showing her the spread.

He wore black leather. His open leather vest with the fluorescent green color on his stomach looked hilarious and he knew Gabrielle wanted to laugh; yet, she didn't. He wore earrings and makeup. His hair was styled by someone else other than Lily.

"You look hot!" he told her.

"So do you. If we weren't in a rush I'd ... Give me your belly," she told him. "Rubbing alcohol will take your paint off." She sprayed him, and began to wipe him gently, so his hard abdominal muscles would be perfect for the shoot.

She looks amazing. Simply amazing. "I know, you'll never let me paint again," he said to her smiling.

"You can paint," she said to him. "Just not on my body ever again."

"I'm gonna paint a picture of you one day."

"No one would buy it," she said jokingly.

"Take off the coat," he said, and she did.

"Do you like?" she asked.

"You look hot!" he told her. "You'll be on the top ten list in no time."

"Don't get me angry," she told him.

"You look hot!"

"You've said. The guys are waiting. Let's go."

They both walked into the studio and Ra'vole had no problem lifting Gabrielle into their arms as the photographer took their picture.

HE FELT THE HAND cupping his shoulder. John placed his hand on hers.

"Hi," Jackie said.

He looked over his shoulder. "Hi," he said with a smile.

"Were you thinking about Mom, again?"

"How long have you been standing behind me?" John asked his daughter, while staring out into Long Island Sound.

"A couple minutes. I didn't want to startle you. How much longer are you going to stay out here?"

"I'm done." He stood.

With an arm slipped around her waist, father and daughter walked toward the beach house.

Chapter 4

"**J**ohn!" she shouted. "I'm stuck in the elevator!"

John took a deep breath and exhaled slowly. He placed his release key into the panel to open the guard shaft doors. The two doors opened instantly. "Stand back," John said, his voice a cautious whisper. "Check the frame," he added, while examining the elevator car. It was six feet above the platform. "Are you all right?" he asked.

"I'm fine!"

He breathed an outward sigh of relief.

"You're not claustrophobic are you?" Mick shouted.

"No," she said with a laugh. "I'm bored!"

Lenny's gaze turned to Mick. "I don't see or hear anything."

"Bobbie, why didn't you sound the alarm?" John asked. "Why didn't you pick up the emergency phone?"

"Are you nuts?" she answered. "This is embarrassing!"

John laughed and looked up into the elevator shaft. "Bobbie, are the lights on?"

"Not the usual ones," she shouted.

"Did you touch any buttons when the car stalled?" John asked.

"No," she said. "Do you want me too?"

"No!" His voice boomed out into the shaft.

"I'll just sit here and twiddle my thumbs then!"

"Mick," John said, "go to the control room, and turn off the mainline disconnect switch." John looked underneath the elevator car. "Bobbie, I'll get you out!"

"WHAT'S HAPPENING?" she yelled.

"Mick's going to lower the car, then the doors will open," Lenny said, "but if they don't, I'm going to have fun with this crow bar."

27

"The elevator's not going to crash to the ground is it?" she asked lightheartedly at first, but then grew nervous. "Is it?"

"Noooo. The elevator's not going to crash," John said from above her. "At least, not with me sitting here," he mumbled.

"What are you doing up there? Why couldn't you just call the elevator company like I asked you too?"

"Then he wouldn't be able to rescue you," Lenny said.

"How you doin' in there?" John asked her. "Are you sick, sweetheart? It's not getting too hot, is it?"

"I'm fine," Gabrielle said. "I should've brought a book."

"What happened, Bobbie?"

"Whaddya mean?"

"What'd you hear when you stepped into the elevator?"

"I hope you're not blaming me for this. Per Bobbie's Elevator Code, I'm not supposed to be trapped alone."

John smirked. "I need to know, so I can figure out what *your* problem—"

"Do you know anything about elevators?" she asked.

"Bobbie, this is *my* elevator, so just tell me," he groaned.

"I scanned my *new* key card and the doors opened," she said.

"Immediately? With normal power?"

"Yes," Gabrielle said.

"Then what happened?"

"I jumped inside." She paused.

"You entered the elevator. Then what?" he asked.

"After pressing the 'One' button, the doors stayed opened. I pressed the button again, but still nada. Then I pressed the 'Door Close' button."

"You pressed the 'One' button twice and the 'Door Close' after that?"

"Yep. And then the doors closed," she said. "Well, the doors didn't close like they normally do—"

"Whaddya mean? Chopping action?" He chuckled.

"No." She giggled. "They closed—uh—unevenly, I guess. Then the elevator went down. Then the power shut down and the lights went on. And then I said, *Noooo,* just like you normally do. *Roy, can you hear me? I'm stuck in the elevator!* I banged on the door. I didn't pick up a red phone or touch any more buttons after that."

"Bobbie," John whispered, "I'm going to rescue you."

She laughed, but then stopped, since the elevator rocked. John wasn't on top of the car anymore. Then, gradually, the elevator descended to the first floor.

KATIE COUGHED, sucked in air while attempting to stand. The jagged rocks sliced her bare feet with each step. Due to having sea legs, she fell to her knees. Now, one bled. She began to crawl from the waves that continued to push her to her knees.

Her purse had opened in the water and all the money was lost forever, she realized. "Damn." She coughed again.

As soon as the water meshed with sand, she sat and turned to face the direction to where the boat was hijacked.

After hearing the explosion on the yacht, she had swam faster toward the lighthouse. Now, her arms felt as if they were still moving, her legs ached from kicking. Her eyes burned from the salt. Out in the water, oiled-flames replaced the spot where the boat was seized and anchored.

The gunfire had fallen silent.

While sitting, she felt the pain shoot through her neck, up through her artery and behind her ear. "Not now. *Please,*" she pleaded with herself. "Not now."

Another bolt of lightning shot into her ear as she reached into her purse. After undoing the zipper to the secret compartment, she dug inside to pull out her medicine.

Katie's head began to throb. A heartbeat settled into the right side of her skull. Like a giant caterpillar, the beat began to crawl, finding its way to different sections of her brain, only to rest for a moment to beat, and then move on. She had lost her wig and her blue-black hair in a boys cut felt as if the strands were trembling, with the ends on fire.

Her hands shook, yet she held down on the lid and turned. While pouring pills into her hand, some dropped into the sand. Without coordination, she placed two into her mouth with her palm. She gagged with no water to escort the pills. She attempted to swallow, and swallow, and swallow. At last, one went down her throat and then another.

While feeling the pressure of the pills in her chest, she crawled toward the water.

Cupping her hands, she sipped the water. Only to find herself spitting. Attempting to emit the salt. "Oh no. Please, not now. Please."

LIKE AN ERUPTING VOLCANO, THE BEACH HOUSE EXPLODED.

As if in slow motion, they turned around.

"My.Babies!" Katie cried out. Then she received a hard jab to her shoulder. Katie fell. With all of her might, she crawled to stand. After another blow from the glock to her spine, Katie again fell to the ground. He ran forward and kneeled behind her to protect her. He held her hands at her waist. And as they melted with the sand, they watched.

She laughed. "Your babies?"

Katie tilted her chin to glance at the woman's throat. The evil woman spit into her hair.

"You fucking bitch!" Katie yelled, throwing sand into the air. She brought her leg up and out and kicked the woman in the kneecap. He fought off one of her thugs when the evil woman fell to the ground. Ferociously, Katie leaped on top of her, and began to strangle her. Again, she couldn't see her face. Someone grabbed Katie and pulled her off. She landed on top of the man's legs.

COUGHING.

She heard the coughing.

"Katie!" he yelled. "KATIE! KATIE!"

"Michael?" Dazed, she sat and collected her bottle. While placing the container back into her purse she yelled, "Michael! Where are you? Michael?"

She saw his shadow running toward her. Was this a dream or reality? At first, she wasn't sure. She couldn't tell until she saw his face. "Michael," she said his name crying.

"Katie, are you all right?" He knelt beside her, touched her face before wrapping his arms around her.

"I am now," she said as a tear rolled down her cheek.

He kissed her while his hazel eyes grew watery. "I was scared that I lost you."

"No, I've been through worse," she said. "I think."

"Come on, love. Let's go into the lighthouse. Are you hungry?"

"Starving."

"I'M SITTING HERE in the dark guys." Her voice sounded strange. "I'm scared of the dark."

"Whaddya mean?" John asked her. "Those lights are made to stay on for four hours."

"Is Bobbie stuck in the elevator?" J.J. Shedel laughed. "Do you have a back-up power supply?" he asked.

"We have a generator," John said.

"Make sure there's power going to the button wires, they should be on after the standby system is hooked up. Have her press the 'Door Open' button. Works every time."

"Brandon, Trevor, come and help me find the generator bypass switch," Lenny said.

"Press the green button," John said.

"The one with the arrows pointing in opposite directions?" she asked.

"Yes," he told her.

"It's dark and I don't know which one it is," she said with a laugh.

"Be right back, Bobbie. Lenny, call me if the doors unlock."

"What about the card reader?" J.J. asked.

"The card won't open the doors," John said, walking away.

Lenny added, "It's not a card reader issue."

"If I swipe this, the doors might open," J.J. said.

"Put your card away," Lenny told him.

He scanned his card. "The power's not on for the card reader, either? Why'd you people disconnect everything? And, if you had power going to those buttons on the inside—"

"Bobbie, press any button, except for the 'Alarm' button," Mick said. "I'd strangle Shedel if I heard the siren."

"Okay."

"No. Don't do it!" J.J. shouted at her. "The elevator will move, and *you* probably took it off its track," he told Mick.

"Lenny," she said quietly. "I pressed them all."

Lenny sat on the floor. "At least you tried," he told her.

"How do you take an elevator off its track?" Mick shouted. "You know nothing about elevators, man."

Bobbie stood in front of the buttons, except she couldn't remember which one was which. She pressed another, then another one.

Irritated, Mick continued, "Shedel, the elevator can't move. There's no power going to that motor, and there is, to the 'Door Open' button."

"How can there be power when she can't see those buttons?"

He blurted out, "If you knew anything about elevators—"

John walked passed the brawl. "The doors won't release, sweetheart," he said. "You're coming out the top."

"*No.*" Her voice now upset. "I thought Lenny was going to pry open the doors."

"Mick's got the bar," Lenny told her, except she didn't respond to his sarcasm. "I'm ready with the bar, Bobbie. I'm waiting for the good word."

"Two minutes," John said.

"She'll be inside for another hour. Bobbie, press the open button. I know what I'm talkin' 'bout," J.J. told John.

Suddenly, Bobbie noticed a soft glow, and then pressed the 'Open Door' button. She held her push with her right index finger.

"Do you have a better idea?" he asked Shedel, as the doors slid open with the power source draining.

"I DID," Katie said, as Lenny helped the left side glide to open. Katie looked around and there was applause from the others. Two men stood in front of her with their hair, faces, and clothing covered with dust, spider webs, and oil. Katie wrapped her arms around someone and kissed the unknown's cheek.

"CAN WE have elevator picnics more often?" she asked.

"John's Elevator Code is different than Bobbie's," he replied, placing a blanket to the floor.

"John's codes always are," she groaned. "I'll tell you now, there's a major conflict with our stairwell codes." She sat. "I think I'll be rejecting John's Elevator Code, as well."

"There's nothing romantic about a cold-hearted stairwell. You're impressed with my beach code, aren't ya?"

"I have to wait five months for you to initiate it. What does John's Elevator Code entail?" she asked.

"John and Bobbie shall only have picnics—on the evening of— when Bobbie gets stuck in the elevator—without John." John sat across from her, and then Bobbie handed him a filled, plastic champagne glass, along with an opened bottle.

"What you're trying to say is, you made sure Al here will never keep me alone with him again, didn't you?" They linked their arms and John took a sip from his glass. "Didn't you?" Bobbie asked again and then drank a gulp full.

"Yep," he said. Bobbie gave an exaggerated sigh, and then he kissed her, as they sat, with the doors opened within the main hall of The Recording Studio. "You named the elevator *Al?*"

"Yep. We bonded. He likes the name."

"What would I do without you? You have the ponytail going on, you're all slaphappy."

"I'm happy I rescued myself before I got sick in your elevator."

"You told me you weren't sick. Didn't Shedel rescue you?"

"Nope," she said.

"Didn't Trevor or Brandon, since—?"

"*I* was the one who pressed the button."

"Then why'd you hug Shedel?"

"You and Mick were dirty," Bobbie said. "Lenny was inspecting the doors. Trevor and Brandon were the paramedics on the scene. They had all that equipment as if Al was in cardiac arrest. And, I did feel nauseous toward the end. I thought if I were to, I'd puke on J.J., since he made Mick so angry. J.J. had no right to interfere—"

"You thought me and Mick were already having serious fashion problems, didn't you?"

"No hard feelings?"

He smiled. "I think you've had too much to drink."

"Me too. A couple sips of grape juice, causes me to get drunk, real fast." She giggled uncontrollably.

"Bobbie, you drank almost the whole bottle. Grape juice causes constipation."

"I'll use prune juice to reverse the effect."

"Okay now, I have serious questions for you. Stop laughing."

"I'm laughing, because ... you ... have grease in your ear." Bobbie fell backward, her laughter hysterical.

John leaned forward, then licked the tip of his index finger, and attempted to place his finger in her left ear. "What'd you think of Jamie and Suzie's reaction?" He pulled her arms to sit.

"Hell, I was in shock," Bobbie said. "Jamie hugged me before Suzie had. They both acted as if *Al* was torturing me. Jamie even looked like she'd been crying." Bobbie took a sip of John's grape juice. "I thanked Jamie for tattle tailing that I was late, in which I wasn't. I showed for work fifteen minutes early."

"You still weren't on time." He chuckled.

Bobbie took another sip. "Did I mention, Jamie spent eighteen dollars on my lunch today?"

"I've lost count how many—"

"Tomorrow Suzie's buying?"

"I gave them the money," John said.

"You did not—" she looked at him wide-eyed "—Did you?"

"Noooo—" he chuckled "—How'd you stay so calm? You were inside Al here, for almost two hours." He filled her glass.

"I know somethin' 'bout Al. Besides him being a roped hydraulic driving machine."

"What'd he tell you?" His voice was nervous. John handed Bobbie's glass to her.

"He's *your* elevator. *Then,* after we're married, he'll be *our* elevator. Then, my elevator code will override yours and we'll have many more picnics." She removed the blanket a tad and then stood the glass near her right side. "He told me you said so."

"I know you're not finished," John said, and then smiled.

"Hm. I trust you with"—she paused—"with—"

"Spit it out."

"—*my* life. You and Mick's grease and grime, was a little overwhelming I must add, and brought tears to my blue eyes." Her voice grew serious. "I knew—you knew—what you were doing. I remained calm for you, since I knew how worried you were."

"No one was worried 'bout you. They were worried about you throwing up on *Al*."

Bobbie moved her face close to his. "I know the truth. You're my hero," she said softly.

John smirked. "I love you," he told her, and kissed her.

"You've said." She smiled, with her lips touching his. Bobbie handed John his empty glass. She looked up and noticed the button panel hanging by the compartment's wires. "I see Al's internal organs have not yet been replaced."

"Maybe, you can assist Trevor with the surgery tomorrow."

"You just sounded like—"

"I'm sorry. I feel like an ass. Do you know about elect—?"

"I was gonna say Jamie, not my father. She always tells me, *'Maybe you can assist tomorrow,'*" she mocked her. "Did the fabulous five figure out what was wrong with my new friend?"

"The consensus is—" he did a drum roll on his thighs "—heart failure."

"Power failure? I noticed Trevor had this device. He seemed to be checking for a magnetic field or electrical current, while Al was detached from his life force. You never told me Trevor had multiple degrees."

"I can never keep a secret from you." John bumped the wall with his forearm and the fluorescent-white lighting changed to a purple glow, her favorite color.

"Ooh, I am so very surprised. I am. I am." She began to giggle. "I thought ... Trevor and Brandon ... *too* funny."

"What?" He smiled at her. "You thought what?" His smile grew wider. "Tell me?"

"I thought ... they were searching ... for a bomb."

"A bomb?" His laughter filled the room. "You never cease to amaze me. Just wait until the guys hear 'bout this one."

"No. Don't you ever tell 'em," she said, laughing.

"With that answer, you are surprised then?"

"Oh yes. I do like your elevator code," she said, scooting closer. "Oh no, I spilled my other glass of champagne."

He smirked. "Bobbie, per my code only *I* do the customizing."

"Don't worry John, grape juice doesn't stain."

"'Course not. Or soak through your favorite blankey."

"My blankey." She attempted to stand, while John pulled her to the floor.

Bobbie sat in John's lap with her legs wrapped around his waist, her palms at his chest. John supported her back with his arms, and said, "Clap your hands."

She did. The sound of instrumental music played through the overhead speaker.

"Tell me," he whispered.

She gave a blank stare. She smiled. "John, I love you."

The door closed.

"KATIE, wake up."

"Huh? What?"

"You just said 'John, I love you.'"

"Huh?"

"You've been dreaming again. Katie," Michael said. "Katie, wake up."

"What?"

"You've been dreaming. You were dreaming, love."

"What'd I say?" she uttered. "What was I dreaming about?" She sat to find Michael sitting beside her with a glass of water and two pills.

"Here, love."

"More pills? I can't Michael. This is all I've been eating."

"They're working. You keep dreaming. What do you remember? You were talking in your sleep. I think you were stuck in an elevator. Do you remember?"

She shook her head. "I don't remember anything, Michael." She took the two pills and a gulp of the water. "We don't know if I'm just dreaming or what I'm dreaming really happened in my past."

"You want to find out don't you?"

"Of course I do. Michael, you know what's more important to me."

"I know, love. I'll find your baby girl."

Chapter 5

John shouted back, "Aimee, why do you have to start shit? Every single morning. I just wanna wake up, have breakfast alone, read the goddamn paper. And you walk in here grumbling and complaining about something. Yesterday was a broken nail, the day before you couldn't find your purse. I want you to move the hell out've my house. I'm sick of this shit. You're not sleeping in my bed anymore. I don't want you sleepin' in my house."

Jackie walked into the foyer and overheard her father and stepmother arguing in the kitchen. They passed her. Aimee now stomped up the stairs, and he followed. Halfway up the stairs, John turned around looked toward Jackie, "Good morning, sweetheart."

"Morning, Dad." She smiled.

Melinda entered the room with a fresh bouquet of white roses. "Good mornin', Miss Jackie."

"What are they fighting about this time?"

Melinda shrugged. "They're fighting started because of comments Miss Aimee made about your mother."

Jackie dashed up the stairs.

Aimee had a vase over her head and was ready to throw. When John picked flowers from the garden, he used to fill the vase for Gabrielle and then after her death, Jackie.

Jackie knew her mother made the vase in high school or perhaps she was younger. Carved into the bottom were her initials, G.N. for Gabrielle Newtonendie. Painted onto white clay were two long-stemmed red roses with thorns and one white rose without.

In the hallway, Aimee threw the vase at John's feet. He took a step back, and the vase broke into many pieces.

Stunned, Jackie murmured, "That was twenty years old."

"Jacqueline!" John yelled. "Aimee, get out of my goddamn house!" He followed Jackie.

"Just because you think that woman saved my life when I was born doesn't mean she has to wreck my life now," Jackie yelled to her father. "You were the one who was shot. You were the one who held me up while bleeding. Wow, she came in when Bernadette left and took me from your arms. If she hadn't you would've gotten up. You don't owe her shit, Dad!"

"Jackie, I'm trying my best to get her out!"

"She just broke Mom's vase! Doesn't Mom mean anything to you anymore?"

"Don't even. You know I loved your mother and still do. How can you ask me that?"

"How could you show her such disrespect by marrying that bitch in the first place?" Jackie slammed her bedroom door in her father's face.

JOHN REMEMBERED the night Jackie came into their lives. While Gabrielle lay unconscious, he took a stroll into the nursery to check on their first-born. There wasn't time to realize the lights to the nursery were not working. Bernadette Malone shot him in the arm. Then one of her thugs came from behind him with a baseball bat. As John lay on his back on the floor with a shattered kneecap, Bernadette placed a plastic strip normally used for identification bracelets around Jackie's neck. Before Bernadette had cut the strip from the roll, she attached it to the glass-sided crib.

Although John had a gun shot wound, he continued to keep his arms in the air, holding Jackie above his head. If he had removed his hand from behind the base of the newborns neck, there would have been serious consequences. Aimee hid herself in the room, and as soon as Bernadette and her hit man left, Aimee ran out from her hiding spot and grabbed the baby from John's hands.

That evening sixteen years ago was still so vivid, however he barely remembered his wedding night to Aimee. He was intoxicated four years ago. He took the nurse and then his backup singer, Aimee, to Vegas. He believes she actually took him. They were married and he called Jackie a few days later. Gabrielle had been deceased for eight years; he was thirty-nine years old, and a drunk. His daughter knew that he was going through a mid-life crisis. He told her he was old, yet not ready to retire. He still loved the music. He loved getting up on stage and doing concerts for millions of people.

Previously, he'd take a break for a year or two and then start record making and touring the world all over again. He'd record an album with his bassist and best friend Mick Harrison (Micky), drummer Lenny Dakota (his stage name Dakota), guitarist Brandon Jones (B.J.), and Trevor La'win, who played any instrument they needed playing. During the summer months,

Robbie and Jackie went with him, but when September came her younger brother and she had to go to school.

He raised Jackie and Robbie in his estate. John had owned this house for many years before he met Gabrielle. Per Aimee's request, they were to stay here and live and per John, he'd never live with Aimee at the new and always renovated beach house. The Ravolie Estate was so huge. His daughter never knew exactly how many people on staff actually lived there. There was someone who took care of the garden, many to take care of the lawn, numerous chefs, and people who cleaned. But John knew them all by name, had even taken time to run background checks, and personally checked their references.

There was an Olympic-size swimming pool out back. John occasionally used it. And, a full-size tennis court where Jackie took tennis lessons. A beautiful rose garden outlined the patio and more roses were up on the terrace. After Gabrielle had died, John rarely tended to the flowers and left their care to the gardener and lawn workers. He brought in his horses from his home in California, but rarely rode.

JUST RECENTLY, Jackie drove past the beach house and noticed her father had built a fire in the pit and watched the waves. Perhaps, he sat on the sand reading a magazine article or a book. Jackie considered that he also talked to her mother out there. She assumed he felt close to her when he was there. In that sand, they were buried alive together one month before her death.

The past four years, he's been unhappy with Aimee. Since the day they had married, they were unhappy together. Jackie knew her father never loved this woman. They drank together mainly after they were first married, but now he has remained sober for quite some time. Aimee and John argued continuously about having children. Aimee wanted to have children and John didn't, but Aimee hated Jackie so much that she didn't understand the argument.

John chose Aimee because he liked her voice when he was drunk, Jackie assumed. So, Aimee sang with him for eight years. After they were married, Aimee never went on tour with Ra'vole again and John found another back up singer. He might have slept with her too, because then she was gone and another one came and went.

Jackie attempted to stay at the other end of the house when Aimee was near, but still, she knew Aimee had men come and go. Jackie noticed her stepmother with the sixteen-year-old boy who took care of the two horses in the stable on Friday nights. Her stepmother sleeping with the boy who was her age made Jackie sick to her stomach. Jackie told her father, but he didn't believe her. Maybe he already knew, but didn't say. Her father always knew more than what he let on.

Rob came over to the house in a limousine, since he now lived with J.J. Occasionally Rob drove J.J.'s motorcycle when he wasn't home. Melinda called him immediately after learning that she had to clean up the broken vase. Melinda always called Robbie. And he seemed to know exactly what to do when it came to his older sister Jackie. Robbie received the pieces from Melinda and walked the flight of stairs to Jackie's bedroom where she remained hidden behind the door.

"Jackie, open up," he said after trying the handle. "Jacqueline! Come on, now! Open up!" He knocked harder.

Jackie stood from her bed, unlocked the door, and she opened it, giving Rob a look of disgust.

He showed her the pieces of the vase, and he shrugged.

She let him enter and he placed the pieces on her bed.

Her brother, although eleven months younger, was taller than she. He was muscular because he worked out with his father lifting weights and was on the dive team at school. He had shoulder-length blond hair, green eyes, and long eyelashes, and he looked exactly like J.J. When their backs were turned, Jackie wouldn't be able to tell the difference if she were staring at their behinds. Well, J.J. was a little taller and Robbie's ass was a little smaller, she thought. Robbie didn't look like their mother at all though, and he didn't have any facial features resembling Jackie either.

"You want to go for a walk and then come back and try to put this vase together?"

"Sure," Jackie said.

Robbie cupped her hand and they jogged down the stairs before Aimee appeared.

The path outside led past the rose garden and the pool, then the sidewalk led to the tennis courts. After walking onto the lawn that her father had once pronounced was his football field, her backyard became a small forest preserve. There was a creek dividing the property between the forest preserve and the football field and in order to get into the woods, a stone bridge over the creek was the pathway. Robbie and she walked hand in hand like boyfriend and girlfriend, but they were mainly just best friends who happened to have the same mother and different fathers.

"Mom would've loved it here," Rob said.

"Maybe."

"Didn't you tell me that Mom loved to go riding?"

"I don't know how many times she rode."

He added, "You told me the day before Mom and Dad were married that Dad took her for a ride on a horse on the beach in Hawaii."

"It was her first time," Jackie said. "On their honeymoon, Dad took a whole bunch of pictures. After that, she loved to ride. Dad said she was a natural. She rode a couple of times after, not here though. She'd never come here and still to this day, I wonder why."

"She would've loved to ride horses through here." Rob continued.

"You think so?" Jackie asked him.

"Yeah."

"I wish when we were younger the beach house didn't burn to the ground. I probably would still be living there. Dad goes there at least three times a week now. I hate the way Jeffrey rebuilt it and so does Dad. When we were younger, it wasn't as big as it is now and it was so warm and homey. Rob you would have loved living there."

"I'm sure I would've."

"Hey, will you move in there with me? You and me? Let's go together. I have to get away from this house. I have to get away from Aimee."

"Dad's going to get rid of her any day now."

"We thought that last week," Jackie grumbled.

"What about school? It's not that bad, is it? Doesn't Aimee usually ignore you?"

"Well, yeah."

"And school has already started, so you'll never see her."

"Well, yeah."

"I already installed a different lock on your bedroom door for you."

"Well, yeah."

"What about that field trip to the insane asylum with your vocational class? I thought you wanted to go. Are you going?"

"Yes, I'm very interested in the psychiatric hospital. I plan to take an internship there once I start college."

"Well, if we moved to the beach house we'd have to change schools and you wouldn't be able to go."

"Can we move after I go?"

"If Dad doesn't get rid of Aimee by then, you'll come live with me and my dad."

"I can't live with J.J.," Jackie said with a laugh.

He laughed with her. They began their journey back toward the house.

"Let's go fix the vase, shall we?" They walked hand in hand into the foyer. Robbie's cellular phone rang to a classic Intensity tune.

"Don't answer it," Jackie said.

"I have to. It's my dad. If I don't answer, he'll be all over me." They sat on the sofa near the three-tier fountain. "Hello? Hi Dad. I'm here with Jackie. I know you want me to help you. All right, I'll be there. I'm leaving now." He ended the call. "I'm sorry, Jackie. Dad bought this train set and he wants me to help him put it together. I didn't think he'd be back so soon."

"What is J.J. going to do with a train set?" Jackie asked.

"Watch it go 'round and 'round." They laughed. "I'm sorry. I'll come back tomorrow after school. We're going to be working on this thing all day and well into the night. I know I'll probably fall asleep in class again."

"What was it he made you finish the other night?"

"A seven thousand piece jigsaw puzzle of a naked woman," he said with a laugh. "I tell you, he's insane. He just wants to spend time with me and he's trying so hard. I have to admit, we do have a lot of fun. But, he's nuts."

"I won't start on the vase without you," Jackie said.

"Promise?"

"Promise." They walked outside to the front of the house where the limousine was still waiting. As Jackie waved good-bye to Rob, Aimee walked outside.

"Jacqueline!" Aimee called out. "I'm sorry for breaking your mother's vase. But, she's dead. I don't think she cares."

Aimee's so ignorant, Jackie thought, and then compared her to Felecia, Mick Harrison's ex-wife. "Look, Aimee. I'm sick of your crap. I'm sick of you apologizing for everything you break that was my mother's. I know you never liked me from the beginning, and you only married my father for his money. You're doin' drugs, you're still drinking, and who knows who you slept with last night—"

"You're not going to talk to me like that! I saved your life you little bitch and your mother was a slut. She slept with everyone. Everyday, she'd have a—"

"Well, Aimee I don't believe that's true. I know it's not true. The whole world *knows* that's not true. What my mom and dad had was true love."

"You should start thinking of your mother as the whore she was, instead of the little miss innocent that she wasn't."

"It takes you hours, when standing out on street corners just to get someone to honk their horn, and when someone does it's a boy who hasn't even hit puberty yet. At least my father is smart enough not to have sex with you. He told me you had crabs and he wouldn't go near you if his life depended on it."

"Yeah, well, we sleep together every night, unlike you. You're sixteen and—"

"Is that why you were locked out of the house and sleeping on the pool deck last night?"

"Excuse me," John said, appearing from nowhere.

They both turned to look at him.

"Your daughter hit me," Aimee then said.

"I did not."

"She lies too," Aimee told John.

Jackie blew out a huff of air, turned around, and walked away.

"No, Jackie. Please come back? Stay here, sweetheart," John said.

Jackie turned around and John held his hand out for her to take hold of. He seemed so exhausted; he was so frustrated with Aimee. Gladly, Jackie took her father's hand.

"Aimee, I have something that I want to say to you."

"What John?"

"Go." He pointed toward the drive. "Just go. You will leave my house today and you won't come back ever. I've got so much shit on you that my head's spinnin'. Just go. Jackie, go in your room. There's a surprise in there for you. Go on now," he told her.

"This is the deal Aimee, you get five hundred thousand, not two million. You get to keep that car of yours and were done."

JACKIE OPENED THE DOOR. Many photographs of her mother that Jackie carried in her purse lay on her bed with a long, rectangular box. Attached to the box a card read:

> My Baby Love,
>
> > I'm sorry! I know I owe you more than that. For the past twelve years of your life, it's been hell and it's my entire fault. I don't know how I can make it up to you. I hope you will forgive me. I love you with all my heart. I fixed the vase as well as I could; it looks brand new. There's a little extra and I hope you like it. I'll even help you put it on your wall. I love you!
>
> Love you always,
> Daddy

Jackie opened the box and found a single, long-stemmed white rose. She assumed her father had picked the flower from the rose garden and then found a box for it. Jackie quickly brought the vase to the sink in her bathroom and filled it with water. He did an excellent job fixing it, she thought, there were no leaks. Jackie took the white rose and quickly placed the flower in the vase and set it on her nightstand examining it. She lifted the vase to see her mother's initials aligned perfectly at the base. Jackie realized he must have done this while she walked with Robbie.

Also, rolled up on her bed was a poster. Jackie unraveled it. It was a picture of her mother. Jackie had one in her wallet and he had blown it up into poster size. When did he have time to do this? she wondered. He had to have done this week's ago. When he cared about her, which was the majority of the time, he always did things to make her happy. She thought when he had done things like this—anything that had to do with Gabrielle—it made him happy, too.

John walked into her bedroom. "Do you like?" he asked.

"I love!" Jackie said, the tears welling. They hugged and Jackie looked up into her father's blue eyes and noticed that not only did he look extremely happy, but ten years younger. "She won't be coming back?" she asked him.

"The locks are being changed as we speak."

"What about the gate?"

"Already done." He had a few tacks in his hand. "Now, let's hang this poster."

Chapter 6

"It's so eerie in here," June said to Jackie.

"Shhh, I'm trying to listen."

"...And this is Tom. He's suffering from dissociative amnesia, also known as psychogenic amnesia. He has memory loss of vital personal information."

The class of twelve walked to the next window. The professor continued, "This is Kathryn. We believe her to be suffering from transient global amnesia, which is the sudden appearance of severe, dreamy confusion lasting from as little as thirty to sixty minutes to as long as twelve hours or more. It is unusual, but not an uncommon syndrome. However, Kathryn also appears to be suffering from dissociative and permanent amnesia. She doesn't have any childhood memories, nor does she have any memories up until she was twenty-one years old. Occasionally, she speaks, but not much..."

June called to her, "Jackie—"

"Professor Kane," Jackie spoke up. "What treatment is available for Kathryn, here?"

"We've been treating her for dissociative amnesia as well. We use therapy aimed at helping the person restore their lost memories. If a person is not able to recall the memories, hypnosis or a medication called Pentothal can sometimes help to restore them. Kathryn has had both. She receives two injections everyday and has for the past two months."

"Have the injections helped at all?" Jackie asked.

"Unfortunately, no." He continued, "Also, psychotherapy can help an individual deal with the trauma associated with the recalled memories. We haven't found anything that will work for Kathryn. She is indeed a special case."

"Isn't hypnosis often used in the treatment of dissociative fugue?" Jackie asked.

"Yes, hypnosis can help the patient recall his or her true identity and remember the events of the past. But even if the hypnosis we've used on her has worked, she simply won't tell us. Psychotherapy is helpful for the person who has traumatic past events to resolve. Again, neither has worked for Kathryn."

Suddenly, Kathryn jumped out of bed and threw herself at the glass window. "My babies!" she yelled, startling the class.

Many began to laugh, despite their career intuition not to. Except Jackie. Instead, her eyes met the fear in Kathryn's. Kathryn looked so helpless, trapped, and lost in her white gown and socks, her arms spread across the window. Her eyes were wide; sweat trickled from the strands of her black hair.

Jackie watched as Kathryn held onto the window and slid slowly to the floor. Then, Kathryn tucked her knees and rocked back and forth.

"Occasionally," the professor continued. "She yells. Screams of the trauma. And, we believe she may have been pregnant at one time and had lost her twins."

"There has to be more to that," Jackie muffled. "Professor, what else do you know about her?"

"On the back of her head there is a scar from some unknown brain surgery, which may mean there was some cerebrovascular disease, but all her brain scans show normal. Kathryn is completely unaware of her own identity." He looked at Kathryn huddled there rocking back and forth on the floor, and shook his head in defeat.

The group walked to the next patient, except for Jackie and June. They remained in front of the glass window, watching Kathryn. "They're not even sure if she's thirty-two years old," Jackie mumbled.

"What?" June asked.

"This is Kevin and as the same as the others he has dissociative amnesia. Dissociative amnesia emerges by stress associated with traumatic experiences. Pay attention, this perhaps might be on your next test. Rape, the military, hurricanes, tornados, or natural disasters, abandonment at an early age, or death of a loved one can cause dissociative amnesia. You may just be asked to name a few...."

"You're obviously interested in Kathryn, aren't you?" June asked Jackie.

Jackie pulled a picture from her wallet and showed June. "Can you blame me?" she asked, handing June the snapshot of her mother, who looked just like a younger version of this Kathryn.

"NOW, I WANT YOU to choose a patient, get to know them, ask them questions. Some will tell you stories; others will not. Try to communicate with them the best way you know how and just be yourselves."

"Can I stay with this patient, Professor?" Jackie asked.

"Kathryn?" He placed a finger to his chin. "Jackie, she doesn't say much. She will not harm you, but occasionally she does have loud outbursts about her babies. She came to the facility about ten years ago. A man brought her here and said that he couldn't take care of her anymore. He told us her name was Kathryn Morris and he called her Katie. Katie Lyn.

"All he knew about her was that her parents had died in a plane crash, she had been a prostitute, and he believed she was twenty-one, but wasn't sure. She had no identification. She barely spoke. She was taking pills for pain due to the flashbacks of her trauma. He said that she was taking some other pills, but he didn't know what they were and that is what led her into a catastrophic state of mind."

"She's been here for ten years?" Jackie asked.

"And still there's nothing we can do for her. That's why two months ago we started with the Pentothal injections."

"Does she always have this blank stare on her face? Is she always so frightened?"

"I've never seen her smile. She'll eat on her own. She'll use the bathroom. Brush her hair. She has never attempted to harm herself."

"Let me stay with her, Professor?"

"All right, but if you don't think you can come up with a fifteen-page report on her then I'll assign you to a different patient."

"Yes, Professor. Thank you."

"Everyone has two hours with their patients."

Jackie used her keycard and the door slid open. The door closed automatically behind her. "Hi, my name is Jackie. Jackie Ravolie."

"ROB, YOU HAVE TO HELP ME," Jackie said.

"You're freakin' nuts," he said, pointing a finger in her face.

"What if this woman is our mother?"

"She's dead, Jackie. You know our mother is dead. We both know it."

"I don't think so."

"Let me repeat what you just said, just so I know I've got this straight. You got this van from nowhere. I'm behind the wheel. You want me to break into a psychiatric hospital with you and steal a patient who looks like our mother. And then, we're gonna take this woman home. You don't even know how to take care of a person like this. You don't even know if she'll harm herself. How can you watch her every second of the day? This is nuts, Jackie! Where's your brain?"

"Robbie, just a week. Or, or let's just keep her for the weekend."

"She's not a dog, Jackie!"

"I'll tell Dad on Sunday and we'll see if anything, a memory, or anything happens for her. I'll show her pictures and talk to her. She looks just like Mom. She has to be Mom."

"You're crazy. Mom's dead. Let me refresh *your* memory. After we found her locket, we told my dad. A crane came and pulled the coffin out from the sand. Mom and Dad were in that box for almost seventy-two hours. They were taken to the hospital. Mom and Dad woke up. Dad survived, Mom didn't. She died a month later. She couldn't breathe on her own. She couldn't hold our hands anymore—"

"Why didn't she, Robbie Jason Shedel? Huh? Tell me! Why did Dad survive and Mom didn't. She had to have been drugged. She had the rash and Dad didn't—"

"She died in the hospital. We were both there. Dad was there. We saw her at the wake and—"

"Yeah, after the wake, Robbie, did anybody see her? At the funeral, the coffin went down, but no body went down with it."

"Stop! She was our mother!" Rob yelled. He placed his palms over his eyes and said, "I'm taking you to that place and lockin' you up with those psychos."

It was silent.

Jackie began, "Did I mention I checked the back of her head and she has a scar?"

"So what?" He paused. "Oh, I see, you think this scar is from when the car hit her when she was fourteen. I'll say it again, you belong in that mental ward with that woman."

"Will you help me or not?"

"You're my half-sister and I love you to death, but—"

"Will.You.Help.Me, Robbie?"

"Even if I did help you, we can't make it in through the security."

"We can." Jackie showed him a keycard with her picture on it, then handed him his. "See."

He looked at his picture. "Fake ID's? Where'd you get this from?" he asked, staring at her in disbelief.

"I asked John Rolando to—"

"Rolando? You.Are.Nuts. If Dad finds out you said two words to Rolando—"

"Well, you know he has a crush on me, and I kind of took advantage of his mob affiliations."

Rob looked out the van's darkened window. "I can't believe this. I can't believe you. My sister wants me to help her commit a crime. Stealing a person from a mental ward...." He scratched his head.

Jeffrey's sixteen-year-old son opened the back door and stepped into the van.

Rob turned around quickly, averted his eyes. "Great. This only gets better."

"Here, take this." Over Rob's shoulder, John Rolando handed him a gun.

"What the hell do I need this for?" Rob asked.

"Here, Jack. I got you two some coats. And, you have your ID's, right?"

"Yeah," Jackie said.

"Here's the plan. You're gonna go in through the front gate and if anyone stops you you're gonna say that you're just checking on your patient. You're gonna take her out the west side of the building and to the sidewalk and that's where I'll be waiting...."

"THE MISSION IMPOSSIBLE theme is running through my head," Jackie said walking the sidewalk with Rob. "I'm so nervous I can't hear anything but crickets. How're we going to pull this off?" Jackie asked him.

"Not sure," Rob said. "We can turn back—" He turned around.

"Not so fast," Jackie tugged on his arm. She placed the fake glasses over her eyes as did Rob. They walked to the front glass doors and she slid her keycard through the device.

"Which way?" Rob asked when they walked to an intersection of the hallway.

"This way," Jackie pointed out. They walked the corridor, took the stairs, and made a right. "She's in this room here." With a brisk jog, Jackie went up to the door, while Rob stared through the glass to view the woman sleeping on her bed. Jackie swiped the keycard.

The woman lay asleep peacefully, wearing a white short-sleeve gown and bright-white socks. The glass door closed behind them. "Kathryn," Jackie spoke softly. "Katie." She jostled her gently.

Kathryn blinked slowly and looked to see who was talking to her through the dim lighting.

"Hi, I'm Rob." He placed a thin sweater over her head and she placed her arms through. Jackie helped place pants on her legs, while Rob gave Kathryn a fake pair of glasses to wear. Jackie set the sides of Kathryn's hair back into a fashionable barrette and Rob fitted rubber-sole shoes on Kathryn's feet.

Jackie smiled at her. "Are you ready to get the hell outta here?" The woman didn't respond, gave a blank stare and a blink.

"Put this on," Rob told her, handing Kathryn a white jacket with a name badge.

"Our car is parked right outside," Jackie said.

"We just need to move quickly," Rob added. "Or Rolando will probably leave us."

Jackie swiped the card. They exited the room, first Rob, then Kathryn, and Jackie. They walked briskly through the hall in a quick pace, not even daring a whisper between them, or a look back behind them, and made the left to another exit where Jackie used the card again.

They hurried down the stairs, out the west side of the building, and behind the bushes to the sidewalk where John Rolando was waiting in the van. Now, Jackie held Kathryn's hand. "I'm taking you home," Jackie said with a smile.

"WE MADE IT," Jackie said, finally breathing, while placing the seatbelt over Kathryn and clicking it into place.

"That was too easy," Rob said. "I'm waiting for the police to come after us at any moment." He continued to scope out the road. "This is a felony."

"I'll get you home," John Rolando said. "You'll be safe when you're home."

"Whaddya mean by that?" Rob asked.

"There's still a chance that the cops could come after us. But I'm not worried. I've got back-up."

"You do? Where?" Rob asked. "I don't see any—"

"I wonder what Dad's gonna do when he sees her," Jackie said.

"Stop daydreaming about that love-at-first-sight crap. He's gonna flip, Jackie," Rob said. "Even my father's gonna have an aneurism."

"J.J.'s too cool to freak out like that. Are you hungry?" Jackie asked Kathryn. "As soon as we get home I'll bring you to the kitchen and you can choose whatever you want to eat. I'll give you a tour of the house. You'll have your own special room that I made up for you. She's gonna like her room, right Robbie?"

"How long have you two been planning this?" There was no answer. Rob looked at Kathryn and changed his tone. "Yeah, you'll love your room. You'll love the house," he added.

"You'll love the house," Jackie repeated. "And, you can stay with us for as long as you want. We'll take care of you."

"But," Rob said. "You need to learn to take care of yourself."

"That'll come later," Jackie said, then gave Kathryn a reassuring smile.

"Yeah, in two days when you have school again," John began.

Jackie interrupted, "I'm gonna pretend that I'm sick."

"You need to go to school. You might be questioned by the school or by the cops, since Monday you met with Kathryn. You know they'll be looking for her. You will be interrogated."

"I *might* be interrogated?" Jackie asked. "You said—"

"And what do you expect from us in return?" Rob asked him.

"Nothing."

"My ass," Rob said. "I don't get it. What are you not telling me, Jackie?"

"This is not the time to talk about this!" Jackie raised her voice.

"Are you sure the cameras weren't taping us in there?"

"I took care of it," John said.

"Yeah, right. Who else is involved in this?"

Jackie pressed the remote control.

"Home?" Kathryn finally spoke when the gate opened to the Ravolie Estate.

"Home." Jackie repeated looking at the huge mansion before them.

"THEY MADE IT," he said into his cell phone. "Just drove through the gate."

"Did you see her," she asked.

"Yeah, I saw her."

"What do you think? Could it be her?"

"I haven't seen Gabrielle in twelve years. I can't be sure."

"Well, does she look like me?" she asked him.

"Truthfully," he said. "This woman is absolutely beautiful. She doesn't look like you at all."

Click.

He heard the dial tone.

LATE INTO THE NIGHT

"I HAVE PICTURES OF MY MOTHER. She died twelve years ago. You just, you just look so much like her. This was my mother." Jackie handed Kathryn the photo.

After she felt her forehead with the palm of her hand, she handed her the picture back.

"My mother was a singer," Jackie told her. "She sang with my dad."

"Here's another one of my father, mother, me, and Rob on the beach at our house, where we lived."

She examined the picture of the four on the beach with the back of the house standing in the background.

Jackie noticed Kathryn's cheeks were beginning to pale. "We used to live there before it blew up," Jackie said.

"It blew up?" Kathryn asked, wide-eyed.

"Yes. Yes it sure did. Robbie and I were inside, but we escaped out the balcony. My mother knew we were alive before she died."

She stood from the bed and began to pace while staring at the picture.

Jackie wanted Kathryn to be her mother. She knew she had to be, but how? She saw Gabrielle in a coffin, at the wake. They all watched while her casket lowered into the ground, at the funeral. Jackie wondered, what if? What if she was alive under those blankets? What if? What if the hearse switched along the drive from the funeral home to the cemetery and no one had noticed the switching of hearses or caskets for that matter? And, furthermore, who? Bernadette Malone was dead.

Bernadette Malone, who was Jeffrey Rolando's half-sister, must have drugged Gabrielle before throwing her into that box with John. Unless, someone else drugged her at the hospital.

Jackie's cell phone rang. "Hello?"

"It's me."

"Hi Roxy. I'm sitting on the bed. Tell me, please."

"Your mother's grave was excavated."

"And?"

"I'm still in Chicago. I'm standing in front of her coffin."

"Open it." There was silence. "And?" The tears welled into Jackie's eyes.

"Jackie," Roxy's voice shattered. "I am so sorry. I am so incredibly sorry. Your mother—"

"Just tell me, *please.*"

Roxy began to cry. Jackie assumed the woman who was also her mother's 'good friend' was now on her knees wallowing in grief. "Oh Jackie, I should have known. This is my entire fault. I should have known ... Claycondine..."

KATHRYN RETURNED from the bathroom.

"How are you feeling?" Jackie asked politely.

"Better." She nodded slowly.

"We have horses. Skippy is the best horse we have." Jackie frantically searched for a picture. "He's so incredibly smart." She rambled, "Did I mention that we have ten bedrooms and eight bathrooms? Four fireplaces, two kitchens, and three living rooms? The list can go on and on. My dad never goes into the kitchen that I showed you, so you need to use that one, until I tell him that you're staying here. Like I said, before my dad and I moved here, we lived in this beach house. Here." Jackie handed her another picture to hold. "Would you like to look at some more pictures?"

"Sure," said Kathryn. But she looked too ill or too tired to be interested.

"After my mother died, the beach house was rebuilt by Jeffrey Rolando. My father still goes there a lot. If you're up to it, I'll bring you there tomorrow. As long as he's not around."

"Tell me more about your mother," Kathryn asked.

Jackie smiled. "My mom was an honor student like I am. She graduated high school with scholarships she never used, because she was a singer and a model and had me when she was sixteen. Well, she died on my fourth birthday. We share a birthday. She turned twenty that day. I loved her very much. Tell me about you?"

The woman looked confused, agitated, began to pace and held her head with both hands. She pressed hard against the sides of her hair and Jackie feared that Kathryn would scream.

"Maybe you need to rest. Come lay down," Jackie said.

LIKE AN ERUPTING VOLCANO, THE BEACH HOUSE EXPLODED.

As if in slow motion, they turned around.

"My.Babies!" Gabrielle cried out. Then she received a hard jab to her shoulder. Gabrielle fell. With all of her might, she crawled to stand. After another blow from the glock to her spine, Gabrielle again fell to the ground. John ran forward and kneeled behind Gabrielle to protect her. He held her hands at her waist. And as they melted with the sand, they watched.

Bernadette Malone laughed. "Your babies?"

Gabrielle tilted her chin to glance at the woman's throat. The evil woman spit into her hair.

"You fucking bitch!" Gabrielle yelled, throwing sand into the air. She brought her leg up and out and kicked Bernadette in the kneecap. John fought off one of her thugs when Bernadette fell to the ground. Ferociously, Gabrielle leaped on top of Bernadette, and began to strangle her. Someone grabbed Gabrielle and pulled her off. She landed on top of John's legs.

"GOODNIGHT, MOM." Jackie tucked Kathryn into bed.

Chapter 7

Jackie yawned and then rolled out of bed. She was about to hurry across the hall to see if Kathryn was awake yet, but then she noticed the woman staring out the bedroom window. "Good morning."

"Hi, Jackie," Kathryn replied.

"Is everything okay?" Jackie asked.

"I'm fine."

"Good." Jackie smiled. "Did you sleep well?"

"Tell me about the night the beach house blew up?"

"Yeah, sure. No problem. So, you *can* talk?" Jackie gave out a faint giggle.

Kathryn stared at her blankly.

"Well, okay then." Jackie sat on the bed, and Kathryn sat beside her. "Well, it was the Fourth of July and you, Dad, Rob and I came home from the fireworks. I was almost four, and Rob just turned three. His birthday is in June. Anyway, we were all sitting on the ground and Rob was frightened of the fireworks. You were trying to calm him down."

Kathryn shook her head.

"I didn't think you'd remember," Jackie said. "I can't remember the fireworks either. Dad told me I couldn't sleep. You and Dad were talking in your room, and Bernadette Malone and her men were outside on the beach with guns."

"Why?"

"Why, what?"

"Why did this Bernadette hate me?"

"Well, she loved my father in this twisted way and my father loved you. From what I know, she tormented my father and threatened him before he even met you. If he tried to leave her, she'd have Grandma and Grandpa, or Uncle Jimmy and Uncle Randy killed."

"So, she hated me because me and your father were in love?"

"Basically. I'll continue. After I told you and Dad that someone was filming a movie on the beach—"

"Wasn't it private property?" Kathryn asked.

"Yes." Jackie smirked.

"This place is a fortress," Kathryn said.

"The Ravolie Estate is, but the beach house wasn't."

"Why not?"

"Don't know. Anyway, Dad placed Rob and I in the closet and threw some laundry on top of us."

"In the closet?" Kathryn placed her hand over her mouth. "You couldn't breathe?"

"No, no, we were fine. Here, let me get you a glass of water." Jackie stood.

"I'm fine." Kathryn grabbed her hand hard. "Continue."

Jackie sat beside her, while Kathryn held tight to her hand. "Then Bernadette came in with her men and took Dad and you away. There were bombs planted within the house and garage that went off simultaneously. The whole house was on fire with me and Rob in it."

"My babies," Kathryn whispered.

"I need my hand back before you break it," Jackie said, jerking away. She looked around the room. "Here, uh, take my pillow instead."

Kathryn set the pillow in her lap.

"You, possibly, out on the beach when the house exploded yelled, 'My babies.' But I squeezed through the rails with Rob and Teddy." Jackie pointed to her old brown bear that sat in a tiny rocking chair in the corner of her room.

Kathryn stood and was about to claim the bear. Jackie thought about it. "No, please." She stood. "J.J. gave me that bear and maybe one day, but not right now," she said with fear of what Kathryn would do to Teddy when it came to her tight grip. Kathryn faced Jackie. "We didn't die in that house." Jackie reached out to hold Kathryn's fingertips without fear.

Jackie was a little shorter than her, but not by much. Her hair was at shoulder length just as hers. Their eyes were the same color blue. Their noses were the perfect shape; their lips neither formed a smile nor a frown. "Mom? Is it?" Jackie's eyes welled up in tears. "Tell me, please? Is it you? Are you alive?"

Together, they wrapped their arms around one another and to Jackie's surprise, Kathryn kissed the side of her head.

"OH SHIT, what do I do? What do I do? Call Roxy. Mom, hang on. I'm going to call Roxy. She'll know what to do."

SHE KICKED THE WOOD with the heels of her leather shoes, but it was solid. No one seemed to be on the outside, and the box wouldn't budge. "Oh my God, John. We're in a coffin," she whispered frantically.

"What?"

"Yeah John—a coffin. Underground. Oh shit."

"It's not a coffin. It can't be a coffin. It can't be a fucking coffin!" He kicked the box again.

She crawled to him already lying on his back. "At least the insane bitch put us together," he said.

"Yes—insane bitch." She rested her head on his chest, draped her right arm over his waist, and squeezed him tightly, trying to fight off her hopelessness by embracing the man she loved.

His left hand found the back of her head. He kissed her forehead.

"John?"

"Yeah?"

"We're going to die."

"I know."

"YOU DIDN'T DIE in that box," Jackie said. "Roxy pick up the goddamn phone!"

"I'M ITCHY," she said.

"Where're you itchy?"

"On my back." He began to rub her back, while her head rested on his chest, her right leg over his, and her arm over his waist. "Does your back hurt? Or your head?" she asked.

"I'm fine," John said. "How 'bout you? You got hit hard, a couple times."

"There's pain, but—I don't know. I'm too scared to feel pain. Think I've got a rash all over my body."

"A rash?"

"Yeah, I'm *itchy.*" She squirmed. Even squirming was hard in such cramped quarters, but she couldn't help it. The itching would not stop.

"I'M ITCHY," Kathryn yelled.

"Rob, you have to help me here!" Jackie yelled into her cell phone. "She *is* Mom. And she thinks she's in the box with Dad. She's yelling 'I'm itchy.' She's crawling around on the floor. She's breaking things. She's—"

"I'll be right there," Rob said.

"I need you to hold her down."

"I'll be right there," Rob said again.

"Jackie?"

"I'm here, Mom. I'm here." Jackie sat on the floor next to her. Kathryn rocked back and forth with her legs tucked in. "I'm here." Jackie sat behind her and wrapped her arms around her.

"Where's your father?" she asked.

"He's probably in the kitchen reading the newspaper," Jackie said. "He didn't hear a thing."

"Good," Kathryn mumbled.

"Oh shit. The newspaper," Jackie said. "Tuesday. You'll probably be in Tuesday's paper. I tried to call Roxy. She believes that you were drugged with something called Claycondine. On Monday, we're going to California and Roxy's going to give you the antidote to Claycondine. I'm going to stay with you. I won't leave you. Listen to me. Listen to me," Jackie said, scooting around her. "Your life ended happy. You and my father were so much in love. We were all happy, the four of us. I know you're scared all the time, but after you receive the injection—"

"It won't work," Kathryn cried.

"Oh *yes* it will. I promise you. Do you trust me? This *will* work. No one knows about Claycondine except for Roxanne Rolando, and this will work. Happy thoughts. Let me give you a happy thought." Jackie searched her pictures. "Here. Here's one. Here's a picture of you and my dad on your honeymoon. John is his name. Remember, his name is John, John Ravolie. Look at his face and try to remember he was the man you rode a horse with."

She took the picture and looked at it. "John Ravolie? Italian?"

"Yes." Jackie laughed. "It's Italian, and you're Italian too."

"I'm not Italian," she told her, shaking her head back and forth, as Jackie shook her head up and down. "I loved him and he loved me?"

"It was like a wonderful fairytale. He loves you. He still loves you. He has never forgotten you."

"HELLO?" she answered. "Hello? You going to say something?"

"Hi," said a male's voice.

"Hi," Kathryn said.

"*Do. You. Know,* who this is?"

"*Uh.* No. Are *you* going to tell me?" Kathryn echoed.

"It's me, your father."

She wouldn't say anything.

"Your father," he repeated.

"Yeah, right," she said, then she ended the call.

"Did you just hang up on my dad?" Jackie asked Kathryn.

"I guess so."

The phone rang. Jackie answered, "Hello?"

"I don't know who you are, but if you hurt my daughter or if you touch her in any way, shape or form, I will have you killed. Do you understand?"

Jackie laughed. "Yes, Mr. Ravolie, I understand completely, and your daughter and I will see you for breakfast," she replied.

AS JOHN READ THE PAPER and finished his coffee at the counter, he felt a chill in the air. Consequently, the chill was actually more of a warm draft. He raked his fingers through his hair and turned the page. He stood from the stool. While reading, he carried the paper in his left hand and walked to the other counter. Beside him, he reached for the pot. He traveled back to the breakfast bar and poured the black liquid into his 'DAD' mug. He walked back to the coffee maker and set the pot down. Again, he felt the draft behind him. He realized the door to the rose garden must be ajar.

Aimee? he wondered. Noooo. She wouldn't dare come back and she couldn't get in anyway. It perhaps was just left open by someone.

He went to the refrigerator to reach in for the orange juice he had freshly squeezed prior, and after he closed the door, she stood in front of him. He looked right through her, as if she was a translucent figure, and then he walked away to place the pitcher on the breakfast bar.

She continued to stare at him. He looked her way briefly and smiled. Slowly, he walked to her and invaded her space. She shied away by turning around, and he stayed directly behind her. John brushed her hair from her right shoulder with his fingertips and brought his mouth down to her pale skin. She tilted her head and he planted soft, wet kisses onto her collarbone, trailing to her ear where she felt his warm breath.

He stopped tormenting her and placed his arms around her waist. While holding her hands at her navel, he kissed her neck. Slowly she turned to face him. For a moment, they stared into one another's eyes. She returned the gentleness of his warm lips when he pressed them firmly against hers. While reaching around her, he trailed her spine with his fingertips, adding a light pressure.

He placed his palm at the base of her neck. As she tilted her chin, he again tasted her lips He stared at her for a moment as she stared lustfully back at him.

His gaze continued to melt with hers. "I love you," he whispered. His hands went to her shoulders, his fingertips brushed lightly down her arms, to her fingers, and her hands linked with his. "You're absolutely beautiful," he told her. "Hi," he said. "I haven't seen you for a while. What should I talk to you about today, huh?"

"Orange juice," she murmured, and then pointed to the pitcher.

"You want some?" he asked her. He turned toward the cabinet and pulled out a glass, filled it half way and set it on the counter. He sat on the stool and began to read his paper again. She sat across from him in arms reach. He looked up to see her gulping down the juice. "You always did like my freshly squeezed OJ."

"More," she asked.

"Sure." He poured another half a glass. "I've waited for you all my life, you know. I have never been able to move on. I visit your grave and talk to you. And, I hear you talking to me. Telling me the answers. I argue with you, yet I'm only arguing with myself. You look and even feel so real to me now. I could make love to you right here on this counter."

She stared at him dreamily as he continued, "You're the only person I think about before I go to bed, and when I wake up in the morning, your picture is the first thing I see. It has always been you. I have never stopped loving you, wanting to be with you, needing you. *You* are what makes me feel complete. You are all I need. All I ever wanted. Many times, I've thought about killing myself just to be with you. Many times, I thought about setting an extra plate at the table for you, filling it with food, but then I wouldn't be able to consider myself sane."

"Please do," she said.

He smirked. "I perhaps would ask the air if I could have what you hadn't finished and then I would take the plate away. I would ask you if you didn't have much of an appetite and then I'd wrap up the food and pretend to tuck you into bed. I've thought about taking baths with you, walks in the woods—"

The swinging door to the kitchen jarred open with a thud, and Jackie and Rob stared at them sitting at the breakfast nook.

"Hey," John said. "On Saturdays, you know I don't make breakfast until nine-thirty."

"Ah, we were hungry," Rob said.

"Yes. Hungry," Jackie repeated.

John looked at Kathryn. She was still sitting on the stool. He raised his eyebrows, and said, "I *am* losing my mind."

"So, ah." Jackie sat beside Kathryn. "What have you two been talking about?" she asked.

"What two?" John asked.

"You two?" Jackie motioned with her fingers.

"You mean? You can see her?" John asked.

Jackie looked at him with crooked eyebrows, while Rob gave a brief nod.

"Seriously? Can you see her?" He pointed to Kathryn.

"I can see her, too," Rob said.

"You guys are messing with me," John said turning around to the stove.

"This is worse than I thought it would be," Jackie said to Rob.

"Dad," Rob said. "Turn around. There is a woman sitting on this stool, and her name is Kathryn."

"She's one of my friends, Dad," Jackie added.

"Oh. Hi Kathryn, nice to meet you."

"Katie," she replied.

"Katie, nice to meet you. I'm feeling very embarrassed right now," he murmured.

"Don't be," Katie said.

"I'm not going to cook breakfast today." He turned off the stove. "Can you ask—ah Phil—if he's preparing lunch? Katie, you're more than welcomed to stay for lunch. I just remembered," John added, "that I have something I have to do."

"Yeah, okay, Dad," Jackie said confused.

He disappeared into the rose garden.

"What happened?" Jackie asked Kathryn.

"He thought I was a ghost."

"Well, you are to him," Rob said.

"I told you not to come to this kitchen," Jackie said.

"I'm going out there to be with him."

"What?" Jackie and Rob said together.

"I think I'm in love."

"Here we go," Rob said.

"I give you five minutes with him. That's all. You hear me?" Jackie said. "Five minutes."

"Let's make a bet," Rob said. "One minute and he's gone."

Kathryn walked out into the rose garden and found John clipping the white roses. "Making a bouquet?" she asked.

"Not sure," he said.

"I'm sorry. I guess I should have stopped you from talking, but sometimes it's better to—"

"You a shrink?"

"No."

"Good. Don't you dare tell Jackie or Rob what happened in the kitchen."

"I won't."

"Good." He walked away.

Chapter 8

Five Days Later

"What's taking the plane so long to touch down?" John paced.

"They'll be here soon. I think that's the one," Rob pointed out.

They watched the plane land onto the runway. Gabrielle and Jackie walked the stairs and stepped down onto the paved cement.

John and Rob jogged toward them. "Did she hurt you?" John asked Jackie, making sure that her head was intact. He took a glance at Gabrielle, who was wearing black slacks and a white button-down shirt with the sleeves rolled up to her elbows. "What do you think you're doing?" he asked Jackie, taking her carry-on bag. "You run off with this woman to California, you skip school—"

"Welcome home, Mom!" Rob said wide-eyed and smiling. He wrapped his arms around her.

Gabrielle dropped her purse and enveloped him as well. "Robbie?" She then looked to Jackie; she nodded. "My goodness. Let me look at you." He held onto her ever so tightly.

"Rob! Let go of that woman. We don't know who she is," John told him, pulling him away.

"You're my son," she said to him, ignoring John's comments. "I have two children," she said, half to herself. "You look just like someone I've been seeing in my dreams."

"J.J.?" Rob asked.

"Is J.J. here?"

"We're not getting him involved in this just yet," Rob told her, picking up her small suitcase.

"So, you must be John?" she asked, turning toward him.

"Yes, I'm Jackie's father," he said calmly.

"Nice to meet you." She held out her hand.

"We've met," he said angrily. "Turn around and put your head down," John told her.

"What?"

"Are you gonna knock her unconscious?" Rob asked him with a chuckle.

"When your mother was hit by that car she had surgery. If this is your mother, she'd have a scar on the back of her head. Gabrielle turned around and lifted up her hair. He placed his fingers on the back of her neck to feel the scar he saw. "We're going to the hospital right now to do a blood test. That's what I think." John said, "DNA tests. Many tests. A variety of many blood tests, urine tests, bone tests, and skin tests. A whole slew of tests."

"Sounds like an excellent idea," Gabrielle said, as she paid attention to her children laughing.

"Then we can move on and you can go back to that psycho ward or wherever the hell you came from and Jackie will stop thinking you're her mother...."

The four stepped into the limousine, and John stared at Gabrielle.

"She looks like her, doesn't she?" Jackie asked her father softly.

He looked away.

"What do *you* do for a living?" Gabrielle asked John.

"You're joking right?"

"No." She shook her head.

"Haven't you ever heard of Ra'vole?"

"No, I can't say that I have. What is it, a famous pizza in the U.S. or something?"

Rob and Jackie laughed, and John formed a smile. He placed a hand over his mouth with his fingers on his cheek to hide it. The olive green garnet on his middle finger sparked her attention.

She struggled to remove his ring. "Can I have this?" Gabrielle asked.

"My ring?" John asked, as if he hadn't noticed her pulling, tugging, as well as grunting.

"Yes." Gabrielle stopped trying. She thought she needed butter.

"Mick gave this to me. It's too big for any of your fingers or your toes."

"I guess that means no, huh?"

"I'd have to buy you a gold chain so you could wear this 'round your neck, but then it would be as if you were wearing Mick's ring, and I wouldn't like that at all."

"I guess that means no, huh?"

And after twenty seconds, her color returned.

"Are you remembering something?" Jackie asked her.

"What did you remember?" Rob asked.

"Well, you see the ring on your father's finger."

"You know who gave this to me?"

"Did you give him the ring?" Jackie asked her.

"No, actually I didn't."

"I'm sure she read about it in a magazine and she knows—"

"Who's Mick?" Gabrielle asked.

"Is it true, Dad?" Jackie asked. "Did Mick give you that ring?"

"It looks like a class ring," Rob said.

"No, it's not. It's his birthstone," Gabrielle added. John gazed out the window and Gabrielle started humming a tune while the rest were silent. At this particular moment, she stayed calm and collected, while John was the flustered one.

"John is a rock and roll star," Rob answered her question.

"What does he do?" She laughed. "Play the bongos?"

"I sing."

"Do you play guitar as well?" she joked.

He continued to look out the window, remembering back to when he did, in fact, play guitar quite a lot when the band toured.

"My dad plays the drums in a rock and roll band, too," Rob said. "Intensity is the name of his band."

"So, I used to date rock and roll stars. Isn't that funny? I think I like jazz and classical music."

"Well, I guess this means you're not Gabrielle. Gabrielle loved rock and roll and she sang rock and roll. She loved the music." They were silent.

"Smell her, Dad," Jackie told him.

"What?" John and Gabrielle asked together.

"Go on," Rob said, he and Jackie slid over, and John had no choice but to move to the other side, next to Gabrielle.

"I am not going to smell this woman."

"He is not going to smell me," she said with a laugh.

"Smell her hair. Smell her arm. Go on," Jackie said.

"Smell her panties," Rob blurted out.

"He will not!" Kathryn said laughing.

"Rob, I am going to throw you over my knee when we get home," John said, laughing too.

"You will not." Gabrielle couldn't stop laughing. "Oh my God. I remember something." She placed her hand over her mouth.

"Oh yeah, what do you remember now?" John asked sarcastically.

"What did I do to you?" John asked her, as she crouched in front of the suitcases, unzipping one. "What are you doing?"

"I'm unpacking and making sure you didn't steal anything."

"Sorry darling, there's nothing in that black bag that I could possibly want."

"You probably smelled my underwear before you packed 'em."

"Your panties are in the first suitcase, I didn't take any."

"No, but you smelled 'em." She stood.

"Do you remember?" Rob asked John.

"It doesn't mean anything. A million people could have arguments about smellin' panties. It doesn't mean anything." His anger suppressed his laugh.

"Tell us, what happened?"

"Your mom was pregnant with Rob. She didn't know if Rob was my son, so she ran. I found her in Connecticut and packed all of her belongings. We argued and then—"

"Your knee!" Gabrielle blurted out.

"What?"

"I threatened your knee cap. And we, Oh my—"

"And we what?"

"In the middle of the hallway," she said.

"What did you do?" Rob asked, with a huge smile on his face.

"Did you kick him in the kneecap?" Jackie asked her curiously.

"No, she didn't kick me in the kneecap," John growled.

"We made love," Gabrielle said. She smiled and closed her eyes. "But before I pulled my pants down—"

"You will not continue with this dream you had about me. There are children in the car."

He gazed at her white-lace panties and pointed with two fingers. "These are nice, different than the ones I packed."

"My boyfriend likes 'em."

"This is very intimate," he said softly. "Do I have your consent?"

"Oh yes," she whispered, "You have my full consent." She closed her eyes; tilted her head back.

"After this, you'll never want to have sex with me again." He slid her panties down, placed his lips to her pelvis.

"Maybe ... not."

"You said you liked my white panties and they were different than the ones that *you* had packed." She opened her eyes.

Rob and Jackie shook hands, as she continued to let her memories convince all of them of her identity.

"How do you know all this?" He grew angrier.

"Dad," Jackie said.

"No. You lived there in Connecticut when she moved to that apartment? You were outside the door when we were arguing? That's how she knows all this. She's not your mother. When Gabrielle was living in Connecticut she probably befriended you at the crisis clinic she was working at, the scar is just coincidence, and she told you all this. How old was Gabrielle when she was raped? You probably know that, too."

"What?" Jackie and Rob said together.

"I don't know how old I was. Would you like to tell me?"

"Fifteen," John snarled.

"I lived through it, and I live through it repeatedly in my nightmares. These are *my* goddamn nightmares, not someone else's. There were three men who raped me in the back of a van, and then those same three men—two of them were shot in the head and the third—his neck was snapped and there was so much blood. If you had pictures, I would be able to tell you who my rapists were and who had killed them." She grew quiet and the tears began to fall to her cheeks. She wiped one with a finger.

"Why didn't you ever tell me?" Jackie asked her father. "How did this happen? Who? Who killed these—?"

"Later!" John shouted in his fatherly tone.

"Now!" Gabrielle raised her voice. "Who was the man in the suit who killed my rapists?"

John was silent.

"Who, Dad?" Rob asked.

"I was in a small room with ugly green carpet and he made them kneel down in front of me, while I kept the pieces of my clothing—"

"Rolando did it," John blurted out. "No more," he said.

The air was quiet until Jackie asked, "How would she know about the beach house? And the box you two were buried in?"

"Your mother probably called her from the hospital, before she died and told her what had happened. She's from a mental hospital, Jackie. She decided to take advantage of you when you thought she was your mother."

"You still don't believe?" Jackie asked him.

"You can believe whatever you like," Gabrielle said. "I never spoke to anyone about these things. And, I've seen these visions. And, as soon as more and more memories come back, I'm sure I'll be able to tell you everything and anything you want to know, in order to convince you of who I am. Intimate things that only you and I know about."

"Well, we're here at the hospital," Rob announced.

"Don't we need to make an appointment or something?" Gabrielle asked.

"I already did. I told you or did you forget already? Tests. A whole slew of them."

Rob and Jackie stepped out of the limousine.

"How old am I?" Gabrielle asked John.

"You don't know?"

"I think I'm thirty-two, but I'm not sure."

"Gabrielle died on her twentieth birthday. August tenth. Years ago."

"This means I'd be thirty-two. Do I look like her? Do I sound like her?" She grabbed his arm to stop him from avoiding the question.

"I refuse to answer that. It's been twelve years. People change."

"Listen to my voice. Do I sound like her?"

"If you're not her, I'll make sure you're locked up for good."

"And if I am?"

"You won't be."

They walked into the hospital together. After their blood was drawn, they waited until the nurse called for them. They gathered in the closed-door room. She began, "After carefully looking over the blood samples that were drawn from the four of you and without knowing the situation or why this was done, the only thing we can tell you at this point is that Jonathan you are Jacqueline's biological father. Jacqueline and Robbie are brother and sister. However, you are not Robbie's birth father. I'm sorry."

"We already knew that. Keep going," John said, while doing a hand roll, and then he began to nervously bite his cuticle.

"Kathryn's blood type, without any doubt *whatsoever*, matched completely with the two children, Jacqueline and Robbie."

"Yes!" Jackie yelled.

"Holy shit!" Rob said. He gave his sister a bear hug.

Then they tackled Gabrielle. "Jackie, you're strangling me," Gabrielle said, laughing while Rob held tight to her left side.

"Are you sure?" John asked, pulling the nurse aside.

"Yes. It matches perfectly. Look at the results." They viewed the papers together.

"No more nurses for you," Rob said tugging at John's arm.

"May I keep this?" John asked her.

"Yes."

"Come on, kids. Let's go home," he told them.

"Me, too?" Gabrielle asked him, her voice crackled.

"You can come, too," John said. "This is unbelievable. Unbelievable. Rob, you're gonna have to tell Shedel and I'm gonna have to call your parents," he told Gabrielle.

"I have parents?" Gabrielle asked.

"Yes. You have parents. You might not like 'em, but you have 'em. You have a brother, too. I have to call your parents. There's a long list of people."

"YOU LIVE HERE?" Gabrielle asked as the front gates opened.

"Does this surprise you?" John asked her.

"I thought we were going to the beach house."

"I told you on the plane," Jackie said. "We don't live in the beach house."

"Yes, I remember. I'd like to see the beach house, though. I have a lot of recurring nightmares about the house blowing up," she told John. "I want to know the exact spot where I cried out for my babies."

"Shit," he muttered to himself. "Yes, yes, it was rebuilt, but not by my choice. It doesn't look the same, but I'll show it to you later. Maybe after you see pictures of how it used to look ... Looking at the pictures and talking about things may stop you from getting the nightmares."

The limousine rounded the circular drive where a rectangular three-feet deep pool sat in the center on a circular plot of land. From the four inner edges, the spray shot into the air and crisscrossed. Gabrielle watched the water fly out from the border in a dance that was so surreal she couldn't think of words beautiful enough to describe it. They stepped out of the limousine, but Gabrielle took an extra moment to watch the dancing waters.

"You coming in?" John asked her; she nodded.

She stared in amazement inside the foyer where a three-tier fountain stood. "Your home is exquisite."

"Dad," Jackie said. "We're taking the bags upstairs. You two can spend some quality time alone to get re-acquainted, while we call J.J."

"You can smell Mom's panties," Rob said, chuckling under his breath.

"DO YOU REMEMBER this house at all?" John asked her, while they entered the rose garden.

"No. I don't believe I've ever been here."

"Gabrielle was never here. She wouldn't come here."

"Why not? It's beautiful."

"She already had her fairytale. Did Roxy say when you'd get your Kathryn memories back?"

"Short-term memory is gone for now," Gabrielle said with a shrug. "And, I'm the lab rat," she said, then blushed for sounding foolish.

"This house didn't belong in our lives. We were only together for five years. When we first met this was her dream house, but I could never bring her here and then when it was possible, she just never wanted to come."

"*I* never wanted to come?"

"*She* never wanted to come. While *she* was dying, I added the two fountains, a tennis court, and a pool, for her out back. She never made it here to see it. A few months later, I brought the horses here." He paused. "Let me get a good look at you."

"Would you like me to twirl around for you?" she asked.

"Be my guest," he replied and she twirled, just like she had when they were married in Hawaii, he remembered. "I knew Jackie would grow up to look just like you, black hair and blue eyes, and, and ... Do you have a birthmark on your hip?"

"I wouldn't call it birthmark. It's like a beauty mark. A little brown spot on my left ... Would you like to see it?"

"No. I couldn't handle you pulling down your pants in the rose garden. I believe you. Come here." He felt uncomfortable, yet he placed his arms around her and kissed her cheek and held her. He released her as quickly as he had taken her into his arms. "Yes," he said. "You're Gabrielle. A little taller. A little heavier. But you're definitely Gabrielle."

"Heavier?"

"Well, I didn't mean anything by it. I mean, you are still attractive for your weight."

"My weight?"

"I'm getting myself into trouble here. Aren't I?"

"Oh yes you are!" she told him laughing.

"You were always petite and you still are."

"Petite? You mean I'm skinny, like a toothpick?"

"You're not a toothpick," John said. "You were never a toothpick. How much do you weigh?"

"You should know better than that, Mr. Ravolie. You never ask a woman how much she weighs."

"Okay. How do I say this?"

"Go ahead. I'm waiting. You're already in way over your head. How are you going to get yourself out of this jam you're in?"

"Kathryn, you are beautiful. Attractive. And I wouldn't mind sleeping with you, but I know you're not that kind of woman and I'm, well, I'm that kind of man." He picked a white rose and placed it in her hair. "But you are beautiful and attractive for being thirty-two years old. You look more now like a super model than Gabrielle did back then. Well, she wasn't a super model, but one magazine did place her in the top fifty as being one of the sexiest women in the world. There, I said it, gave you a rose, and we're done."

"I was only in the top fifty?" she asked, disappointed.

"She wasn't too happy about it back then, either."

"HI DAD," Rob said into the phone.

"Rob-bie," J.J. spoke, sounding like Rocky. "I thought we'd do pizza and a movie. How does that sound?"

"Dad, I thought we'd do something a little different."

"What's on your mind?" J.J. asked.

"Well, Mom, actually."

"Mom? You want to look through some old pictures or videos?"

"No. Dad, are you sitting down?"

"Should I be?"

"I think you need to sit, 'cause of what I'm about to tell you. Dad? Are you sitting yet?"

"Yeah. I'm sitting."

"Jackie went on this field trip with her vocational class. She went to this psychiatric ward and met this woman. And, the next thing I knew I was helping Jackie kidnap her. And we abducted her because she looked like Mom. And we brought her home and are you listening to me?"

"Are you and Jackie in jail?" J.J. asked.

"No. Jackie is sitting next to me and we're in her bedroom."

"Where's Ravolie?"

"Outside, talking to Mom." He paused. "Dad?"

J.J. was laughing. "Ravolie thinks a woman, from a mental hospital, is your mother. Is he taking her for a walk in the rose garden?" He chuckled.

"Take a deep breath. There's more."

"I'm listening." He stifled his laughter.

"We all went for a blood test."

"And what happened, Rob? What did the results show? She was a he—" his laughter was hysterical "—you didn't tell Ravolie, did you?"

"Dad. I hope you're still sitting."

"I fell off my chair"—he laughed—"This only gets better."

"The blood tests showed that Jackie and I are a perfect match to her."

"Can't be possible," he said seriously. "I'm sitting."

"She has the scar on the back of her head from when she was hit by the car."

"Your mother had a birthmark on her hip," J.J. added.

"We haven't asked her to pull down her pants," Rob said. "Dad, she looks a little different from what I remember of her and from the pictures I've seen, but not by much. Her hair is still black, not brown. ...great personality. She laughs a lot. We've figured out that she was drugged by Bernadette with Claycondine before being thrown in the box, and Roxy Rolando had the antidote...."

"WHERE SHOULD I START?" John asked.

"I don't know, but don't take too long. I can't wait another second. I need to know my past."

"I never want you talking to Roxanne Rolando ever again. You hear me?"

"She gave me my memories back. I owe her."

"No, no. You don't owe her anything. The Rolando's owe us big time and after you get your memories back, you'll understand. She looked like you when you were younger. Now, though, Roxy doesn't look like you at all. She gained a lot of weight and you're still beautiful," he added.

"Call me fortunate, huh?" She smiled.

"Before you died—" He paused a moment, realizing how awkward sounding that statement was, and then began again. "—Before you died, you had a rash all over your body. No one knew why you had this rash. Doctors figured it wasn't contagious, since I never caught it. You could've been allergic to the box we were buried in for all we knew. It looked like you had the chicken pox."

He continued, "This morning, Roxy explained to me that once Claycondine is administered into the bloodstream, it causes memory loss, and to the administrator to tell the right dose was injected, a rash would develop on the person it was injected to. Roxy never knew this back then when you were dying. Ryan didn't know either."

"Who's Ryan?"

"Ryan was Roxy's bodyguard at first and then yours. He figured out an antidote so Claycondine wouldn't effect Roxy when she allowed Bernadette to hold her captive. That's a story for a completely different day. How could they have missed this? How could they have not known that Claycondine caused your rash? Someone from Bernadette's mob stole your body between the funeral home and the cemetery. I figured that out today. Anyway, the drug—"

"Claycondine?"

"Yes. It then takes over the body, causing there to be no noticeable pulse and look as if the person isn't breathing. It's used for faking one's death. The person wakes up from an unconscious state after about five days and doesn't remember a thing. Doesn't remember who they are. Doesn't remember their own name or the names of people they've known their whole life. People do remember things like how to count, or how to read, but other than that—nothing."

"Claycondine?"

"It's not permanent. You'll remember who you are soon, I'm sure."

"I woke up in a roach infested motel in Australia with the police handcuffing me. Then this person, Reverend Richard K. Morris bailed me out of jail and claimed that he was my father. I remember—"

"Don't worry. I'll find him."

"That's probably not his real name."

"I'll find him. I need some vodka."

"Are you an alcoholic?"

"Actually, I stopped drinking a few years ago. I've been sober for quite some time, but you're back and I definitely need some vodka."

"Were we alcoholics together?"

"No," he said with a laugh. "When we were together, we didn't drink. You were pregnant most of the time, actually. We drank a lot of grape juice—" He smirked.

"And had elevator picnics?" she asked him.

"Yeah," he said, finding a patch of velvety green grass and then helped her to sit beside him.

"We need to talk about us," she said. "Jackie wants us to get back together. Do you want a divorce?"

"I haven't thought about it."

"Well, if you do, I don't need any money from you. Roxy has already given me—"

"You don't take shit from Roxy! You hear me? You will not take a penny from the Rolandos!" he said with a finger in her face.

"Okay, okay," she said wide-eyed and looking like a child who had just been corrected.

"Gabrielle, listen."

"No John, I understand completely. I'll stay out of your life forever, and in a few weeks, I'll find myself a place to live. I just want to be reacquainted with my children and I want to know my past. I would very much like for you to help me with these memories I have."

"Gabrielle, no. You're missing the point. I don't want you to go. You can't go now. You have to stay and live with me and Jackie."

"I can't stay here in your house with your wife. Where is she, by the way? It would be wrong."

"You have to stay here. Your daughter needs you, Rob needs you, and most of all—" he paused "—I need you."

"Why would you need me? You're married."

"I'm in the process of getting a divorce from Aimee. Holy shit! Since you're alive—I was never married to her legally anyway, right?" This realization brought a strange sense of relief and excitement to John, as if a heavy weight had been lifted.

"Aimee's her name?"

"Yeah, remember the nurse? The singer you never liked? One Chance?"

"One Chance? The nurse? The singer? Oh my God! You.Married. Tuba?"

He laughed. "I *thought* you were dead."

"So of all people you marry Tuba?"

"I could've married Felecia."

"Felecia?" She thought about her. "You wouldn't't've."

"Mick did, but I could've."

"Do you think we'd still be together if I didn't die?" He didn't answer her. "John, when you held me before, I remembered your arms being around me. I always felt so safe, so secure when you hold me."

"I'll hold you again." He asked her to sit in his lap, facing him, and he wrapped his arms around her.

"I'm starting to remember you," she whispered. "I can tell why I loved you so much. We can pretend twelve years went by and we were always together, and we raised Jackie and Robbie together."

"It's not that easy, Gabrielle." He rubbed her back, as she looked into his eyes.

"Don't you love me anymore?"

He didn't answer her.

Feeling suddenly uncomfortable, she removed herself from his lap. She began to pull the blades of grass and twist them nervously in-between her fingers.

"You don't know me anymore, Gabrielle. I don't sing. I'm forty one years old."

"You look the same in these visions I've been getting for the past five days. You don't look like you've aged."

"I love the thought of you being here with me right now, and I'm trying to convince myself that you're not a hallucination. But, I don't know you, and you don't know me. If you knew me, you wouldn't like me. You've changed. I've changed. You're not nineteen anymore; you're thirty-two years old and I'm over forty. I'm just Johnny Ravolie, a has-been singer in a rock and roll band. I can't live in the past. We have a beautiful daughter together. But, really, she's all we have in common anymore—"

"And our memories?"

"Do you understand where I'm coming from?"

They stood together. He began to walk the path back to the house, and she followed.

He felt all he'd done for her was hurt her. She lost her childhood by coming with him and falling in love. She lost the past twelve years of her life because of a woman who was obsessed with him. He loved her. Deep down, he loved her with all his heart, but he couldn't make the mistake again. John knew if he took her back into his life she would end the marriage, hating him. He couldn't risk hurting her or making her hate him. He just couldn't let this happen.

"I want to be a part of you again, John."

"You don't want to be with me, Gabrielle."

"I'm alive, John, and now it's your turn to be alive again."

"It took me twelve years to get this way."

"Just give me twelve hours, and I can turn you back."

They stopped walking and sat in the grass. Again, she sat in his lap. They stared at one another. "My beautiful Gabrielle," he said, placing the strands of her hair behind her ears.

They leaned forward and pressed their lips softly into one another. He suckled gently on her bottom lip, and then placed his tongue to hers. She tilted her head and their tongues touched again momentarily with passion. As John lay back into the grass, he pulled her with him. He remained placing soft, wet kisses to her lips.

Gabrielle's body tingled all over. She had remembered that John had always made her tingle. No matter what he did, or how he did it. Only he could make her feel this way. John felt the same sensations. He knew this was so right, yet so wrong. If only he could make it just a harmless kiss. Yet, he didn't want to stop kissing her. His hardness aligned with her body and he wanted more now than just an innocent kiss. Her body felt so good to touch. Her mesmerizing scent stained his clothes, his nose, as he took each breath. He had never felt this way with anyone else but Gabrielle. His beloved Gabrielle. He wanted to stay like this forever, but knew it would only cause more pain for her. He couldn't stop himself from touching her. They remained laying in the grass with their lips together, kissing passionately, both of them yearning to melt into each other.

She removed her lips from his and asked softly, "How did we meet?"

"You were in a coma."

She giggled and returned her mouth to his.

Chapter 9

*K*nock. *Knock.*

John opened the door to his daughter's room. He peeked inside to see Gabrielle, Rob, and Jackie sitting on the bed.

"J.J. will be here any moment now," Jackie told her father.

"I'll be downstairs making some more calls," John said, leaning against the doorframe. "I'll send Shedel up when he gets here."

"Do you need me to talk to anyone?" Gabrielle asked John.

"No," he answered. "You just get comfortable. Don't try to rush these memories. Next weekend, we're going to have a gathering with some people." John left the doorway.

"'Some' means several hundred," Jackie warned her mother.

Rob looked at his watch. "It's time for you to take your medication." He poured water from a pitcher.

"Is it three pills now and two later?" Gabrielle asked.

"Two now, three later," Jackie said. "Think two-three. Not three-two."

"Good idea," she said, while holding out her hand. Jackie set the two oblong caplets onto her palm, and Rob handed her the glass of water.

"And my final shot of this anti-clayco will be?" she asked, pointing to the capped needle on the nightstand.

"After lunch," Jackie said. "Are you doing all right?"

"I've never felt better in my life," she said after gulping down the pills.

Jackie pulled out a magazine from her hope chest. "This magazine has a four-page spread of you and Dad when he first met you," Jackie said. "And it was the day you woke up from a coma."

Gabrielle read, "'*The Girl He Saved: Johnny Ravolie Saves Fourteen-Year-Old Girl Who Was Hit By a Car and In Coma*' Can I keep this?"

"Sure."

"Did your father ever tell you how insane this was?" Gabrielle asked Jackie, while looking at her daughter's bedroom walls.

"No, but I have," Rob blurted out.

"I love classic rock. I love Ra'vole and Intensity. I've always had pictures on my walls of the bands. Actually, this picture—" Jackie pointed to the magazine that Gabrielle held "—of you and Dad is worth a lot of money. The magazine intact is worth hundreds of dollars. It's just like having pictures of your favorite bands or actors on your wall. Except, it's family. Mom, I love calling you 'Mom'."

"I love hearing it. What about you? Do you like to be called Jackie, Jack, or Jacqueline?"

"Jackie is fine."

"And you?"

"Rob," he said. "I hate R.J.," he stated.

"I bet J.J. and your parents will still call you 'Bobbie'," Jackie said.

"'Bobbie'?"

"A lot of people don't realize it, but it's short for Gabrielle," Jackie explained.

"Jackie, how do you do in school?"

"I'm an honor student."

"Boyfriend?"

"Too many of them like me and I can't pick."

"How many is too many?"

"There are five that are interested in me."

"And you just keep them chasing after you?"

"Yes."

"That's a good thing. And you, Rob?"

"B student. I fall asleep in school a lot because of Dad keeping me up all night. I'm on the dive team."

"Girlfriend?" Gabrielle asked.

"I'm workin' on her," he said.

"How did J.J. handle my death?"

"He turned into an alcoholic," Rob said.

"J.J.?"

"Both of them did," Rob said. "They became best friends. They also went to Alcoholics Anonymous together. They wanted to stop drinking because of us, but they couldn't for a long time. About six months after you had died, *my* dad tried to commit suicide," Rob added.

"Because of me?" Gabrielle asked.

"Don't know," he said. "He dates women, but he never got married. He always loved you."

"I remember you telling me that J.J. said that Mom haunted him," Jackie said.

"At first, he hallucinated too, like Dad does."

"I think we all did," Jackie admitted.

"I never did," Rob protested.

"You call them both 'Dad'?" Gabrielle asked.

"Yeah. They're both my dads. When there was Father and Son Night at school, they both came."

"Really?" Gabrielle asked with a smile. She simply closed her eyes to the happy thought of the two men she loved the most raising her children together. Gabrielle opened her eyes to J.J. in the doorway.

"Hi," J.J. said. "Remember me, your old pal—?"

"This isn't the *Wizard of Oz*," Jackie groaned.

"You must be J.J.," Gabrielle said. "What does J.J. stand for anyway?"

"I told you once, but I'm not going to tell you again."

"I'll remember," she replied. "Where did you tell me?"

"That'll remain a mystery, too," J.J. added. "Until you remember."

"Would you like to see the back of my head or my hip?" Gabrielle asked, and then stood from the bed.

"No," he said with a smile.

"Do you want me to twirl around for you?"

"No. I would like the kids to leave the room, so we could—"

"Eww! Not on my bed!" Jackie growled.

Gabrielle giggled. "I'll have to remember what J.J. stands for now, won't I?"

"Yes. Now, what should I call you?"

Gabrielle closed her eyes; her face turned pale.

"What's happening? Is she doing some kind of voodoo?" J.J. asked.

"She's remembering something," Jackie whispered.

"She's not going to vomit is she?" he asked softly.

"Where did we meet?" Gabrielle asked, opening her eyes.

"At the beach house," J.J. replied.

"Was I only wearing a robe?"

"Yes. You had morning sickness; you were pregnant with Jackie."

"You didn't know my name when you came there, did you?"

"I didn't have a clue, really." J.J. shook his head, shrugging with subtle embarrassment.

"I told you I preferred to be called 'Bobbie' and you said, 'Gabrielle sounds sexy, ah womanly. But if you prefer Bobbie, a stripper's name, that's not a problem.'"

"You're good. You're Bobbie. I'm convinced just by looking at you."

"I weigh a little more, right?"

"No comment," he said, with a sarcastic grin.

"You wouldn't tell me what J.J. stood for on the day we met."

"No, I wouldn't."

"I'll remember," she told him.

"I'm sure you will," he replied.

Gabrielle beamed dreamily at this handsome man wearing jeans and a light-blue button down shirt and he returned the fascinated stare.

"Let's go downstairs and get something to eat," Jackie said.

"I'm starving," Rob agreed.

"Is your first name Jason? Rob's middle name?" Gabrielle asked, wondering.

"Nope," J.J. said. He slipped an arm behind her waist and they walked down the stairs. "It's you?" J.J. asked her.

"It's me. I can't believe it either." She giggled.

"You look awesome! Unbelievably awesome."

"HI, JOHN." Gabrielle waved from below as John watered the flowerbeds on the terrace.

"Hi," he signaled to her, while a cigarette dangled from his bottom lip. "Where are you off to?" he asked. "Your parents will be here soon. Shedel's coming back with a video."

"I'm going for a walk to clear my head." She kept moving toward the tennis courts.

"Sounds like fun."—he shut off the hose—"In the woods?" He set the hose down.

"Yes."

"Alone?"

"Yes. Is there a problem?" She stopped and twirled around, looking up at him as he wandered around the terrace rails peering down at her.

"There're bears and skunks in those woods," he joked.

"I'll be careful." She turned and walked on, rolling her eyes a bit at his charming over-protectiveness.

"No. Seriously. I got a letter from the Forest Preserve. A pipe broke, and I'm not sure where they had to dig. It might not be safe."

"I'll be careful," she repeated. She waved without looking back.

"MR. RAVOLIE, have you seen Mrs. Ravolie?" Melinda asked him when he entered the foyer.

"Mrs. Ravolie?" he questioned. "Oh, you mean, Miss Gabrielle? You scared the hell out've me. I thought you meant, Miss Aimee."

"I meant Miss Gabrielle. What a lovely woman. We were talkin' about the youngens, and she's just the sweetest woman I've ever met. She's too sweet for you," she added, with an elbow to his side. "I bought some clothes for her and I wanted to tell her I put 'em in her closet."

"She's not back from her walk, and it's been a half hour," he told Melinda as he looked at his watch

"I showed you the letter yesterday," Melinda replied. "There was some work bein' done out there—"

"She's fine, Miss Melinda."

"There's a hole." She looked at him with her southern raised eyebrows and stood with hands on her hips. "There's a hole, Mr. Ravolie," she repeated with desperation.

"I'll take Skippy and go look for her," he groaned. "But I know she's fine." He walked away slowly. He pretended to rummage through the mail that sat on a curio table within the foyer.

"Go." She pointed toward the door.

"I'm going," he said. He stepped into the rose garden until he was out of Melinda's sight. And then, he ran.

He ran to the stables where the horse was already saddled. He rode off through his football field, over the creek, and into the woods. "Gabrielle!" He yelled. "Gabrielle, where are you?" He jumped off the horse when he noticed the trench along the dirt path. He looked into the twelve-foot deep grave. "Oh shit. Gabrielle, are you all right?"

"I think I ate a worm." She sputtered dirt out of her lips and shielded her eyes from the sun when she looked up at him. "Black snakes aren't poisonous are they?" she asked, looking back at the ground.

"Red, you're dead. Where?" John asked her.

"There." She pointed to a gardener snake that was traveling over her foot and then slithered away from her.

"Cover your ears," he told her, and she did.

Bang.

With the bang of the gun, she jumped, gasping and holding her breath as she looked down at the twitching remains of the snake.

"It won't hurt you now," John said, placing his gun into its holster. "So, what happened?" he asked, while he adjusted the straps of Skippy's reigns. "You saw the hole and decided to jump in?"

"I was looking at this yellow bird up in the trees. You forgot to warn me about yellow birds."

He stifled a laugh. "Did you hurt yourself? Hit your head or anything?"

"I'm fine."

He lay on the ground and peered over the hole. "Take my hands and I'll pull you up."

She jumped to reach for his palms, but couldn't leap high enough. "I'm too short," she told him. "Can you get a ladder?"

"I won't leave you. Is there a root or anything you can use to climb with?" he asked, searching the pit.

"No, I don't see anything. Plus, I wouldn't be able to hold on."

"What if I took Skippy here and you held onto the reigns and I'll have him pull you up and out of the hole?"

"We can try it, but I don't think I'll be able to hold on."

"As soon as he pulls you up a notch, I'll grab hold of you."

"We can try it," she repeated.

Skippy walked slowly up to the edge and lowered his head. John threw the slack beside her. She wrapped the ends of the two straps around her wrists and clenched it with both fists.

"Put your feet up against the wall as if you were mountain climbing."

"I've never been mountain climbing before. Have you?"

"No." He stepped away from the hole. "Come on, Skippy." The horse took a step backward. "Are you holding on?" John peered over the edge to view her.

"I'm holding on."

"Back Skippy. Pull back, boy."

"I'm off the ground!"

"Pull back, boy," he told the horse again. Gently, he slapped the horse's side.

Bending over her, he placed his hands under her arms and said, "I got you."

"Don't let go of me, John. Please don't let go of me."

"You're as light as a feather, and I would never drop you back in there." He pulled her up and set her feet to the ground. He unwound the straps from her hands. He noticed her trembling, yet he walked away and told the horse, "Good boy."

"You have an excellent horse," she told him as she wiped her pants off and then looked up from her legs to him staring at her. "What?" she asked.

"I rescue you from a gardener snake and a hole, and I don't even get a hug?"

"Sure," she told him, taking a step forward. "But I'll get you dirty."

"I've been dirty before. Besides, I have to take a shower anyway, before I go out tonight," he said walking toward her with opened arms.

"You're going out tonight?" she asked him, taking a few steps back toward the hole.

"Come forward." He took her hand. "Yeah. Is that all right with you?"

She took her hand back. "But my parents are coming."

"That's why I'm going out," he said with raised eyebrows.

"I was expecting you to take me to the beach house."

"Tomorrow. I'll take you tomorrow. This has been a busy day for you. Rising from the dead, plane ride, memories coming back to you all at once, meeting Shedel—you're bleeding."

"What?"

"Your elbow." He lifted her arm to see if it needed stitches.

"New girlfriend?" she asked him.

"A date. I just have a date."

"Oh. Well, I'm going to walk back and see if Melinda is back from shopping. And, I'm waiting for J.J.—"

"She is. She put the clothes in your closet. Would you like to ride back with me and Skippy?" he asked her politely. "I'll take care of your elbow when we get back to the stables."

"Okay," she agreed.

"I'll help you up," he told her, holding onto her waist. "Do you ride?"

"I've been in a psychiatric hospital for the past ten years. What do you think?" She sat onto the saddle.

"I forgot," he said with a sigh and a grin.

"I think the last time I was on a horse was probably with you."

"Move up, I'll sit behind you," he told her, as he placed his foot in the stirrup, flung over his leg, and slowly lowered his body behind hers.

He wrapped his arms around her. As he held the reins, she placed her palms on top of his hands and he signaled the horse to walk slowly.

Back at the stables, Gabrielle sat on top of a wooden picnic table while John pulled the first aid kit from the wall. "So, you were looking at a yellow bird, huh?"

"Don't wanna talk about it."

"If you don't, tonight you'll have nightmares about yellow birds."
He set the kit on the table and lifted her arm gently. "Do you have any other
cuts?" he asked her. "Snake bites?"

"Not that I'm aware of," she said.

He looked at the torn skin hanging off her elbow. It reminded him
of Jackie's scrapes from falling from her bike or roller blades. "This won't
hurt a bit," he said, just as he always told Jackie.

"Like hell it won't," she replied.

He was gentle. He patted her elbow tenderly with an antiseptic
towelette. He made sure all the dirt was removed. Then he spread an
ointment onto her open wound using a circular motion with his finger. Then
he blew softly.

She closed her eyes. The sensation of his breath tickled the inside of
her elbow and trailed to the hairs on her arm. She enjoyed this feeling and it
put a wide white teeth smile onto her face.

She heard John pull the gun from his holster and what sounded to
her as the safety unlocking. She opened her eyes quickly to see them staring
back at her. "Mom? Dad? Oh my God! I remember you!" She jumped up
and ran forward.

John stashed his gun.

Chapter 10

Attempting to sneak up on her, he entered the pool deck quietly. "What are you reading?" John grabbed the book from Gabrielle's hands. He marked the page that she had opened with his finger. "*Luck of the Draw* by Candace Moon?" he questioned, handing it back to her. "Good book?"

"It's okay," Gabrielle said, bending her knees to get comfortable as she lay on her back on the full-length patio chair donning a new black bikini.

"What's it about?" He sat on the lawn chair beside her.

"Don't know," she said, with a shrug.

"Don't know? You're on page 152 and you don't know what it's about?"

"You wanna read it?"

"No, I got my own book. See." He lifted the towel off his shoulder and showed her the book he had hidden under his arm.

"What kind of book is that?" she asked. "*When Money Changes Everything?*"

"It's a sci-fi," he said.

"A sci-fi?" She laughed.

"Snow White—" he looked to the sky "—do you think you'll tan out here at all? There's a big overcast today."

"Who are you callin', Snow White? Have you seen *yourself* in the mirror lately?"

"Hey, look at my wrist." He leaned over to show her his tan line underneath his watch.

"So what? You still look *sooo* white."

"That's it." He stood and threw his book down onto the lawn chair. "This is a tan, these are muscles—" he flexed his right arm "—and this is *you* going in that pool."

"No I'm not." He picked her up into his arms. "No, John!" She laughed hard. "No!" she screamed. "Put me down!"

"Shhh, your parents will come runnin'."

"Help!" she yelled, louder.

"You're going down," he said, swinging her back and forth, getting ready to throw her.

"No, no...." He threw her into the deepest section of the pool. "Help!" she came up wheezing. "Help?" she gasped again.

Immediately, John dove in. He grabbed her from underneath her arms. While he treaded water, she held onto him.

She embraced him in a hug and wrapped her legs around his waist. She turned her head and coughed over his shoulder.

"I'm sorry," he said.

She coughed again.

"I guess I thought you knew how to swim, since you were a great swimmer years ago." Still holding her close to his body, he walked in the shallow end and brought her to the stairwell.

"Do you feel guilty?" she asked as she stood on the first stair, squeezing out her hair.

"Yeah. I'm sorry," he said with regret.

"Since I can't pick you up, that's *my* way of getting *you* into the pool!"

She ran.

SHE SLAMMED the newspaper onto the table. "Have you seen this?" she asked him.

Gabrielle Ravolie is Alive!

Kathryn Lyn Morris, held at the Long Island Rehabilitation Center for permanent amnesia, has a new identity.

For ten years, Long Island Hospital has treated Kathryn Morris for permanent amnesia with no success. Last week, Long Island High School student Jackie Ravolie visited the hospital with her vocational class. Jackie Ravolie, daughter of rock star Johnny Ravolie, claimed that Ms. Morris was her mother.

After several tests and a more powerful drug (anti-clayco) was administered to Ms. Morris, her identity was revealed.

Kathryn Morris's true identity is none other than Gabrielle Ravolie who was declared dead on August 10^{th,} twelve years ago.

Her fraudulent death was more than a shock to her husband, rock star Johnny Ravolie, lead singer of Ra'vole. "My wife is alive! We all thought that she was dead. Instead, Bernadette Malone faked Gabrielle's death, twelve years ago. This past week, we've been having a family reunion. I vow that no one and nothing will harm Gabrielle again," Ravolie said.

"Having amnesia is worse than death," Gabrielle Ravolie said. "Not knowing who you are, not having anything, no possessions, no…"

She began, "Rolando will be on their side. He has strength in numbers."

"I vowed to honor your sister's death with her request."

"What will we do?" she asked him.

"First we get rid of the three children, then we get rid of Gabrielle Ravolie."

"And if Rolando stands in our way?" she asked.

"Are you frightened of Jeffrey Rolando, Elizabeth?"

"No sir. I'm prepared to do anything you ask, even if I have to pretend that I'm Bernadette."

"Well, you are her twin sister."

"We were triplets," Elizabeth said. "But Maureen—"

"I know dear." He patted her hand. "Maureen is not worthy…."

JOHN UNLOCKED the door for her.

"Wow," Gabrielle said, entering the beach house. "I'm amazed."

"This house is yours, Gabrielle."

"What?"

"It's in your name."

"Wow, this is beautiful, John." She looked up at the glass chandelier hanging from the vaulted ceiling. She noticed the light blue walls. She then flashed back to the evening when John first showed her the beach house, seventeen years ago.

"Gabrielle?" He jostled her. "Gabrielle, are you all right?"

"What? Yes, I'm fine. I'm just remembering things. Ugly green carpet."

He chuckled. "I took the carpet out and then there was a psychedelic one you weren't too crazy about either. Your choice would've been dark purple."

"Purple? Yuck. I had horrible taste back then." She walked up the stairs to where the bedrooms were, and John followed. "I don't remember the beach house having two floors," she told him.

"It didn't. When we lived here, there was only the one floor and three short stairs that led into a sunken living room." John continued to show her the upstairs bedrooms before they walked down the stairs together and sat on the sofa, in the living room.

"So, you want me to tell you about Bernadette?"

"If it's too painful, you don't have too."

"It's how I met you, really." John took Gabrielle's hand, stroking it softly, and continued. "Rolando's father was a mobster, the great and powerful Nicholas Rolando. He married Angelique Malone who had three daughters; they were triplets. Nicholas and Angelique were very much in love and they had Jeffrey together."

Gabrielle concurred, "Jeffrey and Bernadette are half-brother and sister. Same mother, not the same father."

"Yes. After Nicholas's death, he passed his power on to Jeffrey, his only son. Bernadette felt that she should be the next great one, since she was the first born of the triplets, but she wasn't Nicholas's blood. Bernadette didn't understand how the process is brought down from father to son and she had her stepfather and mother killed in a boating accident, thinking that she would be the next in line."

Gabrielle said, "But she wasn't."

"No. I was friends with Jeffrey Rolando. When you're in the music biz, you make friends with a lot of people," John added. "One night, Rolando introduced me to his half-sister—Bernadette. In just a month's time, she grew so obsessive with me. She wanted to be my manager, my agent, my girlfriend, my mother, and my father. You name it; she wanted to be it.

"She made sure I wouldn't escape. She had me handcuffed to her or the bed when I went to sleep. Or, she handcuffed me to the metal guardrails attached to the bathtubs in the hotels we stayed in."

"How long did this go on for?" Gabrielle asked.

"Too long, and there was nothing I could do. She controlled me, and everything around me. She started making decisions for the band and she wouldn't let me have any control over my own life. She took away my money and made sure I was her prisoner in every way.

"I could barely talk to my friends and when I did, she'd always be there with her bodyguards. I went on tour, and she came along. The guys in the band didn't want her to come, but I had to insist that she did because she had to always be attached to my side.

"My escape was two hours, twice a week, when we were on tour. A show would last for two hours. After the show, I had to go straight back to the hotel room. She believed that I was gone for two weeks, instead of two hours, and would go ape shit on me."

"How could she do this to you?" Gabrielle asked. "There was nothing you could do? You couldn't get away from her? You couldn't tell anyone?"

"I tried. Believe me, I tried. I even tried to tell my mother, but she didn't understand what I was trying to say. Bernadette threatened me and made it clear that if I did anything to try to get rid of her, she would have my family killed. First, she'd kill Mick and frame me for his death."

THE RECORDING STUDIO
LONG ISLAND, NEW YORK
JUNE 25

"JOHN? Can I talk to you alone?" Mick Harrison asked.

"Whatever you have to say, you can say it to the both of us."

"Come into the studio, would'ja?" Mick asked him.

John took Bernadette's hand. "Hey." John looked toward Lenny behind his drums. Brandon hung up his guitar. Trevor smoked his cigar while staring angrily at John with Bernadette. John noticed the guitar he bought for Brandon smashed into pieces.

"The band's breaking up, man," Mick announced.

"What?" John asked, and shook his head. "We had a lousy night last night. The sound system sounded screwy. But—"

"That's not it!" Brandon said angrily.

"We're sick of this shit," Trevor said.

"And, we're sick of her." Lenny pointed at Bernadette.

"Leave Bernadette out of this!" John defended her.

"She's the one who messed up the set," Mick told him. "She's tellin' everyone what to do. Puttin' her big nose in where it don't belong!"

"Will you leave her out of this? Honey, why don't you—"

"I'm staying," Bernadette said, squeezing his hand.

"Can't you just leave him for one fucking second?" Trevor shouted.

"I'm not going anywhere!" Bernadette yelled back.

"Look, John! We're through. We're firing you. We'll find another singer, someone better—"

"I can't believe this shit. You can't find anyone better!"

"The band can't break up," Bernadette said.

"Well, we just did," Mick growled.

"So, that's it. You've all agreed to this? Mick, we're best friends, man."

"Not anymore."

"What? You gonna keep the name Ra'vole?" John asked.

"We weren't plannin' on it," Mick supplied.

John turned to Lenny. "Lenny—?"

Lenny began, "We want you cut off—"

"You can't fucking do this," John said.

"We just did," Brandon answered.

"That means no more money will come in," Trevor mumbled. "For any of us."

"No more money?" Bernadette gasped.

"Nothin'. Not a dime," Mick said, averting his eyes.

"I apologize man, for ... for ... whatever I did. I don't even know what the fuck I did for you—"

"It's her, man," Mick told him. "It's her!"

"Bernadette means the world to me and you all know that!"

"That's just it, Ravolie," Mick said. "We thought music meant more. Music doesn't mean shit to you anymore."

"It does," John said. "Besides Bernadette, music is my life! What the hell do I gotta do to make this right?"

"Leave her!" Trevor pointed at Bernadette.

"I can't! I'd die without her! Don't you assholes know that I'd die without her?"

"Well then, we're through," Mick said sternly.

"No ... no, we ain't," John said. "We still have one last show to do and we're doin' it and then we're gonna make another recording in this goddamn studio and then—"

"The band can't break up," Bernadette blurted out.

"Awe. Are you still thinkin' 'bout the money Bern?" Trevor said sadly.

"That's right," Brandon said. "Your Johnny isn't gonna receive a penny."

Bernadette grew teary eyed.

"That's not true," John told her.

"Oh yes, it is," Mick said.

"The contract, honey. I'll still receive money," John told her.

"Not enough, though," Lenny said.

"You'll have to sell your house," Brandon added.

"I'm at your mercy." John threw up his hands. "I'll ask it again. What do I gotta do to make things right between ... between all of us. But, I'm not leavin' Bernadette. That's out of the question."

"Then there's nothin'," Mick said.

Trevor began, "We want no part of her—"

"And no part of you," Brandon finished.

"There has to be something. Johnny?" Bernadette whined. "The money?"

"I still don't understand what I did—"

"You'll never understand," Mick said, shaking his head.

"We're not playing the last show," Lenny mentioned.

"But the ... the last show was going to bring in millions," Bernadette gasped. "Johnny loves me, but he loves the music, too. There has to be something that he can do besides leaving me that will make everyone happy and allow him to stay within the band. You just can't fire him like this. I promise that I'll be better company and I'll keep my distance from Jewel. I won't tell her what to choose for Johnny when she's deciding on his wardrobe."

"There's one thing that I can think of," Mick said.

"What?" John asked.

"What? He'll do anything," Bernadette said. "Right, Johnny? You'll do anything they ask, just to stay in the band, just to keep bringing in money?"

"I'll do anything," John agreed.

"There's a children's hospital—"

"A children's hospital?" Bernadette questioned.

"There are children, in Chicago, who are disfigured from burn injuries."

Bernadette sucked in air again.

Lenny pulled out a manila folder and walked to John and Bernadette. He handed the folder to John.

John looked inside. Bernadette peered over his arm; turned her head rapidly from the child in the photo. "What do you want me to do?" John asked.

"Go to the hospital," Lenny said. "Stay with these children for one week."

"Can Bernadette come with me?" John asked.

"Oh, no," Bernadette said. "I couldn't. Johnny you must go alone. You must see these burned children and sing a few songs. It would be a great publicity stunt. Oh, the publicity. The money. People all around the world, will love you."

John told Gabrielle, "It was Mick's idea to send me to the children's hospital in Chicago. As long as I stayed in the hospital, he didn't think that Bernadette would come. No one could come with me; that was the deal. None of her bodyguards. Mick found out from Rolando that she didn't like being in hospitals. She thought of those children in the hospitals as zombies or ghosts. Or, I don't know what her demented mind was thinking. I had no idea that Mick and Rolando were working together until I got there. Rolando was going to have her killed while I was at the hospital.

"After I arrived, a woman sitting in the waiting room handed me a package. I went to the bathroom and opened it. There was a cell phone, a checkbook, fake IDs, and a letter from Mick. You name it; it was in this box. I called Mick immediately and he told me everything was bein' taken care of and I told him how much I loved him."

"I can't wait to meet Mick," Gabrielle said.

"Next weekend," John supplied. "I found out that the last show we did, the lighting was all messed up on purpose. I found out that the guitar Brandon smashed wasn't the one I had gave to him. I don't know how Rolando launders money. But, he switched my accounts into a fake name, and I could get at my money. The hospital was my escape. I brought my dog Charlene with me. The kids absolutely loved Charlene. These kids were saving my life."

"Then what happened?" Gabrielle asked.

"I absolutely loved those kids in the pediatric burn unit and I decided to make a one hundred thousand dollar donation to the hospital."

"Those kids meant a lot to you, didn't they?"

"They sure did. Bernadette was furious," he said with a laugh. "She read about it. Anyway, it was the last day of my full week there and I knew I had to get back to New York. Rolando missed his time slot and since Bernadette wasn't dead yet, she'd be going on a shooting spree.

"I was about ready to leave the hospital and a man and a woman came up to me and told me their daughter was hit by a drunk driver while she was walking on a sidewalk. She was a bright young woman and only fourteen years old. She was in a coma for almost a month now. She loved the band Ra'vole and it was all she ever listened to. It was you, Gabrielle. They begged me to go in and talk to you."

"Did you visit me then? The fourteen year old girl in the coma?"

"Yes. I knew I only had one hour. While you were lying there, attached to a respirator, I fell in love with you. Mick came and took the phone and everything back and secretly left. I then flew back to New York where Bernadette was waiting for me.

"After our last show, the guys in the band told Bernadette that I had to go back to the children's hospital, and there were no exceptions. Mick knew I wanted to come back and stay with you until you woke up. I sang to you and talked to you. I thought that if I did that, I'd help you come out of the coma."

"And I did," Gabrielle said.

"Yes, and Rolando now had a second chance to kill Bernadette."

"You were able to escape again?"

"Yes, amazingly. And, Rolando said that Bernadette was gone this time. I spent so much time with you. My dog did too, in your room. It was so hard for me to take care of her though and Mick secretly came and brought Charlene back home with him. He took care of her at his place. Rolando was protecting my parents, my brother, and my older brother's family. And the guys in the band were working together to form a mob of our own.

"I told Rolando I wanted a beach house. He thought it would be a good idea, especially since he had one and Bernadette and her mob never knew he lived there. He thought she or her people would never find me there, and I told him my plan was to bring you here after you woke up from the coma. You mesmerized me, and I wanted to start a new life with you. Rolando began to build the beach house not just for me, but for us.

"You were awake for two days and Mick called me and told me Charlene was missing. He couldn't find her and Bernadette was still alive and coming to the hospital. She found out about the girl in the coma. I asked you to wait for me. I told you I loved you. I told you that I might have to leave without saying good-bye—"

"And you did," Gabrielle said. "I remember the argument you had with Bernadette in the hall."

"Out in the hall, Bernadette told me to go home. I found my dog bleeding to death. Charlene died in my arms."

"Were you her prisoner all over again? What happened after?"

"Well, yes and no. I'll explain more to you on a different day, okay."

"Sure."

"I kept all these secrets from you and I never told you about Bernadette. Actually, you found out for yourself with Shedel being your private detective."

"She's dead, right?" Gabrielle asked teary eyed.

"Yeah. She's dead, for sure, never to return."

"Are you sure?"

"Yes. She was shot five times and Shedel made sure her brain was splattered." John paused, needing a break from his painful past. "Would you like to take a walk on the beach?"

"Sure."

"Let me get a blanket for us to sit on. Hold on." John walked up the stairs as Gabrielle waited outside on the deck. After he pulled a blanket out of the closet, he removed two towels.

John slid the glass door closed. They walked down the stairs that led to the sand and walked out toward the water.

"The Rolandos' still live about a half mile away—"

"I bet, you still can't catch me," Gabrielle said, smiling.

"You remember?"

"I sure do." Gabrielle ran as fast as she could through the sand.

He caught up to her and grabbed her arm. She fell into his embrace. "You let me catch up to you," he said out of breath.

"I did not," she said.

"You could at least challenge me for once." He spread out the blanket over the sand.

Out of breath, they collapsed to the ground.

"I always did let you catch up to me. Why was this?" she asked him.

"I have a bad knee. I brought towels just in case you wanted to go for a swim. The water is probably too cold tonight, though. I don't think you'll want to go skinny dipping."

"Do you want to? I'm game if you are."

"I brought two towels for you. One for your body, one for your hair. You won't catch me swimming in there tonight. And you won't catch me naked out there either." He pointed to Long Island Sound.

"Impressive," she said.

"What is?"

"Two towels for me? You're thoughtful and romantic."

John and Gabrielle lay on their backs, looking up to the stars. "You can put your head on my chest if you want. I won't bite you, I promise," he said; she did.

"I remember you being romantic," she said.

"I'm not romantic anymore, really, Gabrielle. To be honest, I sleep with a lot of women and then get rid of them afterwards."

"Why?" She turned her body to view him.

"Because I don't love them, I don't need them."

"Do you still love me? Do you still need me?" she asked in a whisper. Her mouth went close to his.

"Gabrielle, I will always love you and I will always need you."

"I love you, John." She placed her mouth to his.

"You're passionate," he whispered and then kissed her mouth tenderly.

He rolled her onto her back and straddled over her. He lifted her skirt to her thighs and held onto her panties with his left hand. He embraced her face with his right.

"I remember you," she said to him. "I love you, John."

Something came over him—something she had never known existed within him. He kissed her wildly and his fingers ripped her panties from her thigh. He grabbed onto her shirt and tore it apart to where she would never be able to use the same buttons again. He dropped the cup of her bra down over her right breast, then did the same to her left, and then kissed her neck harshly.

Instead of waiting for her to open up to him, he penetrated her quickly. After she dug her nails into his back, he took hold of her wrists and pressed the back of her hands harshly into the sand.

"You feel so good, I never want this to end," he said to her with a wild thrust.

"But I do," she said softly.

"What?" He rolled onto his back tugging on his zipper and buttoning his jeans. He pulled his lighter out of his pocket and the pack of cigarettes out of the other and lit one. Together, they lied quietly on the rustled blanket.

Gabrielle didn't know what to say to John. She felt her tears welling up inside her eyes and she knew they were glossy. She was speechless.

"Each time we make love it's like the first time," he said hatefully, and then blew out a puff of smoke.

"Make love? John, I don't remember us ever having sex like *that* before."

Gabrielle lay with the towel hiding her ripped shirt and skirt.

"Would you like me to start a fire?"

"What kind of fire?" she said, still confused, a little hurt, and embarrassed.

"No—" He changed his mind. "—We should head back to the house soon."

"John, what the hell just happened? You tore my clothes. My skirt is not fixable and my buttons for my shirt are here somewhere."

"What we had right now was just sex, a one night stand, and it'll never happen again. You came onto me. I did not come on to you. I told you how I was and I thought you accepted how I am. That's why you came on to me."

"You asked me to stay and live with you," she whimpered. "You told me you still loved me and you needed me."

"I told you what you wanted to hear. I know what women want to hear," he added.

"Huh?" Gabrielle asked, still confused.

John lay on the blanket looking up at the stars, smoking his cigarette.

She stood. "You are a real ass! I am confused right now and still don't remember things. There's one thing that I clearly remembered and that was that my love for you was never stronger. You inserted your thing into me and you can't even apologize for what you did. I'm not one of your whores that you've been doing for twelve years, John. I'm your wife!"

He was silent.

"You have no right to treat me this way! No right! I haven't done anything to hurt you. Your ex-girlfriend Bernadette Malone separated us! I love you and I thought you loved me! I can see now you do hate me! You blame me! How do you think I've felt all these years? Don't you think I've been in pain, too? I didn't know my past, but I went on."

"I don't blame you," he snarled, and sat.

"Oh yes, you do. At least you had Jackie. You had a life. I didn't have anyone! No one cared about me! I'm leaving and I won't be coming back! At least not for you!"

Gabrielle ran.

"Oh shit." John ran after her. "Gabrielle, listen." He grabbed her arm. "I don't know what to say. I need time to think. I love you. I know I love you. I haven't loved anyone since you died. I'm still in this stage where you're not real. What we just had right now wasn't real. That wasn't you and me."

"You're right. That was *you* doing I don't know what."

"You're someone else. You're not Gabrielle. Gabrielle's not real to me yet. Do you understand?"

"Go see a shrink. It was real, John! Would you like me to punch you? I would like to give you a bloody lip right now, or a black eye, or both. Then will you believe I'm real?"

"Go ahead, I deserve it."

Gabrielle punched him in his right eye.

"Damn! Son of a bitch!"

"I'm real all right!"

"Where'd you learn to ... Oh, yeah, I remember."

She then gave him a blow to his stomach.

"Damn!" He toppled over into the sand, holding his abdomen. He gasped, "You're real. I believe you. Don't attack me again." He stood and held her tight to his body, but she wouldn't return his embrace and she wept painfully into his chest. "Please don't hit me again. I'm seeing stars."

She slid the side of her face against his chest. "You deserve this!" She brought her knee up hard into his groin.

He hunched over in scorching pain.

"You will never take advantage of me again, John!" she yelled pointing at him. "Never."

"Gabrielle." He reached out to her. "I died twelve years ago."

"It's about time you rose from your grave. I did."

Chapter 11

Jackie felt that something terrible had happened to her mother. And she had good reason to feel this way. Gabrielle was missing. Three weeks ago, Gabrielle had packed her bags, told Jackie what had happened with John at the beach house, and left the Ravolie Estate in an apparent huff. Jackie assumed that her mother would head for Chicago to stay with her parents. Perhaps she needed more time with them to learn about her childhood. But, Jackie was wrong. Gabrielle never flew to Chicago.

John had hired a private detective to search for her, but so far, Gabrielle hadn't applied for a credit card, or rented an apartment. She had never purchased a ticket for a plane or a train; nor had she rented a car or purchased one. She was presumably using taxis but wasn't using her own name when calling for one. Essentially, Jackie's mother had vanished, not leaving much of a trail for John's detective.

John attempted to find her the best way he knew how and without bringing the media into it. But all of John's avenues in the past three weeks had turned up nothing.

The real world is a big and confusing place for anyone, but especially for Gabrielle, who had spent the last twelve years not even knowing who she was. Jackie's biggest fear was the thought of her poorly confused mother trying to fend for herself in the real world.

For a while, Jackie was angry with both her father and mother for the whole thing. More so with her father. Dad had humiliated Gabrielle out there on the beach; but then her mother had humiliated him, too. John couldn't walk for days. He complained of pain in his abdomen. Above his eye, he had a small lump filled with blood—a hematoma—until the swelling went away. But Jackie still couldn't believe Gabrielle just packed what she had and left. At least she remembered to take her pills with her; even as angry as she was when she stormed out of here.

Three weeks had gone by, and Gabrielle never called. Jackie feared she had lost her mother all over again. Jackie tried reaching Gabrielle by cell phone at least twenty times a day, but her mother never answered. She called the Rolandos' home in California and spoke with Roxy, but apparently, Gabrielle never went back there. No one had heard from her, not even Roxanne Rococo Rolando.

But then, finally, it happened. Her cell phone rang. "Hi, Jack," Gabrielle said.

"Mom? Are you all right? You never went to Chicago. You never went to California. Where have you been?"

"Tied up. I'm sorry I haven't gotten back to you sooner. I needed more time to think before I saw your father again. But Jackie, I stayed here in New York."

"You did?"

"Yes. I've been here the whole time. I've got myself a job and I found myself a house. Do you know where Park Avenue is, near the mall?"

"A house? A job?" Jackie asked confused, and a bit agitated, but still glad to hear from her mother and anxious to see her again. "Of course I do."

"I'll meet you at the park on the corner at ten o'clock."

"In fifteen minutes?" Jackie asked. "I don't think I can—" Jackie heard the dial tone.

"Was that Rob?" J.J. asked, standing in the doorway.

"No. I haven't seen him. That was my mother. She's been here in New York this whole time."

"That explains why we can't find her," J.J. said, sarcastically.

"She found a house and got herself a job. She's been so tied up that she hasn't been able to return any of my phone calls."

"Tied up?" J.J. asked.

"You don't think?" Jackie questioned.

"No," he said with a chuckle. "But, I'm gonna tie Rob up, if he doesn't call me back."

"J.J.?" Jackie said his name in a serious tone.

"She hasn't been a mother to you and doesn't realize she needs to call you immediately after she gets your message, but Rob should know this."

"It's been three weeks, J.J."

"And when does she get your voice mail? At two o'clock in the morning. She wasn't ignoring you purposely, but it sure seems that way," he added.

"I've gotta go. She wants to meet me at the park on the corner of Park Avenue, by the strip mall. She said fifteen minutes. I'm going to be extremely late."

"I'm going with you," J.J. said.

"Nooo," Jackie groaned.

"I have to talk to Gabrielle. Rob will call me back soon."

"*All right,*" Jackie said to him. "Let's take two cars, though."

"Why?"

"I'd like to stay with her for the weekend. She just might ask me to stay with her—"

"I don't think that's going to happen, but *all right.* We'll take two cars."

It took them close to thirty minutes to get to the park and Jackie realized she was twenty minutes late. They quickly were out of their cars, sat on a bench, and waited, watching intently around them for Gabrielle to make an appearance.

"She probably came and left already," Jackie mentioned, frustrated.

"Try her cell," J.J. suggested.

"She never answers," said Jackie, while pressing the buttons anyway. "No answer," Jackie sighed. "Told you. Maybe Mom is watching us from a distance and, no offense, but maybe she just doesn't want to talk to you. Maybe she only wants to see me." She turned her head from side to side looking for her mother.

"Jackie, you watch way too many movies."

"Will you leave for just a moment just in case—?"

"All of you Ravolie's are crazy. She probably came already and left. I'm going to *McDonald's* to get something for lunch. What do you want?"

"I'm not hungry. Why isn't she here?" Jackie asked him, while trying Gabrielle's cell again.

"You don't know your mother well. Actually, you don't know her at all. You didn't even spend all week with her before she left. She's different then she was twelve years ago. I could tell she was unusual. She's the same person, yet she's older. She was more mature, ravishing, a woman. I wanted her." He began to daydream.

"J.J., snap out of it!"

"Why did she leave anyway?"

"Well," Jackie answered, hesitating for a moment and wondering if she should tell. She looked at J.J. who was peering back at her, his eyes begging for an explanation of Gabrielle's sudden departure. "She slept with my dad."

"Where?"

"On the beach. At the beach house."

"Why didn't *I* hear about this?"

"I thought you knew already. I thought Rob told you."

"No. Here I was waiting. I thought I'd give it a week-and-a-half and then I'd make the moves on her. Ravolie beat me to it. Bastard. It's always been like that with us. A contest. With Gabrielle as the prize."

"Well, you might still have a chance. He invited her to stay and live at our home. He told her he needed her and he loved her. And then, after he slept with her on the beach, he told her that he couldn't stay married to her. She left because he told her he just couldn't live in the past."

"Bastard."

"You've said already," Jackie sighed, reaching for her cell phone. "I'm trying her phone again. No answer."

"Now I can't even use those lines—I love you and I need you. The bastard even stole the lines."

"Bye, J.J. Go to *McDonald's*. I'll wait here."

HE CROSSED THE STREET, entered the busy *McDonald's,* and found a place in a long line of hungry people. As he waited to place his order, he turned to look out the window. He noticed a woman who looked like Gabrielle walking the sidewalk with a man accompanying her.

J.J. quickly sacrificed his place in the line and weaved his way through the morning rush of people. As he ran past a large standee of Happy Meal displays and out through the double front doors, he looked recklessly in the direction he had seen the woman walking, but she had already disappeared.

Just then, Jackie pulled up along the curb. "I saw Mom walking this way!" she told him. "I'm going to follow her. Go get your car and call me on your cell." With that, she sped off.

As he walked across the street to his car, he noticed Jackie pass him and round the corner. J.J. watched from his vehicle. A limousine pulled up to the curb, and the woman and man stepped into it. She wore a polyester scarf around her neck and cheap sunglasses, he could tell. J.J. wasn't sure if it was Gabrielle, but he wasn't going to take any chances by not following the limo.

"There she is. And she is beautiful. And now another man is going to beat me to her *again,*" he thought, audibly. He slapped the steering wheel with frustration. "That's not going to happen. Not this time." Then he realized he'd better start his car and follow the limousine before it disappeared.

JACKIE STOPPED AT THE TRAFFIC LIGHT and then decided to make a right. She went in a complete circle. At the intersection, again, she made a left and circled and then the street led into a residential neighborhood. She made a U-turn and went back to the curb where she could park her car. Maybe her mother and the man went into one of the stores, Jackie thought.

Jackie stepped out of the car. She pulled out a picture of Gabrielle, taken long ago. She began to ask people if they'd seen her mother. Most politely said 'no' or shook their heads. Some rudely ignored her, didn't answer, and just kept walking. Because of the scarf and sunglasses Gabrielle wore, Jackie didn't think anyone would recognize her mother from the picture anyhow. Defeated, she placed the old photo back in her wallet.

Jackie walked into a store and was just about to ask the clerk if he saw her when she realized something was sticking to her shoe. She lifted her foot up and peeled the small paper off her leather shoe, recognizing instantly that it was a wallet-size photo. She flipped the photo over and viewed a picture of her mother.

"How bizarre," Jackie said aloud. She went up to the man at the counter, showed him the picture, and asked him if he had seen the woman in the photo. He recognized Gabrielle's face right away, and told Jackie that she was there about four minutes ago looking around and the woman seemed to be acting a bit unusual. Jackie asked the man if he saw which way she went, and he said that she had turned right after she exited the storefront.

Jackie ran out onto the sidewalk and immediately noticed the same man who was with her mother earlier entering a limousine. Before she could get the driver's attention, the limo sped off down the street, ignoring the red light. Jackie stood on the cement cylinder block that held a flagpole and watched to see if the limousine was going forward or if it would turn right or left onto the next street. She saw it make a left and she ran to her car.

She placed the key into her ignition and her car wouldn't start. "What the hell?" Jackie yelled, causing the joggers to turn their heads. "Don't do this to me!" she yelled at the car. Finally, after many frustrated tries and idle threats to the stubborn vehicle, the engine roared. Jackie pressed her foot on the gas and sped out into the traffic. As people honked their horns, Jackie gave many of them the finger. In angry exchange, they returned the favor by offering her gestures and remarks of their own.

She drove into the residential neighborhood and made her way down the street, frantically looking for the limousine. In the process, she got completely lost. All the houses looked the same to her and she didn't know if she had already searched this same street twice or even three times. She braked hard at the stop sign; not realizing it was there until she noticed the pedestrian crossing the street, an older man in a gaudy purple nylon suit, who grimaced at her as he strolled through the intersection way too slowly.

Then Jackie realized she had forgot all about J.J. She picked up her car phone and turned her head to see if she could pass through the intersection. While doing so, she noticed J.J.'s red corvette parked on the side of the road in front of a house. Jackie glanced at the license plate to make sure. Yes, this was J.J.'s corvette.

J.J. found Gabrielle before she had, but why didn't he call her? she wondered. Jackie pulled up behind his car, parked, and began to walk up the sidewalk to the driveway of the white, two-story home. She knocked on the door.

A woman answered. "Yes, dear?"

"I'm sorry. I must be at the wrong house," Jackie said, turning.

"You must be Jack. Why don't you come in and make yourself at home?"

Jackie thought there was something quite peculiar about the woman who stood drying a knife with a towel. She must have interrupted her from doing dishes. "Is my mother here?" Jackie asked her.

"Oh yes, Kathryn is inside with David and J.J. Would you like to come in?"

David? Jackie thought. Who was David? "No," Jackie said. "I was wondering if you would direct them out here? I'm having car troubles."

"Jack, they're in a serious conversation downstairs and they don't want to be disturbed. Kathryn said that when her lovely daughter arrived, to have her come in."

"But this is important. Seriously, I'm having problems starting my car."

"I was told not to intrude on their conversation, dear. Please do come in."

There was something odd about this, and something in the pit of Jackie's stomach screamed at her not to walk into the house. And Rob was the only one who really called her Jack at times. So did John Rolando. She stopped thinking. "Well," Jackie said. "Since, J.J. and *David* are in there. I don't think *I* should interrupt their serious conversation either, but I'm going to go home and get my father, and we'll come back together."

"Oh, splendid," the odd woman said. "The more the merrier."

"I'll be back in a little while," Jackie said. She walked down the driveway, and then gave a short wave to the woman still standing at the front door smiling and staring at her. Jackie noticed a wallet-size photo on the ground. It was a picture of her and Gabrielle. Jackie pretended to drop her purse.

"Oh! Be careful, young lady," the woman yelled out to her.

"I'm okay," Jackie replied. She picked up her purse, sneaking to scoop up the photo as well, and headed straight for the car. She flipped the picture over. On the back, written in an obviously rushed and panicked scribble, it read, 'Call the police.'

Jackie turned the key, hoping desperately that the car would cooperate with her this time. And it did. She drove down the block and turned the corner, only to park the car again. She used her car phone and called her father at home.

He didn't ask Jackie if she was sure. He didn't second-guess his daughter at all because she had never given him reason to. John said that he would be there and the minute Jackie got off the phone with her father, the calls were made, and the proper authorities were aligning their police cars up against the adjacent road. Before John arrived, the police surrounded the house.

There was no word from inside the home. John and Jackie stood together across the street. He embraced her waist as they stared nervously at the house with its blinds all drawn and its curtains all closed. He had a cigarette gripped in his right fingers, which he quickly smoked down to the butt, flicked away, and lit another.

Jackie and John were notified promptly by the police who had assessed the situation that the woman who lived there held J.J., Gabrielle, and even Rob hostage. The driver of Rob's limousine stated that this morning, Rob had met Gabrielle at this house. This was the limousine that J.J. and Jackie noticed Gabrielle getting into with this man, who was actually the woman in disguise. She was forcing Gabrielle to use her cash to purchase things for her in town. However, Rob did not go shopping with them.

The police told John and Jackie that Rob remained unharmed, however was in the downstairs bathroom. At this point, they weren't sure if J.J. was in the bathroom as well or somewhere else in the house. Gabrielle sat on the sofa downstairs near a curtained window.

Jackie decided it was time for her to take charge. She let go of her father's hand and began to walk toward the sidewalk in the direction of the house.

"Jackie, where do you think you're going?" John asked her. "Jackie—!"

"I have to try to get into that house, Dad."

"Are you out of your mind?" He followed her. There was little use in trying to stop her.

"I'm just going to look to see if there is a way," Jackie said. "This waiting is ridiculous. I can't wait anymore, and you're going to die from cancer before they pull them out of there alive."

"Shit. You're my daughter. You think like me. Don't you dare go into that house. Just check it out and see where they are. I'll check out the east side. You check out the west. We'll meet in front of the house again. Got it?"

"Yeah. I got it," she said, but already had her own plan in the works. Instead of listening to her father, Jackie went around to the back of the house. Without the police noticing, she climbed on top of the air conditioning unit located behind a bush, and quickly pulled herself up into an opened window with no screen. She crawled in and landed on a bed. Not only did Jackie think like him, but also she was just as stubborn. This was easy, too easy, she thought. After exiting the bedroom, she heard the scandalous woman's voice. She realized it was coming from downstairs. She walked slowly through the carpeted hallway, praying that the floor didn't creek, until reaching the end of a hall.

Jackie overheard the woman. "You're going to yell out the window and tell them I want one million dollars and I'll let you all go. No... How about three million? One for each of you. Plus, I want my own car to get out of here, and when I get to Canada, I'll trade Kathryn in for another million."

The woman who lived here was deranged, Jackie noticed immediately. She couldn't even make up her mind on a suitable ransom. Jackie was certain she had nothing to do with the mob. She was just a woman who wanted money. She abducted Gabrielle out of jealous greed, knowing how wealthy John and Gabrielle were because of stories she had seen on TV and headlines she had been reading in the papers. This hostile woman knew who the Ravolie's were, as well as the Shedel's, and she decided to hold the family hostage, leaving Johnny Ravolie to bring the ransom money. She wasn't a cold-blooded killer and might have no other weapons besides the knife that Jackie had seen her with at the front door. All she wanted was money, not blood on her hands. Jackie thought of a plan in the hallway.

She anxiously pulled the pistol from her purse and walked down the stairs to the quarter-basement. The bathroom was on the right of her at the bottom of the stairs. And as she had suspected, Jackie noticed the woman only holding a butcher knife and not a gun.

Jackie knew she could take her.

The woman stood in front of Gabrielle with her back toward Jackie. Gabrielle sat on the couch with her hands handcuffed in front of her and her feet tied in an uncomfortably tight and twisted knot, but she didn't seem to notice Jackie. Either that, or she instinctively kept her eyes to the floor, not looking in Jackie's direction on purpose.

Jackie noticed J.J. and Rob in the bathroom. Rob's hands were cuffed to a metal handrail that ran along the side of the bathtub. Jackie noticed a chain was attached to Rob's handcuffs and that chain was clamped to the metal shower curtain rod. Rob's eye was already bruising from the blows he had taken to the face. J.J. sat on the floor beside him, handcuffed as well to the metal rail and a chain suspended from the ceiling to those handcuffs.

Rob noticed Jackie immediately, 'What are you doing?' he silently mouthed with a look of disbelief in his swollen eye.

Jackie shook her head, motioning him not to talk.

She walked up to the woman swiftly, stuck the gun to the woman's head, and said, "Drop the goddamn knife now or I'll blow your head off!"

Immediately, the woman obeyed and dropped the knife to the floor.

"Get down!" Jackie yelled. "Now! On the floor! Your hands behind your head! Now!" Jackie screamed, as she kept the gun pressing against the woman's head. Jackie grabbed the knife from the floor. "Are you okay, Mom?"

"Yes, sweetheart."

Jackie pulled out her cell phone. "Dad, I'm in. Send in the police. The woman only had a knife and is now laying on her stomach on the floor." Jackie pressed 'END' and asked her mother, "Where're the keys to those cuffs?"

"Over there," Gabrielle pointed out and then attempted to undo the rope from her ankles with her cuffed hands.

Jackie waited to retrieve the keys and remained with the gun pressed up against the back of the woman's head. "Don't move," she told the woman. "Don't even look at me. I'm not a cop. I will shoot you if you move."

The police came down the stairs and entered the quarter-basement, and Jackie hid the pistol under her shirt at her waist. She retrieved the keys and undid the handcuffs attached to her mother's wrists.

There had to have been twenty officers with guns securing the scene. The police released Rob and J.J. from the fixtures and they walked out of the bathroom together.

"Don't you ever do anything like this again," J.J. told Jackie. "But hell, I'm glad you did." J.J. laughed, hugging her tightly.

Jackie realized the situation was under control, so she pulled the gun from her pants and set it beside her on the couch.

Gabrielle rubbed her wrists. "I can't believe this. I met her at the grocery store, and she said that she had a house for rent and asked if I wanted to view it, so I went with her. Today, she snapped. She said she knew who I was and that I had money. I can't believe this." Gabrielle shuddered.

At last, John made it down the stairwell. As he walked to them sitting on the sofa John said, "Don't ever pull a stunt like this again, young lady. When I say, 'don't go in the house,' this means don't go in the house."

"That was dangerous," Gabrielle agreed.

"But it worked," Rob said. "I hope that gun's not loaded," he whispered, then laughed as a paramedic brought an ice pack to him for his eye.

"It is," Jackie said with a smirk.

John inspected Gabrielle. Jackie could tell that he wanted to ask her if she was all right. The words seemed to be on the tip of his tongue. But, he didn't.

Gabrielle remained sitting on the couch, rubbing her wrists, and fidgeting. Jackie thought the fidgeting had much more to do with John being in the room than it did from the red marks the cuffs left.

"Dad wants to know if you're all right," Jackie asked for him.

"I can ask her myself," John told Jackie. "Gabrielle, are you all right, sweetheart?" he asked sincerely.

"I'm fine, John. Thank you for asking," she replied.

He hadn't seen her for three weeks. Anyone could tell that he was still in love with her. He just didn't want to admit it. Gabrielle looked up at John and smiled while she wiped the large tears jerking from her eyes.

Without realizing the gun was a problem, Jackie picked it up and swung it around like the cowboys did in the old westerns. Her finger encircled the trigger.

"Jackie, you can put the gun down," J.J. said nervously.

Jackie stopped twirling it around, then asked, "Why? It's my gun."

"Put it in your purse," J.J. whispered. "You could be arrested. You're not even eighteen—"

"Where the hell did you get a—?" John raised his voice.

"I bought it."

"You bought it?" John and Gabrielle questioned together.

"Yes, from school," Jackie supplied.

"Give it to me! You're ... You're grounded young lady!" John told her.

"John," Gabrielle spoke.

"No." He shook his head. "I realize she saved your life, but she's too young to carry a gun. She will not. Give it to me. Even I don't carry a gun."

"Yes, you do," Gabrielle said with a groan.

Jackie still had the gun in her hand with her finger on the trigger. Gabrielle looked up at John, while still fidgeting with her wrists. Gabrielle gave John a glare that told him this wasn't the time or the place to discipline their daughter. Jackie just saved their lives, and all John could think about was grounding her. Gabrielle wouldn't allow it.

"All right Dad," Jackie said, reluctantly. "I'll give it to you, but I bet you won't ground me." Jackie pulled the trigger ever so quickly and water came out of the pistol and shot John in the face. "It's a water gun," Jackie commented, grinning maniacally.

Gabrielle laughed so hard that she held her abdomen.

"It was only a dollar at school. It looked so real, so I bought it. I didn't think you'd ground me for buying a squirt gun." She shot him in the face again, laughing at her bewildered father.

Rob fell to the floor laughing. Rob was with Jackie when she bought it, so the gun was no surprise to him.

"You little brat." John shoved Jackie to the end of the couch and sat between Gabrielle and her.

"Are you going to ground her now for shooting you?" Gabrielle asked, still laughing.

John wiped his face with the bottom of his T-shirt.

Rob sat next to Gabrielle with his arm around her at her other side and the four of them sat closely smashed together.

Jackie glanced at J.J., who appeared a bit dismayed. She thought for a second, that he must be thinking, 'How could Ravolie be so smooth. Why didn't I think of pushing Jackie aside to sit between them?'

Gabrielle stood. She collected her purse and a manila envelope from the bar. "John? Here," she called out to him. "I have something for you."

'Great, *he* gets a present,' thought J.J.

John looked questionally at the outside of the manila envelope and then opened it.

"I was declared legally alive yesterday. All the papers are here."

"What about the beach house?" he asked her.

"I don't want the beach house," she said to him. "Since we don't own anything together and there's nothing to split between us and I'm not going to fight you for custody. All you have to do is sign, and we'll be legally divorced in a matter of weeks as soon as all the papers get shuffled through the red tape."

He skimmed through the papers. J.J., Robbie, and Jackie stared at them from the opposite corner of the room, having an idea of what they were talking so softly about.

"Are you *sure* you don't want the beach house—" She shook her head 'no.' "—You don't want any money from me?" he asked.

"I don't want anything from you," she said. "I made my own money before I died. I modeled. I sang with you. I have enough of my own money to last me a lifetime."

"Is there a clause in here that says you can change your mind later?"

"I made sure there wasn't." She handed him a pen.

He took the pen from her hand and he skimmed the rest of the papers. Jackie thought to interrupt, but somehow wasn't sure how. An officer had, and told Gabrielle and John that they could leave the building now. Gabrielle, J.J., Rob, and Jackie were to be questioned at the police station.

John signed on all the lines he was supposed to. Every damn one of them, and every one more regretfully than the one before it. He placed the papers back into the envelope.

Jackie could tell he purposely dropped the pen to the floor. Jackie noticed her mother crying, and noticed her father's eyes getting glossy as well. As he bent down for the pen, he took his sunglasses from his shirt pocket and placed them over his eyes quickly to hide the onset of quiet tears. And then John picked up the pen from the floor.

"Come on, guys." J.J. insisted. "Let's get out of here." Jackie and Rob stood from the sofa.

Jackie walked slowly to the stairwell, to continue to overhear her parents.

"No regrets?" John asked Gabrielle, handing back the envelope, however hesitating for a second to let it go.

"No regrets," she replied. "May I?" Gabrielle held her arms out and John embraced her ever so tightly.

He kissed her forehead. His hands moved to her shoulders. He then kissed her head. "We better get out of here," John told Gabrielle.

"Sure," she replied with a fake smile on her face.

"Do you want to talk about this divorce thing at all before we go?" he asked her.

"Did you read Section Eight, Point Two?" she asked him.

"What does it say in Section Eight, Point Two?" he asked.

"It basically says that, although we're divorced, you can't stop caring about me and we have to remain friends for life," Gabrielle told him.

"My beautiful Gabrielle. I'll never stop caring about you. You're the mother of my daughter and since you've been alive all this time, you were my only wife. Let's get this done and over with," he said. "You ready to go to the police station? Do you need a ride?" he added.

"Yeah. Can we stop for some fast food?" she asked. "I'm starving."

"I have a taste for ice-cream," he said to her.

She laughed, and he smiled as he took her hand. She let go of his hand for only a moment to grab her purse and the manila envelope, but then took his hand again as they walked up the stairs together.

Chapter 12

Gabrielle moved in to stay at the Ravolie Estate. More than anything, she wanted to be with her children, and the easiest way to do this was to move in with John and Jackie. J.J. had asked her to move in with him and Rob, but Rob nicely talked her out of it. J.J. still lived like a bachelor and he had an excessive amount of parties at his place. Rob was never too crazy about living there either and didn't think it was the right place for his mother.

Gabrielle continued to have her own bedroom down the hall from her daughter. It was not too far down the hall from her ex-husband either.

John and Jackie were the ones who convinced her to stay. John mainly did it because of Jackie. Jackie wasn't sure if he had asked Gabrielle for himself. However, John ignored Gabrielle at times and didn't talk much to her. They saw one another in the morning for breakfast. Later in the day, John said the customary 'hello' and 'good-bye' to her, however they never talked about their marriage, or if he wanted her back.

J.J. was just the reverse.

He visited everyday, practically all day, and he didn't stop getting close to Gabrielle. He stopped all his daily routines just to be with her. As soon as 10 AM hit, Gabrielle and J.J. were walking outside, and they'd sit in John's football field. And they would talk. They'd talk about anything and everything.

"What's wrong?" J.J. asked Gabrielle.

"Oh, nothing," she replied.

"Time of the month?" he asked.

"No." She slapped his leg.

"Remember, I'm your best friend, and you can tell me anything."

"I just feel like my whole life is a new beginning," she spoke softly.

"Can I ask you something personal?"

"How personal?" she questioned.

"You don't have to answer, if you don't want to."

"Promise," she replied, smiling.

"I promise." He paused. "Do you remember the one night we had together?"

"I am so incredibly sorry," she said, blushing.

"You don't remember?" he asked again.

"I remember practically nothing about us."

"You don't remember sleeping together?"

"I am so, so sorry."

"Don't worry about it."

"J.J.?"

"Yeah?"

"Why was it only one night?" she asked.

"Because you were in love with that prick over there." He pointed to John watering the roses.

"Didn't he hire someone to take care of the rose garden?" she asked.

"He's watching us," J.J. said.

She laughed. "Now why would he?"

"He always gets jealous when I talk to you," J.J. said.

"Why? He doesn't care about me anymore."

"How do you know?" J.J. asked.

"We slept together, and after that, he told me. He said we could never be together. *And,* we got a divorce."

"When did this happen?" J.J. asked surprised.

"I thought the world knew we slept together." She raised a brow at him.

He pretended to be in shock. "I didn't know," he lied.

She knew he was lying, since Jackie told her that she had told him.

"Where have I been?" he asked.

"So tell me about the night we had together?" Gabrielle sat close to him. She knew that he was able to smell her hair from where he sat.

"Well, you came over one night. I was having a party. I brought you and Jackie upstairs. I was about to tell the guys they needed to go home." He added, "I had a baby and a woman in the house that needed to go to sleep."

"Go to sleep, huh?" She scooted closer to him.

"Yes. *I* didn't seduce you that night."

"Oh, now I wish I could remember."

"No, no, no. Listen to this. I was just about to leave to go downstairs, and you started ripping off your clothes."

"And you helped me?"

"You do remember this?"

"No. I swear. I don't," she said laughing at her own lie.

"I helped you. Just your bra and then we kissed."

"Then what happened?" she asked softly.

"I went downstairs."

"Yeah, go on."

"I came back up and you were naked under the blanket. I had no idea what was going to happen, and you completely seduced me, just like you're doing now."

"I am not!"

"Oh, yes you are." He moved his face closer to hers.

The spray from the hose came so quickly and left; yet, the side of J.J.'s face was drenched. "What the hell, Ravolie?" J.J. yelled at him as Gabrielle fell back laughing. "He is such a pain in the ass," J.J. said, as he took off his shirt and wiped his face with it. "Can we try it again?" J.J. asked her.

"Sure." Gabrielle leaned close, but not too close and John sprayed J.J. again in the face.

"Damn you, Ravolie!" J.J. yelled at John, who had already disappeared within the roses.

"Were you two always such good friends?" Gabrielle asked J.J., as she continued to laugh. He was drenched this time. Water poured from his hair. And his shirt and pants were wet. John sure had good aim, Gabrielle thought.

"He hated me at first, but then after you died we got close, because of Rob."

"So that was the famous one night stand?" Gabrielle asked. "I need to hear more about this I-seduced-you thing."

"You did," he said. "Completely."

She remembered.

She stared out into the grass in the direction where she noticed John had returned and was again watering the roses. He was watering the white ones. And then he stopped and began to clip some from the bush.

"What are you thinking about? You're not watching him, are you?" J.J. asked jokingly.

"No. No way." She turned her head.

"You were looking at that creep, weren't you?" J.J. continued to joke, since she was blushing now.

"No, he's the farthest from my mind," she said seriously.

"You need a man," J.J. told her.

"What?"

"A man is the hardest thing, huh?" J.J. asked. "Without Ravolie, you can't go on, huh?"

"He rejected me."

"I can help you find a man."

"Yeah, right." Gabrielle threw grass into J.J.'s lap.

"I know this guy who's looking to fall in love and to spend the rest of his life with someone," J.J. mentioned.

"Well, let me tell you what I like in a man." She thought to look at John and describe his facial features, blond hair with blue eyes and no facial hair for he shaved perfectly without ever nicking himself. His chest was waxed. His body was muscular. And he was strong. He knew everything there was to know about anything. He was so intelligent. He knew how to cook, how to take care of flowers, how to work on cars, how to ride a motorcycle, how to kill a moving snake. His tongue, his lips, his...

Her ex-husband had it all, and she loved everything about this man, except for the horrible, hurtful night on the beach.

The way he dressed, the way his hair and orange juice was set perfectly at breakfast, and she wanted to name off the cologne he wore occasionally, since it smelled so good. She wanted to describe the way he walked, talked, and how his mouth was perfect when he ate his food. John was so perfect.

"Okay, what do you want in a man?" J.J. asked her.

"I'm going to find a man who adores me not because I'm rich, but because he respects me for my personality. I'm going to forget all about John. I can't remember much about him anyhow. I'm going to marry someone who's a garbage picker. Maybe we'll even have garbage pickin' kids."

"Well, I know a guy who likes to date women. He would adore you for your personality, and your looks wouldn't matter to him. He's rich, so I can't say he's a garbage picker. I think he has more money than you do."

"Is he a musician? Do I know this person?"

"He's a good friend of mine. He's thirty-eight and he has a kid. I think his kid is fifteen. He's friends with Rob."

"Do you think it will work? I don't want to start something with someone if it's not going to work from the start."

"You won't know unless you try it out. How could he not fall in love with someone as amazing as you?"

"It's me I'm worried about," she mumbled.

"All you have to do is say 'yes,' and I will set up a blind date."

She thought about it. "Yes! How tall is he? You have to tell me all about this man. Is he good looking?"

"Yeah, I think so."

"What do you mean, you think so?"

"He's sexy."

"Oh J.J., thank you so much. You know always when I'm down how to cheer me up, I think." Then they hugged.

They decided it was time for their morning walk.

"Tomorrow, while the kids are at school again, I'm going to be sitting around doing nothing all day," she said. "I can go horseback riding. I don't know how to ride, though. I don't have a job anymore."

"What happened?"

"I quit. Too many people knew who I was. But now, I have all the time in the world to spend with my two children, but they go to school." Then she turned to look at J.J. who had stopped walking. He rubbed his hands together, and if Gabrielle looked hard enough, she thought she would see a light bulb glowing above his head.

"Gabrielle, you know what?"

"What?"

"*You* are going to go to work with me tomorrow. *You* are going to sing again."

"*You* are out of your mind! I can't sing. I haven't sung for twelve years."

"So what. Gabrielle, sing."

"You have to be kidding me."

"No, sing with me. Silent night, holy night," he began.

"J., *you* are embarrassing me."

"In front of who? Mr. Tree over there? Come on!"

Gabrielle began, "Silent night, holy night..." She stopped walking. J.J. stared.

She stopped singing. She looked at him, looked down, and then looked back up at him. "Why are you staring at me?"

"You can't sing, huh? You are so, so damn beautiful. It's killin' me. You have a beautiful voice. Always have. Like an angel." J.J. then placed his hands on her face. "I'll get the key from Ravolie, and you are coming to Bobbie's Place with me tomorrow."

"Bobbie's Place?" she asked.

"The Recording Studio. Didn't John tell you? After you died, he changed the name from The Recording Studio to Bobbie's Place. There's a big purple sign out—"

"Because my favorite color was purple," she sighed.

"Yeah. It's bigger than the sign for the music store. I'm picking you up at six-thirty tomorrow morning, and you better be ready."

"Do I have a choice?" she asked him.

"Yeah, you do. It's either you go to work with me tomorrow or you kiss me right now."

"Eww." Gabrielle pulled away. "I'll go to work with you tomorrow."

"Thanks a lot," J.J. said. "I took a shower before I came here. I brushed—"

"I would like to kiss you also," she said seductively.

J.J.'s hands were still through her shiny, soft black hair. He pulled her close to his face as she leaned her back up against the tree.

Suddenly, they heard the sound of a horse galloping. They looked. John rode passed them, and as quickly as he appeared with Skippy, he disappeared with him down the trail.

Gabrielle laughed.

"He's something else," J.J. said.

"He makes me laugh," Gabrielle replied, giggling.

"I'm going to attempt to kiss you again," he said.

"Do you think he'll ride past—?"

He kissed her quickly. A small peck to the lips.

EARLY THE NEXT MORNING, John went into his car when he saw Gabrielle jump into J.J.'s. They arrived together at Bobbie's Place. John asked Gabrielle, "What are you doing here?"

J.J. explained that he and Gabrielle were going to record a song together.

"But you can't sing," John told him.

"She's going to sing with Scott," J.J. added.

J.J. never told John the night before why he wanted to borrow the key for the music store. And after they entered the store, they took the elevator down to Bobbie's Place—the old—The Recording Studio. John looked as if he didn't like the idea or was jealous because he didn't think of it first, Gabrielle noticed.

J.J. held her hand as they walked the hallway together. "Wow, this place looks the same," Gabrielle said.

"Memories?" J.J. asked.

"A lot of them," she said.

Everyone who was there and noticed who she was said 'Hello' to her, but Gabrielle didn't know who any of them were. She couldn't identify anyone. She finally went into Studio A where she saw the rest of the band. They also said 'Hello,' but she didn't recognize Intensity—Seth, Matt, or Scott.

Sheet music and the words to the songs were given to her and she believed she sang as fine as she did twelve years ago. Her voice was even more developed and everyone loved it. When she sang and looked up, John stood in the window with the engineer. John stared at her. He wasn't going to criticize her; he wasn't going to compliment her, and he wasn't going to speak to her about singing with Scott.

After the three-hour recording session, a very attractive man walked up to Gabrielle. "Don't tell me who you are," Gabrielle said. "I know you!" She wrapped her arms around him. "Mick!"

"You're lucky, Harrison," Seth Edilson said. "She remembers you and doesn't remember any of us.

Mick held tight to her as she held her arms around him. They kissed a small peck on the lips. "Gabrielle," Mick said. "You have to do me this favor?"

"What?" she asked smiling. "Anything for you."

"Felecia says she's pregnant again. Could you ask her who the father of the baby is? She'll tell you the truth."

"Felecia? Where's Felecia?" She looked around the room.

"She's my ex-wife. And she's here. Not here, but in the café. That's her hang out."

"Are you married now?"

"No," he said with a grin.

"Would you like to be?" she asked him.

"Name the place, baby." He hugged her again. "Felecia was your best friend."

"I somewhat remember her," Gabrielle said.

Mick kissed Gabrielle's cheek.

John overheard their conversation. "No. No. No. You will not get Gabrielle involved with Felecia again."

"Why not?" Gabrielle asked.

"You will not talk to that woman!"

"I will talk to whomever I want to, whether you like it or not," Gabrielle insisted.

"Come on." John grabbed her arm.

"Where are we going?" He walked her out into the hallway and then around the corner. Her face turned pale. "A man died here," Gabrielle said, frightened of the memory.

While she continued to point to the office, John pulled her through the hall quickly and to the door for the stairwell. "That woman is nothing but trouble. If you tell her anything about us..."

"About 'us'? There is no 'us'. You made it perfectly clear to me on the beach. Good-bye, John." And she walked away, ran past the mysterious room quickly, and found J.J. exiting the studio. "J.J., why does John not want me to talk to Felecia? And I figured a man's brain was splattered in front of me, in the office down this hall."

He walked past the hallway quickly, and she followed. "There's a magazine article I can show you later. You'll have to read it. Felecia did a lot of damage way back when. No one knows why you remained friends with her."

"And the man's splattered brain?" she asked.

"There's a newspaper article about that too."

"Will you tell both stories later?" Gabrielle asked.

"Sure, but she was the one who told everyone I was Rob's biological father and that the two of us slept together."

"And that was a bad thing?" Gabrielle asked.

"At the time, I guess so," J.J. answered with a slight grin. "And you gave her a black eye over it."

Chapter 13

In the café, J.J. picked out Gabrielle's breakfast for her.

John noticed that all of the food J.J. picked for Gabrielle made her grimace. There were eggs, made with milk. There was sausage, which was well done. Bacon. She tried the bacon, but it was too crisp. John was sure Gabrielle couldn't wait for him to make breakfast for her tomorrow morning. He knew what she liked.

At another table, John sat across from them with Lenny Dakota. John attempted to stand from the chair, but Lenny insisted for John to sit. "Where do you think you're going?" Lenny asked him.

"Nowhere," John said, regretfully, as he sat back down.

"You were going to go over to her, weren't you?"

"She doesn't drink milk. She's lactose intolerant. I was going to bring her orange juice, that's all. She loves orange juice."

"I can't believe she's sitting over there," Lenny said.

"Tell me about it," John mumbled. "My dead wife is back from the dead."

"And you're not with her. You're gonna let Shedel take her away from you?"

"This isn't simple, Lenny."

"After everything you two have been through, you're going to throw it all away," Lenny said shaking his head. "I can't believe you, man."

"It's not that I haven't stopped loving her. I just can't be with her right now."

Lenny shook his head at John again. "You couldn't be with her back then, either, but you found a way."

"And look what happened to her, 'cause of me. She lost twelve years of her life. And now she's back—"

"It wasn't you. It was Malone. Gabrielle's back. And this time you are going to hurt her all over again. She wants to be with you, man. And you won't budge. A long time ago, you told me you two were destined to be together, and now you two have a second chance. How many people get second chances like this? This is a miracle. And you're not taking it. You're whacked, man."

"I don't want to start an argument with you, Len. I just want to give her the orange juice, possibly even a banana. Are we going?"

"Yeah." They stood and John went to the counters, while Lenny walked to Gabrielle's table.

Gabrielle looked up. "Oh.My.God. Lenny!" Gabrielle stood and wrapped her arms around him as he returned the embrace.

"You remember me?" he asked, chuckling.

"You look different, but oddly still the same. Just a bit older, maybe. We have to get together and talk about your new boyfriend," she told him.

"My new boyfriend! You do remember?" He laughed.

"Sure," she said.

"I have to tell you all about this new guy I'm seeing," Lenny said.

"It's not Mick, is it?" she joked.

"How do you remember me? This is so incredible she remembers me, John," Lenny told him.

"Here." John handed Gabrielle orange juice in a tall glass.

"Thank you." She smiled grimly, taking it from his hand.

"No banana?" Lenny asked in a whisper.

John shook his head no.

"Excuse me," she said when she noticed Mick and Felecia walking in together. They were arguing, she noticed, and she remembered it wasn't unusual. "I poured a plate of noodles over that woman, didn't I?" she asked J.J.

"Oh yes you did," he replied.

"Why'd I do that?"

"Because of what I told you earlier," J.J. said.

"Was that all I did to her?" Gabrielle asked.

"No. She had a pillow under her shirt instead of a baby, and you pulled it out. Remember? I'll show you the magazine article later."

Gabrielle walked away from the table and headed for Mick and Felecia Harrison, while John and Lenny sat at their original table.

"Will you two stop fighting?" Gabrielle said.

"Bobbie!" Felecia embraced her. Gabrielle placed her arms around her. "Mick told me that you were back. I just couldn't believe it."

"I remember you," Gabrielle said. "I could never forget you forever."

Mick and Felecia took their food and sat at the table with J.J. and Gabrielle. After a while, Gabrielle and Felecia departed to another table to talk about 'girl stuff'.

IT WAS LIKE old times again. Gabrielle told Felecia everything that had happened until the blind date she was to have on Friday night.

Felecia told her whole story to Gabrielle.

Felecia had a twelve-year-old son named Ron Mace. He was Nick's son. Ron came along because she fell in lust with Nick again, right after she had married Mick.

A few months ago, Felecia and Mick went on a trip together. Felecia thought that Mick would ask her to marry him again, but he didn't. She told everyone that she was pregnant, and that it was Mick's.

A month later, she went to the Bahamas with Nick, because Mick was on a business trip. She told Nick the baby she was carrying was his, too.

Gabrielle attempted to follow all of this.

Then Felecia slept with Nick's brother, Johnny. Johnny and Sharon were married. Sharon was Felecia's best friend and a friend of Gabrielle's, twelve years ago. Sharon caught Johnny and Felecia in a hotel suite and told Mick.

But when Mick was on his so-called business trip, he was having an affair with Sharon.

Felecia told Johnny that the baby was his, too.

Sharon and Johnny were now going to get a divorce.

"So Nick, Mick, and Johnny each think that you're having their baby." Gabrielle asked.

"Yes," Felecia said, regretfully.

"But, you're not pregnant?" Gabrielle asked her.

"What should I do?" Felecia asked, looking towards the floor in a confused and shameful glance. "Why do I do these stupid things, Bobbie?"

The next day, Felecia told everyone that she had miscarried.

IT WAS FINALLY Friday. All week Gabrielle had been trying to get J.J. to tell her about this blind date, but he was impenetrable. J.J. told her that her mystery date wanted to meet her at this upscale restaurant, the Artillery, at five p.m. for dinner, and she was to be picked up by a mysterious limousine at four-thirty.

Gabrielle waited in the foyer for the limo. As she looked out the window, John drove into the circular drive and parked his exotic sports car. He helped a woman out from the passenger side and kissed her right breast.

The woman had short red hair, and Gabrielle could tell she was about his age, ten years older than herself and flirtatious, which sickened Gabrielle. And John was the same with the sluttish looking woman, pawing her all over and grabbing at her body parts. Grabbing her butt, and then both hands were at her tiny waist as they walked happily to the front door.

Gabrielle looked closely at the woman, envying her for having an ass that could fit into that tight, short, skirt and wondering if her own ass would look quite that amazing in such a getup.

Gabrielle backed away from the window as they walked into the foyer together. Still in the shadows, she walked back to see if her limousine had arrived.

"GABRIELLE?" John noticed her standing in the darkness looking out the window. She turned around to see him pushing the woman's lips away and his hand doing a backward crawl out of her skirt.

"Hi, John."

The woman nibbled on his ear and he shooed her away.

Gabrielle wore a navy-blue spaghetti strap dress, which complimented her hips. Her blue high heels matched her dress. Her dress was tight and revealed her soft cleavage. The dress was short, reaching only to her thighs above her knees. She looked sophisticated, as a woman should look, John Ravolie thought. The type of woman *he* should be with. Her shoulder-length hair was in an up-do and her makeup was perfectly placed on her cheeks and eyelids. Her lips were outlined burgundy and filled with a richer, deeper color, which complimented her Italian complexion.

John couldn't take his look off her; she was radiant. They stared at one another, briefly. Gabrielle's diamond earrings sparkled from the dim lighting of the three-tier fountain, which made her blue eyes twinkle as well.

John had forgotten about his flirtatious cheap and easy date as Gabrielle walked toward her coat that she had draped over a chair. "What's all this?" he asked Gabrielle, gesturing to her body and looking her up and down.

"I have a blind date tonight," she told him.

"Where are you going?" he asked, seriously.

"Out for dinner, and then dancing, I presume," she answered

"Is this all right with you?" the woman asked John.

Ignoring her completely, John continued interrogating Gabrielle. "Who are you going out with?"

"Who is she?" the woman asked, becoming obviously frustrated. "Your daughter?"

"She's my wife," John said.

"Your wife?" Gabrielle and the woman asked together.

"Ex-wife." He smiled at Gabrielle for making the mistake.

"And who is this?" Gabrielle asked John.

"This is. This is. I'm sorry." He raked a hand through his hair. "I forgot your name."

"Sahara. My name is Sahara," she said, crossing her arms and rolling her eyes at him in an angry glare.

"Right. Sahara. This is Sahara," he told Gabrielle. "Like the dessert. And this is my ex, Gabrielle."

"Nice to meet you," Gabrielle said, then turned to look out the window. She noticed the limousine pulling behind John's car. "My blind date is here, I have to go. How do I look?" she asked John.

He took her coat from her hands and held it up for Gabrielle to slip her arms through. "Amazing." His voice low and his mouth close enough for her to feel his warm breath on her ear.

"Now, don't wait up for me," she joked.

"Let me get the door for you," he said. He held the doorknob for a moment.

"Aren't you going to let her out, Johnny?" Sahara asked.

"Amazing," he told Gabrielle again.

"Thank you," she said.

At last, he opened the door.

THE CHAUFFEUR OPENED the limo door for Gabrielle, who turned back toward the house just long enough to catch a glance of John kissing Sahara harshly. She wondered if the animals were going to lower themselves to having sex right there in the foyer.

She sat in the back seat to where she found a bouquet of roses and a card attached. The card read, 'I can't wait to see you. I'm sure you look radiant tonight.' She noticed a bottle of unopened wine placed on ice.

She arrived at the Artillery. Immediately, the hostess knew who Gabrielle Ravolie was and seated her at a table for two in the back of the dimly lit but beautifully quaint restaurant.

Gabrielle sat in her assigned chair and waited for her blind date to arrive.

She waited.

The time went by slowly and she fidgeted with her watch, then with the backings of her earrings. She wished she had brought pen and paper with her. Her thoughts drifted to John, and she had an overwhelming desire to be with him right now in the foyer. And who would name their daughter 'Sahara' anyway?

She noticed her hands were shaking and her leg wouldn't stop trembling up and down. She tried to hold her leg to stop the uncontrollable spasm, but it didn't seem to work. She looked at the menu, set it down, and then picked it back up again. She started to think this man, who was her blind date was either actually blind and didn't know where she was sitting or he would never show up. If she had to, she would eat alone and then send J.J. the bill.

The waiter brought her a bottle of wine and she remarked, "I don't think I can drink all this by myself." The waiter smiled, poured a glass for her, and then walked away. J.J. will get the bill for that bottle as well, she thought. She took a sip. Not being a drinker, she knew she had this disgusted look on her face from the taste.

As she was looking at the menu, someone came up to her table, and now a man in an expensively dapper Armani suit stood in front of her. She didn't want to look up to see who this mysterious man was, but then he said, "Hello."

Gabrielle recognized the voice and immediately glanced up to the familiar face. "J.J., where's my date?"

"I'm your date."

"What?"

"I wanted you to think it was an important person, but instead it's just me. Are you disappointed?"

"Did you have to make me wait?"

"I like watching you fidget. Are you disappointed?"

"You haven't been watching me this whole time, have you?" She felt a slight blushing come over her cheeks, while he shook his head slightly. "No. I'm not disappointed. Sit."

"Do you still want to have dinner?" he asked, after he sat across from her.

"Yes, I'm *so* hungry. I was going to order all this food and then send you the bill."

"You were, were you?" He smiled. "I have plans for us tonight."

"I have nothing better to do," Gabrielle replied. "Why didn't you just ask me to come out on a date with you?"

"You would've said 'no.'"

"Probably. I think John was a little jealous when I left the house tonight."

"See, if I told you it was me you wouldn't've had the chance to make him jealous. You would've told him you were going out with 'only J.J.'"

"He walked into the house with a different woman again. He never brings the same one home twice."

"He's going to catch an STD," J.J. replied. She giggled at the thought. "Well?"

"Well, what—?" She thought about the question he had asked her moments before. "—I would love to spend the evening with you," she answered.

After Gabrielle and J.J. ate their delectable gourmet meals, they stepped into the limousine where J.J. opened and poured a glass of wine for her.

"What are you trying to do? Get me drunk?"

"No, just relax you."

They spoke about Rob. J.J. told her about Rob's plans for school and college.

"He wants to be a writer. He writes many stories—good ones, too—and his first book probably will be one about our life history or somethin'. He's always busy, but he always has time for his friends and Jackie. He loves Jackie so much."

"Yes, and Jackie loves him," Gabrielle replied. The limousine stopped in front of an old, classic movie theater and Gabrielle asked, "Are we going to the movies?"

"Maybe," J.J. replied.

"We're a little over dressed, don't you think?" They stepped out of the vehicle and Gabrielle noticed the lights were off inside and there wasn't even a show playing. "J.J., how are we going to get in? The only show today was at two o'clock this afternoon."

He showed her the key in the palm of his hand. He placed it in the lock and tried to push down on the old fashion handle, but the lock or the door wouldn't budge. "This is the key," he said, turning the key in the other direction.

"I'm sure it is."

He pressed down on the lever and said, "There, it worked." He pushed the creaky old door open slowly.

He persuaded her to walk in, and so she did, to the single theatre and down the red carpet of the center aisle.

"Where should we sit?" she asked him.

"Wherever you want."

She walked in front of him and chose a center aisle seat within the middle of the theatre, and he sat beside her.

He told her they were going to see a new movie that no one had seen yet. A love story.

The previews began, and J.J. placed his arm around her. His fingertips tickled her shoulder. Until his hand began to annoy her. He then slipped her spaghetti strap down past her shoulder. She lifted it quickly when a man brought them a bucket of popcorn.

"I feel like a teenager," he said, tossing popcorn into his mouth. "I remember taking girls to movie theatres and doing things we never should have."

"I hope you're not planning on doing those things with me." She grabbed his hand quickly, before it reached her breast.

The lights went out, the pleated curtains lifted, and the movie began. She let loose of his hand, which he took back and placed on her thigh. He smiled widely at her with his white kernel filled teeth glowing through the darkness. She smiled and giggled back at him. She knew he was going to try to get himself into some trouble.

After a minute or two, she noticed his fingers were starting to travel to her inner thigh. He moved his hand closer and closer to her body. Gabrielle snatched it and held his hand in hers when she noticed the man returning with one large plastic container of soda and two straws.

The two lovers on the screen were about to kiss, which inspired J.J. to instinctively tilt her face toward his, place his mouth on hers, and kiss her roughly, passionately. She didn't resist him and kissed him just as much as he kissed her. Then he bit her lip.

"Sorry," he said.

"No problem."

Gabrielle noticed that she felt uncomfortable with J.J., especially when his hand found her inner thigh again. She took his hand in hers.

If John were here, she thought, this date would have been different. She imagined John turning the key and immediately the front door opening. Him picking her up and carrying her into the theatre. Him taking her upstairs and starting the reel himself. Oh my God, she thought. John took me here once, and we did make love on the stage in front of the movie screen, while a movie played. There were no interruptions. What movie was it? she wondered. But she couldn't remember.

J.J. smelled like popcorn. He kissed her differently, not like how John had kissed her on the beach, and not like John had kissed her in the past. When John touched her, her body exploded. When J.J. touched her, her body resisted.

She thought about John as J.J. took his mouth off hers and looked her in her eyes and said, "I love you, Gabrielle."

She didn't want to ruin the moment, however she hated herself after she told him that she loved him too.

He placed his hand in his pocket and pulled out a small box.

"I hope those are earrings," Gabrielle said to him.

"I don't want to disappoint you," he said.

"I won't be disappointed," she said, expecting earrings.

He then opened it to show her a diamond engagement ring. "Gabrielle, will you marry me?"

She gasped, having expected and hoped for earrings or a necklace. "Never before have I seen a ring so—Wow." The ring was enormous, and it looked heavy. It was not the type of ring she would have wanted to wear on her finger for the rest of her life. J.J. didn't really know her. Not her love for orange juice. And not her taste in jewelry either.

"Will you?" J.J. asked again, his eyes pleading for an answer.

"NOW I WANT to show *you* something," Jackie said to her mother.

"What, honey?" Gabrielle asked, still gazing at the bulky ring J.J. had given her the night before.

Jackie returned to Gabrielle's bedroom and she set the ring aside. "What do you have there?" Gabrielle asked, noticing the three cases in Jackie's hands.

"Pick a number? 1, 2, or 3."

"Start with number 1."

"I think it's this one," Jackie said, handing it to her.

"Oh my God! This is the ring your father gave me, when he first proposed to me." It was a marquee with pear shaped diamonds on the side. "Where did you get this?"

"After you died, Dad took the rings off your finger. He gave them to me as a present for my sixteenth birthday. Do you realize these three rings cost close to eighty-thousand dollars?"

"You mean I wore eighty-thousand dollars on my finger everyday?"

"Put them on, Mom."

"Okay," she squealed. Gabrielle placed each ring slowly onto her ring finger and said, "They still fit."

Suddenly, there were two knocks on the door, and it opened. "Look. Dad, the rings still fit," Jackie told her father and Gabrielle showed him her hand.

"No, they don't," John said sternly. "Take 'em off, Gabrielle. Go lock 'em back up in the safe, Jackie. I never want you to wear those again," he told Gabrielle.

"I was just—" Gabrielle couldn't continue.

"Never again," he said in an angry tone as Gabrielle stared at him blankly.

Suddenly, she removed the three rings quickly from her finger.

"Dad, Mom is going to marry J.J. on Christmas Day," Jackie said.

"He can afford to buy her a ring."

"He did." Jackie grabbed the small case from the bed and popped it open, holding it up to her father. "Look."

John took a glance at the ring.

"Here, Jackie," Gabrielle said, trading the three boxes for the one.

"Rob is waiting downstairs for you, Jackie," John said.

Jackie left the room with the boxes.

"Thanks a lot, Gabrielle." He looked either angry or hurt, but Gabrielle couldn't quite tell. "You bring me the divorce papers and then you decide to marry one of my best friend's. You told me that you had a blind date last night."

"I thought I did, and it ended up being J.J."

"Out of the blue he proposes to you and you say 'yes.' You two just decided to be spontaneous. I hope you'll be happy together," he said with an angry face and a disappointed tone. He left the room.

Jackie waited for him in the hallway. "You don't care about her, do you?" Jackie asked her father, as they walked.

"She's going to marry Shedel," John said. "She stopped caring about me."

"How long did you expect her to wait for you to wake up and realize that she's alive?"

"If she loved me, she would've waited forever."

"Don't turn this around on her. You can still stop this marriage from happening, Dad. You know she will always love you."

"She made her choice."

"You made it for her."

John was silent.

LATER THAT EVENING

GABRIELLE TIPTOED into the foyer. She felt as if she was sneaking around in John's house. It would be her last night that she'd spend at the Ravolie Estate, and then she'd be moving in with J.J. and Rob. J.J.'s house was just as big, but not as beautiful or immaculate. There weren't fountains in the foyer. There wasn't a rose garden out back. J.J. did have an indoor and an outdoor swimming pool. But, who cares? Gabrielle thought.

Jackie had told Gabrielle that all the home movies were behind the sliding glass door of the entertainment center in the den. The house was so big that Gabrielle realized she had never been down into this room or in the basement before.

She noticed the light was on. Perhaps Jackie had left it on for her. Gabrielle walked the carpeted stairs and into the small den. This was homey, she thought, while viewing the couch in front of the plasma TV.

Gabrielle opened the sliding glass door.

"Hi."

She jumped what she thought must have carried her feet two feet off the ground. She laughed with embarrassment while turning around. John stood in front of her, holding a guitar. "Where'd you come from?" She laughed.

He pointed to the sound proof room. It was a studio. She didn't realize there was a glass door that exited into another room. Furthermore, there was a two-way mirror hanging on the wall. Perhaps, John had been in the other room playing his guitar and had noticed her when she tiptoed down the stairs, but there was no way for her to have noticed him.

He didn't ask which one she wanted to view. Somehow, he already knew. "It's this one," he told her. He turned the television on, while Gabrielle sat on the sofa. Then, he sat beside her, with an arm behind her head.

Gabrielle wore a modern stylish version of the Hawaiian holoku. Strapless, backless, lined with satin. A stunning train supplied a handle, so she could walk freely.

She walked to the wedding arch with her shoulder-length hair worn in an up-do, with professional makeup, and a fresh French manicure on her fingers and a gorgeous pedicure on her bare toes.

She held a cascade of flowers. Around her neck, she wore a delicate jasmine lei. A Haku lei crowned her blue-black hair with white flowers as well.

John wore a maile lei. The green garland, not sewn in a circle, draped his shoulders. He was barefoot, and wore a white aloha shirt with khakis, instead of the typical suit and tie with black polished shoes that most grooms wore.

Gabrielle spun around in her bare feet.

John had tears in his eyes and a smile so wide as he watched his stunning bride-to-be walk toward him.

When Gabrielle reached the wedding arch, she handed her bouquet to Felecia.

John took her hands in his. "My beautiful Gabrielle." They kissed a deep passionate kiss, until Mick Harrison cleared his throat.

"Welcome to the marriage of Jonathan and Gabrielle. You have been asked to gather here to witness and contribute to the joy of this union..."

"There were shadows for a long time and then there was light. The light was you, Gabrielle. Your love has given me life, and a fresh journey begins for us today. At last, today, we make our two lives one. I wanted you yesterday. I want and need you today, tomorrow, and for all eternity."

The tape played on. "I have dreamt my whole life of having someone as magnificent as you to love, cherish, and honor me as *you* do," she said. "And I vow here and now, to treasure for all of my days, the love we celebrate here today. Let us bring together our lives for ourselves, for our children, and we will find ourselves within one another and them each day."

"Gabrielle, take this white rose as a symbol of my love. It began a tiny bud and blossomed, just as my love for you has grown and blossomed these past three years," said the groom.

The bride took the flower from her groom. "I take this white rose, a symbol of your love, and I place it into water, an indication of life. Just as this rose cannot survive without water, I know I will never be able to survive without you."

"In remembrance of this day, I'll give to you a white rose each year on our anniversary, which is your birthday, and our daughter's birthday." He smirked. "As a reminder of our love and the vows spoken here today."

Gabrielle smiled at him. "And I'll refill this vase with water each year on August 10th. I will be ready to receive your gift, in remembrance of our love and the vows spoken here today."

Minister: "...I present to you the newly wedded couple, Mr. and Mrs. Jonathan and Gabrielle Ravolie...."

John interrupted, "Can I kiss my bride now?"

"—you may kiss your bride now," said the minister, smiling at the happy couple.

"I got to go to bed," John told her. "I'll see you in the morning."

"Good night," she replied.

He walked up the stairs, as the video scrolled on.

John swept her into his arms. They both cried and laughed together as they kissed passionately until John lowered her to the sand.

John picked her up over his shoulder and ran through the sand. On the tape, she couldn't stop laughing as she watched the photographer and videographer running behind them. Before entering the opened door, John loosened the ties with one hand while his other held her derriere. As he laughed, he shut and bolted the door from the inside.

Static filled the screen.

Gabrielle shut off the TV and then wandered into the sound proof room.

She fell to the floor, wailing.

Chapter 14

"Talk," John answered his cell phone.

"I have some news," the voice said.

"Lay it on me."

"They found out about the wedding."

"It's in the media all across the nation," John said.

"It's tentative. Nothing is for sure just yet."

"Nothing ever is. Are they coming after her on Christmas Day?" John asked.

"I'll call you when I have more information."

The call ended.

"MOM, THIS IS SO EXCITING! Dad's gonna give you your wedding present," Jackie said.

"My wedding isn't for another two months," Gabrielle said.

"I know. But then there will be snow on the ground and you can't use your present during the winter months."

"What?" Gabrielle laughed.

"Come on. Come on," Jackie said excitedly, and pulled her mother to the coat closet.

"Will you give me a clue?" Gabrielle asked Jackie, taking her coat from her.

"You'll be going to the Halloween party on Friday night in *style*. That's all the clues you get."

"What kind of a clue is that?" Gabrielle asked Jackie. "Style, huh? What am I going as?"

"J.J. wanted you to be cat woman," Jackie confirmed.

Rob jogged down the stairwell and into the foyer.

"Oh yes, that's right. I'm wearing vinyl. A black vinyl harness bra, vinyl pants, and a vinyl cat mask. How could I forget? J.J.'s a sick, demented creature."

John exited the kitchen and entered the foyer. "You can always pretend that you're allergic to vinyl. We won't tell him."

"Excellent idea," Gabrielle said.

"Look on the bright side," Rob said. "Dad's not making you carry a whip all night."

"Or wear a leash," John said.

"What are you going as?" Gabrielle asked John.

"He never dresses up for Halloween," Jackie said.

"I do, too," John said. "That one year I went as a pirate."

"You took off your costume as soon as you got to J.J.'s," Jackie said.

"Are you dressing up on Friday?" Gabrielle asked John.

"What's Shedel going as?" he asked her.

"The big, bad wolf," Rob answered. "He's got a fur jumpsuit with plaid overalls and gloves."

"Then why aren't you going as Little Red Riding Hood?" John asked Gabrielle.

"Don't place the idea into his head," Gabrielle pleaded.

"What do you want to go as?" John asked her.

"Scarlett," Gabrielle answered, truthfully.

"Scarlett?" they asked together.

"Yeah, from *Gone With the Wind*."

"You'd make a great Rhett Butler," Jackie told her father, nudging him.

"I'd also make a great Johnny Ravolie," John said. He stood behind Gabrielle and placed his palms over her eyes.

"What are you doing?" Gabrielle asked.

"Taking you to your wedding present," John said.

"Jackie tells me you can't give it to me in December." Gabrielle smiled, a bright white teeth smile.

"Nah, you can't use it in the winter months," John confirmed.

"What is it?" she asked with excitement.

"I've got a camera, Dad," Jackie said.

"I've got one too," Rob added.

"Walk forward," John said.

His body rubbed up against the back of hers and she felt that sudden tingle that she always receives when he touches her. Make it go away, she thought. But it wouldn't go away. It felt so good, too good whenever he touched her. She didn't want the feeling to end. She felt her breathing deepen in harmony with his. I have to stop feeling this way if— "I'm going to marry J.J.," she thought aloud.

"I know," John said. "Whose choice was that? Shedel's or yours?" he said into her ear.

"Huh?"

"Forget it," John said.

Rob opened the door.

John led her out onto the porch, and down the stairs.

She realized they were walking through the grass, passing the rectangular fountain, and back onto the paved circular driveway.

John stopped her. He spun her around real fast in circles.

"I'm getting dizzy," she said, trying to keep her balance.

John stood behind her with his hands around her waist and Gabrielle opened her eyes.

Rob took the picture as Gabrielle stared at a jet-black sports car, with a huge red ribbon attached to the hood. She had no idea what kind it was, but it was the coolest sports car she had ever seen.

"Not only do you get the car," Jackie said. "But Dad's gonna teach you how to drive it."

"This is a Tuscan," John said, removing the huge red bow from the hood. "This same type of car was used in that Bugs Bunny movie."

"*Loony Tunes: Back in Action,*" Jackie supplied.

"It can get up to 60mph in 4.2 seconds," Rob said.

"Holy shit!" Gabrielle said.

"If you don't want it, I'll take it for my sixteenth birthday," Rob suggested hopefully.

"Come on," John said proudly.

She went up to the car. "Where's the handle?" Gabrielle asked.

"You have to use a plipper," John said.

"A what?" Gabrielle asked.

"The remote." John laughed. He handed her the key with the alarm plipper attached. "Press this button here—" John showed her "—and there's a button on the underside of the mirror." He took her hand and again the shivers went up her arm. She felt for the button and pressed it. The door magically sprung open.

"Ahh!" She jumped up and down.

"Get in," he told her. She sat behind the wheel. "How does it feel?" John asked her.

"Unbelievable," she said smiling, while Rob and Jackie took more pictures of her and the car.

She placed the key into the ignition. "Before you turn the key," John told her. "There are three pedals down there. The clutch, the brake, and the accelerator. Press down on the brake with your right foot," he told her and she did. "Press the clutch down to the floor with your left foot." And she did.

"Can I turn the key now?" she asked him.

"Go ahead."

The engine roared. "It's so loud!" she shouted.

John reached over and turned the key. "Now get out."

"What?" she asked confused.

He smiled at her. "Get in on the other side and I'll take you for a test drive."

It was a beautiful autumn day. The sun was shining and the leaves rustled as the car glided down the road. "The steering is super sharp," John told Gabrielle, shifting the gears. "You have to be careful when driving this thing," he told her and she nodded. "Every piece of crucial info is displayed in front of you, including the gear-change lights. You never move your eyes from the road for more than a second."

"Got it," she said.

"The pedals pivot. It'll feel weird at first, but you'll get used to it."

"I noticed that," Gabrielle said. "I don't know what to say. I can't believe you got me this car!"

"This isn't just any car, Gabrielle," John said.

"What else does it do?"

"It can fly."

Another thing Gabrielle thought to add to her list: John was also an excellent driver and a serious teacher.

They drove back to the gate for the Ravolie Estate and John showed her the remote that he already had in place on the visor for her to press to open the gate. They entered the circular drive and John stopped the car. "Now," he said. "There are two ways to park this baby. But, I always want you to park it in first gear. Okay?"

"Okay," she said.

"You keep your foot on the brake. Your foot on the clutch. Shift into first gear." He turned off the car. "Then you take your foot off the clutch and then your foot off the brake. Clutch first, then brake. When getting in you brake, then clutch. When getting out you clutch then brake."

She had a confused look on her face.

"Come on," he said with a smile.

They traded seats and Gabrielle got behind the wheel.

"Think of it this way. When gettin' in your right foot goes down first, then left. When getting out, left foot comes up first, then right."

"Got it," she said.

He took a small notepad out of the glove, and Gabrielle couldn't help but giggle. "What?" he asked smiling.

"You came prepared."

"This is serious stuff," he said to her. "I wrote this down for you. " He showed her. "When you're in 0 to 15 you keep it in first gear. 15-30 is second and 30-40 is third, 40-50 is fourth, 180 miles per hour is fifth."

"180!" She laughed.

"I'll be with you when you're going 180," he told her.

"What?"

"I reserved the race track for later."

"No, you didn't."

"Yeah, I did."

"You're not serious, John."

"I am," he said. "Now here's your oral test. What's first gear?" he asked her.

"0 to 15," she said.

"Where's the clutch?"

She thought about it. "Don't remember," she said.

"You want to drive in circles?" he asked her.

"Good idea."

"I'M ALMOST THERE." John told her. "Gabrielle, do not get out of the car. Leave the speaker phone on so I can hear what's going on."

"Here he comes," she said.

"Mrs. Ravolie, can I see your license and registration," the officer asked her.

"Here it is and my insurance card, too. How fast was I going, Officer?"

"You don't know?"

"I was in third gear," she said. "That means I had to have been going between 30 and 40 miles per hour. I saw a sign back there that read 45. I don't believe that I was speeding."

"Will you step out of the vehicle, Mrs. Ravolie?"

"Can I ask why?"

"I'd like you to step out of the vehicle."

"With all due respect, Officer, I'm not leaving my vehicle wearing a cat woman outfit. I'll turn the car off—" and she did "—but I'm not getting out of my car."

"Are you resisting an order?"

"You still haven't said why *you're* pulling me over."

"Keep the car turned off, I'll be right back," he said, then walked to his vehicle.

"John, what do you think he wants?" Gabrielle asked.

"Don't know. But it doesn't sound too good. I'm here. I just pulled up behind the police car."

Gabrielle looked through her rearview mirror and noticed John talking to the police officer. He was dressed as a pirate and had the hook on his hand and a patch over his eye. Gabrielle would've laughed if she was in a different predictament.

John stepped back into his car and Gabrielle noticed the officer walking back to hers, with a hand on his gun. John drove past her, heading for the party.

"Sorry about that, Mrs. Ravolie. We just wanted to make sure that the car wasn't stolen and that it was indeed you who was driving it." He handed Gabrielle her license, registration, and insurance card.

"Thank you, Officer. I can go now?" she asked.

"Yes," he said.

She pressed down on the brake with her right foot and pressed the clutch down to the floor with her left. She turned the key. She loved the loud roar of the powerful engine. "What was that all about?" she asked John, while heading back onto the roadway.

"He just wanted to see what you were wearing," John's electronic voice said. "If you have any more problems, give me a call. I'll meet you at the party."

"See ya there." Gabrielle ended the call.

Her phone rang.

She smiled thinking it was John again. "What's taking you so long?" J.J. asked.

"Well, like I told you, the mask didn't fit properly, so I got a new one. Would you believe I just got pulled over for nothing?" Gabrielle said.

"Pulled over?"

"Yeah, by a cop."

"What'd he want?"

"He wanted to make sure the car wasn't stolen. John wasn't too far behind me—"

"How long will it take for you to be here."

"Fifteen minutes," Gabrielle said.

"Love you," J.J. said.

"Love you, too." Gabrielle ended the call.

She kept the windows closed. It was too cold of a night to have one open. Regardless of the heat wafting out of the vents, she was still cold beneath the tight thin layer of vinyl against her skin. Why did she agree with J.J. to go as cat woman? She knew she would have been much warmer in an elegant dress if she had gone as Scarlett.

A drop of rain fell onto the windshield, then another, and another. She turned the wipers on. "John thought of teaching me everything," she said aloud, then yawned. "What would I ever do without him."

JOHN ARRIVED at the party, parked his sports car, and entered through the front door. The party was in full swing. People were getting high or drunk. And then he noticed the big, bad wolf with a beer can in his hand.

"How do you drink that with your mask on," John asked him.

He lifted up his head and J.J.'s face was completely in view under the huge muzzle of the wolf.

"Where's Gabrielle?" J.J. asked.

"She should be here in about fifteen minutes." John chuckled. "She drives 15 under the speed limit. Where're Jackie and Rob?"

"Don't know," J.J. said.

"How much have you had to drink?" John asked him.

"Second beer."

"Cut yourself off at four."

"I will, man." J.J. walked away.

John looked around the room for Jackie and Rob. He knew they'd stick together. They usually did at these parties and with a group of friends.

"Hi Johnny." He turned around.

"Hi." He looked at a beautiful woman with long straight brown hair to her waist. She wore a French maid costume.

"I brought you a drink," she told him.

"I don't drink," he said.

"This is non-alcoholic," she said.

"Is it safe?"

She took a sip, then licked her lips. "Positive," she said, handing him the plastic cup.

He took a sip and realized it was strictly fruit punch.

"I'm Lilah," she said, and pointed to a name badge that she had pinned onto her costume.

"Nice to meet you." He took her hand and kissed it. As he held her hand, he took her upstairs.

THE SMALL DROPS turned into a downpour and without taking any chances, Gabrielle decided to pull over. She yawned again. Her eyes burned. Her eyes were so heavy. They wanted to close and she wanted to sleep. "I've got to get home," she said aloud.

Gabrielle opened her eyes wide and pressed the button for the window to go down and then back up. She decided she should drive home now before she fell asleep in this parking lot. But what would she find at home anyway. It would be loud. The bands would be up on stage or the DJ would have a fast dance tune playing. Besides, she'd have to play host to her fiancé's guests.

J.J. had parties at his house practically every night. John may have had a different woman almost every night, but at least she didn't have to cater to his guests.

Most of all, she missed John. While she was out in the tennis courts batting the oncoming ball, he would stand near the rose garden and water the roses. He would wave to her, and she would wave back. There were a few days where the two of them actually played tennis together. At J.J.'s there was no tennis court, but J.J. said when the spring came he would have one installed for her.

At John's, Gabrielle would take a swim and he would show in his bathing suit. They would swim on opposite sides of the pool, but at least they were together. If she sat in the lawn chair to read a book, he would always ask if he could sit in the chair beside her and she would allow it. She would read a romance novel and he would read science fiction. It was as if they raced to finish their books, and one day when she told him that she was done, he took it out of her hand and threw it onto the deck near the pool. He wouldn't get up to get it and so she did and he stood behind her, picked her up, and threw her in.

After he had, she pretended she had hurt her foot on the bottom of the pool. He felt sorry and crouched in front of her to examine her foot. He even told her it looked a little bruised. Then, she took both of her feet and pushed him backwards into the heated swimming pool.

J.J. had an indoor pool where the sun found its way in through the glass skylights and windows. When Gabrielle opened the door to use the pool, J.J.'s all night party guests were still camping out on the deck. She didn't know what type of alcohol or bodily fluids were mixing with the chlorine in their pool, making her morning swim much less appealing.

At John's, she went to the stables and brushed the horses, and he would show to do the same. He rode along side of her on Skippy and showed her how to get Malaysia to jump over the hurdles. His knowledge of horses impressed her. Most things about him still impressed her.

At J.J.'s, there were no horses, and she hadn't bothered to ask him to buy her one.

Throughout the Ravolie Estate and its grounds, John treated her with full respect. He never expected anything from her, not a one-night stand and he never touched her sexually or made comments about how beautiful she was or how sexy she looked or how her hair looked like a rat's nest when he found her at one a.m. making a sandwich in the kitchen.

J.J. would always have to touch her in private places, especially when other people were around, as if he owned her private places and was trying to show off his property. Although he respected her, he made her feel uncomfortable. One night, J.J. and Gabrielle sat in front of the television watching a movie with some of his friends. J.J. held her in his arms with a blanket covering them to keep Gabrielle warm. Rob was in the room as well. J.J. continued to reach for her with his fingers, as she continued to keep his hands away. He whispered in her ear, "Please let me. I want to give you an orgasm."

She whispered, "No," and was insistently angry.

He continued anyway, thinking of it as a game. She kept grabbing his hands, pulling him away, but finally gave into his attack. When he accomplished what he was set out to do, she left the room. He never followed her to the bedroom.

Jackie, John, and Gabrielle would sit for breakfast in the kitchen talking. When the women were finished eating, John would take their plates, rinse them, and then place the china in the dishwasher. John knew what she liked to eat and what she didn't like and he ate from her plate at times after Gabrielle would hand it to him. She would save certain fruits off to the side of her plate for him to eat.

At J.J.'s she would hand her plate to a stranger who wasn't there the day before. J.J. and she rarely ate breakfast together. However, Rob and Gabrielle would eat together, while J.J. remained sleeping from the party that occurred the night before.

JOHN WOKE UP. He sat on the bed and looked around the room. He realized the woman had vanished. He attempted to stand, but then fell onto his back. The room spun. His vision was hazy. He knew immediately that Lilah drugged him with the fruit punch. He didn't sleep with her though, he thought. He passed out before it happened. He was fully dressed. His second thought was Gabrielle. He stood from the bed and opened the door. He almost fell again. His vision was so blurry as he passed the costumed people in the hallway looking at him. His hearing had collapsed with his vision. Sounds blended. He felt as if he could hear people's thoughts, especially when they looked at him.

"Have you seen Gabrielle?" his speech slurred, while asking someone he didn't know.

"She's not here!" the devil shouted.

He stumbled down the stairwell, and ripped the eye patch from his eye. He looked around the crowded room filled with people. It was dark and the disco light trailed the walls around the room. People were dancing. He looked for the big, bad wolf, but couldn't find Shedel. He spotted Trevor La'win in a mobster costume, smoking a cigar. John fumbled through the crowd, bouncing off them, as he attempted to walk in a straight line. By the time he got over there, Trevor was gone. "Gabrielle. I have to find Gabrielle," John said to himself. He found his way to the stage.

"What do you need?" the disc jockey asked him.

"Turn on the lights," John said.

"What?"

"Turn on the fuckin' lights!" John growled. He went up to a speaker and spilled it off the stage. In a rage, he began pulling the cords from the stereo equipment.

The lights came on and someone grabbed John from behind, which caused him to stumble and fall to his stomach.

"What's goin' on, John? What's goin' on?" the voice said into his ear.

John went into a crawling position and dragged his body to sit. He turned and noticed the man's legs. He wore brown paisley pajamas. The print seemed to be swimming within the fabric. John raised his head to view his face. "Mick," John said. "I've been drugged."

Many jumped onto the stage. John heard many voices repeating 'What's going on, what's going on?'

John grabbed the paisley pajamas and Mick crouched. "Have you seen Gabrielle?"

"Shit," Mick said and stood.

In John's blurred state, he noticed many legs walking away and jumping off the stage.

"Dad? Dad?" the voices called out to him.

John looked to see Jackie and Rob crouching next to him. Jackie took his hand. They spoke to him, but he had no clue what they were saying. "Listen to me," John said. "Stay together. Rob, do not leave Jackie alone."

"I won't, Dad," Rob said, and John understood.

It was too long.

He couldn't tell what was going on, but while sitting there on the stage, he noticed a microphone hanging from the table. He grabbed it and slid the switch. He yelled, "Gabrielle!" He attempted to stand and yelled again into the microphone, "Gabrielle!"

He could barely open his eyes, however he threw the microphone to the floor and jumped down from the stage. He walked again through the crowd of people.

He couldn't figure what was going on. He was sure they tried to tell him, but he couldn't comprehend what they were saying. Something told him to open the front door, and he peered out into the pouring rain. The rain fell hard, he could tell. The lightning lit up the sky. The thunder roared. And he yelled her name.

He shuffled toward the hundreds of cars parked on the lawn. He grabbed onto them for support as he searched. And then he saw a dim light. A purple, fluorescent light. He remembered he had added the bulb to the Tuscan, so when Gabrielle opened the door ... he walked faster. He scraped his arms on mirrors. He tore his pant leg on someone's license plate. He reached the Tuscan with its door open and fell beside her.

Gabrielle lay on the ground in the mud. Her mask lay beside her, and when John placed his hand under her head, her hair was full of muddy water. The vinyl she wore was drenched with warm beads of rain all over it. He checked her pulse—she had one. He checked to see if she was breathing— she was. He lifted her into a sitting position.

John sat up against the car with her in his lap. He reached into her coat she wore and pulled out her cell phone. He knew if he pressed the number 2 and held it down, it would call Rob's cell.

Rob answered, "Mom!"

"I found her!" John noticed Gabrielle held tight to the plipper. He took the key ring out of her hand and pressed the alarm button and the car's lights flashed and the horn sounded loudly, and John set the phone down to the ground.

Gabrielle's eyes opened to the sound of the alarm.

"Hi, sweetheart," John said.

The crowd of people came and J.J picked Gabrielle up into his arms.

"WHAT'D THEY DO TO MY CAR?" John yelled into his cell phone.

"Carbon Monoxide came in through the vents," the voice said. "I called you."

"When you called, I was already drugged. Next time, call me a few days before shit like this happens!"

He ended the call.

Chapter 15

Christmas Day

As Gabrielle had her hair set into her veil, John sat alone on a stool at Bobbie's Place, composing a song in Studio A.

Finally, he knew where he needed to be. He needed to see his daughter in her emerald Maid of Honor dress. And, though he hated to admit it to himself, he needed to see Gabrielle, walking down the aisle to marry one of his best friends.

J.J. Shedel had asked John to be one of his groomsmen, but John had to turn Shedel down.

"I just can't," said John. "It will cause a mayhem with the press if I'm in that procession, and you don't need that at your wedding. It would just give them something to scowl at." He reasoned with Shedel, knowing full well, that the real reason was that he couldn't bear the thought of being in his ex-wife's wedding. It just wasn't right. If she had married someone else, maybe. But not in Shedel's and Gabrielle's wedding.

J.J. had asked Nick Mace to stand in John's place, and Nick jumped at the chance.

GABRIELLE SAT AT THE VANITY swearing at herself in the mirror for far too long, until she heard the knock.

Slowly, she opened the bedroom door to see her father.

Michael Newtonendie stood in his black suit with her bouquet in hand. He hugged and kissed his daughter in an embrace that became much too difficult for either of them to release, until Gabrielle realized her tears were wrecking her makeup and she needed to wipe her eyes.

"Are you ready to walk down the aisle with the man you love?" he asked her.

"Do you mean J.J. or you, Dad?"

"Me, of course." He patted a blemish on her cheek with his handkerchief.

She hugged him again.

JOHN LEFT BOBBIE'S PLACE and returned home. Just as he was undoing the zipper of the bag for his suit, Gabrielle was receiving help entering the limousine, where she would ride to her ceremony with her father. Michael continued to say the right things and knew better than to mention John Ravolie. He knew that one reference of John might convince his little girl to force the driver to set out into the opposite direction of the church.

JOHN WRAPPED HIS TIE around his neck and tucked it snugly under his collar. He drove quickly down the street, ignoring any traffic signals, until he appeared a few blocks away from the church. The ceremony had drawn a ridiculous amount of traffic, and John now found himself sitting in the line of onlookers.

He glanced in his rearview mirror and realized the same piece of hair he had attempted to keep down was still curved up into the air. While attempting to smash the strand down, he noticed the street sign and remembered that taking the one-way road would dead end at the side of the church.

Instead of driving forward, he shifted the car in reverse. Luckily, no traffic came from behind. Then he spun the car around and parked in a 'NO PARKING,' spot on the side of the road, beside the church, ignoring the rules yet again. As he walked to the front doors, he noticed many limousines in line, and realized they were the cause of the annoying traffic jam and all the horn honking. "It can't be over yet," John muttered to himself. "It must just be starting."

J.J. STOOD PROUDLY at the altar with Rob as his best man, Seth Edilson and Nick Mace at his side, while Jackie walked first, Felecia Harrison, and then Roxy Rolando in the rhythmic pace that all bridesmaids know so well with their pretty bouquets clutched in front of them just below their chest. The music grew louder when Gabrielle entered the corridor with her father. After the audience rose, they stared in awe at her. Her dress was white, and extravagant, with a long train trailing behind her as she walked gingerly. With real white roses in her hair, the veil covered her face. She took a deep breath in and put on a wide smile. A mock smile from cheek to cheek might help fool them into thinking that this was the happiest day of her life, even if it wasn't.

With her father's arm linked with hers, she took a step onto the white runner. As she smiled, she noticed herself looking around for John, but he wasn't there. She glanced toward the altar, where J.J. stood smiling at her and nervously shifting slightly from foot to foot. And she wished he were John.

This is ridiculous. Get John out of your head, now and forever.

As she arrived at the altar, she realized that she hadn't seen John in any of the pews as she scanned them during her walk. She couldn't feel him watching her either, so she knew he didn't come. She recognized her mother and her brother, Jeff, with his family sitting in the first pew. Her mother cried joyful tears; her brother gave a slight wave.

She looked toward Jackie. Jackie shrugged as if to say, 'Dad's not here.'

Gabrielle realized the world was in this chapel watching her. It was too late to turn back time to the proposal at the movie theatre and tell J.J. 'No'... She didn't want to marry him, even though she knew that he'd always protect her, love her, take care of her, and never intentionally hurt her. When she spent time with him these past few months, she continued to fake her love for him, always thinking of and yearning for John under the surface. But now, she was here, in this church, with this bouquet, wearing this ridiculously lavish dress, and she knew she would be with J.J. for the rest of her life.

OUTSIDE, John walked the stairs in the front of the church where many men in black were waiting. Rolando's men, John knew. Shedel wasn't thrilled about the mob waiting outside and inside the church either, however he wanted to make Gabrielle happy, since she had asked Jeffrey Rolando's wife Roxy to stand up in the wedding. Intensity members Matt Hayden and Scott Cuder were standing outside as ushers.

"Can we see your invitation, Ravolie?" Matt asked, jokingly.

John shook hands with them and then lit a cigarette. "I must've forgotten the invitation in my other suit," he said, patting down the pockets and smiling at Matt with a fake look of panic.

"Go on in," Scott said.

John entered the church with the lit cigarette between his fingers. When he realized he was smoking, he threw it to the carpet. He stepped on it with a freshly polished shoe and noticed the spark before a small flame. Rapidly, he smothered the small fire with the bottom of his other shoe and picked up the half-smoked cigarette. He noticed the pewter wall pocket holding holy water. He popped the cigarette inside and heard the sizzle.

He gazed into the chapel and noticed that he had missed Gabrielle's and Shedel's wedding vows, and the minister's asking for objections. Shedel was already reaching to kiss his new bride. John was too late.

150   *Falling Roses: The Years Between*

He thought about lighting another cigarette and realized again he was in a church. Mr. and Mrs. Shedel were running down the aisle and ran past while John remained hidden in the dark shadows of the atrium. "I'll see her at the reception," he reassured himself.

GABRIELLE AND J.J. were supposed to dance the night away. Gabrielle's feet were starting to hurt, but she continued to dance—without shoes—with her bridesmaids and her daughter. J.J. took off Gabrielle's garter and threw it to Seth. When Gabrielle threw her bouquet of red and white roses, Jackie caught it in the air among a scuffle of other single women desperate for a chance. Gabrielle and J.J. forced Seth and Jackie to dance, and Gabrielle couldn't help noticing that Jackie seemed disappointed when Seth danced only one dance with her and then walked away. But Rob filled in where Seth left off, and Jackie danced the next song with him.

Felecia and Mick attempted not to argue and cause a scene. So, Felecia didn't dance with Nick or Johnny. For Gabrielle's sake, she danced with other people to avoid the argument that would be sparked by Mick's accusing glares if she had danced with the two of them.

While Gabrielle and J.J. were dancing, she sensed that John was in the room, and she began to look around for him. John had taken a seat at the bar. He had asked for a shot of vodka, which Gabrielle knew he'd never drink.

"What's wrong, sweetheart?" J.J. asked.

"Nothing. I am so happy," she told him. And she wasn't lying since she had seen John. She closed her eyes and placed her head on J.J.'s shoulder. After a minute, he had stopped dancing, and she opened her eyes to John beside them.

"May I have this dance?" he asked.

"I'll be around," J.J. told her.

John took her hand and said, "You look beautiful, Gabrielle."

"Thank you," she said.

He pressed her body close to his and she laid her arms over his shoulders.

"You're trembling?"

"I've had a little too much to drink," she whispered.

"May I kiss the bride?" he asked her.

She nodded and they kissed the perfect kiss as the song ended.

"Good-bye," he said to her, releasing her arms from his shoulders.

"Good-bye," she said, letting go slowly. At first, she walked backward toward the door to take one last look at him.

J.J. waited for her and placed Gabrielle's coat on over her gorgeous white wedding dress. "Wait here. I'll make sure the limo's here," J.J. told her.

"Okay," she said. She waited for her husband to return.

Mick, Trevor, Lenny, Brandon, and John took the stage. A soft, slow tune began to play. She had heard this song many times before. It was a song from the past.

"I love you," John sang. "In the morning, I'll be there to comfort you." She walked closer to the stage, while couples danced and she stared at John as he sat on a stool singing to her. "I'm sorry that I never told you. I wish that I could hold you.... I love you."

A tear fell to her cheek. She wiped it and turned toward the door when the song ended.

"Can I ask you three questions?" John asked from behind her.

She turned to look at him. "Sure."

"What name are you going by?"

"I'm sorry, I don't understand the question."

"You kept Ravolie, didn't you?"

"Why do you ask me questions you already know the answer to?"

"My second question. Why is your name Gabrielle Ravolie Shedel and not Gabrielle Shedel?"

"I'm sure *you* know the answer."

"Because you were mine first."

"That wouldn't've been—"

"I am your first, your last, and your only," he told her.

"What is your next question, John?"

"Why did you do this to me?"

She stared at him, remembering the words he had just said to her and the meaning behind them. John's wedding ring. And she looked at his hand—he wore it. Years ago, she had it engraved with those words.

Gabrielle didn't know how to answer his last question. She wanted to be with John. She loved him. Her body and her mind would be his whenever he was ready to be with her. She felt guilty escaping from her true feelings and marrying J.J. She loved J.J., but only as a friend not a husband. Just then as her thoughts were wandering and questions were looming in her head, J.J. walked up to them before she could answer John's question.

"Shedel, congratulations," John said, shaking his hand. "She's a lovely woman," John then said and looked at Gabrielle intensely.

J.J. placed his arm around her. Gabrielle wanted J.J. to take his arm away from her waist. She felt smothered by him. Gabrielle took one last look at John, before she and J.J. walked away and she said, "J.J. makes me happy."

Gabrielle and J.J. ran outside into the snow and rain. They found the limousine parked farther down the street than they anticipated, and the driver opened the door for them as they forcefully slid on the ice and into the car.

When they arrived at the hotel, J.J. picked her up and carried her into the room, approaching the bed with his bride in his arms. He set her down slowly, took off her heels, and set them to the floor. This time he was gentle with her. Then he took off her veil, and Gabrielle reached behind her to undo her train from her dress. J.J. unzipped her dress slowly. He took off her panty hose and she stood before him, wearing a white satin slip.

Exhausted, she lay on the bed while J.J. undressed. He slipped under the covers with her. It was four in the morning and J.J. whispered in her ear, "I love you."

"I love you, too," she lied. Her love wasn't the kind of love he wanted or should have from her in return.

"I wish we could be like this forever," he said encircling her left breast and pushing his torso close to hers.

"We can J., we can be."

"I just hope you have no regrets."

She turned to face him and said, "None at all. I love you with all my heart," she lied again.

Then they made love in complete silence. And afterwards, J.J. fell promptly asleep.

But Gabrielle's mind wouldn't let her sleep. Inside her head, she yelled at herself to stop thinking about John. She thought about how John would have made this wedding a fairytale for her. He'd be awake right now, they'd be talking, and laughing and eating strawberries with whipped cream, or doing something incredibly sexy with food. Even if, they both were extremely exhausted. Because, exhausted or not, John could never get enough of her, nor she of him.

Or, they would be taking a hot bath together and he would be soaping up her body, kissing her neck. She wished him to give her a foot massage. They'd stay awake all night and in the morning get on the plane for Hawaii—his plane. They'd make love in the air, and then fall asleep during the long flight and awake to find themselves in Maui.

Finally, her thoughts and the exhaustion of the day brought her to sleep.

The next morning Gabrielle was held tightly within J.J.'s grip. There were two knocks on the door.

"You have got to be kiddin' me," J.J. whispered and sat.

"Don't answer it." Gabrielle pulled him to her and kissed him passionately. "I want you to make love to me."

"Right now?" he asked her.

"Yes," she replied.

"We have to get dressed. We have to get on a plane and go to Hawaii," he told her.

"We can make love again right now and still have time," she suggested.

"We have to take showers."

"We can take one together." Gabrielle kissed the corner of his mouth, looking at him pleadingly.

"There's no room for the both of us," he said, standing.

She knew she'd be second to take a shower and most likely—yes she was sure of it—the water would be cold.

Hours later, their plane arrived on the beautiful island of Maui.

Today, they went shopping and bought items for their children. Gabrielle secretly purchased a few items for John. When they arrived back at the hotel, they placed their swimsuits on and headed out to the private beach.

As they were near the shallow end, they had their arms around one another and kissed passionately. For a moment, Gabrielle forgot about John. The current began to push them back to shore and they lay there on the sand to watch the sunset and the waves getting stronger.

"I bet you can't catch me in those waves," J.J. said.

"I bet you I can," Gabrielle insisted.

J.J. ran into the water and dove into the high waves. Gabrielle followed. The waves crashed over their heads.

J.J. began to cough. He yelled to Gabrielle who drifted from him, "Go back!" He threw up an arm, pointing.

"No! I'm not ... leaving ... without you!" she yelled.

At last, she bypassed the waves and treaded water beside him. They held hands. He choked on the salt water and gasped for air.

While lying on her back, she held onto him, until the waves settled. Then she pumped her legs to bring them back to shore.

"J.J., wake up!" she yelled, noticing he wasn't breathing. She pinched his nose to blow air through his mouth, however air wouldn't move into his chest. She began to panic, realizing no one was around. She didn't have a cell phone. Even if she did, how would she call 9-1-1 in Hawaii with a New York phone?

Gabrielle tried to blow air into his mouth again. When she placed her lips on his, she received more than a response of breath. J.J. began to kiss her, and laughed loudly at her.

"You were faking!" Her voice cracked into a sputter.

"That was a great rescue." He pulled her on top of him; Gabrielle let loose of his grip and stood. She was so angry she couldn't speak, and she ran from him.

"Wait!" He chased her, grabbed her arm, and turned her toward him. "Hey. I'm sorry. Hey, look at me. I'm sorry. I love you. I didn't mean to hurt you."

"That was so cruel! You scared me to death," Gabrielle cried out. "I thought you were dead. There's no one around. I couldn't call for help. I felt helpless. How could you?"

"I'm sorry. Wasn't it funny at all?"

Gabrielle looked away, wiping her tears.

"Just a little bit?" he asked, showing her his thumb and forefinger. J.J. kissed the corner of her mouth. "This honeymoon isn't getting off to a great start, is it?" he asked her.

She shook her head no.

"No regrets?" he asked.

Again, she shook her head no. Although she had wished she was with John right now, instead of J.J. John would have made their honeymoon as romantic as possible and he would have never pulled a stunt like the one J.J. just pulled, she thought.

At 6:30 a.m., Gabrielle awoke to the two knocks on the door. "Gurreat." She yanked her body out of the grip J.J. had locked on her.

To her surprise, it wasn't room service. It was John.

"Oh my God. John. Did something happen to the kids?" she asked immediately.

"No. No," John said. "Things are fine. Is Shedel asleep?" He looked toward the bed at J.J. face down, covered with the blankets, and snoring. "Get dressed, get your purse, I want to show you something."

"What are you doing here?" she asked in a whisper, as she let him inside and John closed the door.

"I had to come out here for business. There's a nightclub that I want to buy. Come on." He smiled at her. "Get dressed."

Already, she didn't believe his story. "You came all the way to Maui, *today*, to purchase a club?"

"Since you were in town, I thought I'd ask you for advice," John said.

"You want *my* advice?"

"Yes, but first put something on, would you? Get rid of the sheet."

She looked down at the sheet wrapped around her body. "What should I wear?"

"Bathing suit, shorts, and running shoes. Don't forget your purse."

"I should wake J.J."

"Let him sleep. He won't even know you're gone."

"I should at least write him a note."

"Okay, I'll write it."

"No," she said sternly. "You will do no such thing." She pulled out a pen and paper from the drawer. "What should I write?" she asked him.

"I took a walk on the beach and I'll be back soon," John said.

That's what she wrote.

Gabrielle gracefully went into the bathroom where her suit was hanging and placed the one-piece royal-blue bathing suit on over her legs and lifted up the straps around her shoulders. Her brush contained J.J.'s hair, which she carefully removed and then placed the brush through hers. And then she clipped her hair in a barrette.

"Hurry up," she heard John say.

JOHN SAT ON THE BED BESIDE J.J.

"It's working so far," J.J. said to John.

"She's coming with me. You have the gun?"

"Yeah, in the drawer," J.J. said.

"You remember the plan?" John asked him.

"I thought of it."

GABRIELLE ENTERED THE BEDROOM and asked in a whisper, "Is J.J. awake?"

"No. You ready?"

"Let me find my sandals," she said, still whispering so as not to wake up her husband.

"Put those on, instead," he said, pointing to her gym shoes. "And where's your purse?"

She placed her purse over her shoulder and over her head. "Okay, let's go," Gabrielle said.

John shut the door.

J.J. GRABBED THE GUN from the nightstand and got dressed quickly.

GABRIELLE AND JOHN took a stroll along the white sandy beach. Gabrielle stopped and John let her lean on him while she removed her shoes that had accumulated sand.

"ROOM SERVICE." J.J. heard the voice. He placed the gun in his pants, under his shirt. He opened the door and the man came in with a tray. J.J. lifted the cover, grabbed a piece of French toast, and left the room.

"HERE." He took her hands in his. "I'll carry your shoes."

She allowed him the privilege. "How far is this nightclub, anyway?" she asked.

"Not far." He looked around, scoping out the beach.

"What is this advice you want from me?" she asked him.

"Well, let's sit over there." He pointed to an old wooden, outdoor restroom. "In the shade," he added politely.

"I thought we were walking to this nightclub."

"We were, we are, but I thought we'd just sit for a minute, so I could tell you about it." They sat on a slab of cement side by side. "Do you have your pills with you?" he asked her.

"What?"

"Your pills? How many do you have?" He took the purse strap from around her head and off her shoulder.

"I don't have my pills with me," she said.

He took her purse from her hand. He opened it and began to scan the contents. Then, he dumped it into the sand. "Where're your pills?"

"I don't have them with me," she repeated.

"What?"

"I'm going back—" She stood and he pulled her to sit.

"Where're your pills?" he asked again.

"You're scaring me," she said.

"Tell me." He pressed the buttons on his cell phone.

"I left the bottle in the bathroom."

There was no answer, and John ended the call. He looked at her blankly, and immediately noticed the red beam of light on her forehead. "Oh shit!" He pulled her down. Bullets hit the wood where she was sitting. He opened the door of the bathroom. "Go!" he yelled.

She crawled inside. "Was someone just—?"

"Yes, damn it!"

In the stall, John had a carry-on bag. He opened up the window. She stood on top of the toilet, and he pushed her onto the low roof. She slid down and he tossed the bag to her. He slid down just as fast with a gun in his hand, took the bag from her and said, "Let's go!"

They ran.

"Follow me," John said, and he led her into a parking lot. They got low between two cars. John unzipped the bag and handed her a vest. "Put this on," he told her.

"Are we going on a boat?" she asked.

"No, that's a bulletproof vest." He helped her button it.

"It's so heavy," she said. "I can't run as fast."

"Trust me, when these assholes are shooting at you, you'll run."

"What is going on, John?"

"What do you think?"

"The mob is attempting to kill me."

He squatted and looked around the car. "I don't see anyone," he told her.

"What about J.J.?" Gabrielle asked.

"Shedel's gonna meet us. Are you ready?"

She nodded.

They ran.

Random gunfire hit the sand. The pellets were too close, too close to her feet. She screamed and ran as fast as she could alongside John.

"The park, let's go," he shouted.

SHE RAN UP THE WOODEN PLATFORM as John ran up the other end. She ran across the bridge and met him behind the tunnel slide.

He sat, with his back against the entrance of the slide, and she sat on top of his legs facing him within the pocket-sized space.

"Now what do we do," she whispered.

John pressed the buttons on his cell and Gabrielle noticed he was calling J.J. "She doesn't have her pills," he said into the phone. Call off the chopper." John ended the call.

"What is going on?" Gabrielle asked angrily.

"I love you, Gabrielle," John said.

"What?" She shook her head.

"I love you, Gabrielle," he said again. He pulled her face close to his and kissed her mouth.

She pushed him away, and attempted to get off him.

"I want you, Gabrielle. Only you, for the rest of my life."

The tears came flowing with her rapid heartbeat. "Is it safe for me to leave?" she asked him.

"Don't ever leave me again."

"You ... You—" She pushed herself away from him. "—and J.J. set me up. Where is he?" She looked over the slide. I bet he's watching us from somewhere. Where is he?" She looked around the beach, but didn't see him. "I don't love either one of you." She stomped over the bridge and John followed her down the wooden platform. "He pretends he's going to drown to see if I would save him! Were you watching yesterday? What is this anyway?" She unbuttoned both sides. "Rob's paintball vest?" she asked, throwing it to the ground. "The two of you are obscene, stupid and egotistical! You're both dirty and rotten, and love doesn't mean anything to either of you!"

Then Gabrielle spotted J.J. coming toward them. "This whole honeymoon has been a disaster!" Gabrielle slapped J.J. across the face. "Are we even married? You are a disaster! I don't love you! This has been the worst seventy-two hours of my life!" She stomped through the sand.

"Listen to me," J.J. pleaded

"Save it for the judge!"

Her anger led to wailing tears. She ran from them back to the hotel. She wept while she packed her belongings. "My life can't get better than this," she said to herself as she shoved her clothes and things into the bag with frustrated haste.

J.J. OPENED THE DOOR to the hotel room and found Gabrielle packing.

"Why did you do this to me?" she yelled.

"I did this *for* you," J.J. told her. "I asked Ravolie to come here."

"Why?" She placed her suitcase on the floor and sat beside him.

"I read your journal."

"You did what?" she gasped.

"I don't know how you married me when you still love him. You've always *loved* him. And he's ready for you now. So, go be with him. Go spend the next two weeks with him. Ravolie is ready. He wants you. And I can't be with someone who I know is wishing she was with someone else."

She was silent.

"Don't be angry with him. I came up with the plan. I asked Ravolie to come here. I wanted to see if you'd go with him, and you did. And then a helicopter was going to pick you two up and take you for a ride that you'd always remember. Go get your pills and take that ride."

"You'd give me up that easily?"

"I'm not selfish. I want to see you and Ravolie happy. Yes, I love you, but you love him more. I came up with this plan 'cause I care about both of you and want you to be happy. He'd take you on an adventure. And we'd see if you came back to me. May the best man win."

"So, you both thought of me as a prize? Did you plan this months ago?"

"Yes. No. Yes."

"How can I love either of you? You were firing an air gun and shooting pellets at me," she said with disgust. "Why didn't you use real bullets?"

Chapter 16

Six Months Later
June

"**O**h no," Gabrielle said as she looked down the hallway.

"What?" Jackie asked.

"Here comes your father," she mumbled.

"Mom, just talk to *him*." They stopped walking.

"I don't want to," she whispered.

"Why not?" Jackie groaned.

"I have nothing to say to him *today*." Her voice muffled.

"Are you still angry?" Jackie asked.

"No." She shook her head.

"Then talk to him. Tell him how you feel. You still love him, don't you?"

"Sometimes it doesn't matter how a person feels." She looked up and noticed John, merely a few feet away.

"Just talk to him," Jackie said quickly, and then smiled at her father.

"Hi, munchkin." He wiggled her ponytail.

"I'll leave the two of you alone," Jackie said, departing quickly.

"Hi." He smiled sheepishly at Gabrielle.

"Hi, John." She began to fidget with her tennis racquet. She looked past him and to their daughter, walking away from them. "It's a beautiful day to play tennis," she said, and swung her racquet. "Are you going this way to water the roses?"

"No," he said with a chuckle. "Actually, I wanted to have a word with—"

"A word with me? What'd I do wrong for you to want to have a word with me, and why do you bother watering those flowers?"

"You did nothin' wrong. And, I like to water those roses. It's relaxing."

Suddenly, he was too close, invading her space. There was no other place for her to look except directly into his eyes, and her mouth was only an inch from his. He set his fingers on her chin to raise her head.

"I'm ready," he whispered.

"Ready for what?" she asked angrily.

He let go of her chin and took a step back. "You sure know how to throw off a mood."

"What mood? There was no mood," she lied.

"I never apologized," he said, looking regretful.

"You're ready to apologize? For what this time? What'd you do?"

"I'm sorry. I'm sorry for—everything. I'm sorry for hurting you at the beach house. What I did to you that night was wrong," he admitted.

She stared at him blankly, waiting for more.

"You're not like other women. I didn't make love to you on the beach. I just had sex with you that night, and that was wrong. I was wrong. When it comes to sleeping with women, I'm selfish and egotistical to say the least. I want to change—for you." He crossed his arms.

"Go on. Please tell me more," she inquired, swatting the air with her racquet.

"Will you forgive me for what Shedel and I did to you in Hawaii? At least, let me try to win you back? I'd like to start by taking you out for dinner tonight. You can go get dressed and out of that leotard thing you're wearin' and I'll drive you to dinner to a nice romantic restaurant, just the two of us."

"I've forgotten about what happened between the two of us on the beach," Gabrielle said. "And, I forgave J.J. and you for what you two did to me in Hawaii. But, in spite of that, it's over. Neither one of you received me as your prize. What you two did to me was the best thing for all three of us. It happened months ago. And—and—dinner outside of the home, without Jackie, is not necessary."

She continued, "The only reason why I'm living under the same roof as you is because I just wanted to get to know my kids, like I told you in the first place. All this time, I've been learning that I'm a damn good mother. I might not have a good relationship with their fathers, but at least I have good relations with them."

John said, "I've seen you with Jackie and Rob and you are an excellent mother. Again, I apologize. I don't think of you as a prize or a possession. You have my complete respect, Gabrielle, and you should know that."

"It's over and done with," she said. "I know you respect me. What you do in your own house is your business. Since I've been living here, you've respected me in front of the kids, and Hawaii—I forgive you for that outrageous, ridiculous, insane—"

"I thought you would've had your pills with you," John said. "I had a chopper set to pick us up. I was going to take you for an aerial ride. I don't know what I thought I was doing. Or, what it would've led to. I don't know. It all happened so fast."

"What would've happened?" she asked angrily. "Tell me. Did you think you'd be able to seduce me on my honeymoon? Were you not attracted to me until I was a married woman? Someone you could never have again? Did you only want me because you didn't have me?"

"Christ," John said. "I'm not here to argue with you. You got it all wrong."

"Do I now? I know what you would've done, if I did have my pills with me. Later in the day you would've had sex with me, and J.J. would've watched," she sneered.

He chuckled.

"That wasn't supposed to be funny," she said.

"You're the only woman who ever makes me laugh. I don't laugh with anyone else other than you and the kids. When we're all together, I never want the moment to end."

"Don't change the subject. After J.J. watched us, you would've made me feel like trash for the second time. I got the picture at the beach house. If I did play your game, gave into you, would you have slept with me again, and do the same thing to me twice?" She paused with a serious, agitated face and glared at him. "Please, answer the question."

"I hurt you so much at the beach house. I wasn't going to do that again. I hope you understand how Shedel felt. He needed to know."

"I know what he needed to know. He found out now, didn't he? And, so did you!"

"He didn't want you to be miserable with him," John raised his voice. "Even though, he's so much in love with you. He sacrificed you, because you didn't love him. He's not selfish!"

"Am I supposed to believe what you two did was honorable? I did love J.J. I wasn't miserable with him. I was willing to spend the rest of my life with him. I told him there'd be no regrets, and I meant it. I'm not a liar."

"Come on, Gabrielle. You're talkin' to John now. You didn't love him. You were miserable with him. And hell, you wouldn't've spent the rest of your life with him. Perhaps another week. Or, maybe until I came to rescue you—"

"Rescue me? Mmmhmm," she mumbled.

"Yes. You didn't love him then and you don't love him now. I know what you did love, though."

"You and J.J. have me all figured out, so please tell me? What do I love to do? Manipulate the both of you? Is this what you're gonna tell me? Do you seriously believe I love teasing you both with the prospect of having me? Do you think I'm that cold and cruel of a person?"

"No, but you said it." He pointed to her. "You loved making me hurt. You loved making me jealous with him."

"It's always about you! I never made you jealous and I never tried to. I wanted you, John. Since the day, Jackie came back into my life and showed me your picture. I wanted you. You made it perfectly clear that you didn't want me." She continued, "You use to parade women upstairs to your bedroom. Hell, last year, you had a new woman in your bed each night. You're hurt? You're jealous? I'm doing this to you?"

"You noticed?" he asked her.

"How could I not? Who were they? Hookers?"

"I stopped dating completely because I want to be with you."

"I thought you got the clap."

"You thought they were hookers?" John asked her.

"If I let something happen on the beach in Hawaii, I know what you would've said."

"See, you haven't forgave me. Tell me, sweetheart, what would I have told you?"

"'Oh Gabrielle, I can't live in the past,'" she said sarcastically, mocking him. "It's exactly what you would've said."

"No. My words would've been quite different."

"I'm waiting to hear this." She put on a fake smile.

"Gabrielle, I needed time to adjust to you being alive again. I keep thinking, when I see you, you're not real. When we had sex, at the beach house it was as if I was dreaming and then while we were—you know—I told myself it wasn't real and I was with someone else. Ever since the day that I thought you died, I've never let myself be close to anyone. Not anyone."

"Wake up, John. You're not dreaming anymore. I'm alive now. I am here standing before you and I am hungry because you won't love me in return."

"Hungry?"

"Angry." They laughed from her mix up in words.

"I said I'm ready now, and I'll take you out to dinner if you're hungry," John said. "I want you now. I need you now. I'm sick of being lonely without you. I'm sick of watching you alone without me. I want to be in love. I need *your* love."

She swung her racquet from side to side.

"I'm ready for you now," John said. "I will be for the rest of our lives. I want to marry you again. We should've never gotten a divorce. Damn those papers."

He continued, "I apologize that it took me so long to realize it, but I've finally figured out that you being here isn't a dream. I don't want to fight you out my life anymore I want to fight for you to be in it. Are you listening to what I'm trying to say? Will you look at me when I talk to you? Will you stop fidgeting like crazy with that damn tennis racquet and look at me?"

"I'm not fidgeting!" she screamed, embarrassed.

"What are you doin' with that racquet?" he asked her.

"I'm getting ready to swat you with it."

"You have to be difficult, and I deserve it," he said.

"Damn right, you do," she mumbled. She paused for only a second and then said with a wisp of frustration in her voice, "I am alive, John. You're not dreaming. I'm here. I'm real."

"It took you long enough to speak and when you do, you tell me you're alive? I already realize this now. Here I am, begging for your forgiveness and proclaiming I want you, I need you, and I love you! Why can't you say, 'all right John, let's start over? I'm still willing if you are.' And—and—why don't you ever come to my bedroom at night?"

"You never come to mine!" she yelled back.

"I always come to your room and you never open the door!"

"You never knock!"

"You want me to crawl?" he asked her. "I still have a bad knee, but I'll crawl. You want me to beg?"

"Yes, crawl and beg!" she yelled.

"You are always looking to pick a fight with me! Well woman, I'm sick of fighting with you! It took me ten damn months to get you out of my dreams and into my reality and to get enough courage, I even practiced my lines and saw a shrink!"

"Did you sleep with her, too?" Gabrielle asked in an angry tone.

"Yes!" He paused, reconsidering the question. "Hell, no! Who? My shrink?" They laughed at his confusion. "You hurt me too, you know," John said. "You were the one who forgot about me. I never forgot about you," he said seriously.

"You're still going to blame me? All this time you blame me for our twelve years apart?" Gabrielle felt her anger roaring inside of her.

"No," he stated.

"Then why'd you just say—?"

"Here we go again," he huffed.

"Yes, I think you do. You do blame me. It's not fair. I never forgot about you. If your shrink told you to say that to me, you're both wrong. I remembered you. I always have remembered you. I never was able to see your face in my dreams or know your name, but I always felt your presence and knew you were out there.

"The day we found each other again, it was you who gave up on us," she said pointing a finger at him. "It wasn't my fault that we've lost twelve years going on thirteen together. I've been ready to start again, where we left off. I may not have known your name or where you lived, but my God, I never stopped loving you." She paused. "Even when I was with J.J., I never stopped loving you or even thinking about you."

She continued, "I want to hate you for everything you've done to me the past ten months, but I can't. You treat me like shit and the reason you do better not be because you think I forgot or you didn't realize I was alive. This can't be the reason why. It doesn't make any sense because neither of those things are true. I've never forgotten about you, and this whole time I've been real and alive, right here in front of you."

"It's because I needed you!" he cried out to her and he grabbed her by the head, held her with one hand, and with the other held onto the racquet she continued to swing while she had talked. He stopped the racquet and then kissed her passionately.

He pulled his face away from hers. "Awe. Damn it. You bit my lip. You bit my freakin' lip!"

"I need you to believe I'm real and you're not having a dream to where you'll wake up and I'm gone. Did your shrink tell you that if I broke your kneecap you'd believe in me? What's it gonna take for you to believe in me?"

"Come here. You better not bite me again." He grabbed her body and pulled her close to him. Again, he kissed her passionately. Instead of biting him, she hit him over the head with the racquet.

"Why the hell did you do that?" He took the racquet out of her hand and threw it down the hall. It bounced off the wall, just barely missing the exquisitely framed photographs of Jackie and the brass sconces, and onto the floor.

"Because you told me not to bite you again," she said with a giggle.

"I would like to bite you right now. My lip feels like it's bleeding." He kept his right hand on the side of her head while he felt his lip with his left hand, looking to see if there was blood.

"It's not bleeding, and you better not dare bite me." She smirked. "John," she said seriously. "I am alive. I've been alive all this time and you never came searching for me, for me." Her voice crackled. "*I'm* not holding a grudge. Please remove your hand and don't kiss me again." She turned her face from his.

Brushing up against her, he led her back into the wall. He held her arms to her side. He paused for a moment. Letting go he said, "Well, are you coming to dinner with me or do I have to eat alone?" She didn't answer. Again, she looked away. "Talk to me? Please look at me? How do you feel?" He took his hands off her.

"About dinner? I'm hungry."

"How do you feel about us, silly? Are we going to start where we left off?"

"Who wants to know?" she asked him.

"Jackie, Rob, Shedel, Fred the gardener—I do."

"What do I tell you in your dreams, baby?" She looked into his eyes.

"As I cry in your arms you tell me you'll never leave me again." John's eyes began to gloss.

"I still care about you. Maybe. I think. As for leaving you again."

"Do you need me or don't you? I know you won't leave me again. It'll never happen again."

"What difference would it make?" she asked him. "Why do I need to tell you how I feel? It wouldn't matter. Obviously, my feelings seldom matter."

"Don't you understand what I'm trying to tell you, woman? I'm not looking for a one-night-stand here, baby. We start over from the beginning. You tell me you're in this for the long haul. You sign a contract that you'll never leave me. We sleep together. We eat together. Maybe we'll make more babies together, and, and, we just do every damn thing together."

He let out a sigh and continued, "You and me, me and you together forever. You need to tell me if this is what you want. I need to know now. Our future together depends on your answer at this very moment. It would make a big difference in our lives."

"I'll think about it." She began to walk away.

"I don't believe this shit," he mumbled. "There is no one on this earth that makes me so excited, so lucky, and so damn frustrated but you. Don't you walk away from me! Don't walk away! Gabrielle, if you don't stop—I'm going to grab you and throw you down in the middle of this hallway. I'll make love to you like I've never made love to you before."

Gabrielle then stopped walking.

"Why'd you stop?" he questioned her.

"Do I always keep walking in your dreams?"

"Yes, actually you do," he said, scratching his head.

"Well, I stopped so I could pick up my racquet."

She leaned down. Her short skirt uncovered her derriere and he noticed the thong— "Well?" He walked up to her, pretending not to have noticed how sexy she was underneath that short skirt.

"Well, what? I thought you were finished." She turned to face him.

"You have a nice ass." He couldn't help himself.

"Thank you." She looked at the ceiling and began to swing her racquet again.

"That's it? You're not going to tell me, 'John, I remember how we use to be. I love you. Yes, I'll take you back.'" he asked her, thinking maybe it was too late. Maybe he had just waited too long to tell her he was ready. Now, she was a different person. And, just as he had feared, Gabrielle hurt because of him. This time, *she* wasn't ready for him to take her back. At this point, he would do anything she asked just to be with her again.

"No," she replied.

"Then, what are you going to say?" he asked, confused.

"Nothing," she said.

"You have to say somethin'. You can't make me crawl and beg for the rest of our lives."

"I don't have to say anything," she mentioned.

"*Yes*, you do," he huffed.

"What would you like me to say?" she asked him.

"I just told you!" This was too much for him to take. It would take a lot of crawling and begging, he thought.

She turned around and began to walk down the hall again. He followed her and said, "Does this mean I'll have to cook you dinner and bring it to your room tonight? Does this mean I have to pick flowers for you? Draw your baths and give you full body massages every day and night to win you over? I'll do anything, baby. Anything. Even crawl or beg." He followed closely behind her.

She stopped and he almost fell over her.

"Why don't you come to my room in about twenty minutes?" she told him. She turned around to look at him. "I'm going to change. I'm sweaty. I need a shower. Then, maybe you and I can fight some more before you take me out to dinner."

"Christ. It's about time, woman. It was a pleasure doing business with you." They shook hands.

He fell to the floor feeling mentally exhausted. "You take my breath away," he said. On his back, he lay in the middle of the hall with his arms and legs sprawled.

She stepped over him and stood with her legs straddling across his chest. He could look up her skirt again. She leaned over him, and said, "No. You'd need a breath mint for that." She walked away with her racquet.

"A blue breath mint?" he asked her.

"You taste like stale cigarettes," she told him. "You better do something about that breath before you come up to my room. And, you better be there in twenty." She continued walking.

"I have to quit smoking for her," he thought aloud.

AS SOON AS SHE CLOSED the door to her room, she locked it and screamed, "Yes!" And then covered her mouth with her hands, hoping she didn't yell too loud. Gabrielle jumped into the shower and when finished ran out with the towel around her head.

She grabbed her brand new black lace negligee from the hanger. The sheer netting on the back made it look backless. She slipped her legs in quickly. Tightly fitted, she brought the spaghetti straps over her shoulders. She placed her legs through her red dress and realized she forgot to put on her panties.

Underneath she wore a teddy. Since it was something to wear when two people were intimate, she thought she didn't need to wear panties anyhow. Since time was running out, she wouldn't be able to grab a new pair of underwear and place it on her and then redo the teddy, so it would fit perfectly onto her body for John, and then zip up her dress— With both hands, she tugged on the zipper and realized it wouldn't budge. She couldn't do it alone.

"Damn," she said. "Jackie!" she called out, but knew her daughter wasn't near for her to hear her. "Where is my daughter when I need her?" Then she heard a knock on her door.

"Thank God," she said, unlocking the door.

"May I come in?" John asked.

Gabrielle had hoped it was Jackie. Had it been twenty minutes already? she wondered, holding the door shut. "You can come in after you count to ten. I'm not dressed yet," she told him.

"It's not as if I haven't seen you naked before," he told her through the door. "And I've seen that sexy blue thing you're wearin' twice now."

While bolting to the bathroom, she attempted to zip up her dress. She knew as soon as she took her hand from the knob, John would walk right in without counting first. It would be just like him to do just that.

As John waited, he sat on the bed and smelled her pillow. "Gabrielle, are you gonna hide in the bathroom all evening?"

"No." She walked toward him with her arms holding the dress up over her breasts.

Quickly, John removed the pillow from his lap as she turned around to place her back to him. "I should have known," he said sarcastically.

"Zip it," she ordered, feeling frustrated.

"What's this black thing you're wearin' underneath it?" He placed his finger on the teddy where the sheer met the lace outlining her derriere.

"Are you going to zip it, or shall I find something else to wear? An old flannel frock, maybe?"

He ran his fingers gently up her spine.

"My daughter is not around to help me with my dress. You're the one who invited me out to dinner, so I need you to zip up my dress." She challenged herself not to whisper and attempted not to show him emotionally how she enjoyed him touching her. Physically, she had goose bumps. Mentally, she was tingling with every fiber of her being. She hoped he couldn't view her closed eyes within her reflection in the mirror.

Instead of John zipping up her dress, he asked, "Why don't—Why don't we stay right here? Instead of dinner, I'll have something brought up here for us to—to eat."

"What do you do in your dreams?" she asked, looking over her right shoulder.

"Take you out to dinner." He remained touching her spine with his fingers and undressing her with his mind.

"And then, what happens?" she asked.

"We never make it there, since you can't zip up your dress and I won't do it for you."

She turned to face him. "And what do we do when we stay here? Do we eat?"

He placed his hands on her hips. Swiftly, he pulled the dress to her ankles.

"Thanks. How romantic. I'm not one of your cheap thrills you bring into your bedroom, and we're in my bedroom now." She began to fidget with her wrist.

His gaze fell onto her body in front of him. He could view the outline of her breasts, her nipples, and her navel. He wanted to reach out and touch her, place his mouth to her abdomen. He placed his index finger on her belly button and encircled it as he swallowed. He then looked up at her face; she looked down at him with an eyebrow raised. She folded her arms.

"I know you're special," John said. "You're the mother of my children. You're the love of my life. I'm not sorry for pulling your dress off you, though. This sexy thing you're wearing—I see it's brand new." He pointed to the tag, attached to the spaghetti strap. "Do you have scissors?" he asked. "I'll get the tag for you."

She walked gracefully over to the nightstand as he waited on the bed. She picked out the scissors from her drawer and gently placed it into his hand. She leaned over him as he lightly pushed her hair aside to cut the tag. He then leaned over backwards and placed the scissors back on the nightstand.

His hands gently removed the two pieces of the tag and plastic that held it together as she kneeled over him. Without asking, he caressed her neck with his mouth, and moved his hands up and down her hips and then to her backside. As he pressed her toward him, he nibbled on her ear and then brought his mouth to hers. He pulled his mouth away, teasing her. He grabbed her and pulled her on top of him. Laying back he said, "Gabrielle, I don't want to live in the past."

"You're an ass." She attempted to move away.

"No, Gabrielle." He held her hands and her body close to his. "Let me continue." He sat and she wrapped her legs around his torso. "I love you, and we both know you love me."

"No. I don't." She smiled at him.

"Yes. You do." He returned the seductive look.

"Are you going to let me go?" she asked.

"No, I'm not," he teased.

"Are you going to tie me up?" she joked.

He chuckled. "I would like to. But no, I didn't bring any rope with me." He then pulled her head down, her mouth intimate with his lips. He placed his mouth to hers and his tongue entered.

She returned his sensual desire, feeling weak to his touch. "What do you want from me?" she breathed into his mouth.

"I want you to love me for who I am now. Not for who I was then. I don't want to start from the beginning. I want to start fresh from this moment on."

"How do I know this is not one of your tricks again?"

"You can't open your eyes."

"Shut up! You're a jerk."

"You love this jerk, don't you?" He kissed her again.

"Stop," she said. "Let go of my wrists."

"Why? You like—you like fighting."

She shuffled, until their fingers joined.

"Now, since I have you like this." He paused. "There are so many things I want to tell you." He kissed her again.

"And here I thought you've already told me everything," she said sarcastically.

"I want to be with you, forever. From this moment forward, I'm going to be a changed man for you."

"A changed man, huh?"

"You want me to be romantic. I'll be romantic," he said. "You want the fairytale. I'm gonna give it to you, baby," he whispered.

"What fairytale? Is this something from the past?" she asked him.

"Well, yeah."

"Tell me, what is this fairytale all about?"

"Well, you always wanted the big white house with the fountains and the rose garden and the pond out back—and horses."

"I have all of this now," she said.

"Do you want another purple corvette?"

"A purple corvette?" She laughed. "What else have I asked you for?"

"Well, you got your two kids, a boy and a girl and you had a career in singing. Do you still want to sing?"

"No, I don't like singing," she told him. "I'm nervous when I sing. You gave me the fairytale already, it seems."

"I guess you have different dreams now, huh? What can I possibly give you that you've always wanted?" he asked her.

"The question is: What can we possibly give to one another that we don't already have?"

"There's one thing I can think of," John said.

"Forever?" Gabrielle whispered.

"Forever," John whispered, kissed her, and smiled.

"Till death do us part," she replied.

"Even then," he told her.

"Will we be together?" she asked.

"Yes, Gabrielle. We will always be together."

He flipped her over. Kneeling over her he asked, "Why are you so beautiful?"

"Because I am," she said, flipping back on top of him.

John then took off his shirt and she unbuttoned his pants. He kissed her again and said with his eyes half opened, "You smell like strawberries."

"A new shampoo," she whispered.

"I like it ... a lot."

He helped her with his pants. They looked into one another's eyes. "Are you going to take this tight, sexy, black thing off you or do I have to rip it off you?" he asked, as she sat on top of him.

"You just ruined my moment."

"I did?" he asked. "You're joking, right?"

"No. You just said something J.J. would've said."

"You'd better be joking." He placed his hands behind his head and looked up at her.

"No. You forgot about romance already. It looks like nothing is going to happen between us now. You said you were going to order food in."

"I knew it!" he said.

"Knew what?"

"You never liked Shedel being all touchy feely with you. He always had his hands all over you and you hated it." He pointed at her as he looked at her beautiful eyes looking back at him. "He fondled you in public and you couldn't stand him for it."

"It took you this long to realize—"

"Don't ever compare me to Shedel again." He smirked.

"Well, then you'll have to always please me first." She smiled at him, flashing her eyelashes.

"I knew it! He doesn't know how to please a woman."

"You will stop talking about him, right now. Or, or, nothing is going to happen between us."

"I'll take it off you ... slowly," he said as he sat and wrapped his hands around her shoulder blades.

He slid the straps down off her shoulders, first the left and then the right and pulled her arms through gently as the front fell slowly. He gradually pulled the garment down her straight, smooth legs to her ankles. She gently kicked it to the floor. He placed his head back to the pillow behind him. Steadily, she slid on top of him. Again, he sat and kissed her chest while lightly rubbing her shoulders.

"I want to make love to you right now," he whispered. "I can't restrain myself any longer."

"Do you?" she whispered, placing her hands on his chest.

"Yes, baby. I do." Her breasts touched his chest as they kissed again.

"Now what are you going to do to me?" she asked him, after noticing he had seen her goose bumps.

He grabbed the pillow, removed the pillowcase, and wrapped it around her upper torso. She set her arms down and the pillowcase remained tightly in place.

"Do you have cigarettes in your shirt pocket?" she asked him.

"You wanna wear my shirt instead of the pillowcase?"

"Do you have cigarettes in your shirt?" she asked again.

"I'll quit first thing tomorrow," he told her.

"Maybe, I'd like one afterward," she told him.

"Do we need protection?" He reached for his pants.

Grabbing his hand she said, "I'm protected. Is the door locked?"

"The door is bolted shut," he told her.

He adjusted himself as she sat on top of him, "Are you ready?" His voice was low.

"Yes," she whispered.

He penetrated her, and she moaned in delight. Their bodies moved so slowly together and when joined they knew their insides were perfectly matched.

"Talk to me," she said. "Tell me *your* fantasies?" She leaned back in her sitting position as their hands united.

"I'm going to tell you ... all the things ... I've always wanted to tell you."

Gabrielle moaned with pleasure.

"I will love you always. I have never stopped loving you." He then paused.

"Don't stop talking to me," she said.

"This is so hard to do, you know? Talk and make love to you at the same time—" He couldn't continue.

"I like when you talk to me. You feel so good. Don't stop moving." She moaned.

"You feel so real," he told her.

"I am real." She moved her body with his.

He opened his eyes. "You're so beautiful." He watched her. "So perfect."

"Tell me ... more." She kept her eyes closed. "Tell me your fantasies?" she asked him.

"You. You're my fantasy, and if I'm dreaming—"

"You're not. We're here together, making love. You feel so good. Promise me—"

"Anything baby. Anything you want."

"I only want you forever."

"I promise you, baby. Oh God. Oh, Gabrielle, slow down baby. You, you are going to make me—explode," he then whispered.

"Explode for me," she whispered, and stopped moving her body.

She was about to lean down and kiss his lips when he said, "Don't move. I can feel you wanting more."

After a while, they opened their eyes together. "I love you," John told her, with tears in his eyes. "I always have and always will. Can I keep you forever?"

"I won't die again. I promise." She began to cry.

He sat and held her, as their bodies remained joined as one.

THEY LAID IN each other's arms talking playfully. John tickled Gabrielle under the sheets.

He ordered fresh fruit along with dinner delivered to her bedroom immediately. After a knock on the door, John stood quickly, took the tray from the butler's hands, said "Thank you" by rushing his words, and ran back into bed, placing a strawberry into her mouth.

"These are the best strawberries," he announced.

"Mmmhmm," she mumbled.

"And the best cherries." He placed one in his mouth. As she kissed him, she pulled the stem from his lips with her teeth.

They loved one another's company and it felt so right for both of them to be together and find one another again.

Suddenly she said, "John, I want something from you."

"I've lost count. I already gave it to you, how many times?" He laughed as he poured her a glass of the bubbly non-alcoholic champagne. "But I will take your glass and if you want to—"

"No silly. I want something different from you this time."

"I'll give you anything you want," he whispered. "I'll even fondle you in front of Shedel tomorrow."

"John!" She laughed. "I don't recall you ever, I mean *ever* writing a song for me?"

"What?"

"You have never written a song about the way you feel about me. The way we feel about each other."

"You're joking, right?"

"No. J.J. wrote at least a hundred songs about me. A lot of them were sexual, but you, darling have never written a song about us. Not even one."

"I wrote songs about you. When you were in a coma, the day we were engaged for the first time, when we got married—" he pointed to her

"—and after you died, that's all I did was write songs about you. Oh yeah, I wrote a whole bunch of 'em."

"You never sang any to me."

"Sure I did."

"Well, if you did? Of course, I don't remember. No, I don't think you've written any songs about me, and I do think there's a guitar J.J. bought for me under this bed."

"All right, you got me. I did write one song, only one about you."

"You did?" she asked, surprised.

He reached down and grabbed the guitar from under the bed. "This is a nice guitar."

"You can have it. I don't play." She giggled.

"Why would Shedel buy you a guitar?" He made sure it was tuned.

"So he could play while I sang and danced."

"No way. Shedel doesn't know how to play guitar. He doesn't know how to play drums real well, either."

"We're off the subject now of you singing this song you wrote for me."

"You don't have to dance for me," he said. "But, you better not laugh at me either. You have to promise you won't laugh."

"I promise. How bad can it be?"

"I can't think of the words or the chords." He sat there laughing with the acoustic guitar in his lap.

"I'm waiting," she said smiling and laughing with him.

"You promised you wouldn't laugh."

"You're laughing, therefore I'm laughing. Please sing it to me."

"I can't think of the words."

"You *are* going to write me a song one day soon."

"It's way too hard for me to do. There are no words to describe the way we feel about one another. Our love is way to powerful for any words written. Almost thirteen years later, and I think we have our proof that we are destined to be together. I did write many songs before for you when you were alive. I did."

"And this past year, since I've been back?"

"I've written one."

"Which one? Sing it to me."

"I can't think of the words," he told her laughing again.

"See. You never have, have you?"

"It's hard to write a song about the way you feel about someone and then record it and sing it in front of millions of people, knowing they know what this song is all about. Songs about us are sacred. I'd write one and then I'd throw it out for no one else but me to know I had written it."

She gave him a look as if she didn't believe him.

He said, "All right, I'll sing you one song. Oh, Gabrielle." He played the guitar. "Oh, Gabrielle, Oh, Gabrielle how I love the way you smell ... Oh, baby, my Gabrielle."

"Shut up, no more singing."

"No. Wait. Second verse. Oh, Gabrielle, Oh, Gabrielle I love the way your feet smell ... Oh, baby, my Gabrielle."

"You are done! You idiot." They were laughing so hard together they were crying.

He placed the guitar on the floor.

"Don't ever write a song about the way you feel about me or how I smell." She laughed as she kissed him.

"I don't know how you do it, but you always smell good and you taste so damn good." He kissed her lips. "And you always look incredible."

"Tell me, seriously—" she began.

"Oh no, the serious look," he joked.

"Your fairytale? You gave me mine when I was younger. I know you gave me the world. What about your fairytale? *Your* dreams? In your forty-two years did you get everything you ever wanted?"

"All I ever wanted was you, and before you, I only wanted to be a singer in a rock and roll band. You gave me a beautiful little girl, and you gave me a son."

"But, he wasn't your biological son."

"But, Rob is my son."

"I know what I can give you now," she told him.

"No. No. Jackie almost killed you, and with Rob, you were lucky. I can't lose you again. Don't even think about it."

"We'll talk more about it some other time." She smiled at him. "What else do you want?"

"I want to marry you again, tomorrow."

"Tomorrow?"

"Yes." He chuckled.

"What about today?" She laughed along with him.

"Today's too soon. We have to get to know one another better, go out on a few dates before tomorrow."

"What if we're not sexually compatible?"

"Now, that's one thing about you that hasn't changed."

"What's that?"

"Sex. That's all you ever thought about back then and it's all you ever think about now."

"That's not true!" They laughed together.

THEY WERE IN LOVE. They always would be.

All night, John stayed in her room and they wouldn't fall asleep. Not once, did he want to leave her and she didn't ask him to. When the morning came, he allowed her to sleep as he sat in bed beside her. He kissed her forehead, placed a pad of paper in his lap, and began to write a song—a song he knew they'd record together.

Jackie knocked on the door. "Mom, are you awake?" She entered. "Dad? Oh.My.God!"

"Cigarette?" he asked her.

"Dad?"

"Shhh, your mother is still sleeping."

"Wow! You and Mom, finally."

"What do you want, Jackie?"

"I want to borrow Mom's earrings." She snatched them from Gabrielle's vanity. "Took you long enough."

"Get." He pointed to the door.

John kneeled over Gabrielle and kissed the corner of her mouth. She turned over and he kissed her again. "I love you," he whispered.

"The door was bolted shut, huh?" she asked him.

"It was. Before the food came up," he whispered and she fell back asleep.

AS GABRIELLE READ THE SONG JOHN WROTE, she had tears in her eyes, or what John considered falling roses. She understood what had taken John so long to come back to her. Droplets of her tears fell onto the piece of paper. While attempting to wipe the drops away, she smeared the ink. She crawled back into bed and thought to read it again when the door opened and John entered the room.

"Good morning, baby," he said, then lay beside her. "It's actually the afternoon, so good afternoon, sweetheart."

"Good afternoon." They kissed.

"I wrote a song," John told her.

"It's not what I had expected," she replied.

"You wrecked it. You cried on it," he said, while looking at the paper.

"I understand now. I do."

"I'm sorry for not coming to you sooner."

"I love you more than you love me," she confirmed.

"That's what you think. But it's impossible." He kissed her passionately.

"Would you like to go to Bobbie's Place and record this? You and me?"

"It's personal. Is this a duet?"

"You couldn't tell?" He smiled at her. "I called my engineer, and he'll meet us there in a couple of hours. I'm going to carry you out of here in just a sheet, we're going to sing it together, and then I'm going to carry you back here and take the sheet from you."

"I can see now what the future holds for me."

"And what might that be?"

"A sheet."

He smirked. "Do you like the song?"

"Do you feel we can record it together?"

"It's so personal, I know. I think I can do it if you're there with me."

"Is it called Falling Roses?"

"No."

"Then what is it called?" she asked him, confused.

"Falling Roses."

"It's beautiful." A tear came from her eye.

"Falling roses," he then said to her and wiped the tears from her eyes.

"The song's beautiful," she told him again. "And there's no references to how I smell."

"I see there's some changes that already need to be made," John said.

"No. I love it just the way it is. If there were any changes, we'd figure it out when we sing it. Hum it for me?" she asked him.

"I'll sing it to you." John sat beside her and reached to the side of the bed where he had left the guitar standing. "You sing first." He looked at the piece of paper and sang her part. He continued singing and said, "We both sing this falling roses part. It should go something like this."

She sang with him. "It sounds wonderful, John."

"So does your voice, sweetheart." He then kissed her. "Go get some clothes on."

"No," she said sternly.

"Why not?"

"Because."

"Because why?" He smirked.

"There's something you have that I want," she said in a sexy tone of voice.

"And what might that be this time?"

"Come closer and I'll show you."

"It's bad luck to make love before you record a song together," he said, then kissed her.

"But *baby*." She kissed his neck.

"I have to go round up the guys. I don't know where Lenny is today. And, if I can't find Len, I'd have to ask Shedel to play drums."

"All right," she pouted. "Go. I'll get dressed."

"I can round up the guys after we make love." He straddled over her. "And after you eat. I brought up brunch." He leaped up from the bed and opened the door. He brought two trays into the room. "Breakfast in my right hand, lunch in my left."

"I'll take both," she said.

"How do you eat so much and gain so little?" He opened the covers of the trays and set them on the bed beside her. He placed a piece of bacon into her mouth and then the other half into his.

"Did you shower already?" she asked him.

"No. I've been waiting for you," he replied.

"Let's go," she said, as she kissed him quick.

"What about food?" He stood.

"I told you, I get nervous when I sing." John lifted her into his arms. The sheet came off before he brought her into the shower room.

GABRIELLE STOOD IN FRONT OF THE MIRROR fixing her makeup with John standing behind her blow-drying his and her hair.

"I have to keep some of my clothes in your room from now on," he talked loudly over the blow dryer.

"One of us needs to change rooms," she agreed.

"We need to choose another room together that'll fit all of our clothes. I'll be right back."

"Are you doing that now?" She laughed at him.

"No. I need clothes, though. There's a couple kids that wander the house sometimes, and there's one that'll be home from school soon."

She kissed him good-bye.

As he left, she sat in front of her vanity continuing to blow-dry her hair and humming *Falling Roses*.

John came to her room to get her, placed the lyrics in his pocket, walked downstairs into the foyer arm in arm with Gabrielle.

John opened the door.

A man with a child stood in front of them. He asked, "Is Kathryn here?"

PART TWO
~~

Are you a fantasy?
Are you here with me?
(Gabrielle)

I don't see you.
I don't believe in you.
But you're here with me.
(John)

I guess you're here, because
I can see you.
I know you're here,
You've cried on me
(John)

I guess you're here because,
You say you need me
I know you're here,
I can breathe you in,
(Gabrielle)

You tell me your real
But I pretend
(John)

Don't wake me up
Don't want this to end
(Gabrielle)

I've known I've hurt you
I've felt your tears
(John)

And all I can feel now
And all I can feel now
(John and Gabrielle)

I felt your Falling Roses.
Falling tears from your eyes.
I felt your Falling Roses.
And I believed when you cried.
I felt your Falling Roses.
Before you said good-bye
I never want to feel again.
(John)

Chapter 17

Gabrielle peered at the man with the girl in the doorway and then turned toward John.

John shrugged his shoulders.

"Katie, it's me," gasped the man. "Michael."

"Do you recognize him?" John asked Gabrielle, as he glanced at her and noticed she was suddenly pale.

"John?" She looked over her shoulder, and then at Michael standing behind the young girl with his hands on her shoulders. "Catch me."

"KATHRYN, LOVE! Wake up!" Michael yelled into her ear.

"Back off!" John shouted, as he carried Gabrielle to the sofa within the foyer and set her down gently. "Who are you?"

"I'm her husband."

"Not possible," John said. "If you married her twelve years ago, *I* was her husband. She was already married."

"She's my wife, Kathryn."

"Where's your proof?" John asked him.

He dug out a crumpled piece of paper, folded in fours, from his pants pocket, and handed it to John. John unfolded it. "She's our daughter, Chastity," Michael said.

"Hey, is she going to be all right?" Chastity asked John, while sitting next to Gabrielle.

Gabrielle began to come to, squinting to focus her eyes and managing a cotton-mouthed whisper, "John?"

"I'm here, baby." He went to her side. "Do you know who he is?" John asked her.

"No." Gabrielle sat, attempting to focus on something within the room.

Swiftly, John turned around. "Get out of my house!" He threw the paper at him. "Anyone can get a marriage license. Where's the document showing you were legally married?"

"I have pictures—" he reached inside his jacket "—Pictures don't lie."

"*Oh* yes, they do," said Gabrielle, trying to stand.

Swiftly, John pulled out his gun and aimed it at Michael's head.

"No! Daddy!" Chastity gasped.

"Slowly," John told Michael, sternly.

Michael pulled out his wallet and handed it to John.

Nonchalantly, John walked toward Gabrielle while viewing the pictures of a younger Michael. A nineteen-year-old Gabrielle wore a not-so-fancy wedding dress. Then a photo of Michael, a baby, and Gabrielle together, with Gabrielle holding the baby snugly in her arms. "I've seen this picture before," John said, showing her. "It's from a magazine article," he said, hiding the gun in its holster. "That's you, holding Jackie." With a hand on his gun, John turned around and said to Michael, "Don't come any closer."

"Are you sure?" Gabrielle asked John.

"Jackie would know," he said, placing a hand through his hair.

Gabrielle took a glance at the girl.

"You're my mother," she told her. "That's what my dad says."

"Do you remember him?" John asked Gabrielle again.

"No. I don't remember him or her." She swallowed hard, and her lips and mouth felt so dry. "Can you get me a glass of water? I need to take a pill. What happened to my purse?"

"I'm not leaving you alone." John picked up the receiver from a phone sitting on an end table and pressed a button.

Nervously, Melinda entered with a glass of water and handed it to John. Just as quickly as Melinda appeared, she disappeared behind the swinging door to the kitchen. John took Gabrielle's purse from the floor where she had dropped it when she fainted, and opened the bottle of her medication. He handed her a pill and she then motioned for a second one.

"How could I have had a daughter as Kathryn and not know about it?" Gabrielle asked herself, while studying Chastity's facial features. "Let me look at you? You are so precious." Gabrielle smiled at her. Chastity wore a sailor jumpsuit. The fashion for a six-year-old. Her black hair was in pigtails. "You have my hair color; but your face—Oh my God, you look just like Jackie."

"Who's Jackie?" Chastity asked her.

Gabrielle turned toward Michael who hadn't taken another step beyond the entryway. He was a grossly thin man, pale skin, with dark brown hair. His prescription lenses covered his dark-brown eyes. A thick moustache sat unevenly above his upper lip. The cuffs of his pants were stained and crusty with days' worth of dried mud; one of them was torn, and the other frayed.

"Get out of my house!" John then raised a fist.

Jackie was just about to walk in the door when John shoved Michael backward. She stepped aside as Michael came tumbling toward her and then fell onto the front porch. "Air mail," Jackie said.

John ushered her inside the house. "Now stay out!" he commanded, slamming the door closed. "Why aren't you in school?" John asked his daughter, fuming angry and red around the collar.

"School's out for the rest of the day, Dad." He gave her a blank look. "School's *over with* for the rest of the day. Look at the time. I thought it would be more educational if I—" Jackie viewed her mother sitting on the sofa. "Mom! What the hell is going on?"

Michael opened the door and let himself in announcing, "Kathryn is my wife!"

"No, she's not!" John yelled back. "And her name's not 'Kathryn'!"

"Is too!" Michael shouted.

"Is not!"

"Is too!"

"Is not!" John put up his fist again and was about ready to send Michael through the opened door.

Pop. Pop. Pop. Pop.

"Get down!" John yelled, scrambling to the floor.

Chastity screamed. Gabrielle crouched to the floor. Chastity crawled toward her father who lay on his back, shot multiple times.

"A man was just murdered in my foyer!" John yelled into his cell phone.

Ka Boom!

"His goddamn car just exploded in my driveway!" John yelled again, crawling toward the door to shut it.

"Mom, are you all right?" Jackie sat beside her on the marble floor. She was shaking almost as much as her mother. "Do you need a pill?"

Gabrielle's face was as white as a ghost. Even the color on her arms was pale. "I've already taken two," Gabrielle told her daughter. She was teary-eyed, trembling, and looked more weak and frail than Jackie had ever seen her.

John heard the shoes slapping from behind him. "Holy shit!" Rob said, crouching next to John. "It's like World War Three out there. Is he dead?" Rob looked at Michael where Chastity, Gabrielle, and Jackie were hovering over him. Chastity was crying and sobbing loudly for her father.

"Get over here, now!" John yelled into his phone. "Rob, go downstairs and get a gun for your mother and Jackie."

"Who's she?" Rob pointed at Chastity.

John threw him the key to the gun case. "Your other sister."

"Katie," Michael took another breath. "You screamed for me ... but I was too late. I couldn't take care of you." His body began to shake, blood drained from his mouth. Tears welled into his eyes as he gave Gabrielle one last look. He took his final breath. His eyes remained opened and Gabrielle shut his eyes with the palm of her hand.

SHE OPENED THE DOOR to his office. With each step, her heels clicked on the hardwood floor. He sat in his brown leather chair with his back facing her, and he gazed out the large window as she approached. She could see the smoke rising from his cigar. "Michael London is dead," Elizabeth Malone told him.

"And the girl?" he asked her.

Elizabeth was silent.

"And the girl?" he asked again.

"Still alive and in the house being protected by Rolando's men. But sir, why must we kill an innocent child? Chastity London is of no threat to us. My sister never knew Gabrielle Ravolie was pregnant."

"She's a Ravolie!" The man spun his chair around and slammed his fist down angrily on the large desk.

"And wasn't alive when Bernadette was!" Elizabeth reasoned.

He stood and stubbed his cigar. "You're right," he said calmly.

"Why should we waste our efforts on a thirteen year old girl, when it is Jackie Ravolie and J.J. Shedel who murdered my sister? They should be our first targets. Michael London was a waste of our time."

The man was silent, brooding, and contemplating.

"We had our chance at the Shedel wedding. And *he* blew it."

"Our goal is to have Johnny Ravolie suffer, Elizabeth."

"And killing a man that Johnny Ravolie didn't even know in his foyer and blowing up that stolen car on his lawn is not enough. That didn't cause Ravolie to suffer at all, and I'm not satisfied with just that."

Again, he was silent.

Elizabeth continued, "Who is this man that's going after Jackie Ravolie? Is he dependable? Does the girl even know who he is? How close is he to her?"

He wouldn't answer.

"Why won't you let me go? Who is more conniving than me?" She brought her mouth down to his ear and said, "I won't fail you."

GABRIELLE'S EYES JERKED OPENED. She heard the whistling, and looked over to see that she was in her bedroom. J.J. sat in a chair at the edge of the bed, facing her.

She sat in bed. "J.J.?" She felt her heart race, her throat begging for water, while her nerves trembled within her skin. J.J. merely stared at her.

It was an awkward silence, and Gabrielle didn't know when J.J. would speak or what he might say when he did.

She began, "John and I found each other again. He loves me, and you know how much I love him," she confessed. "He wrote a song about us, and we were going to Bobbie's Place to record it. Then, this man showed up unexpectedly at the house. Michael said we were married and that the girl he was with, was my daughter. The mob murdered him in the foyer. The car he drove blew up in the driveway."

J.J. stood and took the tissue box from the dresser and threw it at her lap.

"Don't need one," she said. "Where's my purse?"

He pointed to the nightstand, still silent with pain.

Gabrielle looked over her shoulder and noticed the bottle sitting there. She continued to tremble as she attempted to turn the lid. It dropped to the floor. "Sonofabitch," she groaned, removing the comforter and rolling out of bed. She got on her hands and knees on the hardwood floor, gathering the pills and putting them back in the bottle. She was trembling uncontrollably, and her hands shook as she placed the tiny pills back in their place.

J.J. crouched and handed her a few he had picked up as well.

"This Michael guy comes to the house and says he's my husband...." She rattled on as J.J. handed her another pill.

"How many pills have you taken?" he asked her.

"Don't remember." She gave out a fake laugh. "He's with a little girl who's thirteen years old named Chastity. What should I do?"

"You take a paternity test, which you've already done."

Gabrielle glanced at her forearm and noticed the Band-Aid.

He took the bottle from her, tightened the lid, and placed it back onto the nightstand. "No more of these," J.J. told her.

"What are the results?" she asked him.

"You were pregnant when you died," he said.

"What?" Her eyes widened. "Who?" was her next panicky question.

"Chastity *is* yours and Ravolie's."

"Who knew I was pregnant when I died?"

"Everyone."

"Well, I didn't. Why don't I know this? Why didn't anyone tell me?"

"We all forgot to mention it to you, I guess. At the time when you were dying, we all thought you wouldn't be bringing another child into the world.... Gabrielle ... Gabrielle."

"John?"

"No, it's me J.J. you're blacking out."

"I did have a baby. J.J., I remember having a baby. I have to call John." She closed her eyes, remembering. "I was screaming. It was a girl. As soon as I had her, she was taken from me." She opened her eyes and looked at J.J. "What if I did marry this Michael?"

"You didn't."

"He has a marriage license and pictures of us, married."

"They're fake. Jackie said so. Since Jackie didn't have one of the photos, she gave it to Roxy and she found no altercations. You did meet this man before."

"I need to call John." She looked around the room. Rapidly, she removed the pillows from the bed, scavenging for the cordless phone.

"You need to calm down," J.J. said.

"I need to remember Michael."

"Slowly. You need to remember these things gradually. You don't look good. Roxy gave me another set of pills. I'm so sick of you being used as a lab rat," he said, while she continued to search the bed by the headboard.

"What the hell did you do with the phone?"

"Nothin'. It's there by your foot."

On all fours, she turned her body and viewed the edge of the bed where the cordless phone lay half-hidden by the overturned comforter.

"Don't take any more of your usual pills today," J.J. told her. "Per Roxy's orders. You're dealing with 'New trauma now' she said."

"I don't need pills, damn it. I need the phone. Where's John?"

"Downstairs, on his cell phone," said J.J. "Sit," he ordered. J.J. walked over to the wet bar and filled a glass with water. He reached inside his pocket and took out a bottle.

"What are you doing?"

"I'm getting you your other pill," J.J. said. "It's a good thing Michael told Chastity everything about you. Another dose of Claycondine was what caused you to become a vegetable. Michael couldn't take care of you and brought you to that psychiatric hospital." J.J. sat down next to her on the bed, looking at her pitifully, as if he felt sorry for her. "Do you comprehend, Gabrielle, what you've been through?"

"I know what I've been through before I died, due to the first ten injections Roxy gave me. The pills *have* helped a great deal with the lightning bolts in my head. Every day I remember something new."

"Let's do a quick recap of your life as Gabrielle," J.J. said.

"Why?" she asked, annoyed.

He began anyway. "You were hit by a car, in a coma for two months, kidnapped, your ear was cut open with a knife, in which that tape—"

"Tape?"

"Let me finish. Bernadette taped it and sent it to John and I watched it many years ago."

"Does John still have the tape?"

"What the hell? You wanna watch it? Gabrielle—you're messed up and don't even realize how screwed up you really are."

"I think I like it better when you sit and stare at me—and when you called me Bobbie," she groaned.

"You were raped by three fuckers who were then killed in front of you. At Bobbie's Place, another asshole had his brains splattered all over you. Ravolie's van blew up and threw you to the ground while you were in labor. Do you remember that yet?"

"No."

"Good. Don't *try* to remember that. Don't *try* to remember anything else. Let the memories come naturally."

"Why shouldn't I *try* to remember?"

"Because—look at you. You are gonna crash hard if you remember all this shit too fast. You're gonna end up being a mute. You're gonna end up being back in that psychiatric hospital in a coma, reliving the past of a house blowing up with your babies inside it or somethin' even worse."

"Are you done recapping?"

"No. You were buried alive in a coffin."

"At last—" she threw up her hands "—I'm dead."

"But you're not," J.J. added. "You're just stripped of all these horrible memories."

"And the good ones, too," she reminded him as she gazed down into her lap.

He handed her the glass of ice water. "You've been eating those damn pills Roxy gave you like candy, Gabrielle. And now the bitch gives you another set to deal with more trauma in your life—" he handed her a flat, round, blue pill "—you had a baby stolen from you, you were a prostitute, and you spent over a year with Michael who took care of you before taking you to a hypnotist who was then murdered beside you.

"Someone else came in the room while you were under hypnosis, but you woke up screaming for Michael. When he got in the room, it was too late. Claycondine already passed into your veins and you looked dead. Michael strangled the man who did that to you. That's where these little blue pills come in."

He continued, "You were a breathing vegetable by then, and Michael couldn't take care of you. So, he admitted you to that psychiatric hospital. Do you even know how many times you blacked out today?"

John opened the door. "Hi, sweetheart. Sorry. I wanted to be here when you woke up. I just had a few phone calls to make, since we're not gonna make the duet. What's wrong? What's with the angry look on your face?" He got into bed beside her and slipped an arm behind her head, while J.J. still sat on the other side with his back facing John.

"We've been recapping my life as Gabrielle *and* Kathryn," she told John.

"I left him alone with you for five minutes, I swear." He glared at J.J. "What's wrong with you, Shedel? Don't you know when to stop?"

Gabrielle laughed. "He doesn't do too well, John. When I'm sickly, he turns evil. I remember when I had Rob." Gabrielle laughed insanely again. "You gnawed at me, 'Is he my son?'" she mocked her husband.

J.J. and John looked at one another with eyebrows raised.

"I don't gnaw," J.J. groaned.

"Is it true, John?" Gabrielle asked.

"Is what true, baby?"

"We have another daughter?"

John gave J.J. a dirty look, wrinkling his brow, and pursing his lip, and his skin began to turn flaring red again like it had when Michael came to the door.

JOHN RAVOLIE arranged the funeral for Michael London, after Chastity begged that her father have a suitable burial. John just couldn't resist her pleas. He felt so sorry for her loss.

Members of Ra'vole, Intensity, Mace, Camelot, and Divide attended the cemetery for the proper lowering of the casket. Close to thirty men concealed guns, knives, special radios, pagers, and cell phones within the pockets and compartments of their black and gray suits.

After faking Gabrielle's death, the mob sold Gabrielle to the Morris's for $30,000 Australian dollars. Never dying in a plane crash, Reverend Richard K. Morris and his wife Hailey stole the baby girl, before reentering America. In Australia, the home that Katie had the baby in didn't even belong to the Morris's. It was an abandoned home that was scheduled for demolition two weeks after she had the baby. Until she met Michael, Katie lived on the streets for a year, if one could call it living.

Sometime after Michael admitted Kathryn into the psychiatric hospital in New York for special care, Michael's detective who had searched for Katie's stolen baby for over a year had found the Morris's, who were now calling themselves 'Rev. Richard Kane' and 'Hanna Kane'. They were living in a small town on the outskirts of Georgia when Michael London stole Katie's daughter back from the family that had unjustly adopted her. Chastity was two years old when Michael found and rescued her from the kidnappers.

After Chastity told the story she knew, John had his people find the Kane's. Within twenty-four hours, the Kane's were under arrest by local police and brought to the closest jail.

The State of New York filed formal charges against the Kane's, indicting them on felony charges of kidnapping, as well as misdemeanor charges of unlawful restraint, which violated Gabrielle's right to be free from cruel, inhuman, and degrading treatment. Charges in Australia ranged from a secret method of coercion to obtain Gabrielle's consent, to denying her of all legal rights and snatching her newborn baby while she was still in labor.

Michael and Chastity had been running from the mob for the past ten years. Before meeting Katie, Michael was a boat mechanic, enabling him the opportunity to steal a boat belonging to Jeffrey Rolando. He also taught part-time as a History professor at the local college. For twelve evenings, he had picked up a prostitute in the boat he had borrowed from Jeffrey Rolando without permission. He didn't even know Jeffrey Rolando, but almost lost his life in a yacht explosion eleven-and-a-half years ago that was meant to kill Rolando. A case of mistaken identity with a horrible outcome for Katie and Michael.

Michael London missed Katie, and had read the recent articles in the paper that his Kathryn was actually Gabrielle Ravolie. He found out where she was living and took Chastity home. This life running from the mob was a cruel, punishing one. He had barely any money. It took thousands to continue to move, change vehicles, claim new identities for both himself and Katie's child that he was now raising and trying desperately to protect. As soon as the mob found out Michael's new place of employment or Chastity's new identity in a new school, they were on the run again—and Michael had to carry around the guilt that it was all because he borrowed or stole a boat to spend time with the woman he loved. Until reading the headlines, Michael never knew why the mob was after Katie, or her baby. However, the mob was after Michael for killing one of their men.

For the past ten months, Gabrielle Ravolie, a.k.a. Kathryn Lyn Morris, had been in the public eye. Headlines of tabloid newspapers read: *'Gabrielle's Alive!'* or *'Gabrielle's Getting Married, But Not to Johnny!'* There were articles written in major newspapers around the world. Articles written in well-known magazines, which reminisced the love story between Johnny and Bobbie and refreshed their readers' memories of how John had saved her from a coma and now, how her daughter Jacqueline Marie had found her. The print media and Internet were overwhelmed with pictures from long ago. It wasn't too difficult for Michael to find some to alter for the day when he knew he needed them.

He raised Chastity as if she was his own daughter, never married, and since he truly loved Katie, he imprisoned his life to protecting her daughter.

For some unknown reason, instead of calling the local authorities, John phoned Jeffrey Rolando to clean up the mess—he commissioned him to get rid of Michael's dead body and the metal scraps on his lawn. Rolando was completely accommodating. He did blame himself for not acting fast enough when Bernadette had abducted John and Gabrielle on the Fourth of July, thirteen years ago.

John and Gabrielle's decision was to keep Chastity as close to them as possible and safe within the walls of the Ravolie Estate.

Outside the mansion, Rolando's men were in position all day and throughout the night. Three guards were at the gate. Four heavily armed men were on the roof. Absolutely no one was allowed in or out of the estate, or on the grounds when nightfall came. Within a day, John had all forty-seven windows of the house removed and replaced with bulletproof glass, and the locks were all changed with new keys given only to a few of the trustworthy staff.

John and Gabrielle decided they didn't want anyone new within their home. There were enough people on the grounds installing video cameras or an electric fence where the woods met the lawn. John thought immediately about the horses and had them removed from the property. Animals were always Bernadette's first targets. John feared that he would lose Skippy and Malaysia.

Since this mob was following in Bernadette Malone's footsteps Jeffrey used the help of his wife, Roxanne. She was more than gracious to provide any information that she could. Roxanne Rococo Rolando continued to blame herself for Gabrielle's amnesia. Bernadette had injected Roxanne with Claycondine many years ago as well, however Roxy had taken anti-clayco to prevent the amnesia. If only, she had administered it to Gabrielle when they were both safe and out of harm's way, but she didn't. And she wasn't sure why.

Gabrielle and John knew Michael London was a good man. Gabrielle remembered they had never been officially married, but Michael had taken care of her. He gave her herbs and vitamins repeatedly to help her combat her memory loss in the safest way he knew and could afford. She remembered the day Michael took her to a hypnotist. The next thing she remembered was Michael taking her to Long Island Hospital. He cried. And, he kissed her good-bye on the lips while he sobbed. After telling Katie that he loved her, his last words were, "I'll find your baby girl," he whispered in her ear. "I'll find her, and I'll take care of her."

JOHN AND GABRIELLE walked with arms around each other down the hall to John's room, the master bedroom. He pulled the covers down allowing Gabrielle to lay there. He walked around the bed to lay beside her. She turned to face him. They stared into each other's eyes. He placed an arm around her and she snuggled the side of her face into his chest.

"Hold me. Just hold me, John. Don't ever let me go," she murmured.

"I won't, sweetheart. I'll never let you go again." He kissed her head.

"I'm sorry we couldn't make the duet together. I wanted to go."

That was three days ago, John thought. "Don't worry, baby. We can do it some other time," he told her, realizing her sleeping pills were kicking in.

"I love you. I love you so much. We've found one another again and we have proof that we have another daughter together," she told him.

"I know. Don't cry."

"That means, John, that we can have more babies together." She looked up at him.

"And we're gonna have a lot of fun trying," John told her, kissing her forehead.

Gabrielle smirked. "Just when I feel safe, we happen to be in danger—again. This is insane. Why does this keep happening to us? Why can't I have the fairytale that I've always wanted without all the red roses with thorns spoiling it?"

All Gabrielle wanted was to be safe and secure for the rest of her life. At last, John realized that it was never about the material things. John said, "I guess when two people are meant to be, there are obstacles they have to face together, but in the end there's nothing that'll keep us apart."

"John, the mob is going to come after Chastity, and Jackie, and you and me. Then they're going to go after Robbie and J.J."

"Look at me." Gabrielle held onto his shirt. Crying heavily, she could barely breathe. "Look at me," John said again.

"I can't John. I'm so frightened."

"I'll protect you. I'm here and there are guards outside the house. No one will hurt our children or us. You have to believe me. Do you trust me?"

"Yes, you're the only one I do trust."

"Okay, then. Rolando will do what he has to do to protect us. He'll take good care of us, okay?"

"No he won't," Gabrielle said with a giggle of disgust.

"You're right, he won't." John chuckled. "But I will. I'll keep you safe. *My* men are out there, too. Lots of them. Do you believe me?"

"Yes, I believe you."

"As long as no one shatters my knee cap again, I'll be able to keep you safe." He attempted to joke, but she didn't laugh. "Will you please stop crying?" he asked her.

She yawned

As her eyes remained closed, John wiped her tears with his thumbs and forefingers. He kissed her lips. "Goodnight, Gabrielle," he whispered. Already, she had cried herself to sleep. He held her all night while he lay awake. John realized *he* didn't feel safe. But he had to pretend to be brave and unrelenting for the sake of his three children and Gabrielle. Fear was not an option. And, he'd never make the same mistakes again. This time, he would protect his family. He decided to stay awake all night to watch over Gabrielle. He loved watching her sleep. When the night ended and she had made it safely to morning, he took one of her sleeping pills and fell asleep in the arms of the woman he loved.

Chapter 18

August First
Two Months Later

At Bobbie's Place, everyone listened to the final cut of *Falling Roses*.

I felt your Falling Roses.
(You felt my falling roses.)
Falling tears from your/my eyes.
I felt your Falling Roses.
(You felt my falling roses.)
I believed when you cried.
(You believed when I cried.)
And I felt your Falling Roses.
(You felt my falling roses.)
Before (I never meant to say) I said good-bye.
You never want to feel again.   (Gabrielle)

I know you're here
I can see   (John)

We'll be happy again
You'll see   (Gabrielle)

I love you, Gabrielle   (John whispers)

At last, Gabrielle and John had the chance to make their duet together. J.J., Chastity, and Jackie stood, along with the rest of Intensity, to watch and listen as Ra'vole recorded the song, which was the tale of how Gabrielle's death had changed John's life. He had raised two kids, and was never really the same after he lost her. The lively rock-and-roll tune had a life of its own, even though there were painful verses about John's refusal to believe Gabrielle had returned. John knew when he wrote it that *Falling*

Roses would reach single men who had lost their wives or raised children on their own and that it would give a hope and a new meaning of finding true happiness with the one that you loved.

IT ONLY TOOK John and Gabrielle four takes to record the song to their satisfaction. *Falling Roses* was then mixed and recorded by Dillon, an old friend and co-worker of John and Gabrielle's. After the final cut was finished playing over the speakers throughout Bobbie's Place, everyone applauded. John and Gabrielle kissed one another publicly, paying little attention to the fact that J.J. could view them.

Gabrielle walked away from John. She exited the studio and entered the hall.

"Hi," Seth said, stopping her. "Your birthday is coming up in a couple of weeks, isn't it? How old are you going to be? Twenty-one?"

"I'll be thirty-three," Gabrielle said, smiling and blushing a little with his obvious compliment. "I hate the number three," she whispered in his ear, nudging him with an elbow. "What'd you think of the song?" she asked with eyebrows raised.

"Sounds good, real good. I have a question for you."

"If it's about J.—?"

"No. No. Can we go someplace private, though?"

"Private?" she asked him, looking into the hallway.

"In one of the offices?" he asked her.

"Hold on," she said. "Let me tell John, okay?"

"Yeah, sure." He waited patiently.

Gabrielle walked back into the studio and did a double-take at Lenny. Everyone was laughing at him, which was par for the course for the clown that he was. The tips of Lenny's drumsticks were hanging by his nostrils while he tied his shoes.

Gabrielle laughed hysterically while she attempted to tell John, "Seth ... wants to ... talk to me ... about somethin'. I'll be ... right back." She kissed him.

"Don't be away too long—" John laughed "—we have to open the champagne."

She giggled, while glancing at Lenny and then noticing the extravagant bottle of grape juice John had sitting beside him on a stool.

"Chas?" Lenny called out to her. "Can you help me? I have something stuck ... up my nose."

Gabrielle giggled again, shaking her head at Lenny's silliness as she pushed on the glass door and into the hall where Seth waited. "Lenny's so juvenile, but that's why I love him," she told Seth.

Seth led her into an unoccupied office space. "Maybe you should sit," he told Gabrielle.

"Okay." She sat in the desk chair with one leg over the other. "I'm sitting."

"John and I have been friends for almost twenty years." Gabrielle smiled at Seth waiting for him to continue. "How do I ask you this? I can't ask John. He might rip my head off. I'm thirty-six years old, and I know there are laws. She'll be seventeen."

"Woah! Hold on! Hold on! Nooo," she contemplated while shaking her head back and forth.

"You were young too, when you married John," he defended himself.

"Marriage?" Gabrielle looked around the room in a panic for something to fan herself with. "John's ten years older than me. Ten!" she raised her voice, while opening a desk drawer, finding an empty file folder.

"I know. But you know me. I'm a good guy. Can I please take Jackie out tonight?" Seth asked her.

She fanned herself. "She's too young, Seth." Gabrielle sucked in air. "You're older than her mother."

"But, I'm not older than her father. I won't do anything to her. I don't want to break her heart. You know me, Bobbie. John knows me. You know, I'd never hurt her."

In the hall, Jackie and Chastity passed the room. Gabrielle noticed through the glass window, Chastity waving to them and she waved back, with a fake enthusiastic expression on her face. "Have you and Jackie talked about this?" She blinked and looked at Seth who seemed to be sweating at the brow.

"We talked earlier about doing something. I know how she's into pictures and I have some from the old days that I said she could look through and if she wanted some she could have 'em. Bobbie, I like talking to your daughter. She's very mature for her age. I just thought we'd spend some time together, that's all. If you don't trust me, trust your daughter."

"I do trust Jackie. But I still have to talk to John about this. She's his daughter too, you know."

As if on cue, they heard the two knocks and John opened the office door. "I brought the champagne in here for you," he said to Gabrielle, and placed two plastic glasses on the desk. Beginning to pour he asked Seth, "What's up?"

"I'd like to take your daughter home with me tonight," Seth said.

"To look at old pictures," Gabrielle added quickly.

"If you touch a hair on her head, I'll break you in half."

It was *that* easy? Gabrielle asked herself.

"I won't touch her. I won't hurt her. You know me."

"Pick her up at seven," John said.

"Seven," Seth repeated. "What time do you want her home?"

"Eight," John and Gabrielle said together.

"HOW ARE WE supposed to eat dinner and look at pictures in one hour, Mom?"

"No, Jackie," Gabrielle said.

"*Please?*" she pleaded.

"Ten thirty," Gabrielle said, trying to be reasonable in spite of the wincing she could see John doing out of the corner of her eye.

"Twelve, Mom?"

"No later than one. You hear me?" John pointed at Seth.

"Mom, Dad, thank you so much," Jackie said then kissed her father on the cheek. Seth accompanied her to the café for lunch, not glancing back at her parents.

"One a.m.?" Gabrielle asked John, placing an arm around his waist.

"Nothing's gonna happen," John confirmed. "He knows better."

JACKIE PUT ON HER BEST DRESS. She wore a deep-red satin strapless dress and satin shoes to match. Seth arrived in the circular drive and rang the bell. John shooed away Frank, the butler, and opened the door instead.

John looked at his watch. "You're ten minutes early," he told Seth.

Jackie walked down the stairwell gracefully.

"I feel like I'm taking her to prom," Seth uttered.

"She looks so beautiful—so much older. Don't you go getting any ideas," John said, pointing a finger at him.

Seth helped Jackie into his old, beat-up van. Since there were tinted windows and no back seats, Jackie knew this van was in use for mob dealings or to hide Seth's rock-star identity. Seth was like her father; he didn't drive around in extravagant cars, or wear expensive clothes when he wasn't in the spotlight, even though he could have afforded it. While Seth placed the van in drive and encircled the driveway Jackie asked, "Where are we going first?"

"How about dinner?"

"Oh good, I'm starving," she said. "My stomach's growling."

"What stomach?" Seth asked. "You're so skinny."

"Is that good or bad?"

"Ah, it's good. You're the thinnest girl I've been out with."

"No, I'm not," she said with an eye roll.

"Yeah, you are."

"What about that Nicole chick, you were going out with?"

"That Nicole chick was a dumb broad. I wish I never laid eyes on her. We never dated. I just went to a few places with her."

"Just like you've been to a few places with me?"

"No, you're different, very different. She was seeing other guys, and you're not."

"Maybe, I am."

"No, you're not."

"How do you know?"

"A certain someone told me."

"Who?" she asked.

"He would like to remain anonymous."

"Who told you?"

"Robbie," he answered.

"My brother? What else did he say?"

"Nothing."

"I don't believe you."

"I could never lie to you. Plus, your father would kill me if I hurt you. He even told me he would split me in half, and I believe him."

"My dad told you that?"

"Yes."

"I'm embarrassed." She noticed her leg having a spasm.

"Why should you be?" he asked. "Parents are parents."

"Nevermind," she replied.

"No, tell me?" he asked her.

"No, why should I?" she joked.

"I don't know." He sighed.

Not another word was said until they arrived at the restaurant. The van ride made it more than clear just how uncomfortable they were with each other. *Let's talk more about my parents.*

Jackie started to open the door and Seth said, "Wait, close the door." He skirted the front of the van and opened the door for her. He picked her up out of her seat and placed her feet to the ground. She stared at him and his eyes melted with hers for a moment.

Jackie felt tingly, but she tried to hide her feelings.

They walked side by side into the restaurant and sat at a square table in the back of the room, which had a red rose in a vase at the center of the small table. "The rose is for you," Seth said.

She took it from the vase and placed it up to her nose. "I've never been here before."

"It's nice, isn't it?"

"Dark and romantic," she conveyed.

"I use to come here all the time."

"Oh," Jackie said with a sad expression on her face.

"No, not with a girlfriend. My mother, when I was sixteen. She taught me how to dance on that very dance floor. Would you like to dance?"

SETH REALIZED how close he was holding her to his body, and noticed people were staring at them. He looked like her father. He was old enough to be her father. But Jackie held tight to him, too. She was captivated by the thought they were there on a date. She hadn't grasped the people who were staring and really didn't care anyway. After the slow song ended Seth asked, "Why don't we go back to the table?"

"Okay," she said.

Again, there was an awkward silence. Seth decided to ask, "So, how did school go?"

"Good. Real good. I got straight A's."

"Are you going to go to college?"

"Most likely. After, I graduate."

Seth looked around the room and noticed people still looking and whispering.

Jackie then looked around the room, and finally noticed the same. "Do you think they recognize you?" Jackie asked him. "Or do you think they recognize me?"

"They think I'm too old for you. Come on, Jackie. Let's face it. I care about you. I care about you a lot. If I were to marry anyone, it probably would be you. I feel sickened with myself to feel this way toward you. I feel like a pervert."

"There's nothing wrong with you caring about me," she said annoyed.

"Yeah there is, Jackie. Wake up. Look around you. Society doesn't see a sixteen-year-old and a thirty six-year-old having a relationship. Society sees us together right now as child molestation."

"No, Seth. I think you see it this way. You haven't touched me or laid a hand on me. We're friends. You're J.J.'s best friend and he's practically a father to me. Now that I think about it, he's still my stepfather. I think maybe you should stop worrying about what other people think, because nothing has happened between us. Hell, if something did, I wonder how guilty you would feel then."

"Come on, Jackie. Let's get out of here."
"We haven't even ordered yet."

"LET'S GO." He stood and walked away from the table and she had only one choice, which was to follow, leaving the red rose on purpose in the vase. They walked to the van and Seth unlocked the door for her and went around to the other side. She opened the door and jumped up to sit while he turned the ignition.

"Are you going to take me home now?" she asked him.

"Is this what you want?"

"Is this what you want?" she asked in rebuttal.

"No." He paused and then decided to give her a compliment. "Your hair smells good."

"Thank you." After averting her eyes, she looked out her window into the dark.

"You use the same shampoo as your mother?" he asked her.

"Do you not like it?" *Why are we comparing my hair to my mother's?*

"Would you like to come back to my place?" he asked her.

"Sure." Tears started to flutter into her eyes. "How do you feel about me?"

"What do you mean?"

"How do you feel about me?" Jackie asked again.

"I already told you."

"No you didn't."

"I care about you too much. I shouldn't."

"What's wrong with caring about me?"

"There's nothing wrong with caring about you," Seth said. "It's wrong of me to care about someone as young as you are."

"I don't understand."

"I love you, Jacqueline. There, I said it."

"What?"

"I love you. I think you're beautiful and intelligent for your age. I love you. I know you feel the same way about me."

"Because *Rob* told you?"

"No, because of the way you are when you're around me. You're shy; you tremble."

"I do not."

"Yeah, you do."

"When? When have I trembled?"

"At J.J.'s and your mother's wedding," he said. "When the two of us were dancing. You were shaking, the whole time. I felt it. A man as old as me can tell these things. I walked away from you, because I wanted to be with you. I wanted to take you home with me."

"Instead you took Nicole home with you?"

"Yes, I did."

"And you slept with her?"

"Maybe." Now, he looked guilty, and knew with those words he had hurt her. They then pulled into his driveway and Seth opened the garage door with his remote control.

"Well?" He opened his door and removed himself from the vehicle to walk around to the other side and he was going to open the door for her, but she rolled down the window instead.

"Well, what?" She smiled at him.

He walked away from the van and unlocked the door entering into his home. "You've never been to my house before. Do you want to come in?"

"Is Nicole here?" she half-joked, half-snapped.

"No." He laughed at the question as he pushed the door open. Jackie opened the door to the van and followed him into the house.

"I'll turn on the radio." He then walked over to his stereo and pressed play on his CD player. "I would like to dance with you now," he said to her.

"Since no one is watching," she added.

She walked up to him and draped her arms over his shoulders. He clasped his hands behind her back and his breath was warm against her ear. He did make her tremble, as her whole body tingled. And then her stomach growled loudly.

"I told you I was hungry."

HE PLACED HIS KEY into the keyhole and turned, and the key shattered. "Damn thing," Rob said, then rang the doorbell.

He waited.

He rang the bell again.

Frank appeared wearing his flannel pajamas. "Hi Rob, what are you doing here?"

"Looking for Jack. Is she around?"

"No. She went out with Mr. Edilson."

"Seth Edilson?" Rob asked wide-eyed.

"They were going to dinner and then back to his house to look at some old photos or something," Frank said, walking away.

"Are Mom and Dad here?" Rob asked.

"They went back to Bobbie's Place after I packaged up some fruit."

Rob chuckled. "Okay then. I have nothing better to do on a Friday night, I'll just make myself at home."

"What was for dinner?"

"Steak," Frank said, disappearing into his hidden room beside the foyer.

"I'll think about it," Rob said. He was about to walk up the stairs to his old bedroom when he heard a phone ring. He looked around the foyer and noticed that John had left his cell phone on the curio table. He answered the way John always did. "Talk."

"Can you hear me?" the woman's muffled voice asked.

"Yes, I can hear you."

"It's Seth."

"Seth?" Rob asked.

"He's going to kill Jackie."

"What?" Rob asked.

"Keep her away from Seth," the voice said, and then the call ended.

Rob threw the phone down on the table and ran the stairs into the basement.

"NOW, THAT'S AN OLD ONE," Seth told her as he took a bite into his sausage pizza.

"Is that me playing J.J.'s drums?" Jackie asked, while lying on her stomach on the pullout bed.

"Yeah. You had to've been six," Seth said. "You want another piece?" he asked, grabbing a slice from the box.

"No thanks. I'm full."

"Jackie?" Seth placed a hand on the album and closed it. He looked into her eyes.

"No more pictures?" she asked.

"You can take the album with you," he told her. He picked up the pizza box and moved it to the coffee table. Again, he lay beside her with a hand holding up his head. He looked into her eyes. "Do you want me to make love to you?"

She didn't answer.

"We've never even kissed each other and here I am asking you if you want me to make love to you—"

"I'm a virgin." She placed her lips close to his and he reached out for hers.

"That's nice," he said. The doorbell rang. "Who could that be?"

"Do you have to answer it?" she asked him in a mere whisper.

"Yeah, I should." He slid the album toward her. "I'll be right back." She smiled.

He walked up the creaky stairs to the front door and yelled to Jackie, "Hey, it's Robbie!"

"Rob?" she questioned. She heard the door open.

"Hey, man," Rob said. "Is my sister here?"

"Yeah, she's downstairs," Seth said.

Quickly, Rob jogged down the stairs.

"What are you doing here?" Jackie asked him.

"You wouldn't believe it if I told you. But, I'm here to take you home."

"Home?"

"Yeah."

"What's goin' on, Robbie?" Seth asked.

"Dad will tell you tomorrow, but for now I have to take Jackie home."

"I have until one. What's wrong, Rob?"

"Now, Jackie!" he raised his voice.

She grabbed her purse and stood from the futon. She could see the terror in Rob's eyes. "See you tomorrow," she said to Seth.

"Do you want to take the album?" Seth asked her.

"Tomorrow," she replied, looking longingly into Rob's eyes.

While behind her, Rob shuffled Jackie out the door. He opened the door of his mother's Tuscan, and Jackie got in quickly.

"Are you going to tell me what's going on?" Jackie asked when Rob sat behind the wheel.

"We're going to the beach house, and I'll tell you there."

"The beach house?" she asked him.

"You look incredible, by the way."

"Thanks. But tell me now—"

"I went to your house, I was in the foyer, and I heard a phone ring. Dad left his phone there. Mom and Dad went to Bobbie's Place." Rob shifted gears. "I answered Dad's phone and a woman said that Seth was going to kill you."

"What?"

Rob looked out the side mirror to see if anyone was following them. "I couldn't believe it either. This doesn't make any sense. Tonight's the first night you've ever been to Seth's and this woman calls and says he's going to kill you. Now she didn't say he was going to kill you tonight, but I brought a few guns with us just in case."

"This is insane!" Jackie said, pulling her hair down. "Why are we going to the beach house?"

"Because if he is after you, he'd go toward your house or mine and he'd be able to get in. He wouldn't think we'd be going to the beach house and—"

"Good thinking. But, I don't believe it Rob. I don't believe Seth would try to kill me or you or Mom or anyone."

"We'll stay at the beach house tonight and go home in the morning."

"Let me try Mom's cell phone."

"I've already left her a message."

"Did you say we were going to the beach house?"

"No. I just said that we both were safe and we'd call tomorrow morning. I talked to my dad and told him that you and I were goin' out tonight and we'd be out until morning."

"Good idea," Jackie said.

"He was upset that we didn't have bodyguards with us, but I'm so sick of not having any freedom."

"I agree. Since Seth is one of Dad's men, he didn't make me go with someone else. See, I don't get it. Dad trusts him. We all trust him. If you didn't show up, Seth and I might've had sex."

"What? Are you crazy, Jackie?"

They pulled up into the driveway at the beach house and Rob pressed the remote for the garage. He pulled the Tuscan in and closed the door.

"ARE THINGS GOOD between you and Shedel?" John asked Gabrielle.

"Yes. Why?"

"He hasn't aggravated you, has he?"

"No," she replied as she took off her shirt in front of him. He helped to lift her shirt over her head.

"Turn around. I want to look at your butt in those tight jeans you're wearing."

"Do you want to look at my butt with my jeans off?"

"*Mmmhmm,*" he murmured.

She unbuttoned her pants as her back was facing him and he sat at the edge of the bed.

"Take it off nice and slow," he told her.

She began to wiggle slowly and provocatively out of her jeans as he watched. "I need to sit down to take these things off." She laughed as her jeans were at her ankles. She turned to face him, tripped, and fell onto his body.

John placed his hands through her hair. His right hand trailed to her mouth. She wrapped her lips around his finger and he slowly pulled it out of her mouth. "I want you, baby," he told her as he pulled her body forward and he leaned back. She kissed his neck and his chest, then moved her tongue and lips to his navel, and began to unbutton his pants with her teeth.

"How much do you want me?" she asked, looking up at him.

"You know how much I want you." He took her hand and placed it to where she could feel she had aroused him. She crawled on top of him as he held her head close to his lips.

"Can I be on top tonight?" he asked her.

"You can be on top and on bottom, backwards—" she kissed him "—inside-out, upside-down or any direction you want to be. As long as you please me and I know you will."

"You know I will," he told her.

"Just make it quick," she snapped. "I'm tired and want to go to sleep."

He smirked. "I'm tired and want to go to sleep too, but I'm going to make love to you first."

"Can I just lay here and do nothing while you make love to my body?" she asked him.

He took her limp arm and shook it gently. "Will you let me do anything to your limp body?"

"Anything you want," she said.

"Ooh, I like the sound of this," he whispered. John shut the lamp off and they made love before they fell asleep in one another's arms.

Chapter 19

"Nice outfit," John said to her, as she climbed through the bedroom window.

"Thanks," she said, pulling the mask up over the bottom of her face.

"I've gotta say, you were pretty good out there. Are you wearing tabi boots?" he questioned with a grimace.

She rubbed her head and shook out her shoulder-length sandy blond hair. "Tabi boots make it easier for me to climb ropes and scale walls."

"Whatever turns you on, babe."

"I wanted to look more like a ninja, okay. I wanted to wear a shinobi shozoko."

"Instead he sends you as a cat burglar, I understand. Did you have to use your commando warfare tactics on the dogs?" John asked her.

"I just gave them a slight concussion." She sat on the bed beside him.

"He's not going after my horses, is he?"

"Not even a twinkle in his demented, pea-size brain."

"Good. What'd you bring me?"

She tugged on the zipper between her breasts as John watched her reach inside to pull out two, 3 ½" x 5" books and reached them forward to show him.

"Damn, those are small," John said.

"I told you they were."

"I was talking about your breasts." John smirked.

ROB FLIPPED THROUGH CHANNELS.

Jackie walked in front of him with a T-shirt and shorts in hand. "Can you help me with my zipper?"

He unzipped her partway, down to mid-back, and she wandered off to change behind the partition. "Shut off the TV," she told him. "We need to talk about this." She continued undressing and talking to him from behind the dressing wall. "You don't think Seth would come after me, do you?"

He pressed the power button. "Did he do anything weird with you tonight? Anything to scare you?"

"No. Seth was being Seth. Only in a different sort of way."

"What do you mean?" Rob asked her.

"Nothing, really."

"Come on. We have no secrets between us. What happened between you and Seth?"

"Nothing. We had a shitty time at this restaurant. It sucked."

"How so?" Rob asked.

"We were dancing, and I thought people were staring at us just thinking, 'How cute—a father and daughter dancing'. But Seth was convinced they were staring at us due to our age difference, and it bugged him that they were thinking about him like some child molester, I guess. We never even ordered dinner—we just left." She appeared from behind the partition in the T-shirt and shorts. "He took me back to his place where he ordered us a pizza and we looked at those old pictures like he had promised. He told me that he *loved* me."

"What?" Rob asked, making himself comfortable on the sofa as he stared at her strangely.

Jackie couldn't tell if it was a stare of disbelief or partial disgust. "That was odd, I guess," Jackie said. She sat, lifted her legs, and then lay back, using Rob's chest as a pillow.

"So now, it's making perfect sense," Rob said.

"What is?" Jackie asked, looking over her shoulder.

"He was going to force himself on you and then, afterward, when you were off your guard, he was going to kill you."

"Rob, you're scaring the livin' crap out of me. You think he'd kill me in his house even after he asked my parents if he could take me out? It just doesn't make any sense. Everyone knew I was going out with him tonight. This wasn't a secret."

"Not everyone," Rob said, peering down at her. "I didn't know."

"You weren't at Bobbie's Place today," Jackie told him

THE PHONE WAS RINGING.

Gabrielle rolled over. "John, sweetheart. The phone." She turned the knob to the lamp, looked beside her at the empty space, and crumpled covers. John wasn't in bed. "Hello?" she answered.

"Gabrielle it's me, Roxy. What's going on?"

"What do you mean, 'What's going on?'"

"What's happening? I haven't heard anything."

Gabrielle looked at the wall clock, twelve-thirty. "Roxy you woke me up. What's going on?"

"Jeffrey found out that someone is going after Chastity tonight."

"What?" Gabrielle asked, shocked. She sat in bed wide awake now.

"The last I heard, someone was there on your property," Roxy told her. "They have the dogs involved looking for this man."

"Oh my God." Gabrielle dropped the phone, opened the door to the bedroom, and ran out into the hall.

She came across Jackie's room and slammed open the door and flipped the switch. Jackie wasn't in her bed.

She ran down the hall screaming, "Chastity!"

"OH, SHE'S AWAKE," she said, donning her mask.

"She knows, too," John said, hiding the books in the nightstand drawer.

"I'll see you in a week," she said with one leg out the window. "Love you," she whispered.

"Be careful," he told her.

The door slammed open. "Oh my God, John!" Gabrielle shouted. "What's going on?"

"It's okay." With a gun in his hand, he comforted her. "It's okay."

"YOU THINK MOM and Dad are home from having their elevator picnic?" Jackie asked Rob.

"Maybe," Rob said, reaching for his cell phone. He dialed John's number.

"Talk," John answered.

"You're not going to believe this," Rob said.

"We've got some trouble here at the house," John told him. "You and Jackie together?"

"Yeah," Rob said.

"Don't come home, and call me in the morning."

"Sounds good," Rob said and ended the call. "Dad says there's some trouble at the house," he told Jackie. "He doesn't want us coming back there tonight."

"Seth?" Jackie asked.

"He didn't say." She was quiet as her head rested on his chest and she looked up at the ceiling. "You okay?" Rob asked her.

"Yeah. I'm just thinking."

"Me too," he said.

"About what?" she asked him.

"You."

"I wouldn't've had sex with him, if that's what you're thinkin'."

"Oh, I know you wouldn't have," Rob said reassuringly. "I know you better than you think."

"Thank you," she said.

"For what?"

"For coming for me when you did." She turned her body to the side.

"You have no idea what was goin' through my mind." Rob admitted, "I thought you were dead already."

She tilted her head back. Her mouth was an inch from his. She pecked his bottom lip with a childish kiss. "Thank you," she said again.

"Anytime."

JOHN OPENED THE DOOR, and Gabrielle peered into the bedroom where Chastity slept. Nick Mace sat beside her in a loveseat with his feet reclined.

"See, she's fine," John said.

"Have you heard anything?" Nick asked them.

"No. The last I heard, someone's still out there," John said. "There's only one though, so I know we'll find him or he'll leave. He can't get into the house. There's only one-way in and one-way out," John reminded Nick.

They heard someone in the hall walking toward the room. Mick appeared and said, "He's gone. He ran into the forest and just vanished. Even the dogs couldn't sniff him out."

"Are Shedel and Seth still on the roof?" John asked him.

"Yeah," Mick said.

"Have Shedel come on down," John ordered. "I need to talk to him." Mick left the room. "Nick, I want you on the roof."

"What about Chastity?" he asked.

"We're going to stay here for a while," John told him.

Gabrielle kissed Chastity's forehead. "I love you," she whispered to her sleeping daughter.

"SO, WHAT SHOULD WE DO?" Rob asked her. "Play charades?"

"No." Jackie yawned. "I'm too tired."

"You want me to carry you to bed?" he asked her.

"I'm comfortable right here," she said, giving him a slight squeeze.

"I'll bring you upstairs," he told her. He then picked her up and carried her up the stairs into one of the bedrooms. He set her down on the king-size waterbed.

He pulled the T-shirt over his head and unbuttoned his jeans.

"You're sleeping in here with me, right?" Jackie asked him.

"You want me to?" he asked, placing the guns in the drawer of the nightstand.

"I don't want to sleep alone. I feel stupid, but I don't think I'd be able to sleep if you slept in the other room and left me in here all by myself."

He stripped to his boxers and said, "Move over, then." He lay on his side behind her and draped an arm around her torso.

She lifted the comforter over their bodies. "What is that hard thing poking me in the—" she half-whispered as she reached for him.

"HEY." J.J. entered the bedroom to find Gabrielle asleep in John's lap on the loveseat.

"Hey, man," John said. "I heard from Rob. I think he and Jackie are at the beach house."

"That's what I was thinkin'," J.J. said.

"Don't tell anyone where they are, okay?"

"I won't. Did you get what you needed?" J.J. asked John.

"I have a lot of reading material," John said.

"Good."

"What'd Seth say?" John asked him.

"Rob stormed into the house, fear in his eyes, and told Jackie that she had to leave with him. Jackie didn't ask any questions, and they left in a hurry."

"Good," John said.

"They'll be home by morning," J.J. said.

"Shit. Tell Trevor and Brandon to check the cars. Mine's not in the garage, and I bet—"

"I'm out of here," J.J. said, leaving the room quickly.

"ROB, I'M SO SORRY," she said with a laugh. "I'm sorry. Come back to bed."

Standing at the edge of the bed embarrassed, Robbie Shedel looked to the floor and scratched his head.

"It was just so hard—"

"Shut up, Jackie."

"I thought it was a gun." She laughed again. "Seriously."

"A gun, huh?" He jumped into the bed. "How would you like me to squeeze your tits and say, I thought they were pillows or cantaloupes?" With both hands, he grabbed her, squeezing her breasts. She laughed loudly. And as he poked and tickled her, she squirmed underneath him. He held her wrists above her head as she lay on her back. He looked at her with some strands of her hair in her face. She blew a strand of hair out of her mouth and wore a huge smile.

They stared into one another's eyes, their smiling eyes fading into curious, wanton gazes.

"Shit," Rob said, then leaned down to place his mouth to hers.

They kissed a deep, passionate kiss and he released her wrists to slide his hands over her arms and her breasts. "God. I can't help it. I want you, Jackie," he said with his voice shaking with desire. He lifted the T-shirt up and over her head, and then kissed her neck and gently began to nibble her cleavage. He slid her shorts down her smooth, tan legs and over her knees. She lifted a leg, allowing him to pull her shorts down to her ankle. She lay looking up at him in a cherry-red bra and panties. He straddled her. "Please stop me now if you don't want to do this."

"I want to," she said softly, her eyes barely open.

"There's no turning back," he said.

"I want to," she said again.

"Are you sure you want to do this?" he asked again.

"Yes. I love you, Robbie, and I know you truly love me," she said passionately.

He kissed her neck, nibbled her earlobe, and traced her cleavage again with his lips. He set his hands gently on her small hips.

"Are you sure? Are you sure you want me to make love to you?" he asked.

"Yes. I want you to make love to me. I want you," she confirmed again in a longing whisper.

He took off her bra and Jackie realized she felt naked and embarrassed. They were in the dark, yet after his eyes had time to adjust to the moonlight he would see her small and undeveloped breasts. She knew how many women Rob had been with, and how could she compare to them? He knew that she was inexperienced. She didn't know if her body would please him, since he had been with older women before, grown women who knew what they were doing and had the bodies to do it with.

"Well, what do you think?" she asked him as she lay in front of him in the nude awaiting his approval.

"About what?" he asked, then smiled at her.

"My body. What do you think about my body? Am I too fat?"

"Fat?" He chuckled. "I've never been with anyone so beautiful before. Your skin is so smooth, your lips are moist, your breasts are real and your nipples—" he placed his mouth and his tongue to her left breast "—they're perfect," he said to her. "You, Jacqueline Ravolie are perfect. You're the woman of my dreams." He kissed every inch of her body where no boy or man had touched or caressed before. He kissed her inner thigh and she knew where his mouth would venture next.

Her breathing deepened. She wanted more as she placed her hands within the blond strands of his hair. He tickled her purest essence with his tongue. She felt her whole body quiver in pleasure as the rush of contentment went into the pit of her stomach. Then, the heat enveloped her abdomen.

"Wow," she said, her body shaking uncontrollably. "That was incredible."

"Tell me about it," he said, breathing deeply.

"Can we do that again?" she asked him in a mere whisper, as she held tight to his moist back, while feeling his hard abdominal muscles against her body.

"After." He smiled down at her.

DAWN

KA BOOM!

Gabrielle's eyes opened, and she felt John sitting behind her awaking also to the loud blast.

Chastity sat up in bed. "What was that?" she asked, confused.

"My car," John mumbled sleepily. "They blew up my car."

"Well, at least they didn't try to kill you in it," Chastity said.

"I better make sure no one was in it. Christ, what if—"

Gabrielle stood rapidly, and John ran from the room. "We'd better go. C'mon!" Gabrielle said, grabbing Chastity's hand, and they followed quickly behind him down the stairs.

Melinda stopped her. "Cup of coffee, Miss Gabrielle?"

She glanced inside the cup and noticed creamer was used. "Not milk?"

"Soy," Miss Melinda said.

"Thank you." Gabrielle smiled and walked outside.

Many were standing around looking at the smoldering tires and shattered glass. The staff already had begun to pick up the pieces. The doors of John's midnight Chevy Corvette convertible were imploded from the blast and the trunk was unidentifiable.

Gabrielle picked up the waterfall emblem from the front stoop. It had been dismantled from its affixation to the console of John's beautiful car.

John argued with Trevor and Brandon, "I thought you checked my car last night!"

"I did. We did," Trevor said, standing next to Brandon Jones.

"And?" John waited for the answer.

"We noticed a timer bomb dead center on the underbelly of the car. We pushed your car farther away from the house."

"You couldn't disarm the bomb?" John asked. "You two know more about bombs than you do about music."

Trevor argued, "If you noticed that it only had one minute, would you disarm the bomb or move the car quickly away from the house?"

"What do you mean?" John asked.

"We didn't know when it was going to blow. It had a timer bomb on it, but it showed one minute. That was five hours ago. We figured the safest thing was just to move it away from everyone, but honestly, even that was risky for us. It could have blown us into bits any minute."

"As soon as we pick up all the pieces we're going to see if it has a photo-electric switch," Brandon said. "That would mean—"

Trevor interrupted, "The bomb was designated to go off as soon as enough daylight hit it."

"Due to the photo-electric switches," Brandon added, "the bomb was disabled all night, although a timer had to have activated the circuit."

"Do you think you can find the timer in this rubble?" John asked them.

Trevor and Brandon began to search the grounds, rummaging frantically through the debris.

John placed a hand over his face, peeked through his fingers for one last glance at what was left of his car, and shook his head.

ROB AND JACKIE pulled up in the Tuscan. Jackie ran out of the car toward her father. "What happened, Dad?"

"No one got hurt," John said. "There was someone on the grounds last night and he got close enough to place a bomb under my car."

"Was it Seth?" Jackie asked.

"What?" John asked her.

Rob began, "I answered your phone yesterday. A woman called saying that Seth was going to kill Jackie."

John told them, "After you left Seth's house, he called Shedel, Shedel called me, and then I got a call from Rolando tellin' me someone was on the grounds. Everyone came here. Seth is on the roof now with Shedel. My sources told me that someone was after Chastity. I guess it's a good thing you answered that call, because then I would have left the house. Someone was out there and it wasn't Seth. The dogs were following a trail and two of them almost lost their lives. Where'd you go last night?"

"Beach house," they said together.

"Thought so."

"Let's go in the house," John said, placing an arm around each of them.

"I'm going to go upstairs and shower and change," Jackie said. "Are you sure, Dad? Are you sure Seth isn't trying to kill me?"

"Positive. Rolando was sure the mob was after Chastity last night. Why would someone call my phone and give me an anonymous tip that one of my men is going to kill my daughter?" He answered his own question, "The phone call was from someone to deter me away from the house. That has to be it. I've known Seth for seventeen years, baby. He's been here all night helping the family. He hasn't slept. Before you shower, why don't you go bring him up a hot cup of coffee."

"Shower, then change," she said, while walking away.

She then went to her room where her mother was sitting on her bed watching the early morning news.

"Mom, what are you doing in here?"

"Waiting for you. How was your date with Seth?"

"It sucked."

"Seth's the reason why you've never dated anyone recently, isn't he?"

"Yes," Jackie lied.

"I could tell you love him. But, you're confused, because he's twenty years older than you are, and you don't know when you're going to see him again, since he's a rock star. And, he could be cheating on you—rock stars are notorious for that."

"Mom, it's like you can read my mind."

"I married your father once, remember? What are mothers for?"

"Mothers aren't supposed to know everything."

"This mother is. Jackie, you two, did something, last night?"

"What kind of 'Something'?"

"You know?"

"What?" Jackie asked concerned.

"Sex."

"No Mom. Seth didn't say we had—?"

"It's written all over your face. I'm not mad. I knew it was going to happen."

"Then why'd you let me go?"

"You were begging. I didn't want to break your heart. Plus, if I told you, you wouldn't have listened to me. It was your decision and I'm sure you made the responsible choice. Come here." Gabrielle then hugged her daughter tightly. "I love you, sweetheart. Did you lose your virginity to him?"

"I love you too, Mom," Jackie replied, not answering her question.

"Why don't you get something comfortable to wear and I'll tuck you in. It looks like you haven't slept."

"I haven't," she said. "Mom?"

"Yes, sweetheart?"

"Why does it hurt so much?"

"He's older."

Gabrielle then left the room and went into another. Gabrielle smiled, as she looked at her other daughter who was sleeping peacefully. Gabrielle then walked into the bedroom she shared with John. He sat in bed reading a small green book. "What you reading?" Gabrielle asked him.

"Some old book I pulled from the shelf."

"Did Rob drive Jackie home?" Gabrielle asked him.

"Yeah. They were at the beach house all night."

"I'm glad."

"Rob picked up my phone last night and a woman said that Seth was going to kill Jackie. He freaked out and took her away to the beach house," John said.

"She didn't sleep at all last night. I'm going to go tuck her in. Would you like to come with me?"

"Did she and Seth?"

"Yes."

"No way. I'm going to kill him."

"John."

"I know, I know. We're ten years apart and they're twenty years apart. I've known this guy for seventeen years and he's not going to hurt her. I just don't want him to be my future son-in-law, though."

"It appears she's not happy with herself since she slept with him. Maybe, it's because she thought he was going to kill her."

"I can't deal with this right now, Gabrielle. She's my little girl."

"The truth is John, I don't think she lost her virginity to him. If it makes you feel any better about the situation."

"Jackie's *not* a virgin?"

"Well, for sure not after last night."

"He told me he wasn't going to hurt her."

"And, he didn't," Gabrielle replied.

"He told me he wasn't going to touch her," John said. "I'm gonna run to the roof and punch the livin'—"

"What if your baby came on to him?" Gabrielle asked John.

"She is a little provocative, isn't she?"

"Come on, let's go say goodnight to our daughter?"

They walked through the hall into Jackie's room. Gabrielle kissed Jackie on her forehead and then John did the same. She was already sound asleep. John and Gabrielle left the room with their arms around one another.

"She is one beautiful little girl," Gabrielle said.

"It's because she looks just like her gorgeous mother," John told her.

"I love you, John."

"I love you too, Gabrielle." They walked into their room together.

NOON

QUIETLY, HE ENTERED HER BEDROOM where she slept peacefully. He knelt beside her and touched her face gently. She opened her eyes to see him watching her. "Seth's not out to kill you," Rob said. "He was worried about us last night."

"That's good to know," Jackie said.

"I have to go home with my dad."

"Will you come back later?" Jackie asked him.

"I thought you'd never ask," he said, smiling and brushing the hair away from her cheek.

Chapter 20

Midnight

"Shh, someone's going to hear us," he said.

"I can't help it," she giggled. "This is too much fun."

"We're going to get caught if you're not quiet," he whispered.

She covered her mouth with her hand.

John took Gabrielle's other hand in his and they jogged down the stairwell.

Frank, the butler, was still awake in his bedroom watching television with the door slightly ajar. "Who's there?" he hollered loudly.

"Just me," John said.

"And me." Gabrielle giggled. "We're just—"

"Going to look at the stars," John said with a laugh. He opened the front door.

Barefoot and in just her panties and bra, Gabrielle ran out the front door and toward the fountain in the center of the circular drive. John ran after her in just his boxer shorts.

She quickly jumped in, managing to not even make a splash. A little more cautiously, John jumped up on the base and attempted to tiptoe into the heated pool.

Immediately, two spotlights shined onto the water and the rectangular base, creating a bright reflection from the fountain that blinded Gabrielle and John.

Laughing, they both went to their knees and placed their backs up against the inside of the fountain's base. Suddenly, the water came dancing out from the walls. The majestic fountain lit up in bright shades of pink, blue, purple, and green from the bulbs surrounding it.

"Show yourselves, or I'll shoot," the gruff and angry voice said through the megaphone.

IN THE DARK, they sat together in the shallow end of the heated outdoor pool. She had wrapped her legs around his waist. He tilted his head and kissed her, then tilted his head the other way and kissed her lips again.

With their bodies joined, they bobbed slowly, rhythmically, and romantically together.

"Have I told you yet ... that I love you?" Jackie asked Rob.

"Your body's telling me. Hold me tighter if you need to. I want to be so deep inside of you. I want to be closer to you than anyone will ever be—"

"I'll never let anyone else into my heart," she whispered in his ear.

"Neither will I," he said.

She began to breathe deeply. She arched her back, with her arms resting on his shoulders, and her hands clasped at the base of his neck. "Go deeper," she whispered.

She leaned forward again; her eyes were barely open when he kissed her mouth.

"I love you." His voice was low.

"I love you," she muttered through a deep breath.

With another move, he climaxed within her, and the two moaned in pleasurable ecstasy together.

JOHN BACKED AWAY from the wall. On his knees, he turned to face the house. He held his hands above his head. "Don't shoot!" he yelled. "It's me, Ravolie!"

"Who're you with?" the man asked.

"Gabrielle!" John shouted.

"Mrs. Shedel, show yourself."

She blushed, with a smile so wide, laughing hysterically under her breath. She lifted an arm above the base for the man on the roof to see, and then she gave a slight backward wave.

"How do I know for sure that it's you?" the voice asked.

"Come out here with me and show yourself," John said.

"I'm only wearing a bra and panties, John. I'm not moving from this spot."

"Show yourself," the voice said again. "And I'm not sure I believe you're Ravolie, so don't make any sudden movements."

"That's one of Rolando's men," John said. "If you don't show yourself, he's going to start shooting at the fountain."

"No—"

"She'll be right out!" John yelled and began to pull her arm.

Bullets hit the water.

"It's me, Gabrielle!" she screamed. Next to John, she held her hands above her and stood in the thigh-high water, showing her half-naked body to the men on the roof.

HAND IN HAND, they walked through the rose garden.

"What was that?" Jackie said, hearing the shooting. She grabbed Rob's hand and the two ran into the house, immediately noticing Frank and Melinda looking out the windows in the foyer.

"What's going on?" Rob asked Frank, finding a spot beside him.

He chuckled. "Your mother and father attempted to go for a swim and were busted in the fountain."

"Oh my God. Are you serious?" Jackie laughed. And found a spot next to Melinda to look outside, too.

Chastity came running down the stairs. "What's going on?"

"Mom and Dad are skinny dippin' in the fountain," Jackie told her.

"Nooo."

"I caught them leaving," Frank said. "The sharp-shooter on the roof doesn't believe who they say they are and is giving them quite the runaround."

"They're going to get themselves killed," Jackie said, tossing Rob a concerned glance.

"Well, I'm not going out there to identify them," Frank added.

"I'll go to the roof," Rob said.

"DON'T MOVE. Step out of the water so that we can make a clear identification."

"You've got to be kidding me!" Now she was angry. While getting to her knees, she looked up into the air and yelled, "I'm not showing you my body again!"

Now, John was laughing.

"I'm sorry for the interruption. As you were," the voice said. The two spotlights were turned off.

She turned around to face John. She was red-faced with embarrassment and a touch of anger. "You couldn't just get into the water quickly, like I did." She splashed him. "You always have to be the slow-poke."

"Slow-poke?" he questioned, laughing.

As he walked backward, she moved forward on her knees, splashing him, until he was up against the wall where a beam of water splashed his head harshly.

Gabrielle laughed.

He moved away quickly and grabbed her hands. "How would you like to get it in the head?"

"No!"—her laughter hysterical—"No!"

THE NEXT DAY

THE THREE WOMEN in the hallway intensely watched Seth Edilson through the glass windows of the engineer's room of Studio B. Their backs faced the glass wall of the café.

The dark haired women watched the two slender, longhaired blond bimbos with Seth. The groupies were hugging him and one, he kissed, a small peck on the lips. *Bastard,* thought Gabrielle. With Jackie in the middle, Gabrielle stood on her right and Chastity on her left. As if on cue, Gabrielle crossed her arms, then Jackie, then Chastity.

"Should we kill the bastard now or later?" Gabrielle asked her daughters.

"Jackie," Chastity said. "It may not be all as it seems. Why don't you speak to him?"

"What should I say to him?" Jackie asked her sister and her mother.

Chastity answered, "Just say 'Hi' or 'Hello, Seth. What are you going to do today'?"

"That's lame," Jackie said. "He's here at Bobbie's Place. Intensity is renting out Studio B. I'll use my common sense and ask a sensible question."

"But men are so stupid. Even a stupid hello always works on them," said Gabrielle. "And then kick him in the balls."

JACKIE GAINED ENOUGH COURAGE to open the glass doors of the engineer's office. The room was equipped with soundboards and a glass window to view the rest of the band members inside the studio room.

"Hi, Seth. What are you doing today?"

"Hi, sweetheart." He kissed her on the cheek. "Jane and Judy, this is my one and only true love, Jacqueline Marie Ravolie."

"Jackie will do," she said.

"Hi, Jackie," Jane said.

"We've heard a lot about you," Judy said.

"Why don't you girls go talk to the others? J.J. is desperate; go bother him."

Jane and Judy then walked away and entered the sound proof doors into the studio.

"Hi," Seth said, gazing right at Jackie.

"Hi," she replied, not knowing what else to say to him. She felt uncomfortable again. Not knowing how to say the many things she wanted to tell him. *First off, I don't want to see you anymore. I don't feel the same way about you. I'm in love with my brother.*

"Would you like to move into a private room and talk? I'm not embarrassed to be with you. Not here. We can talk here, if you want." She just shrugged her shoulders. "What's wrong, Jackie? What happened?"

"No, I had something in my eye." A teardrop fell. "I think it's almost gone." Her voice cracked.

"You make a terrible liar. Come on, let's go into the other room." They went into an office and Seth closed the blinds to its window. "Tell me, what's wrong? Did I hurt you? Is this about the other night at my house? I was going to call you yesterday, but I slept all day and I assumed you were sleeping in, too."

"I did," she said. "I did sleep for most of the day," she admitted. *Until Rob came, and we made love in the pool.*

"What's wrong?"

"Well, I don't know how to explain this," she mumbled. "It's, um, it's, I—I was—" *Shit.*

"You were what?" Seth asked her. "I hurt you, didn't I? What did I do to hurt you? Please tell me? I'm so sorry. But I need to know what I did, so I don't do it again. I was rude. I was rude the other night. I'll take you somewhere special soon. When we make love for the first time, it'll be perfect."

"I thought ... just." *I don't want to have sex with you, ever!*

"You thought, what? Jackie, look at me." He tilted her chin. "You can tell me anything. We don't have to be uncomfortable with one another."

"I know. I've never really felt awkward. Jane and Judy? I saw you kiss Jane, and it offended me. I feel so ridiculous. Our kiss was a dream come true for me but seeing you with Jane, now I feel like ours was just a one-night thing. Was it, Seth? After the other night, if you don't love me? If our kiss wasn't good enough for you? Please, just tell me. Yes, I'll be hurt, but I'll live."

"Jackie, come here." He then hugged her like a father would his daughter. "Sweetheart, I know there are a million things running through your mind. I want you to look at me when I tell you this. Come on, look at me. I'm in love with you. You are beautiful. You're everything I want and love. I'm not uncomfortable anymore, because I know how you feel about me, and you know now how I feel about you. I'm in love with you,

Jacqueline. When you turn eighteen, in one year, I would marry you. That's if you'll have me. Did I mention Jane and Judy are my cousins?"

"Your, what?"

"Jane and Judy are my cousins."

Shit. Shit. Shit. "Here I am getting jealous of you kissing your cousin." She laughed.

"I thought it was pretty cute," he said.

"Why didn't you tell me?"

"I didn't realize why you were upset. Come here, sit."

She sat on his lap. *Just get me out of this room.*

"What's going through your mind?"

I feel like a child on Santa's lap. "I'm unsure now. Whatever it was has now—disappeared. Jane and Judy bothered me, a little. What was going through your mind? We should be honest with one another. Right?"

"I thought you were breaking up with me, because your mom or John told you that you should because of our ages. I thought you thought I didn't want to be with you anymore. And then J.J. told me that you thought I was going to kill you—"

"Are Jane and Judy twins?"

"Yes." He smirked. "They are." Seth then kissed her cheek. He then kissed her lips, a soft gentle kiss. "I have something for you." He reached into his pocket. "It's my ring. I wear it all the time."

"Was this your class ring from high school? No, I couldn't."

"I want you to have it." He slipped it on her middle finger.

They heard a knock on the door, and Gabrielle walked in. "Did you tell him he was a bastard? Did you kick him in the balls?"

"No, Mom," she said blushing and embarrassed.

"Is everything all right?" she then asked.

"Fine, Mom," Jackie said.

"The band needs you, Seth."

"Tell them I'll be out in a minute. I'm talking with my favorite girl."

"Okay. I'll tell them." Gabrielle then left the room.

"Seth?"

"Yes?"

"My mother thinks we had sex the other night and I kind of said we did."

"You, what?"

Jackie jumped off his lap. "Thanks for the ring."

"YOU TWO need to get the hell out of there," she said into his ear.

"I'm not leaving my home," John said into his phone.

"Leave the place empty. Maybe we should blow it up."

"You're not going to blow up my house!" John said, angrily.

"We need to blow up something," she told him.

"What about this convention?" John asked her.

"The Rolandos will be there," she said.

"So, we tell them," John said.

The phone went dead.

GABRIELLE BEGAN, "Can I ask you something?"

"Of course," John said in a whisper.

"How do you know when a man truly loves a woman?"

"He can taste her. That's how I knew I loved you. I could taste you and yearned to taste you when I thought I had lost you. So, if a man doesn't yearn to taste a woman—"

"So, now what?" she interrupted.

"We wait."

"Wait for what? Wait for them to kill us, or us to kill them? We're in a ditch, John. It's four o'clock in the morning and we're full of mud."

"You need to add some to your face," John told her. "Seriously, like this." He added a stripe of mud on both of his cheeks.

"I will not," Gabrielle said.

"Then *I* will do it for you." He placed mud on both sides of her cheeks, her forehead, and her nose. "Follow me."

"What is this supposed to do?" she asked, crawling on her elbows and knees beside him.

"Not sure," John said, "but we look good."

"How can you have a sense of humor at a time like this." They heard the helicopter.

"Get down," he said, pushing her into the water. "Don't make any quick movements," he told her. Their bodies were below the murky water of the retention pond, and their faces were above the mud.

"We've been through worse and we're not going to die," John said.

"How do you know?" she asked him.

"You've already died once before and I'm a rock star—" She smirked. "—Rock stars only die in planes or in bathtubs. Helicopter's gone. Let's go."

Gabrielle rolled to her stomach and crawled next to John to the grass.

He handed her the gun. "The safety's on," he said.

"Thanks."

He took her hand and they ran toward the barn. Quickly, John lifted the wooden lock and they hid themselves inside. The stench of the stable went unnoticed under the hay that was stuck to their camouflage clothes.

"Just great," Gabrielle said.

THE NEXT MORNING

"HELLO?" Jackie answered.

"Good morning, sweetheart."

"Seth?" she asked.

"Who else would it be?"

"It's six-thirty in the morning," she said.

"Yeah, I know. How about going swimming?"

"How about you let me sleep?" she asked.

"Don't you want to be with me?" Seth asked her.

Hell no. "Of course I do," she said.

"Okay, get your bikini on and let's go swimming. I'll be right over."

"Men," she remarked. Jackie found her bathing suit hanging in her closet and placed it on with a T-shirt over it, and jean shorts, and walked downstairs. She told Melinda who had already begun the morning dusting in the foyer to tell her parents she was going swimming with Seth Edilson and she didn't have time to write them a note.

"At six-thirty in the morning?" Melinda asked.

"Seth wants to," she replied.

Just then, John stomped into the foyer from the back entryway, followed by Gabrielle. They wore green camouflage outfits—pants and shirts—encrusted with mud and hay. Their faces were muddy; their hair was thick with goop.

"What happened to you two?" Jackie asked loudly and in shock.

"You didn't see us," John said, still walking and tracking mud through the foyer.

"This was your father's idea of a secret late night rendezvous," Gabrielle told her, tracking mud behind her. They walked up the stairwell leaving a trail of filthy footprints with each step.

WHEN SETH ARRIVED, Jackie hopped into his van, kissed his cheek, and placed her head on his shoulder. "Where are we going?"

"To the beach house," Seth said. "Do you have a key?"

"No. But we can still swim. Wake me when we get there." She placed the side of her face on his right thigh. Seth placed his hand on her back. Then he began to stroke her hair.

"What are you doing down there?" he asked her.

"Sleeping," she mumbled.

"Oh," Seth said. "You know, these jeans I'm wearing are tight around my waist. Do you think you can loosen them for me?"

"Yeah, sure," she moaned. Jackie took her left hand and unbuttoned his pants then pulled on the zipper a tad. She knew exactly what was on his mind and knew precisely what he was after, but changed the subject suddenly. "Seth, you're so thin; you're like a toothpick," she said to him. "How could these possibly be tight on you?"

"They're old. These shorts are tight around my fat legs."

"Seth, you don't have any fat on your body. It's all muscle," she reminded him.

"Oh, is that what you call it?"

"Hello. Look at my legs." Then she tried to remove her head from his thigh, but the steering wheel was right above her head and she realized she was stuck.

"What about your beautiful, long legs?" Her legs were bent, with her feet in the air and he placed a hand on her butt, as she struggled to slide her head out from underneath the wheel.

"That's fat," she said, attempting not to let him notice she was indeed stuck. She gave up trying to slide her head out and thought it was time to tell him, "Seth, I'm stuck."

"What?" He looked down at her head.

"My head's stuck. I can't get out."

"Can you wait until we get to the beach house?" he asked her.

"Yeah, I guess I'll have to. Are we almost there?"

"We'll put some butter down there and get you out." He chuckled.

"Seth, this isn't funny." She attempted again to remove her head from his lap and from underneath the steering wheel.

"Since, you're stuck. Do you think you can scratch my right thigh? Your hair is making my thigh itchy right underneath your head."

She tried to scratch his right thigh with her long nails over his jean shorts. The muscle ached in her left arm and she couldn't move it.

"No, it's not working," he told her. She slid her right hand to where his knee was and tried to place her hand up his shorts to scratch his thigh this way. "No, no, it's higher up. I'm real itchy now." He wiggled his butt. Then, he stopped the moving vehicle.

"I don't see how I can scratch you where you want me to scratch."

"Well, can you unzip my pants and stick your hand down them. You have to do something for me, since you're stuck."

Jackie rolled her eyes at his pathetic attempts. She reached her arm in underneath the steering wheel and above her head as her face was turned toward his stomach.

"Are we at the beach house, yet?" she asked him.

"I'm itchy. Please?" he asked sweetly.

She unzipped the zipper with her right hand and then moved her left hand down into his pants, and she began to scratch his right thigh. "Is this where your itch is?" she asked him, hurting the muscle in her arm.

"Up a little," he said. "No, no Jackie, the other way. Toward me." She tried to scratch harder with her long, red fingernails. Seth then pushed the seat back and she was able to lift up her head.

"You mean, I could have came out of there the whole time?"

"Yeah."

"That was so cruel!" she said angrily.

"I know," he replied and laughed.

She decided to place her hand in between his legs and started to rub him.

"Now, wait a minute," Seth said. "That's no fair."

"Yeah, it is," she replied.

She felt his softness beginning to get hard. "Are you going to lock my head under the steering wheel ever again?" She squeezed.

"Ah, no." Seth was laughing, yet seemed to be starting to feel the pain.

"Do you mean, no?" She squeezed a little harder.

"I like what you're doing." He smiled at her, and she squeezed even harder with her whole hand wrapped around his manhood.

"No!" He then gulped.

"My mother would tell me to bite the head off," she said seriously, and then lowered her face.

"No!" Seth laughed and picked up her head with both hands.

He was looking out the window and into the sand. "I think—I see your brother," he said.

"Rob?" She leaned over Seth and looked out the window, past the sand. "Yeah, it's Rob," she said to Seth. "We better get out and see why he's here."

"ROBBIE, what are you doing here?" Seth asked him.

He looked toward Jackie. "Right after you told Melinda you and Seth were going swimming, she called me, so I decided to come here. I figured you'd come here to the beach house. There's nothing like a good swim at seven o'clock in the morning. Besides, Melinda wanted to make sure you were all right."

"We can take care of ourselves," Seth said.

"I know this, but Miss Melinda wanted to make sure there's 'No hanky panky' going on or 'Sex on the beach'. Those are her words, not mine. Miss Melinda is worse than Mom."

They walked closer to the water and Rob said, "Look, I'll leave you alone."

"Be careful, little brother!" Jackie yelled to him as he jogged toward the water.

"The current can pull you under!" Seth shouted. "It's strong out today!"

"Don't worry about me, Sis! I'll be fine!" he shouted, walking backwards.

Jackie watched Rob swim off into the waves until she couldn't see him anymore. Seth and her stayed close to the shore and he held onto her as they sat within the shallow water. Seth kissed her neck and caressed her shoulder.

All she kept thinking about was Rob. *Where was he? Why hadn't he come back to shore? It's been a while, and even he couldn't swim out there for long, especially in that undertow.*

"You know, Seth? I don't see Rob," she told him.

"He's probably over the waves. They're so high. He's over there somewhere," he pointed out and into Long Island Sound.

"Let's go find him," she said.

"Let's not." He kissed her shoulder again. "You're worried about him, aren't you?" he asked.

"Yes. He's my little brother."

"Okay. Wait here. I'll go look for him." Seth stood and began to jog over the waves, until he could dive into the water.

After a minute, she yelled as loud as she could, "Seth? Did you find him?"

There was no reply. She walked into the water and stood where it was knee high to look, but still she did not see either one of them. She knew there was something wrong. She ran through the water and onto the sand to the porch of the beach house where a life preserver and two life vests were hanging. Her father always made sure these were here for them to use, although they never had to use them.

Jackie ran into the water with the life jacket around her and the other one sitting in the tube as she kicked over the waves to where she spotted Seth hanging onto Rob. Seth was laying on his back with Rob on top of his body. Jackie handed Seth the life preserver as they both tried to place the vest behind Rob's back.

They tried to get over the waves and back to shore with Rob, but they couldn't. Jackie began to perform rescue breathing on Rob. It appeared that the more they tried to get over the waves and back to shore the more they swallowed water. The three of them remained where they were and floated. Rob kept bouncing in and out of consciousness.

It only took minutes before the sun shined brightly and it appeared as if the tide had changed. Seth and Jackie swam as fast as they could to get back to shore with Rob who was unconscious again.

"Go! Go to the car and call 9-1-1! Now!" Seth shouted as he pulled Rob's body to shore.

Jackie ran as fast as her sea legs could carry her to the vehicle.

Seth placed Rob gently on his back on the sand, and immediately began trying to resuscitate him by giving him CPR.

Jackie's hands shook furiously as she dialed 9-1-1 into Seth's car phone to summon help.

Chapter 21

"Jackie?" Gabrielle called out to her as she, Chastity, and John rushed into the hall with six bodyguards behind them.

"Oh, Mom," Jackie let loose of Seth's hand. "It's all my fault," she said, crying. Gabrielle held her close. "We should have stayed together," Jackie added.

Gabrielle held Jackie's head under her chin and looked directly into her eyes. "No Jackie, it's not your fault. Rob knew how to swim well. It was a complete accident." She held her daughter close again.

J.J. rushed out of the elevator. "What the hell happened?" He went toward Seth.

"Jackie and I were swimming near the shore," Seth explained. "And Robbie went out over the waves. I went after him. The tide was too strong for me to pull him back to shore. Jackie came with a life vest.... The doctor came out a little while ago. Robbie's breathing is real shallow. They might put him on a respirator soon. J.J., there's something wrong with his heart. It was as if he had a heart attack out there."

"He's sixteen years old," John said. "How could he have had a heart attack?"

"I don't know," Jackie whimpered. "I don't know."

In the waiting room, Jackie sat between Seth and Gabrielle on the sofa with John next to her holding her hands tightly in his. J.J. paced for a moment, sat in a chair, and then stood and paced nervously again.

They waited.

The door opened, and the doctor entered. Everyone tried to read his expression for answers, but they couldn't determine what he would say. Immediately, J.J. went forward and Gabrielle stood beside him with John at her left side.

"Mr. and Mrs. Shedel, your son is not well. I hate to bring this to your attention, but Robbie can't breathe regularly on his own. Your son has

233

dead tissue laying within his heart. Has he ever complained of chest pain or had trouble breathing?"

"No. No," J.J. told him.

The doctor asked, "Not even when bike riding or running? Any type of exercise?"

"No," John told him. "He's always been healthy, strong."

"He hasn't been healthy for quite some time, Mr. Ravolie. It will only be a while until his heart stops beating and he then will stop breathing. I'm afraid no matter what we do, he's not going to make it. I'm sorry, really."

"Oh, God. No," Gabrielle bellowed.

Jackie placed a hand over her mouth as the tears ran down her face. She felt like screaming, and then buried her head within Seth's chest.

"I'm sorry," the doctor said again. "If this was caught years ago, there may have been something we could have done. He needs a heart transplant. We're looking. But, he doesn't have much longer. He's conscious now, and he's asked to see his sister."

Feeling lightheaded, Jackie stood.

"We're giving him morphine so he's comfortable."

"There's nothing we can do?" John asked as he tried not to show his tears. "We can do a media alert. Have every radio, television station, newspaper, announce that we're looking for a donor."

"His lungs are even filled with fluid. He can barely breathe. There's nothing we can do."

John refused to quench his hope, and quickly pressed the buttons on his cell phone to call Mick Harrison.

"May I go in to see him now?" Jackie asked.

"Go ahead," the doctor told her.

JACKIE ENTERED THE DARK AND DREARY ROOM, where Robbie Shedel was resting. She sat down timidly in the chair next to his right side. "Oh, Rob," she cried out softly.

"Jackie," he said in a strained whisper, opening his eyes. "Don't blame yourself. Wipe those tears." He reached out to her. "I don't want to see you cry. I'm going to ... die."

"No, no," she said, "I won't let you. I won't let you die. You can't die on me. I can't lose you. I love you so much."

"I can't breathe," Rob said. "And they told me my heart is bad."

"Didn't you know about your heart? Did you know? Why didn't you tell me?"

"No. No. I didn't ... know."

"What happened in the water? Do you know what happened out there?"

"I just ... got a leg cramp. I didn't know."

"I don't understand, Rob. I don't understand. This can't happen to you. I love you."

"I love you, Jackie, more than ... you know. Hey." He squeezed her hand tightly. "Let me go." Rob started choking.

"I can't ... let you go. I'll never be able to let you go. You are not going to die on me."

"Do ... something ... for me?" he asked her, between shallow coughs and sputters.

"What Rob? I'll do anything."

"Get the key."

"I know where the key is. What's in the drawer?"

"A book. Complete it for me."

"After Mom and Dad are married again?"

"Yes."

"What should I name it?" she asked, smiling at him as the tears passed her chin.

"*Falling Roses.* Just like the song."

"Oh, Rob."

"Go now, okay? Be with Seth. Let me go."

"I can't be with Seth. I don't love him. I've always loved you. I never wanted to be with anyone else, but you." She kissed his lips and he returned her kiss, passionately. She cried and watched as her brother slipped in and out of consciousness.

Slowly his eyes opened again. She kissed him again and he returned her kiss.

"Jackie?" Rob said her name softly.

"You want me to get Mom?" Jackie asked.

"Yes, and Dad."

"All right," she said, walking away slowly and not daring to look back at him.

JOHN AND GABRIELLE entered Rob's room together.

Gabrielle placed her hand over her mouth when it hit her that her son was really laying there dying. The machine beeped softly. Two IVs dripped near his left side. She wiped her face quickly with her palms as she and John walked up to him.

"Hey, little man," John said.

"Hello, darling," Gabrielle said, wiping her eyes again.

"I love you," Rob uttered.

"Oh honey, I love you," Gabrielle said, leaning over and kissing her son's forehead.

"You are ... my father," Rob told John.

"I know," John said. He moved so that Gabrielle could sit beside her son. John stood behind her chair, as she sat. She held Rob's right hand.

"This wasn't ... Jackie's fault."

"We know," John said.

"Make sure Jackie knows," he replied.

"I will Rob. We will," Gabrielle told him.

"She loves Seth," he told them.

"I know, sweetheart," Gabrielle said.

"I'll try not to stand in their way," John told him.

"I'm dying. I can't breathe."

"You'll be fine," John said. "You're going to make it. We're going to find a donor for you—"

"I'm not scared. I know ... I'm going to die."

"Rob, you are not going to die," John continued and then Rob started choking. He squeezed Gabrielle's hand with his right and with his left he held tightly onto the bed rail.

"I'll get J.J., okay?" Gabrielle said, while Rob continued to cough and gag. While still holding his hand, Gabrielle kissed her son on his cheek and noticed one of her tears had fallen onto his face. She wiped it with a finger, kissed him again, and said, "I love you, Robbie. I love you so much, my baby boy." He smiled at her.

She departed the room to retrieve J.J.

John took Rob's hand and Rob squeezed it with all of his might. "You were always my son, and you'll always be my son," John told him. "I love you so damn much."

"I love you, too, Dad," Rob told him. John kissed the top of his head, and brushed his knuckles over his mop of blond hair. It was hard for John to let go of his hand, but he did and exited the room.

When John entered the waiting room, J.J. held tight to Gabrielle as Seth held Jackie close to his chest.

"Go on," Gabrielle said to J.J. She then walked to John who opened his arms and held her, while attempting to stop his own tears.

"HEY ROBBIE," J.J. said upbeat, while entering his son's room.

"I love you, Dad," he replied and began to cough uncontrollably.

"I know. I love you, too. Everyone loves you. There's about a hundred people waiting on the first floor. You're going to be fine."

"I'm not ... getting better," Rob said.

"How do you know?" J.J. asked him. "You're at a hospital. You are getting—"

"Pain in ... my chest. Bad."

"Nah, you'll be all right. I bet, if you fall asleep, you'll feel better tomorrow morning."

"Dad?"

"Yeah, Rob?"

"Sit. Don't pace," Rob said, almost with a smile on his face.

"Okay."

"Promise me?" Rob asked.

"What do you want me to promise?" J.J. asked his son.

"You'll ... fall ... in love ... again. But, not with Mom."

"You better go to sleep now and I *will* see you in the morning," J.J. told him, pointing at him.

"I won't wake up," Rob replied.

"It's a promise, but you will wake up," J.J. told him.

"I love you, Dad." Rob then took in one last breath and exhaled painfully.

"I love you too, son."

"CODE BLUE ..." They heard over the intercom and came rushing out of the waiting room. Everyone who had gathered in the hall overheard the heart machine. The beep was a flat line and it seemed to grow louder and louder with each moment. J.J. stepped back as the doctors and nurses shuffled him out of the way to perform CPR and try to rescue his son.

Gabrielle didn't try to hold back her cries as she nestled herself in John's arms. Her pain was so piercing that Jackie echoed it into Seth's chest.

J.J. remained in the room, holding Rob's hand, and crying heavily, until finally he appeared in the hallway. J.J.'s eyes were swollen, his face was wet, and as they looked at him, he confirmed Rob was gone.

"No!" Jackie ran, and Seth followed. She entered the elevator quickly. One of her guards slipped inside, while the doors quickly closed. Seth stood outside the elevator, and pressed the button anxiously numerous times. Another elevator opened its doors as he hit the button hard so he could follow her.

Gabrielle walked away from John so she could weep in J.J.'s arms. Rob's mother and father wept together, holding one another. "Why him?" J.J. asked her.

"I don't know why," she wailed. "I don't know why."

"I can't take this anymore," J.J. told her, and he let her go from his embrace.

"J.J.? Where are you going?" Gabrielle shouted as he went toward the elevators as well. He pressed the button, waiting for the next elevator to return to the floor.

Gabrielle stood beside him. "Where are you going?"

"I don't know!" he cried out as the doors opened and he walked in and disappeared. John walked slowly toward her and placed his arms around her. She tilted her head back into his chest as they stared at the metal doors of the elevator.

Gabrielle turned her body around to face John. "Why did He have to take my son? Why, John? Why!" She hit his chest softly with her wrists.

"I don't know, baby," he said. Again, she cried in his chest.

"I'm going to take you home, okay?" John asked her, pressing the button. He lifted her pained limp figure into his arms when she didn't reply.

WHEN SETH FOUND JACKIE, she was staring out a window on the third floor, over a retention pond. "Jackie," he said, cupping her shoulder.

"Oh, Seth." She turned around. "Rob told me to be happy with you."

"Jackie, I don't know what to say at a time like this. I've never lost anyone this close to me before. I don't know what you're going through. I'm here for you, though. I'm just here for you."

"Just say you love me," she replied.

"I do. I do love you. Jackie, you have to be strong. I do know that your mother is not as strong as you. You should go be with your mother."

"You're right, Seth. I don't know what I was thinking."

"Come on," Seth said. He slipped an arm behind her waist and they entered the elevator side by side. When they stepped out of the elevator on the floor where Rob's body was still in the room where he had perished, John was still absorbing Gabrielle's pain. Mick and Felecia Harrison had come up to the floor with her son Ron Mace. Due to their arrival, Gabrielle and John couldn't leave the floor just yet.

"Mom," Jackie cried out.

"Oh, Jackie." Gabrielle set her arms around her daughter. "It's not your fault, honey," she reminded her.

"I know," Jackie cried.

"Chastity's still downstairs with Lenny. She's fine," Mick told John.

"I couldn't wait downstairs any longer," Felecia added.

"How did this happen?" Ron asked.

"I don't know. I don't know," John said. "Rob had a bad heart no one knew about. Rob didn't even know himself."

"John, I stopped the media release, but if there's anything else I can do for you—?" Mick questioned.

"Actually, there is," John said. "We need to find Shedel. He just left. He was on the edge, you know."

Felecia and Ron went up to Gabrielle and Jackie. Ron hugged Jackie and Felecia hugged Gabrielle. "Chastity is fine," Felecia told her. "She's downstairs with Lenny and I'll go downstairs and tell her—"

"No, no," Gabrielle said. "Don't tell her about Rob. I will."

JOHN, MICK, AND SETH drove up along the curb near the beach house. They noticed J.J. beginning to walk into the water, still wearing his clothes and shoes.

"Wait here!" Seth told John and Mick. "I'll stop him." He ran down the hill and onto the sand, throwing his shoes and socks aside before running into the water. "J.J.!" Seth called out to him. As if in a trance, J.J. continued to walk into the water, slowly. "You idiot! What the hell are you trying to do?" Seth stood behind him in chest high water. Seth placed J.J. into a headlock and turned his body around to face the shore. "Move," Seth told him. "Walk," he said as J.J. fought him.

"Let me go, Seth!" J.J. yelled, not able to get out of Seth's embrace.

"Do you want me to see my best friend kill himself?"

"I have no one to live for anymore!" he wailed.

"Yes, you do!" Seth told him.

"Don't you see, Seth? I don't have Gabrielle! I don't have Rob!"

"But, Gabrielle cares about you. I care about you. You have many people who care about you and who you care about!"

"No one gives a damn about me, Seth!"

"If I didn't care about you, would I be out here? Risking my life to save your crazy ass? Come on, J.J.! We have to be strong! We love Gabrielle and Jackie! They're gonna need us now. Come on!" Seth let go of the headlock he had on J.J. and continued to push J.J.'s back to force him to walk forward. When J.J. stopped walking where the water was knee high, Seth gave him another push forward. Seth stopped pushing J.J. when he realized he wasn't being hesitant. Seth wished it were this easy when he had pulled J.J.'s son out of the water.

He wanted Robbie to be alive just as much as J.J. did. He blamed himself for not getting the kid over the waves and onto the shore fast enough. Still though, Robbie didn't drown; it was his heart that Seth couldn't save.

John was telling Mick how Shedel's actions to Robbie's death had pissed him off. Here Shedel was running off like a child. When they lost Gabrielle, J.J. Shedel was a grown man with some serious, suicidal issues. Due to the loss of his son, again Shedel wanted to take his life also, but he failed to think how much more miserable that would make Gabrielle and even Jackie feel. Shedel was so selfish, putting people through pain like that. John couldn't say anything to Shedel and wouldn't when Seth got him to the van. Mick agreed with John. They walked to the car, while Seth and J.J. walked closely behind.

"Seth?" J.J. uttered.

"Yeah, man?" Seth asked him.

"I didn't want to off myself," J.J. said.

"Yes you did," Seth replied.

"Thanks," J.J. mumbled.

"Anytime." They slapped one another on the back. "You better not pull any stunts like you did back then after Gabrielle died. You hear me? You better not try to off yourself again with a loaded pistol in your mouth. You hear me?"

"I won't," J.J. said.

Chapter 22

The minister who had so recently married Gabrielle and J.J. now stood beside their son's casket and closed the lid over Rob's young body.

Gabrielle and J.J. walked closer to the back of the room as the minister began to speak to the visitors. When he was finished with his memorial message and prayers, he motioned for Gabrielle and J.J. to come forward to speak to the people who mourned with the family.

Gabrielle Ravolie Shedel took a deep breath as she viewed the audience filling the pews. So many people had come to pay their respects to Rob and her family.

Jackie admired her mother so much, especially in moments like this one when she could look up to her with respect. Jackie hoped she would grow up to be just like her mother one day—gleaming with beauty, talented, loving, and supportive. Gabrielle was strong most of the time, even if some life's worst moments shook her now and then.

Gabrielle stood next to J.J. and held his hand, knowing he needed her love and support in this difficult moment. It was hard for him to begin, so she began for him, "I want to thank you all for coming today," Gabrielle said. "J.J. and I."

Tears then flooded into her eyes. She paused, took another deep breath, and continued, "Most of you knew our son Robbie. Some of you are just friends of J.J.'s and mine, and you just came to be here for us on the worst day of our lives. Just recently, I've gained another daughter, and now I've lost my son. It's not fair. It's not fair that I didn't get to know Chastity sooner. It's not fair that I wasn't here for Rob's childhood. It's not fair John and I lost twelve years of our lives together. And, it's not fair God gave Rob a weak heart and we had to lose him."

She then looked at J.J. "It's just not fair," she said again. "I missed twelve precious years of Robbie's life. I've only known him for a short while, but I've grown to love him. I've always loved him. He was and he still is a wonderful young man. I will never forget him." She let loose of J.J.'s hand and then ran down the two stairs and outside toward the parking lot.

John followed her with worried eyes then stood from the pew and walked down the aisle swiftly after her to be sure she was okay.

J.J. stood in front of the people with red, teary eyes and said, "At one there will be the burial at the Waitlin Cemetery." He choked back tears, and continued, "Rob. Robbie my son. He was the perfect son. He was smarter than I was. He loved everyone and everything. He loved *you*, Jackie." He motioned to her.

J.J. looked at Jackie who attempted to smile at him. She motioned with her lips, 'I know.'

"He loved music," he added. "He loved animals, and he loved to write stories. He wanted to be a writer. He liked to write books. He was good at painting, building sandcastles, cooking, and good at picking up his dirty laundry. Even picking up mine."

There was a moment of hesitant laughter.

"Jackie, come here?" he asked. She stood and walked over to him. Her eyes were beyond swollen and the tip of her nose was a cherry-red. "Would you like to say something?" he asked her.

Jackie thought about it. There were many things she wanted to say. She started with, "Rob was my best friend. He looked out for me as if he were my older brother, not my younger brother. He was—" She became speechless with tears. "—He was perfect," she muffled.

J.J. then walked away and out of the room, leaving her.

Chastity realized Jackie's insecurity. She walked up to Jackie and took her hand. Jackie smiled at Chastity, and the girl smiled back. They were sisters. Jackie didn't have a younger brother anymore, but she did have a younger sister that she had to look out for. Gabrielle was right with what she said. Mysteriously, Rob's death had led Chastity to them. She had lost her brother, but she gained a sister. Something didn't seem right with the world.

"GABRIELLE."

"Oh, John," and they placed their arms around one another as J.J. walked up to them.

"Oh, J.J." Gabrielle let go of John, and J.J. placed his arms around her.

"I'll leave the two of you alone," John said. "I'm going to see how Jackie's doing."

Gabrielle nodded.

"Are you all right?" J.J. asked her.

"I don't think I'll ever be all right. I want him back!" she said.

"*You* want him back?" He let go of his embrace. "How do you think I feel? I'm going to get those divorce papers soon. Rob was the only thing I had, which was a part of you, and a part of me!"

"No, J.J. Don't. Please, don't do this." She put her hands over her mouth to yawn.

"You have to hear it, Gabrielle! I thought you and I somehow would grow to love one another. Thing's would work out between us. You would come back to me. I guess there's no way of having you, or any part of you."

"Oh, J.J." She went forward to place her arms around him again. Again, she wanted to be in J.J.'s arms, so she could feel Rob close to her heart.

J.J. rejected her. "No, Gabrielle. This is the end! I can't play these games anymore. You talk about not being fair. This isn't fair—to me." He walked away, leaving her standing there in misery.

The crowd departed for the cemetery. When the room was empty, Jackie lifted the casket cover to reveal her brother laying there. She knelt in front of the casket. Somehow, Jackie thought Rob would be able to hear her better if she did so. She placed her fingers gently over his fingertips.

J.J. AND JOHN went up to the hearse and talked to the minister and the funeral director, while Chastity walked up to her father. He placed his arm around her.

GABRIELLE ENTERED THE ROOM where Jackie was staring motionless at Rob's face.

"Hi, honey."

"He looks as if he's sleeping," Jackie said to her.

"Yes, he does," said Gabrielle.

"It *is* all my fault. If I didn't go with Seth swimming, Melinda would have never asked Rob to watch over Seth and me. This would have never happened."

"Oh, Jackie. Stop it. Don't blame yourself. Stop this. Stop this right now, and I never want to hear you say it again. He was the one who swam too deep in the water. It was his heart that gave out on him. You didn't do anything wrong."

"He told me it was a leg cramp." She sniffled. "There's something important that I need to tell you. It's bottled up inside of me and I need to tell someone—"

Seth came into the room. "I'm sorry I'm late, Gabrielle; Jackie."
Then he hugged them.

"Seth, I would like to be alone now, please?" Jackie asked him.

"I'll go find J.," Seth replied, after he kissed Jackie's lips.

Seth left the room and Gabrielle asked, "What did you want to tell
me?"

Jackie shook her head. "Nevermind," she mumbled.

"Will you tell me later?"

Jackie nodded.

"Would you like me to leave, too?" Gabrielle asked her daughter.

"Yes, please, I want to be alone with Rob for a little while longer."

"I'll tell the funeral director."

"Thank you," Jackie said.

"I love you, Jackie."

Jackie hugged her mother and said seriously, "Mom, I love you,
too. Mom?"

"Yes, honey?"

"Wouldn't it be a miracle if Rob came back to us, just like you
did?"

"It would be more than a miracle," Gabrielle mentioned and
smiled.

"Mom, do you think I should check under the blankets? Just in case,
Rob is still alive?"

"Honey, go ahead, but I don't think so," Gabrielle said. It was
horrible, but it was something Jackie and Gabrielle had to do for themselves.
They pulled the blankets down and checked his arms, wrists and hands, and
of course, there was no IV in either one. Gabrielle placed her wrist up to his
nose and hoped for some faint sensation of air coming from him. When she
knew there was not, Jackie did the same.

"Do you think we should open his eye to see if there is any eye
movement?"

"No Jackie. Oh, God, no. We will not open his eyelid."

"What would happen if I opened his eyelid?"

"I don't know."

"Does the eyeball pop out?" she asked seriously.

"Let's not find out," Gabrielle pleaded.

He was gone. Still, Jackie didn't believe it. She leaned over and
set her ear to his chest, to listen for a heartbeat, but there was none. Then,
Gabrielle did the same.

Jackie slid the stem of a white rose through the opening of his
clenched fist.

Gabrielle said softly, "I love you, Rob."

"OH, ROB," Jackie said to him. "I love you so much. I wish you would come back to life, just like Mom did." Again, she rested her head on his chest and suddenly she heard Rob's heart beating. "Rob! Rob! I knew you would come back to me," she said in disbelief.

Rob walked out of the coffin. He weaved her hair through his fingers, as John always did to Gabrielle, then Rob spoke, "Jackie darling. You know I love you, and I want you to be happy."

"Yes, but how can I be happy without you?"

"Shhh, listen to me. Jackie, promise me you'll stop blaming yourself for my death, and don't blame Seth. Will you promise me?"

"I promise you, Rob."

"All right. I have to leave now."

"No Rob, don't leave." He then stepped into the coffin, laid down, and Jackie went to kneel down beside him and set her hand on top of his.

"I love you, Jackie," he whispered. She placed the side of her head on the edge of the casket.

"Jackie, Jackie, wake up," Gabrielle said to her lovingly.

"Mom. Mom. Rob's alive!"

"No, Jackie. You fell asleep for over five minutes."

"No, Mom. He was alive. He told me not to think it was my fault."

"Oh, honey, you were dreaming."

"Yeah. You're right." She realized. "I love you too, Rob."

Gabrielle placed a red rose on his chest. Together, they closed the coffin.

Seth, J.J., John, Mick, Ron, and Nick and the driver of the hearse, carried the coffin to the vehicle.

It was only a matter of minutes after, that Jackie's brother, lover, and best friend, was lowered into the ground forever.

"WHAT ARE YOU THINKING?" Gabrielle asked John.

"I was just going to ask you the same thing," John replied.

"Oh," Gabrielle answered. "I was thinking about J.J., and if he is all right. I know Seth, Matt, and Scott are staying at his place, but I'm sure J.J. feels alone."

"He's fine," John uttered.

"I can't believe he's gone, John. He's gone. He was my son only a few days ago, and now he's dead. He was running and laughing and so full of life and so full of energy. No one even knew about his heart. Rob didn't even know he was sick. This whole thing doesn't make any sense."

"I know, Gabrielle." He pushed her hair away from her eyes. "I loved him so much," he said and he kissed her on her lips.

"Oh my God, John, I am so sorry."

"Sorry for what, sweetheart?"

"I haven't even asked you." She removed her head from his chest and sat up in bed.

"Asked me what?" He fixed the pillow up against the headboard so he could sit as well.

"Rob lived with you for thirteen years. He was your son, too. I am so sorry. I haven't even considered that your pain could be as overwhelming as J.J.'s or mine for that matter. I've been so selfish. Please forgive me?"

"Gabrielle, no, I haven't felt like you've neglected me in any way."

"I have been so preoccupied thinking about J.J. I am so scared that he will try to kill himself."

"He's not going to kill himself."

"Jackie told me after I died, he tried."

"Yeah. One night, Seth found him with a gun in his mouth. Shedel was drinking. But, he won't Gabrielle. He has so much to live for."

"What does he have to live for now? He doesn't have me, he doesn't have Rob, our divorce will be hitting him very soon, and then you and I will be married. What does he have to live for now?"

"The same thing he's always lived for. The music. Intensity. After I lost you, I moved on. It takes a while, but he'll be able to do it. Intensity are probably writing a song right now together, and Seth's keeping J.J. away from the drugs, and I know they're not drinking."

"How are you moving on? Has reality hit you over the head yet?" Gabrielle smiled at him.

"I will not see a shrink again, if that's what you're asking."

"No, but how are you staying so strong?"

"I have you to take care of me." He smiled at her.

"I don't feel like I have. I know I haven't been taking care of you at all, but you've been taking excellent care of me."

"Reality hasn't settled in yet." He kissed her.

"How can I help you?" she asked him.

He touched her soft hair. "My son. My sixteen-year-old son drowned, and today we buried him. Even though he wasn't my biological son, I felt as if he was. He was my son. I taught him everything I knew.

"I changed his diapers. I threw birthday parties for him every year. I even dressed up as Santa and shoved myself into the fireplace for him. I taught him how to ride a bike, and he tried to teach me how to roller blade and snowboard.

"I went to every baseball game and every dive team competition he ever had. I never missed a single one. Even when I was on tour, I made sure I was home on time to watch him play ball and then I'd go to his little league pizza parties with him. He would introduce me as his dad. 'This is my dad,' he would say. 'And this is my dad, too,' and he would introduce J.J." John's voice cracked as tears ran down his cheeks.

Gabrielle began to cry as well, as John continued talking and sobbing. "I never missed 'Father Son Night'. J.J. and I both would go with him to make dinosaurs out of clay or the solar system. Whatever it was, I never missed the opportunity, and I thank you for allowing me to have this opportunity. He was our son. To me, he was always—he was my biological son for the first thirteen years, and then he was my son for the rest of his short life. Gabrielle, I loved him so much. I am going to miss him so much. I loved him."

"I know. Let it go. Let it all out, sweetheart," she said.

He cried and held onto her and let himself go into her arms.

IN THE MIDDLE OF THE NIGHT, John received a phone call from California.

Falling Roses had hit number one, and John had to leave. He was to meet Lenny, Trevor, and Brandon at his California home, after he met Mick and flew there with him. It was a once-in-a-lifetime opportunity to meet with a top-of-the-line management company who was promising to give them the world. Ra'vole, Intensity, Mace, Divide, and even Camelot would play anywhere and everywhere together, with Ra'vole headlining the tour. This was going to be so big and he had to go tonight, but Gabrielle wasn't happy about it at all.

Jackie and Chastity stood outside their room, overhearing their mother and father arguing, while their father packed his suitcase. John knew Gabrielle wanted him to stay with her; he knew she needed him, but he had to go. He said, with Ra'vole being on tour, they wouldn't be prisoner in their own home waiting for something to happen to the house, or to the kids. The tour would give them so much publicity, and would give Jeffrey Rolando more time to catch the person or people who were coming after Chastity.

"What about my birthday? It's in three days, you know. John, it's not just mine, it's also Jackie's. We need *you* to be here," she argued exhaustedly. "And because of Rob. You know both Jackie and I are hurting. We need you here."

"I'll call you," John said. "Bye sweetheart," he said to her and kissed her on her angry pursed lips, and then he left the room to kiss his two daughters good-bye quickly.

Chapter 23

J.J. Shedel's house cleaner entered his bedroom while he was still in bed. "Mr. Shedel, I don't mean to bother you, but these papers just arrived in the mail."

"More bills?" J.J. asked.

"No," she said. "I believe these are the divorce papers you told me you wanted as soon as they arrived."

"They came so soon?"

"It's been eight months," she told him. "Would you like them now?"

"Yeah, bring them to me." He wouldn't lift his head from underneath the covers.

"Thanks, Darlene."

"You're welcome, Mr. Shedel. You need to get out of bed." She opened the blinds to let the sunshine in.

Before she left, J.J. had asked her to tell everyone he didn't want to be disturbed for the rest of the day, but he would visit with his wife if Gabrielle indeed came over. He then called Gabrielle and told her to "Come over," since he had the papers.

WHEN GABRIELLE CAME TO THE DOOR, before Darlene or the butler made their negative comments, she quickly ran into the elevator that brought her to the second floor.

J.J. was in the shower as she went into the bedroom. "I'm here," she shouted for him to hear.

"Be right out," he said. Still wet, he stepped out of the shower room with just a towel wrapped around his waist.

"Gur-reat," she said. "Where are the divorce papers? And where are your clothes?"

"Gabrielle, I'll be done in a minute. Can you wait on the bed?" Gabrielle sat, while he went back into the bathroom. She placed her purse on her lap and then padded down the pillow at the headboard.

"'I'll be out in a minute,'" she said aloud mocking J.J. "I want a divorce, and what does he say? 'I'll be out in a minute.'" Gabrielle looked over onto the nightstand and picked up a picture of her and J.J. on their wedding day with Rob standing between them.

J.J. walked out of the bathroom wearing still only the towel around his waist.

"I thought you were getting dressed."

"No, I was brushing my hair. I see you have a wedding picture in your hand."

"Yeah, well, I'm putting it back. And I was looking at Rob in the picture. He looks so happy." She set it back, face-down, on the dresser.

"Would you like something to drink? Scotch? Margarita? A glass of wine, perhaps?"

"You better not have any alcohol in this house. Where are the papers?"

"Wine?"

"I don't want any wine. J.J.—?"

"Before I tell you where they are, I have two questions to ask you."

"And the answers to your questions are Gabrielle Ravolie and yes, I'm happy. J.J., where are the papers? Why are you tormenting me? I've waited and I've waited."

"Number one question: Why didn't you bring Mr. Ravolie with you? Number two question: I guess you already answered, but I'll ask it anyway. Are you keeping Shedel as your last name? Until you change it to Ravolie?"

"J.J., where're the damn papers?"

"Here's your drink." He handed her a glass of water and said, "You know, Rob didn't want us to get a divorce."

"Don't ever try to make me feel guilty by using Rob's name. Don't bring up my son like that again. That's just a shitty thing to do."

"Our son, in case you forgot."

"Where are—"

"The papers?" he continued for her. "Right next to you. Next to the phone, under the lamp."

"I know where the phone is," and she picked up the small lamp and took the envelope. She pulled the papers out of the envelope quickly and began to skim through them.

"Do you need a pen?" J.J. asked.

"No," she said. "I have one in my purse."

"You need black."

"Where does it say—?"

"Fourth paragraph; second line."

"Oh. I didn't get that far yet. You don't mind if I make myself comfortable, do you? There's a lot to read."

"No, after all, it's our bedroom."

"Right," she said, obviously frustrated with him, and then she took off her shoes and laid back. "J.J., this is all wrong. I don't want any of your money and I don't want two-thirds of the house."

"I gave you the tennis court for a present. It's yours, whenever you want to use it. You have the right to use it, whenever."

"J.J., I'm just going to sign this. I give up. These papers are all wrong. You're giving me way too much money."

"I'd give you more, but I have to keep something." J.J. stood beside her and he still had on just a towel.

"J.J., please get dressed. There's some things here we need to talk about."

"There's nothing in there that we need to talk about." He sat beside her, next to her left side.

"What are these stocks and bonds and CDs?" She pointed out. "I never even knew they existed. I don't want them. Please get dressed and stop hovering over me."

"Why?"

"You're scaring me," she joked with a serious tone.

J.J. placed his arm around her and started to bring it closer and closer to her chest. "J.J.! Stop it!"

"Come on, Gabrielle. We were married only for seventy-two hours, and you want a divorce, because I played one fucked up joke on you."

"Two fucked up jokes on me, which proved I didn't love you. I love John."

"Then why'd you marry me?"

She waited. "I thought he'd never take me back. I guess I was settling."

"Can I have the papers?"

"Why? Don't tell me it'll take another year for you to change these again."

"You signed in all the places you needed to sign. I'm not going to do anything with them," J.J. said.

"You *will* file them tomorrow, right?"

"Maybe."

"J.J., *please.*" Trusting him, she handed the papers to him. "Here."

He walked around the bed, still wearing only the towel, and placed them back where she had found them. Quickly, he removed the towel. Wearing boxer shorts, he straddled her.

"What are you doing?"

"I want you, one last time."

"Get offa me!" She pushed. She put her shoes on and then she picked up the papers. "I'm going to look these over with John and my attorney."

"Yeah, sure," J.J. said. "You're just scared to admit how you feel."

"And tell me J.J., how do I feel?" Gabrielle asked.

"You feel the same way about me as you do about John."

"J.J., if it makes you feel better, you keep dreaming about us. You'll be miserable for the rest of your life and you'll lose your best friend."

"I've already lost you as my best friend."

"If you keep pulling stunts like this with the towel and these papers, yes, you're driving me farther and farther away. Yes, I care about you J.J., but not the way you want me to." She shook her head, walked out of his mansion, stepped into the Tuscan, and drove off.

As she drove down the street, she passed the post office and quickly turned around to drive the car up to the mailbox. She pulled the papers out of the manila envelope and made sure she had signed each line with the black pen. Gabrielle then placed the papers in the self addressed stamped envelope, and licked it closed. She opened the lid of the mailbox to slide it in quickly.

As she drove down the road, she thought about what J.J. had said. She didn't love him like that. There was no way, no how. John had only been gone for less than twelve hours and she already missed him so much that it hurt in the pit of her stomach. She was bored. It was one hot afternoon. What could she do? She could go sit out back at the swimming pool while Rolando's men aimed their binoculars at each crevice of her body. She knew her daughters were just as bored as she was. And Gabrielle hated that there had to be sick slobs watching her and the girls, every time they ventured outdoors. What could the three of them do together—alone?

She looked through her side view mirror and noticed the one car escort. Buzz and Sonny drove an armored F350 Crew Cab Harley Davidson. It looked like a black pickup truck. They always kept their distance. Occasionally, she did forget about them. They were good men, in their forties, with families and children of their own. Then she noticed the other car, a white Ford Excursion passing the side of the pickup on the two-lane highway. Now, Sonny and Buzz weren't directly behind her. With

Sonny driving, she noticed he had retreated into the left lane to pass the Ford Excursion.

The Ford then smashed its left side into the right side of the pickup truck.

"Oh shit!" Frantically, she pressed the numbers on her phone.

"Hello?" she heard the voice through the speakerphone.

"Let me speak to Jeffrey, now! This is Gabrielle Ravolie!"

"Hi, Gabrielle," Jeffrey answered.

"I'm driving west on Clare Mountain Road! Sonny and Buzz are in trouble! A white Ford Excursion is trying to knock them off the road."

"Okay, Gabrielle. Calm down," Jeffrey told her.

"How can I calm down?" She noticed another hit to the Harley Davidson pickup on Buzz's size. Buzz began to shoot out his open window.

"Do you have a gun in your car?" Jeffrey asked her.

"I have a 9mm, and I know how to use it."

"Don't worry about Buzz and Sonny. You just pick up speed and get yourself away from there. The guys can take care of themselves."

She looked at her speedometer. "I'm already going 85!" she shouted. "I don't see them. The Ford is coming after me!"

"Gabrielle hit your cruise control and stay at ninety. Watch the road, don't look back," Jeffrey told her.

"I don't see them. They're too far behind me. They could be dead!" Gabrielle screamed.

"They're not dead. Is the Ford catching up with you?"

"He's almost here. What should I do? What should I do?" she asked in hysteria.

"Don't hit the brake, just turn your cruise control off."

"Okay, I did."

"Tell me your speed."

"85," she said.

"Now, what's your speed?"

"73," she said. "They're shooting at me. They realize that the body and the windows are bulletproof. They're coming closer."

"And soon they'll realize that your fuel tank is armored too," Jeffrey said.

"The Ford hit the back of my Tuscan. He's going for another blow. He's going to flip me over!" she yelled.

"What's your speed?"

"65!" she shouted.

"Punch it!" Jeffrey told her. "Hit the gas now!

She did.

After she had passed the intersection, she noticed the military vehicle, the size of a Hummer, come out from the side street. Immediately behind her, it hit the Ford Excursion and pushed it diagonally on the road. She heard the gunfire and then the Excursion exploded. In a sea of smoke and flames, she noticed there was no damage done to the Hummer looking vehicle and then, she noticed the Harley Davidson truck with Sonny and Buzz driving through the fire.

Until just now, she hadn't realized the Tuscan was slowing down. She was doing 45 now.

She heard Jeffrey's voice, "Gabrielle, are you all right?"

"Yeah," she said, shifting gears.

"Are Sonny and Buzz behind you?" he asked.

"Yeah," she replied.

"Is—? Is Buzz dead?" Gabrielle asked him.

She waited for an answer.

"They're both just fine," Jeffrey said.

She pressed the button on her speakerphone to end the call.

WHEN SHE ARRIVED HOME, she pulled into the circular drive as Sonny pulled in behind her. Their tires were still smoking. She stepped out of the Tuscan and looked at the back end of the car where the bullets had dented the body and the back end was smashed up from the single blow. It would never drive the same, she thought.

She entered the house and heard voices coming from behind the kitchen's swinging door. She opened it a tad and looked in at her two daughters sitting on stools at the counter playing a board game. They were doing some bonding, and Gabrielle thought not to interrupt or scare them with what just happened.

Feeling exhausted, she held the handrail as she walked up the stairs.

She decided she was going to take an unexpected trip to Hawaii. It would bring back memories of when her and John were married if she stayed at what she had called "A hut" when he had brought her there that first time. If John could go to California in the blink of an eye, she could go to Hawaii. She wrote John a letter:

Dear John,

J.J. will not leave me alone. I have to get
away from here. This divorce is taking so
long. I'll be in Hawaii, if you need me.

I love you,
Love Gabrielle

She packed her bags and left the note on the curio table in the foyer. Without saying good-bye to Chastity or Jackie, she left in a limousine that took her secretly to the airport just as she asked.

WHEN GABRIELLE DEPARTED THE PLANE in Hana, Hawaii, a man in a jeep awaited her arrival.

"Hello, Mrs. Shedel. I've been waiting for you."

"Oh, please. Don't call me—My name is Gabrielle Ravolie." He helped her into the jeep.

He drove her to the beach house, which John still owned after all these years. Not too far away from the secluded house, which remained buried behind ohea trees was where John and Gabrielle were happily married. This was the wonderful place neither one of them had been to since they were married sixteen years ago, she thought.

She looked outside, which was the same as she remembered it. Memories flooded into her head of when John and her arrived there for the first time so many years ago. Her making rude remarks and making fun of the house, how it looked on the outside. It looked so small. It looked like a hut made out of straw, buried behind tropical trees. She had expected this glamorous house on stilts with glass windows and a huge deck hovering over the ocean. Instead, there was a small wooden porch, which looked like it would crumble as soon as it rained.

The driver opened up the one door as it dragged on the porch and he latched it to the front of the home. She remembered the horse, how it magically appeared, and was tied to the front banister. She remembered how John helped her onto the horse and he then sat behind her and held onto the reins. With the horses stride, she turned her head and her and John kissed.

The outside of the house looked the same as it did when she was there before and in the videotape she had watched repeatedly of John and her getting married.

The man placed her bags inside and when he returned he stared at her.

"Oh, I'm sorry," she said, opening up her purse, which she had wrapped around her shoulder.

"Oh, no Mrs. Ravolie, just looking at your face, looking at the house, is payment enough."

"Please, I would like to give you something," she told him.

"Mr. Ravolie has taken good care of me and my family for many years. Will he be accompanying you on your stay here?"

Gabrielle then realized the reason John never sold any of his homes. The one he had in Florida or the one he had in California or the beach house for that matter. It wasn't about the homes; it was about the people who lived there or who he paid to take care of the grounds. He didn't care about the homes; he cared about the people, and she realized at that very moment that she loved him even more.

"No. He won't come," she answered the man's question.

"Enjoy your stay," he told her.

"Thank you," she replied.

After he departed, she walked through the door and noticed the air conditioning was kicking in. She lay on the bed and stared at the wooden beams above her. Then, she glanced at the wall. She noticed a painting of a girl, which looked just like her when she was younger.

"What happened, Gabrielle? You used to be so full of life, so full of energy."

She looked at the artist's signature. John had painted this picture. He must have returned here after she died. She smiled and closed her eyes. After a while, she stood and began to unpack her items and placed them in the dresser drawers.

She placed her bathing suit on and walked the beach. She found a spot in the sand and began to cry. "Why me?" she asked.

She swam into the ocean until she knew she shouldn't swim any further, and then swam back to the beach. As she stood out of breath, she collapsed down on the sand, melting into tears as she fell.

"Gabrielle, Gabrielle, your husband is here to see you!" She looked up from her crawling position and stood. She looked off into a far distance to see the Hawaiian man yelling to her with J.J standing beside him.

Gabrielle began to walk the other direction and found herself running.

He dropped his bags and ran after her. "Gabrielle!" he yelled.

"I can't take this anymore. Why won't you leave me alone? I don't love you! I love John! I can't take this anymore!" She ran through the sand, not turning back.

"Gabrielle! Gabrielle! It's me! It's John!" He grabbed her and for the first time, since they met so long ago, he caught up to her, without her giving in to him. He held her and kissed her cheek and her chin and they melted to the ground. He pulled her bathing suit straps down off her shoulders and kissed her neck and her breastbone on her right side of her chest. His intentions were to make love to her right then and there.

"I'm sorry. I thought you were J.J.," she spoke.

"We should file a harassment case against him. I'm sick of him hurting you. I don't understand what's taking this divorce so damn long. I want you to forget all about that maggot. I want all of you right now. Don't even worry about Shedel. I want your mind, your body, your soul. Come on." He then picked her up and carried her with her legs gently placed over his left arm and her arms hanging loosely around his neck.

He stopped to pick up his bag and then carried her to the beach house through the open door and placed her gently on the bed.

"You look so exhausted. Have you eaten anything?" He grabbed the phone from its receiver and said, "Pizza?" he confirmed with her. "With everything on it, no anchovies." He placed the receiver down, only to pick it up again. "Watermelon? And lots of it. You look so exhausted. You need to take care of yourself, baby. I need to take care of you."

It wasn't until then that she noticed he wore a suit and tie. "John, you look so handsome."

"I wanted to look nice for you. I missed you. I was gone not even a day, and I already missed your beautiful blue eyes, your soft, shiny black hair, your body touching mine. Your tongue in my mouth." He kissed her passionately. "I missed you, baby," he whispered.

"I missed you," she said, returning another kiss.

He sat her limp body up and gently pulled the straps down off her shoulders while she held onto him. While he slipped her arms through, she covered her body with his chest. He brought the bathing suit down over her soft curves, grabbed the soft white sheet from the drawer, and wrapped her in it. He picked her up into his arms and then placed her tenderly back onto the bed with her head resting gently on the pillow.

He removed his suit jacket along with his tie, loosened the buttons of his shirt, and then took it off. He turned around, kissed her, smiled, spoke to her, and told her how much he loved her. The man arrived with the food and John placed it on the coffee table next to the bed as the man closed the door behind him.

He loosened his pants, lay on his side beside her, and placed a small piece of watermelon in her mouth.

"*Mmm,* this is so refreshing," she said to him, not able to open her eyes.

"You feel so hot and look like you're suffering from heat exhaustion," he told her.

"You came back here after I died?" Gabrielle asked him.

"It was five years after your death, I came back here alone. I sat on the beach and I drew a picture of you and hung it on the wall before I left. I haven't been back here since."

They lay there together and ate. John carried her to the beach and she sat in his arms within the beautiful seventy-four degree air, and they watched the splendor of the Hawaiian sunset. He then carried her back into the house. All they wanted to do was spend time alone together. They didn't laugh, nor did they cry, they were silent as they held one another. They didn't even make love. That evening, they just held one another. And it was beautiful for both of them.

John knew he had to keep this secret from her. He looked at her and saw she was so exhausted, so sick with grief and in so much pain. She was so unhappy J.J. was prolonging this divorce. She was so scared the mob would come after Chastity and then Jackie. And she was still missing Rob a great deal. They needed this vacation together, but after two sunsets and when the sunrise came, he told her she had to go back home and he had to go back to California for yet another meeting.

"John, I don't want you to go back to California."

"I have to sweetheart. We found each other and now I need to find the music again. I want to do this. This is my dream and I know in your heart, this is your dream too. You've always wanted to sing on stage in front of millions of people. You still do, right?"

She shook her head to tell him she didn't know what she wanted.

"We'll sing *Falling Roses* together, every night to millions of people. Please don't stop me from pursuing our dream."

"All right, as long as I am a part of it," she confirmed; she did want to sing with him.

"You are my fairytale, Gabrielle. You're the biggest part of my dream, and the most important part of it. Music always comes second to you. We need to do this together. I need to go back to California to get things all settled, and you need to stay at home with the girls. As soon as I get back, I'll tell you everything and we'll be in for the best times of our lives, I promise you. Do you believe me? I'm doing this for you, for us."

"Yes, and I am happy that you are."

"Can I ask you something?" he asked her.

"Sure."

"What the hell happened between you and Shedel? Was there anything else that happened besides him finally receiving the papers after all this time?"

"He told me that he knows I love him and you equally."

"Is this true?"

"No. I love you, John. Only you. Just you. You are my first and you will be my last and for always. Only you, John. I love you, I need you, and I don't need nor do I want anyone else," she said with complete conviction in her eyes.

"I believe you," he told her.

"I wish *he* would believe me."

"He didn't believe you?"

"I don't want to think about him, John. Please, just hold me. Just hold me, don't ever let me go."

They left Hawaii together, and arrived stateside back in New York. Gabrielle went into a limousine, and went home, while John stayed on the Ra'vole plane and flew back to California.

Chapter 24

Giovanni Caruso was a gambler, drinker, and a cigar smoking man. And, he was no stranger to smuggling cigarettes, alcohol, and pharmaceutical drugs, while managing to build up a small drug ring in southern California. His rabble rousing hadn't really caused him much trouble as of yet, but the unfortunates who worked for him often found themselves arrested for prostitution rings, while Caruso was never linked to the crimes. They knew better than to rat him out.

At sixty-two years old, Caruso was a chubby man, weighing three hundred twenty pounds, with a wide nose and a deep dimple on the right side of his face. His two sons, Vincenzo and Luigi had inherited his hazel eyes, as well as his temper, but not much else from him. While their father was carrying around three hundred twenty pounds at any given time, the twins weighed less than two hundred and stood 5' 10". Unfortunately, a mother could only love their identical faces—and they had never met their mother.

Elizabeth Malone found their foolish attempts at looking handsome and manly laughable at best. The dye job that had turned their hair an obviously faux midnight black was such a pitiful attempt, as she knew that underneath the façade they were both Italian blondes.

John Ravolie remembered how they had lured him and Gabrielle out of the beach house. It was Luigi who had given Gabrielle a blow to her spine.

Giovanni coerced Elizabeth's sister, Bernadette Malone, to kill their mother, Angelique, and her husband, Nicholas Rolando. To Bernadette Malone, Giovanni Caruso was her power, her protection, and an infamous Sicilian Mafia boss. But he fooled her, because anyone in those circles knew that in reality, Caruso was the head of one of the least powerful Mafia families in California. He could coerce Bernadette into believing his delusions of grandeur, since he knew she was obsessed with him, and his fascination with Bernadette was what caused him to carry on with her crazy ideas about doing Johnny Ravolie in even after Bernadette herself was dead and buried. It wasn't long after Bernadette's death that Giovanni Caruso ventured into sleazy dealings with black market babies. There were many Elizabeth knew about. And only one illegal adoption John had cared about.

To Elizabeth Malone, Giovanni Caruso had a quiet, but ominous and deadly voice. But that didn't diminish how much of a fool he really was in not knowing how disrespected he was among his peers. It was time for him and his sons to die.

With Elizabeth behind the wheel, she and John left Caruso's land by driving through the opened gate. Earlier, John was surprised at the size of Giovanni Caruso's home. It looked like a small hotel. It was a large bit of land, wherein was nestled a red brick mansion, protected by barbed wire, electronic sensors surrounding the land, cameras, and guard dogs.

Elizabeth Malone wanted her revenge—she needed vengeance in the powerful way that only losing a parent could cause, and she needed Caruso to pay for what he had done to the mother she loved. She was certain that Bernadette would have never killed her mother and Nicholas if Caruso hadn't coerced her to. With the murder of Giovanni Caruso and his two sons, Elizabeth hoped that justice would finally be served and that the secret criminal society who had destroyed her mother and continued now to go after John Ravolie and his family would come to an end.

Elizabeth Malone explained the operation to John and why and how it should be done.

But first, John had a dog he had to find.

AUGUST 10

AT 10 A.M., Gabrielle poured herself a glass of red wine and sat at the kitchen table drinking. It was their birthday, both Gabrielle's and Jackie's, and John was still out in California making a magnificent business deal. While she understood why he had to go, she sure wasn't happy about being alone on her first birthday back from the dead.

"Mom." Jackie came into the kitchen.

"What do you want?" Gabrielle asked in a drunken stupor, sounding angrier than she meant to.

"I think you should stop drinking, especially if you've been taking your pills along with the wine."

"Jackie, I'll tell myself when to stop when I want to. Leave me, leave me alone!" she said in an uncontrolled angry huff.

"No, Mom, I think you need help. You can't deal with Rob's death. It's just obvious."

"I can deal with Rob's death perfectly fine! I'm perfectly fine! Do you understand me?"

"Yes, Mom, I wanted to ask you."

"Can't it wait?"

"No."

"What the hell is it?"

"Well, I—"

"Don't stutter! Talk to me! Just spit it out, Jackie. Damn it."

"Can I go out with Seth? Only for two hours. We were going to go swimming—at a pool."

"No, no. Absolutely not! You're not going out with Seth! You're not going out with Seth ever again! You hear me?"

"But, Mom?" she pleaded.

"You heard what I said! If you ever think about kissing, talking to one another, holding hands, or doing anything else to one another, I will beat the hell out of you! Do you understand?"

"You're drunk!"

"Do you think I should let my seventeen-year-old daughter go out with a thirty six-year-old man who's just using her for a cheap thrill?"

"That's not true!"

John entered the kitchen.

"Thank God you're home," Jackie said.

"What's going on in here?" John asked.

"She's drinking."

"We've got another problem," John said. "Where's Chas?"

"Upstairs," Jackie said.

"Go get her," John told her. "Why are you drinking?" He took the bottle and poured what was left of the wine down the kitchen sink.

"I missed you," she said.

"I missed you, too, but I didn't hit the bottle over it." He looked at her with a disappointed grimace.

ON THE HOT AUGUST MORNING, the little malnourished dog merely six months old, went wandering the forest in search of food, in search of water. The collar around his neck was tight, and the green box with the flashing light bothered him. He had only been wearing it for a short time, but it was beginning to bother him already. Yet, he couldn't manage to remove it from his neck. He attempted to get it off with his paws, and he chased his tail for a bit, still there was nothing he could do. Since he hadn't eaten for days, the aroma of the barbecued food was intolerably tempting, and he went forward following the beckoning to his little curious nose.

"THERE IS A DOG OUT THERE," John said to the room full of people. "I don't know what kind it is. Don't know if it has rabies. What I do know is that this dog is carrying a bomb around its neck. The bomb is attached to its collar and if you take the collar off it will remove the clip and it will explode like a grenade."

"So, we search the grounds," Gabrielle said. "It's like a scavenger hunt, but we'll all be looking for a dog."

"If you find the dog, don't go near it, use the radio and Brandon will take care of the dog and the bomb around its neck."

"Why don't we call the bomb squad?" Jackie grumbled.

"Because we just don't need the publicity," J.J. said.

"And, Brandon and Trevor *are* our bomb squad," John added.

"For sure there's a dog out there?" Chastity asked.

"My sources tell me there's a dog out there."

"And your sources told you that if I saw this collar on the dog," Chastity asked, "the first thing I'd do would take it off and it would kill me?"

"I guess the mob thinks that my daughters are gullible." He placed an arm around her waist.

"Are you going to kill the dog?" Gabrielle asked in a mumble.

"If we get the dog wet, maybe the collar will be loose enough and we can pull it off its head. If it's a big, mean dog, we'll have to tranquilize it and give it to Rolando."

"No," J.J. said. "We'll only give it to Rolando if it's foaming at the mouth."

"Great. I was going to take a nap, and now I have to search for a stupid dog," Gabrielle said, standing from her stool and wobbling a bit.

The men left the kitchen to search for the dog. Jackie and Chastity left together.

Gabrielle stared at John. "I came home, didn't I? We can celebrate your birthday tonight, okay? Alone, just you and me. No alcohol." He held her.

"She's going to have another nervous breakdown," J.J. said. "This shit has got to stop." He left the kitchen.

"Gabrielle, baby. Gabrielle, listen to me?"

"Forever?" she looked up at him.

"Forever," he told her.

"Till death do us part?" she asked.

"Even then?" he asked her.

"Even then," she told him.

"Will we be together?" they asked together.

"Yes, Gabrielle, we will always be together," John confirmed as always.

"I have to go apologize to Jackie. I am so sorry for yelling at her. God, you're right. I just shouldn't drink at all."

"She's probably out searching for the dog by the tennis courts."

JACKIE AND CHASTITY sat on a bench next to the tennis courts.

"Wow, I'm speechless," Chastity said. "I can't believe it. No one would have—"

"Rob and I truly loved each other. We never talked about the future of our relationship. We knew there wouldn't be a future, per say. I guess we'd have to change our identities and move away if we wanted to start a new life together, but that never even came up. We focused on the here and now of being together. I could never love anyone else, but Seth thinks I'm madly in love with him. He expects me to have sex with him soon, and I just can't do it. How do I get rid of Seth, Chas? What do I do?"

"Can't you just tell him that you don't want to see him anymore?"

"Believe me, I've tried to, but somehow everything's turned around backward and I end up walking away still in a relationship with him."

"Do you have any feelings for him whatsoever?" Chastity asked, trying to sound wiser than her age.

"He annoys the crap out of me. That's the only feeling that I have."

"Where is he now?"

"Gate duty," Jackie said.

"Here comes Mom."

Jackie looked to see Gabrielle walking the path toward them.

"I'm so sorry for yelling at you, Jackie. You can go out with Seth today for as long as you'd like, and do whatever you want with him. I don't care. All I want is for both my girls to be happy. I love you both so much." She sat between them. "Any sign of this dog."

"No," Chastity said.

"Rolando's men are on the roof with binoculars," Jackie said. "I'm sure they'll find him sooner or later."

"They're always watching us," Chastity added.

There was a rustling in the bushes. "What was that?" Gabrielle asked.

"A rabbit," the girls said together.

"What are you and Dad going to do today?" Jackie asked Gabrielle.

"As soon as I sober up a little, he's going to take me to the shooting range."

"Sounds like birthday fun," Chastity said.

"I'm going to look at the target and try not to see J.J. standing there," she added, managing a tipsy smile out of the left corner of her mouth. "Food's almost ready. You girls hungry?"

"Sort of," Chastity said.

"Not really," Jackie said.

As they began walking toward the house, they heard barking in the distance. Just as they turned their heads, the little Terrier came bounding toward them.

"Awww! It's a Toto," Gabrielle said.

"It looks like Toto found us," Jackie said. "Come here. Come here boy or girl or whatever you are." Jackie clapped her hands.

The dog continued to run toward them, looking as if he had found his long lost mother.

Gabrielle called on her radio, "The dog found us. It's a cute little Toto dog."

"I'm not picking it up," Jackie said.

"Neither am I," Chastity added.

The dog rubbed up against Gabrielle's ankle and she placed her radio into the pocket of her jean shorts. "Well, let's take a look at you," Gabrielle said bending down. She picked up the dog gently. He didn't weigh more than a can of coffee, it seemed.

"Does it have fleas?" Jackie asked.

"Don't know, but this little guy is definitely in need of a bath and a hair cut." Her nose wrinkled at the fragrant aroma of the little canine.

John, Brandon, Trevor, and a few others came running down the path toward them.

"This poor thing has been wearing this heavy collar around its neck," Gabrielle said. "It's pretty tight. I feel so bad for him. He can hardly hold up his little head."

"Don't take it off!" John said alarmed.

"I won't," Gabrielle told him, shaking her head and rolling her eyes.

"Can we get the dog wet and see if the collar will slide off?" Chastity asked.

John took the dog from Gabrielle's arms. "Let's go into the garden." John turned the hose on and the dog went crazy after the spray. He leaped into the air and barked, and shook off the cold water and then went wild again. The girls laughed while watching the dog loving the spray of the hose. John turned it off, and the dog continued to bark at the nozzle.

"You're definitely cute," John said, picking the Terrier up into his arms. Slowly, John took the collar from his neck and passed it to Brandon. "I think the consensus is your name is now Toto," John said looking into the dark brown eyes of the puppy.

"You're going to let me keep him?" Gabrielle asked shyly.

"Happy birthday, baby," John said, kissing her. And the dog licked his chin.

"You want some barbecued chicken, little fella?" Gabrielle asked Toto, as if she was talking to a baby.

He barked and wagged his tail happily as if he understood and was excited about dinner.

"YOU'RE ALWAYS SO DISTANT when you're with me," Seth said to Jackie. "Why?"

"I'm sorry. There's just so much that's been happening. I can't think straight sometimes."

Again, he kissed her lips passionately, while she tried desperately to do the right thing and think of him instead of Rob. But she couldn't. The way Seth touched her was different. The way he held her wasn't as warm or as safe as the way Rob had made her feel, and it seemed she'd never be able to rid her mind and heart of how she felt when she was with her brother. The touch of his hair. The way he set his lips to hers. The way their hands fit snugly together. How their bodies united.

Seth undid the button on her shorts.

She took her lips from his and pushed his chest away. "Look, I'm sorry. But, I'm not ready. I'm not ready for this."

"Are you really a virgin?" Seth asked her, sounding both concerned and excited all at once.

"No!" she stated. "Seth, I have been going through one thing after another and I just can't bring myself to relax or to have sex with you right now. Don't you understand?"

TOTO BARKED and jumped up onto the bed.

"Can I give you your birthday present now?" John asked Gabrielle. "I've been waiting all day to give this to you."

"I love surprises." Gabrielle squirmed.

"You have to sit at the edge of the bed," John said; she did.

Toto sat beside her.

John reached inside the bag and pulled out a treat for Toto, and then reached inside his pocket and placed one knee to the floor. "Gabrielle, will you marry me?" He placed the marquise with pear shaped diamonds on the side of the ring, onto her finger.

"I'LL WAIT UNTIL YOU'RE READY," Seth said.

"No you won't," she snapped. "Why do you have to be so nice?"

"You want me to be mean to you? I don't understand, Jackie?"

"Argh. You just don't get it." Jackie sat at the edge of his bed and buttoned her pants.

He skirted the bed, leaned over to look into her eyes, and then pecked at her lips. He took her hands and then knelt down in front of her. He had something in his hand and it was pressed in-between hers and his.

"Okay then. You bitch, will you marry me?"

HE KISSED HER PASSIONATELY, deeply. They rolled under the covers. Now she was on top of him. "It's a good thing—" she said in-between his fervent kisses "—you brought Toto to Chastity's room."

"He'd be barking at us the whole time," John said quickly. Then savored her neck once more. He placed a hand under her head and entered her body again. "Happy birthday, sweetheart."

They moaned in pleasure.

His phone began to ring. "I have to get that," he said. Under the covers, they rolled to the floor together. He reached inside his pants to pull out his cell phone, while he continued to kiss her. "Talk," he mumbled into his phone.

"Caruso knows. He's coming after me." Elizabeth's voice sounded frantic and desperate. "I'm still on the property and can't get out, John." Just then, the gunshots in the background rang out so loudly that both John and Gabrielle could hear them coming from his cell phone.

"Oh my God, John. What was that?" Gabrielle asked, sitting up quickly and pulling the sheet up over her breasts.

"Bethy, hold on," John said. He pressed a button on his phone and then dialed code #8024688. He pressed the talk button. "You there?"

"Yeah," he heard her say. Then there was random gunfire. He pulled the phone away from his ear. "Sorry to call you. I couldn't remember the code," she said.

"It's hard to remember things when people are shooting at you," John said. He heard the explosion of the front gate of Caruso's lodge. "Are you out?" he asked.

She closed the car door, and John heard the tires squeal. "Thanks," she said.

John ended the call.

"Who was that?" Gabrielle asked him.

"An old friend in trouble." He smiled seductively at her. "Now, where were we?"

"OH, WHAT THE HELL." Jackie said and popped the button on her shorts. She pulled them down to her ankles and pulled her shirt up over her head.

"Now, we're talkin'," Seth said, pulling his shirt up and over his head.

She stood in front of him naked. "Do you like?" she asked and began to twirl around.

He pushed her forward on the bed. "I want," he told her, getting behind her. He kissed the back of her neck and then flipped her to face him. "I want you," he said deeply.

"Let's just get this done and over with," Jackie said, nearly rolling her eyes.

She hated herself afterwards.

GABRIELLE HEARD THE DOG barking from down the hall. "I think Toto wants to go outside," she said, rolling over. John lay beside her, sound asleep. "I'll take the dog out," Gabrielle said, while yawning. She walked the hall to Chastity's room.

She attempted to turn the handle, but the door was locked. "Chastity, open the door sweetheart. I'll take Toto out for you." She knocked softly. "Chastity, open the door," she said loudly over the dog's barking. Gabrielle knocked harder. "Chastity!" Gabrielle began to slap the door with her palms. "Chastity!"

"What's going on?" John asked tying his robe.

"Toto won't stop barking and Chastity won't open the door."

"Chas, open the door!" John knocked hard. "Chas!"

Gabrielle moved over and John slammed the side of his body into the wooden door. The door didn't budge. "Come on, Chas! Wake up! Open the door!" John yelled. He slammed the side of his body into the door again.

"What's going on?" Jackie came from down the hall.

"Have you noticed if Chastity is a sound sleeper?" Gabrielle asked her oldest daughter.

"No," Jackie said. "She doesn't snore."

John busted the door down and the dog came running out of the room. John gasped for air. "Don't look!"

But, Gabrielle ran past him. "My baby!" Gabrielle screamed. "My baby! Nooo! Nooo!" She held her daughter's dead body in her arms.

Jackie slid to the floor. Toto sat in her lap. The dog had her sister's blood all over his paws and now all over her.

Shocked and sickened at the sight, John glanced up to see Chastity's blood was still glistening in the crudely written words 'Guess Who's Next?' just above the headboard of her bed.

Chapter 25

Eight Weeks Later

Gabrielle and Jackie sat on the bench next to the tennis courts. They stared out into the grass. "We've been doing this a lot lately," Gabrielle said, breaking the silence.

"You want to play tennis?"

"Nah," Gabrielle answered.

"Go to the shooting range?"

"Nah," she said again. "You want to talk about Rob?"

"Do you?"

"Sweetheart, what's on your mind? I feel like you're so distant from me. I feel as if there's something you want to tell me, but you won't—"

"Mom, will we ever get away from the mob?"

"I don't know, sweetheart. But, nothing is going to happen to you, and that's a promise. Your father and I will let no one hurt you. No one. They will have to kill me first—" She paused.

Jackie noticed Gabrielle looking far out into the distance. There was movement in the forest. Gabrielle stood quickly to get a better look.

There was a woman walking out of the woods. Mysteriously, a helicopter rose above the trees and away from the property.

Jackie stood beside Gabrielle as they both stared at the woman who walked over the bridge and entered the field of green grass.

John walked toward Gabrielle and Jackie from behind, but he knew they were staring at Elizabeth Malone in curiosity and perhaps worried confusion. Elizabeth came too soon, and he didn't have time to tell Gabrielle or his daughter that she was coming—to stay.

Jackie screamed.

Gabrielle stood in shock, as John now ran toward them.

J.J. had already ventured down the roof access and into the backyard when he noticed the chopper. He, too, peered suspiciously at Elizabeth moving closer to them.

Gabrielle was almost certain that Bernadette was now standing next to her and Jackie. She noticed John had a gun on him, but didn't reach for it. Quickly, Gabrielle stretched for his pistol, but she wasn't fast enough.

"It's okay," John said, holding her arms to her side. "It's—" Jackie fainted.

Gabrielle lowered herself next to Jackie. While sitting beside her, she continued to look up at the woman in disbelief.

"Hello John," the woman said.

"That *was* my daughter, Jackie. Gabrielle, are you all right?" She nodded.

"Jackie, wake up," John said, jostling her gently. "It's okay, Gabrielle. She's not Bernadette," he told her sweetly. "Shedel, can you run into the house and get something that smells bad? For Jackie?" John crouched. "It's okay." He touched Gabrielle's cheek lightly. "This is Elizabeth. Beth, this is my one and only true love, Gabrielle." He smiled at Gabrielle, but his smile didn't seem to melt the astonished glare on her face.

"I sure know how to make a grand entrance, don't I?" Elizabeth said to John, shrugging apologetically at the accidental havoc she had caused with her arrival. She looked at John's beloved Gabrielle who continued to stare at her in a trance, and then to Jackie who was starting to regain consciousness.

"Better late than never." John stood, then hugged Elizabeth. "I'm glad you made it here. It took you a while, but you made it."

"Caruso is so furious with me," Elizabeth said. "I am so sorry to hear about the loss of your daughter." Elizabeth looked down at Gabrielle. "I swear, if there was anything that I could've done that evening—"

J.J. ran back to Jackie, who was now coming to, but still groggy. He placed a bottle of rubbing alcohol underneath her nose. Almost immediately, she opened her eyes to find her mother sitting beside her, and looking up at Bernadette. Her father remained calm, looking down at them. "Who the hell is she?" Jackie asked. "A Bernadette impersonator?"

"Gabrielle, Jackie, this is Bernadette's sister, Elizabeth Malone."

"I'm sorry I startled both of you." Then Elizabeth looked at J.J., who was also disturbed by her appearance, but could tell she definitely wasn't Bernadette. His eyes gaped at her and wouldn't blink. This woman standing in front of him looked so much like the woman he had ultimately killed, yet her hair was more brown than blond and her nose wasn't shaped like Bernadette's at all. Her body was petite but with perfect curves and not scrawny or bony. They had always called Bernadette a toothpick when they knew her eighteen years ago. Elizabeth was no toothpick.

"I'm sorry I shocked the three of you," she then proclaimed.

"It's my fault," John said. "Because of Chas and—" he paused and winced with the sting of the loss, and then continued "—Because of everything that's been going on, I didn't have time to explain the whole story to Gabrielle and Jackie and to tell them you were coming."

"I had to come in through the woods so no one would notice me."

"Well, it's hard to sneak around in a helicopter. We saw it," Gabrielle mentioned.

John uttered, "I'll tell Rolando it was just—"

"Something Felecia did for my birthday," Gabrielle said. "After the fact."

"Sounds like a plan, sweetheart." John smiled at her for thinking more clearly.

"What do you want?" Gabrielle asked, not realizing John had asked Elizabeth to come.

"I want to help," Beth answered.

"The mob, or us?" Gabrielle asked.

"I understand the fear you have within you. I understand your feelings toward me are probably hateful. I have done nothing to you or for you. I might look like Bernadette. I am her sister. But, I am nothing like her. I want the harassment your family's been living under all these years to end. I want the mob to leave you alone. I think it's time we finish them once and for all, don't you?"

"So, you're here to help us?" Gabrielle said, as John helped her to stand.

"Yes."

"And what do you want in return?" Gabrielle asked her.

"Ending this is all I want," Elizabeth told her. "They killed my mother."

"There are three of you?" Gabrielle changed the subject again, just as John thought she would be fine.

"Yes. There were three of us," Beth told her. "We were triplets. Bernadette was born first, than me, and then Maureen."

"How can you help us?" Gabrielle asked.

"Let's go inside," John signaled. "Someone may have seen the helicopter fly near the property, and Jeffrey can't know you're here." Just then, John's cell phone rang. It was Rolando.

J.J. draped a pale Jackie over his arms and carried her.

They sat in the dining room. John pulled his bag from under the table and handed it to Elizabeth.

Jackie continued to feel faint, but knew her father trusted this woman, and she trusted her father's judgment. First John and Beth started to speak about Chastity's funeral, which led Gabrielle to talk about it, and then Jackie and J.J. were drawn into the conversation as well.

As they reminisced about Chastity, Gabrielle remembered that she was so innocent, so young. Gabrielle loved her and her eyes filled with tears showed it. Chastity was different, unusual. Throughout her thirteen years, Chastity never had time to make friends or feel safe, but here she was starting a new life, and she wanted to make the most of it.

Chastity was artistic and had drawn many pictures of Michael London; she mainly drew pictures of him. Although John was her father, and they were beginning to bond, she continued to feel love for Michael—he had, after all, raised her and had taken care of her. John accepted pictures of Michael that she drew. Then one day, she sketched an amazingly lifelike portrait of John himself. John loved it and had it placed in glass and hung in the hallway that led toward the rose garden. Chastity was pretty for her age and looked just like Gabrielle when she was fourteen, John thought, but she had his eyes.

Everyone said Chastity looked like Jackie, but Gabrielle's first daughter knew differently. Gabrielle and her Chastity weren't close; it just happened this way, but Gabrielle did love her. They only knew one another for a few months before she was taken from them. Chastity vanished from their lives just as fast as she had appeared on the doorstep with Michael London.

Elizabeth said, "I want you all to know that I knew nothing of what Caruso's plans were that night. He found out that John and I were working together. Someone saw us together on his property. Or, Caruso just thought—I completely denied ever meeting 'Johnny,' but he pulled out his own gun on me and I pulled out mine. He allowed me to leave his office, but then he sent his men to find me. I've been living with him for the past five years. I gained his trust, which I thought would be the best way to destroy him and his two sons. Caruso told me what his plans were, and there was someone at your wedding that was going to kill Jackie. I still don't know who that person is. I don't know if—"

"Seth?" Jackie asked. "Were you the one who called and told Rob that Seth was going to kill me?"

"I'm sorry I lied to you," John began. "It was a ploy to keep you and Rob away from the house for the night."

"I came to test the property to make sure that you'd all be safe and Rolando's men were not cutting it. I was able to enter Chastity's room. I stayed for maybe—"

"Five minutes," John said. "And then you got that call from Roxy." He looked toward Gabrielle.

"The house isn't safe," Elizabeth added. "If I can break in. We know Caruso's men can break in. I think we should all move into J.J.'s house."

"Are you nuts?" J.J. asked.

"My men are out there now," John said. "I don't know why we ever get Rolando involved. He's got the man power, he's got more resources than I, but—"

"We know, John," Gabrielle said. "He's an idiot."

The next topic of discussion was of the near future. Although Jeffrey Rolando had already caught the person who killed Chastity, they didn't know who was coming for Jackie and ultimately Gabrielle. Beth didn't know who the person was either, but she knew Giovanni Caruso and the mob he led were behind the master plan.

It took a while for the five of them to feel comfortable with one another.

It was very difficult for Gabrielle and Jackie to completely trust Beth, knowing that she was related to that evil Bernadette, but she had the plan, she had the resources to get Caruso and his mob into one place, and she and John had a brilliant idea to remedy the situation. Their plan didn't include Jeffrey Rolando or his wife Roxy, and that was exactly what John had wanted.

John didn't want Rolando to be a part of this. John had already lost his daughter because of Jeffrey's carelessness, yet another mark against Rolando to add to the list of unforgivables in his head. First, Rolando had introduced him to Bernadette. He couldn't protect Gabrielle from being kidnapped by Bernadette. Then, Rolando kidnapped Gabrielle and that evening, his men brutally raped her. He never came to the beach house when the alarms went off, and Bernadette had busted through the door with Vincenzo and Luigi. They had buried him and Gabrielle in a coffin, and despite all his connections and resources, Rolando never found them. Rolando's men were watching the property the evening when one of Caruso's men entered his home. John knew that there were gaps in Rolando's defenses. He and Gabrielle had tested the property out a few times. The night when Elizabeth came onto the property with Bernadette's diaries, she was able to make it into the house, into Chastity's room, out again and place a bomb under John's car, and then leave through the forest. Rolando's men weren't reliable. John had known that all these years, and now the unfortunate proof was in the loss of his little girl.

The day after Chastity's death, John removed every one of Rolando's men and hired his own. Today, Mick, Brandon, Trevor, and J.J. were on the roof. Lenny and Nick Mace were at the front gate. Only they knew that Elizabeth Malone was coming. John apologized to Gabrielle and Jackie for not telling them that he and Beth had been secretly meeting. Two months ago, John had visited Caruso's home to plot out where the explosives would be buried. Since Gabrielle had been back, Elizabeth had actually been in frequent contact with John, and she was the one who had given him the information about the dog coming onto the property. Everyone on the property today had known of Elizabeth's imminent arrival, except Gabrielle and Jackie. He simply hadn't had time to discuss it with them.

Five days later, after much rehashing, discussing, and considering all aspects and possible outcomes of their play, it was a unanimous decision that the five of them couldn't carry it out without the help of Jeffrey and Roxy Rolando. They would need them to put an end to all this nonsense once and for all. The family agreed to allow Jeffrey and Roxy Rolando to help them, one last time. But John only hoped Jeffrey Rolando wouldn't screw this up as he had so many other things with which he'd been trusted.

"NOW, I WANT YOU to be on your best behavior," Roxy told Jeffrey in the limo, which pulled slowly into the entrance of the Ravolie Estate.

"Something's not right here," Jeffrey said. "Why would Ravolie invite me for dinner?" he asked his wife.

"It was Gabrielle who invited us. She's a lot more forgiving than John. You have screwed up so much; I'm surprised John doesn't have a price on your head. You know he blames you for not keeping Chastity protected."

"Do we have to go into this now, Roxy?"

"And, I thought you didn't have a conscience." The driver opened the door. Roxy stepped out first, followed by Jeffrey, who buttoned his suit jacket.

Gabrielle immediately opened the door. "Hi Roxy," she said with a smile on her face and hugged her close. Gabrielle's smile turned into a frown when she viewed for the first time standing in front of her—Jeffrey Rolando.

"Hello, Mrs. Shedel." He took Gabrielle's hand and kissed the top.

"Please, call me Gabrielle," she said, and then she smiled at his subtle flatteries.

"Gabrielle. It's lovely to meet you again after all these years," he told her.

"Please come in," Gabrielle said, turning from the entryway and entering the foyer. "I actually have a gift for you, Jeffrey."

"For me?" He raised his eyebrows.

"Chocolates." She handed him a box.

"We haven't had those in—"

He continued, "I don't know how many years. So, who's all coming to dinner?" Jeffrey asked.

"Well, would you believe it? John and J.J. are cooking—together. Jackie wasn't feeling very well, so she's upstairs throwing up." Jackie then came to the stairwell. "Oh, there she is," Gabrielle pointed out.

"Hi, Roxy," Jackie said. "Mr. Rolando," she added, as she came down the stairwell.

"Let's go into the dining room, shall we?" Gabrielle smiled.

They passed through the kitchen where John and J.J. were arguing and obviously frustrated over the meal that they were preparing.

"You're gonna burn it!" John shouted.

"No, I'm not!" J.J. shouted back.

Gabrielle continued to smile as she opened the swinging door to the dining room, with Jeffrey and Roxy in tow. Jackie stayed in the kitchen.

"Hi, Bethy," Jeffrey said, then pulled out his gun.

She already had hers pointing at him.

"No one is going to kill anyone in my house," Gabrielle said. "Put your guns away."

With their guns drawn, their eyes looking as if they were two angry wolves ready to charge at one another, they remained focused on one another and neither one would put their gun down, regardless of Gabrielle's demands.

Chapter 26

"She doesn't work for Caruso," Gabrielle said. "Put your gun down." She placed her hands angrily on her hips and glared at Jeffrey, who still wouldn't relinquish his weapon. "John!" Gabrielle yelled.

John rushed into the dining room, looking relatively harmless in a white apron. But everyone knew John was not harmless, apron or not. "Look, Rolando. Bethy doesn't work for Caruso. Put that thing away and listen to me."

"What is she doing here?" Jeffrey asked him.

"Sit down," John ordered to the ladies. Jackie passed from behind him.

Gabrielle sat and then Roxy did next to her. Jackie seated herself beside her mother.

"Will you please put the gun down, Jeffrey," Roxy told him. "Sit. Let's listen to what they have to say. I'm sure John can explain."

Jeffrey sat next to his wife, but cautiously kept the gun in his hand. His years of dealing with Elizabeth and her people had left him skeptical of their innocence.

J.J. entered with a disgruntled look on his face, carrying a dish that was still on fire. Quickly he slipped the hot plate onto the table and sighed with embarrassed disappointment.

"Maybe we should order a pizza," Jackie said, trying not to laugh.

BETHY EXPLAINED hers and John's plan to Jeffrey and Roxy, as well as her opinion of how it should be accomplished and what the motives behind it were. After listening to her intently, the Rolandos agreed they would help them gather as much information as they could, all of which would be kept confidentially between only the seven of them. No one outside of the house would be made aware of their plans.

They worked all night and into the next day without sleeping. Even between yawns and constant trips to the bathroom, Jackie kept her eyes open and her food down. The nausea had gotten the best of her.

Bethy had prepared an invitation list compiled of at least two hundred people, and Jeffrey had just as many, if not more. The seven of them assembled the lists together and checked them over to make sure no one was invited twice. Gabrielle set up the template on the computer for the invitation and used the exact wording Bethy had told her to use so that no one would be suspicious, and the invites were printed on stationary that Bethy had stolen from Giovanni Caruso's home.

"What happened to the person who was supposed to send out the invitations?" Roxy asked Elizabeth.

"Dead," she replied.

"Thought so," Roxy muttered.

The seven of them made sure they wore gloves so there would be no fingerprints. They knew they were dealing with suspicious types who might check into anything and had the resources to do so. They placed self-adhesive stamps to the envelopes and used water to seal them so that saliva could not be tested. They were sure not to put return addresses on the envelopes, and the next afternoon, J.J. and Bethy drove to Canada to mail them from an unrevealing postmark.

While Bethy and J.J. were traveling, Seth visited with Jackie at his house.

She so wanted him to be involved, and she wanted him to know what the seven of them were doing inside the house. She needed someone to talk to—someone to know what she was going through. She was scared for her life, and she couldn't really confide in her parents. While Jackie wanted Robbie, her brother, she knew it wasn't possible, and Seth was the next best thing, even if something inside her told her he wasn't the person she should be confiding in about this. Lives were at stake, particularly her own and her mother's, and she promised herself that she would keep the secret from Seth, no matter how tempting it was to let him in on it. She just couldn't tell him. She had to keep it a secret. If anyone overheard her talking to Seth or if anyone knew other than, the seven of them, the leak might somehow cause their plan to backfire and blow up in their faces. Jackie just couldn't take the risk of talking to Seth or anyone else, no matter how much she wanted to or felt she needed to.

The problem was that Jackie felt as if Seth did care about her, and she knew he would stick by her through this horrible ordeal. But J.J., who considered Seth his best friend besides John, even convinced her not to say anything to Seth about it.

Although Mick Harrison and the rest of John's best friends knew that Elizabeth Malone was staying at the Ravolie Estate, John would not tell them the plan or even mention Caruso's name. Even the house staff, maids, Frank and Melinda, Phil—the cook, and the lawn crew were sent away from the home to live at J.J.'s mansion for four days with pay, leaving the cooking to John. He didn't mind cooking for everyone as long as J.J. stayed out of his way in the kitchen.

The plan had to stay inside the family and, for all intents and purposes, J.J. was still considered family. Jackie, Gabrielle, John, Bethy, J.J., Jeffrey, and Roxy were to remain the only ones 'in-the-know' about the things that were going to transpire.

Bethy also told all of them many things about the mob none of them were aware of. Everyone, Jeffrey and Roxy included, had been completely oblivious to the severity of what they had been up against all these years and the amount of power Bernadette Malone actually had since she was the first born to Jeffrey's mother.

Gabrielle's and Jackie's lives were simply a game to these people, who dedicated their lives to continue Bernadette's work simply because she was the first-born. It's not that they didn't respect the Rolandos, but their first loyalties were to Angelique's daughter and not Nicholas's son, and that meant they had to carry out Bernadette Malone's agenda first and foremost. There were people Jeffrey didn't want to invite to this party, but he knew Bethy was right. They had to tie up all the loose ends, and some of those people were a threat to both he and Roxy, and John's family as well. Everyone who would continue Bernadette's work had to be abolished. Bernadette had left behind plans, and Jeffrey still wouldn't have the control he needed as long as Caruso's mob were around to carry them out.

Bethy told them Caruso's plan was to have Jackie murdered alongside Gabrielle. They were to be burned alive after being tortured at Caruso's estate in California. His secret home was called Dream Lake Manor, the home of the mob's annual extravaganzas. Elizabeth Malone attended and falsely sided with Giovanni, though if Jeffrey had asked her to, she probably would have switched her falsified loyalties. Jeffrey always attended these yearly meetings, but seemed to be out the door as quickly as he arrived.

Everyone had problems, and the mob bosses were a vengeful sort who wanted everyone killed who caused them any type of problem. Jeffrey didn't want the mob to run this way and his parents never allowed for this. Jeffrey hadn't lost complete control. It was only five hundred and twelve people, out of the thousands, who were not on his side and affiliated with Caruso instead. Even though it was a low amount, the number still saddened

Jeffrey, and until now, he never knew how he could save John and Gabrielle and fix the mob at the same time.

Bethy also showed the two diaries that Bernadette had written in many years ago. The diaries had interested John, hoping to develop some sort of understanding of Bernadette and what led her to do so many horrible things. Why was she so obsessed with him? Why did she wear fur coats inside and outside in the summer? Did she even have a conscience?

Bethy knew. Bernadette hated animals, but loved to wear their skins on her back, almost like some sort of brag to the world that something had died for her vanity. Bernadette hated children because she was jealous of anyone who was younger than she was. Bernadette especially hated children who were burned either in a house fire or in any way.

When she was only seven years old, another child who was five, poured gasoline on himself and thought he wouldn't burn after he lit himself on fire. This boy wanted to show Bernadette he would not die; he got the idea from watching a magic trick on television. The boy told Bernadette only the gasoline would burn, but she knew differently, but still his story was convincing, and she wasn't sure. After the boy began to burn, he ran after her pleading with her to help him. She thought it was all part of the magic trick and the fire would not kill him. While still barely alive, he screamed for her to help him with a piercing shriek that she never quite forgot. She was scarred for life when the boy died in front of her and she thought even when he was dead he still spoke to her.

Besides her irrational disdain for animals, she also wore the furs for protection. Since the furs came with a flame retardant tag, Bernadette thought that the fur wouldn't catch on fire, therefore neither would she—ever.

Bethy also gave them helpful information on how to win this war with the mob. She was their teacher and Jeffrey's leader as well. Bethy also showed them maps and pictures of where the mob gathered to have these meetings. There were special rooms that she had already cleverly rigged with explosives. One push of a button, and the whole California retreat would burn to the ground. Bethy trusted only one man to do this, and it was Jeffrey. He couldn't back down from this task, so he had to go to California, make his guest appearance at the party with his wife, walk out the front door, and push the button in the locked box across the front lawn to detonate the explosives. He would murder five hundred and twelve people all at once.

This was how the war was to end. John knew they would end it once and for all this time, with Beth's experience and input and valuable knowledge from being on the inside with the culprits.

As Jackie had promised, she continued writing Rob's book for him. She knew exactly what Rob would have called this whole thing—'The War Between the Mob and the Falling Roses.'

"THAT'S ALL OF THEM," Bethy said, after pushing the last envelope into the mailbox. She skirted the front of the car and stepped back in.

J.J. drove away from the post office. "So, do you prefer 'Bethy' or 'Elizabeth'?" J.J. asked her.

"Bethy, actually," she replied with a smile.

"You sort of look like Bernadette, but not really."

"I'll take that as a compliment," she said.

"Do you always like to take charge—be in control?" he asked her.

"I've had to be independent my whole life. I lived with my father for the longest time. He's safe from Caruso."

"You never answered my question," J.J. said.

"Do I like to be in charge?" she asked.

"Yeah," he said.

"No," she muffled her answer.

"Have you ever heard of Hawthorne Woods?" J.J. asked.

"Yes," she said. She grinned as if it was a place fond in her memories.

"Would you care for some paint ball?" he asked her.

"THAT WAS SHEDEL on the phone," John told Gabrielle. "Him and Bethy are staying in a motel tonight," he added.

"Really?" Gabrielle asked. "Do you think—?"

"They're doin' it?" John asked her, sliding into bed. He kissed her lips with passion.

"I JUST WANT to think about you tonight," Bethy said, helping J.J. strip off his T-shirt.

"What about tomorrow night?" he asked her, while popping the buttons on her blouse.

"I'll be with someone else," she said and smiled.

"That's what you think," he said, pulling her body close to his.

THE HARDEST PART was the war against the mob took time. The timing had to be perfect. All the people who wanted to seek out Bernadette's revenge had to be gathered at one meeting, an annual meeting which none of the five hundred and twelve invited would not dare miss. The ones that could be trusted by the Ravolies and the Rolandos were left off the invite list. It would keep them safe from the explosion that wasn't meant for them.

If someone happened to mention to Jeffrey or Bethy they had not received the invitation, they were murdered. Jeffrey knew he couldn't trust anyone who was too curious, and that most likely, those people who would complain about not being invited would be the same people who were feeding information back to Caruso so that Jackie and Gabrielle could be killed. The ones who were loyal to Jeffrey and Bethy did not ask them about an invitation, and that was how the seven knew they had no contact with anyone who had received one.

DECEMBER

J.J. HAD ASKED Bethy to move in with him at his mansion, because there was less of a threat of anyone noticing she was there than if she were to stay at the Ravolie Estate. That evening, everyone gathered at J.J.'s house, except for Jeffrey and Roxy Rolando.

THEY WALKED OUT the front door. "It's kind of chilly tonight," Roxy said, zipping up her jacket.

"Are you sure you want to take a walk?" Jeffrey asked her.

"It was getting a little stuffy in there. People were arguing." She glanced around her, noticing that the house guards were watching them and listening in. "Just a short one," she added for the house guards to hear. She hooked her arm in his.

Jeffrey announced into his cell phone the count of exactly five hundred and twelve people and Bethy said the magic word over her cell phone.

As he and his wife stood next to the telephone pole, his wife shivering and looking nervously behind her, Jeffrey reached into his pocket for the metal key and placed it into the box. He reached for the button on the detonator, knowing his black leather gloves would prevent anyone finding fingerprints.

This would be the last meeting, the five hundred and twelve people were to have, and would prevent Caruso sending his two sons, Vincenzo and Luigi, to abduct Gabrielle and Jackie, who were meant to be tortured in Dream Lake Manor and then burned alive at the stake after their Christmas Day abduction. But after these sick last wishes of Bernadette's were eliminated, the women and men who felt obligated to carry them out would follow Jeffrey Rolando as their new leader. Even Caruso himself would be forced to abandon his power over what was left of his mob.

But this is not what Jeffrey wanted.

He didn't want to be the leader of a vengeful bunch who were constantly out to seek revenge on innocent people. He didn't want the title nor did he want any part of this mob. He was into money laundering. He didn't need prostitution rings, or wanted any part of smuggling pharmaceutical drugs. Those were pennies to him, and the risks far outweighed the benefits. And having three children of his own, he couldn't imagine his daughters or son being abducted while his wife gave birth.

The net was what carried the money. The net was what took up his time, and was where all his new money came from.

They were all in the house.

All five hundred and twelve of them, partying their hearts out the way they always did at parties like this—drinking or eating, snorting cocaine, shooting up heroin, on crystal meth, committing suicide, or talking or dancing or sleeping together.

With the movement of one metal button, the doors and windows locked simultaneously, but everyone was so busy that they paid it no notice, unless someone tried to open them from the inside.

Five hundred and twelve went in, but no one was allowed out, except for Jeffrey and Roxy who had already walked to the end of the property line.

At ten o'clock sharp, after the doors and windows had been electronically jammed, Elizabeth Malone gave her half-brother the order, "Do it," she told Jeffrey.

He pressed the button on the detonator.

The bombs planted within the home and outside on the property ignited. Giovanni Caruso's home blew in an explosion so loud and so thunderous it felt like an earthquake to the closest neighbors who lived twenty miles away from the estate. Bombs went off simultaneously in the outdoor pool, in the trees, and even the metal food trays that were rigged with electronic beacons. The ones who thought this was a reunion for the mob to go over the final plans to kill Gabrielle and Jackie Ravolie were now dead, and no one knew it was the keen minds of only seven people who had planned all of it.

Jeffrey placed the detonator back into the box on the telephone poll. He locked it up with the key. Arm in arm, Jeffrey and Roxy ran to their armored car and vanished from the property.

CHRISTMAS DAY

JOHN AND GABRIELLE, Seth and Jackie, J.J. and Beth sat around the Christmas tree opening presents, celebrating life.

Jackie stood and said, "I have an announcement to make!"

Everyone smiled happily and waited eagerly to hear what Jackie had to say.

"I'm getting married to Seth!" she said proudly.

"The hell you are!" John yelled, pointing a finger at Seth Edilson.

"Over my dead body!" Gabrielle yelled.

"Let her marry him," Bethy said cheerfully; J.J. kissed her neck.

"I'm beginning to like you," Jackie told Bethy, sitting back down to snuggle closely with Seth.

"I'm beginning to dislike you," John said, pointing a finger at Bethy.

"Dad, I'm seventeen."

"You're in high school!" Gabrielle and John groaned at the same time.

"I'm pregnant."

"You're what?" they said together.

Since Jackie was pregnant, Gabrielle and John allowed Seth to marry her before the baby was born in April. Gabrielle and John were also married on the same day in Hawaii. Along with J.J. and Elizabeth. Instead of Jackie continuing school to work with the mentally and physically disabled, she made Robbie Jason Shedel's dream come true and published his book. A biography about their mother, *Falling Roses*.

Epilogue

He awoke gasping for air.

He attempted to scratch the tape from his skin. After pulling the tape off halfway, he ripped the IV out of his left hand, leaving a stream of blood running down his hand onto the sheet and the floor. He sat upright, noticing another set of tubes, immersed in fluid, and connected to another IV that was inserted in his ankle. He pulled at the tape, loosening the needle enough to remove it from under his skin.

He stood gingerly, ready to collapse at any moment as his queasy legs trembled beneath him. He tried to walk throughout the dark hospital room, but observed himself stumbling and was surprised at how weak he was. A moment later, he noticed a strange itching on his forehead, and reached up to investigate. He pulled a patch off his face and threw it to the floor. He began to pivot in small circles, until he stumbled into a wall. He almost fell, but gained his strength to stand upright.

He opened a door and walked through, unaware of the unsteady broomstick standing there that toppled and hit him on the head, knocking him to the floor. Obviously, he had walked into the closet. When he fell, he noticed clothes. He ripped off the nightgown and placed himself into pants and a hospital jacket.

He left the room and stumbled hazily into the bathroom. Still dizzy and unsure of himself, he slapped cold water on his face. He then cupped his hand and drank it. His throat was numb and dry. His stomach flat, empty and hollow. He left the bathroom, completely forgetting to turn off the running water. He opened the door to reveal a dark hallway, but after a few seconds, his eyes adjusted enough for him to see the 'ELEVATOR' sign with the big white arrow, and another arrow in the opposite direction indicating 'STAIRS'.

He opted to take the stairs.

He stepped down slowly one by one to find himself falling and hitting his head. He noticed blood with his hand and wiped it. His vision toggled in and out from focused to blurry. To prevent himself from continuing to fall, he decided to slide down the stairs on his back until he realized there were no more stairs to slide down. He used the handrail to steady himself on his feet and leaned to look out the window of the exit door. There were cars parked neatly in a parking garage. He opened the door and slithered up against the wall, and, a moment later, had slid down the wall and was sitting on the floor. Suddenly, as if out of nowhere, he saw the bright headlights of an ambulance.

He crawled quickly as he could around the corner of the building. The ambulance parked abutting to him and he sat silent and still. The paramedic stepped out of the ambulance, walked behind it, and whistled a tune to the staircase. A tune he couldn't quite recognize in his hazy grog, but knew he had heard before.

The man used the mirror of the ambulance to balance himself as he stood. He looked inside the window and noticed the keys in the ignition. He stumbled to the other side, opened the door, and sat himself abruptly in the driver's seat. He turned the key and then placed the ambulance in reverse and stepped on the gas pedal, immediately ramming into another parked car. Quickly and frantically, he placed it in drive, turned on the lights, pressed on the pedal, and drove out of the parking garage. His vision slightly blurred, and his dull practice of driving hindered him from driving without swerving, but in a few moments, he was in a straight lane and seemed to be moving at a steady pace.

After three hours of driving, he pulled into the cornfields.

He noticed his head bleeding, again. He parked the van to tend to his injury, and decided to survey the vehicle for things he may need—like clothes. His search was short, as he couldn't hold attention to the task at hand with his muddled head and shaky, aching body. He became fatigued, lonely, and full of terror, which led him to curl up in a ball on the cot in the back and fall asleep for the night.

The next morning, he awoke in mass confusion, totally unaware of where he was or how he had gotten there. Then, he saw the sunrise. His eyes focused on the golden glare within the clouds, but his mind could not make sense of it. He suddenly remembered what he had been doing before the sleep took him, and he scrounged the ambulance for more useful items he may need. He found a razor. He looked into the rear view mirror and placed the blade carefully to his face. He did not recognize himself underneath a scraggly beard and mustache. He was taller than he remembered himself to be, scrawny, and so thin that his ribs showed through his skin. He looked through the glove compartment to find only registration and insurance card.

He stepped out of the ambulance, walked behind it, and glanced at the van's license plates. Pennsylvania? he asked himself. He walked back into the vehicle with a face that was clean-shaven, but razor burned for lack of shaving cream. His motor coordination was still off a bit, and he realized he had cut his face in many places. But he hadn't hardly noticed the pain of the nicks, and pain didn't matter anyway. He turned the ignition, drove backward through the cornfields, and out onto the road and drove. The vehicle started puttering as he found himself swaying into the gas station. He filled the gas tank and went inside the store.

"You don't look too good, doctor," the woman behind the counter said.

He ignored her while grabbing handfuls of bagged food and pop. He walked out the door.

"Hey, you need to pay!"

Still ignoring her, he walked slowly into the ambulance and stepped in. A police officer arrived just as he turned the ignition.

The woman yelled, "Stop him! He's stealing!"

"Step out of the ambulance, son." The officer looked through the opened window. He had a hand on his gun.

Cautiously, he leaned downward to pretend to look underneath the seat for money, planning to sneak and shift into drive and rush out of there. Instead, he spotted a wallet and a gun. He grabbed the wallet and opened it to find nine hundred dollars. The paramedic must have been paid yesterday, he thought. Still, without speaking, he handed the officer a one hundred dollar bill. He took a piece of paper out and scribbled, 'Deaf. Can't talk.' The officer took the money, and gave it to the woman.

He received his change and then sped off.

Although he could hear, he didn't know if he could talk. He opened his mouth to try to speak, but nothing would come out. He tried to say, 'Hi,' but couldn't. Many times, he tried before he had success with uttering the word 'Hi'.

"Hi, my name is Jay *Jay*-son. Hi, my name is *Jay*-son. Hi, I'm Jason. Jason is my name," he practiced.

After a long ride to New York, Jason found a hotel to sleep in for the night. He knew in New York no one would find a stolen ambulance, and he didn't care. He ditched it. The next morning he planned to do exercises to rebuild his strength, and he even treated himself to a short shopping spree for clothes that he so desperately needed. His thoughts had cleared enough that he knew he had to find a woman. He knew she was in New York. And he knew that Jacqueline Ravolie was the woman he had loved and cherished since the day he was born.

He had to find her.

... To Be Continued

Printed in the United States
77232LV00003B/76-108

9 781425 999346